SHAKESPEARE AT POOH CORNER

V KNOX

a fantasy

'NO THING IS TRUER THAN TRUTH'

('VERO NIHIL VERIUS')
- the motto on the de Vere family's coat of arms

Edward de Vere, the 17th Earl of Oxford
– the true poet playwright courtier
who wrote under the pseudonym

WILLIAM SHAKE-SPEARE
1550 - 1604

'SHAKESPEARE AT POOH CORNER' the **third edition**
ISBN 978-1-0688498-1-7

Front cover – from a portrait of Edward de Vere, the 17th Earl of Oxford - c. 1590
Back cover illustration – Hedingham Castle – the de Vere family seat in Essex, England. Birthplace of Edward de Vere. 1550 - 1604

cover design by Veronica Knox
edited by Silent K Publishing
formatting by Charity Chimni

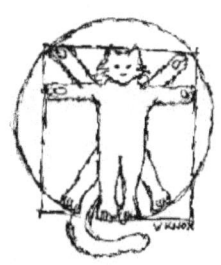

SILENT K PUBLISHING
Vancouver Island, British Columbia, Canada
https://veronicaknox.com

THE TABLE OF CONSCIOUSNESS

THE BACK MATTERS

Hedingham Castle – the birthplace of Edward de Vere – Essex, England

for
Sarah
&
david

THE SCHOOL of HARD KNOCKS

THE FORMATIVE YEARS

chapter 1

THE DARK WOODS

*"In the middle
of the journey of our life
I found myself
within dark woods
where the straight way
was lost."*

DANTE ALIGHIERI

– The Inferno

Are there ghosts? *Not a chance.* Do the stars foretell the future? *Of course not.* Could it be true that numbers rule the universe as alchemists of old once claimed? *Perhaps.* But why does the number 19 haunt me, so? *That* is the question!

I lost Hope first. Hope, my wife of 19 years, died in childbirth on December 19th, 2019, at 19 hundred hours. Our twin girls were born 19 minutes later, 3 months premature after an invitro pregnancy at the onset of Covid 19. My address is 19 Oxford Street. My newborn babes were expected to die within the hour. I was powerless.

In desperation I tuned my car radio to an FM station that promised an escape of soothing music and heard a raunchy pop song for my troubles. Mick Jagger serenaded me with a disturbingly accurate sound byte: *'You better stop. Look around,'* he sang... *'Here comes your nineteenth nervous breakdown.'*

Its up-tempo message hit a newly coined *'jagged'* nerve and laid eggs in my brain. So, I stopped and looked around and what I saw appalled me. Despair weakened my knees, I fell to the ground gasping for breath, marshmallow helpless.

At Hope's funeral, my mother-in-law, Queenie, stared into my soul for the longest time before delivering one of her famously meanspirited body blows. She made her way towards me and raised her voice so the mourners would hear her wholly inappropriate scathing verdict "Henry, you were a mistake," she shouted. "An odd duck. Delusional. Hackneyed. You'll never finish that novel you started."

The surviving twin, Lily, a fragile Christmas child, lived her first six months of life in a glass manger. My mind was mostly offline during her first months of life, mired in the lying wasteland of pointless hocus pocus.

The day I felt depression and grief collide into chaos was likely the nineteenth of something, but I'd ceased watching a calendar for the second shoe to drop.

A sobering trail of Lily pads disappeared into the foreseeable future as far as my befuddled brain could fathom. I followed each one like a dummling.

The Bermuda triangle of hopelessness materialized spiritually, physically, and figuratively. Okay… one out of three. The fourth dimension, woo-woo, was the fluff of fairy tales.

But in an inexplicable flash of fourth dimensional insight, it occurred to me that a Bermuda triangle on steroids might become a pyramid – a realization, given my rapidly imploding nerves that indicated I was on the slippery road to Lalaland to take up a mothball life at the outer limits of New-Age nonsense. I was a completely unstable one-sided pyramid. Peculiar. Terrifying.

But then science way beyond quantum physics dropped a third shoe.

It was early days when Nurse Stone, all of four-foot eleven, dressed in pink hospital scrubs, waylaid me in the hospital lobby looking worried. "Mr. King, I feel I must tell you something," she said.

She looked away twisting her wedding ring for courage. "Where do I start," she said to herself. "It's strange. But I've given the matter some thought, and I prefer to think it's something too extraordinary to ignore. Quite wonderful really. So, here it is. The facts of life don't make a lot of sense during a tragic loss but what I have to tell you is a fact of death. Take it for what it's worth. Meeting Lily has changed my life. I'm not crazy and I don't believe in ghosts but please, hear me out."

I was only paying mild attention until the 'g word', prepared for anything but a ghost story. Renee Stone hemmed and hawed her way into a confession of sorts. "I believe Lily knows when you're on your way here," she said. "I mean, she physically reacts when you enter the lobby. I know it sounds mad, but I've checked it out." She pulled a small device from her pocket. "This is my personal beeper linked to Lily's monitor." She gestured to the entrance. "The moment you come through those doors an alarm sounds in here. It's your daughter saying hello. She's calling you." Renee hesitated. "And then there's the lights and the cloud." She was flushed, stuttering. "Can we sit down. There's coffee in the family lounge. I'm on call but I have a few minutes."

I raised my eyebrows and sighed. "Nineteen minutes, I'll wager."

A sound issued from the device in Renee's hand. "That's Lily. She knows you're here. She's happy."

I started to leave but turned back. "Lights *and* clouds?"

"There are times Lily glows incandescent when she's in Delta sleep. A radiance emanates from her incubator not in an eerie way but as a beacon. She's critically fragile but her life signs rally substantially when she's suffused with light. I'm not being irrational when I say she's dreaming about you."

I remained unmoved and examined my fingernails. Even to my own ears my reaction sounded indifferent. "Right, and ...um, the *cloud*?"

Renee scowled but looked me full in the eyes without flinching. "Quite the opposite. An ominous vapor the size and shape of a brain occasionally hangs over Lily's incubator like a floating stalker, and when it does her breathing becomes labored. It's caused more than a few scares I can tell you. Not everyone can see it or the light. I haven't told anyone else. I'd like to keep my job."

"Are you saying something wants to harm Lily."

"I'm saying something is *jealous*. Don't get me wrong. I don't consider myself psychic or special in any way, but rest assured all is well. I've had a vision of you taking Lily home." She touched my arm. "I wish you well, Mr. King. And as unlikely as it sounds, I think you've been blessed with a curse meant to serve all three of you."

Nurse Stone's story reminded me of the scene in the pantomime Peter Pan where Tinkerbell lay dying, begging for her life because no-one believed in her. Peter had to incite the children in the audience into a rousing cheer to save her. Every child rallied to Tink's aid by clapping their hands until her light grew stronger.

I'm skeptical of all things metaphysical but I stayed after visiting hours when Nurse Stone was on night duty so she could message me when Lily was in the deepest state of Delta sleep.

Lily's beacon was faint at first and sometimes it seemed I imagined it, but I saw the cloud right enough. So, contra to my well-established bias against all things otherworldly, I began repeating a mantra to lift my spirits and tell Lily I loved her:

I believe in fairies! I believe in fairies! I believe in Lily!

Not to sound blasé, but I took *two* daughters home from the hospital.

The cloud escorted us to 19 Oxford Street where it hovered over Lily's cradle like a bad fairy for 19 days.

That said, my mother-in-law waiting at home, was another curse. She had no respect for me, no energy to love Lily, and no desire to engage the compassion necessary to care for the granddaughter she blamed for her daughter's death. But her doppelganger phoned it in. She changed her granddaughter's diapers, made the formula, and babysat like an automaton. All the while, her eyes remained lifeless in a permanent state of grief, mourning her only child.

I got the whiplash end of her tongue as I'd always had from the moment we met, but fanned by grief it exceeded toxic levels harmful to Lily who shrank from her touch and became prone to whimpering in her sleep.

Nevertheless, Lily's progress was mysteriously illuminating.

The name Queenie may have sounded like an endearment to strangers, but the truth was far from it. Queenie was the perfect title befitting the vain, cruel, haughty creature she seemed entitled to be. Her real name was Tish. I gave her the pseudonym Queenie, due to my last name being King, which she hated – an ironic title for an unworthy son-in-law of common ancestry who was never good enough, rich enough, or talented enough for Hope.

Queenie never forgave me for bestowing my name on her

precious daughter, and I must admit, it had once humored me to see her flinch, payback for the times she'd publicly ridiculed me. But now it rang hollow, so I called her Tish again to let her know how incensed I was for her treatment of Lily. It irked her. How I wish it did more than that.

After I read Lily 'Alice in Wonderland', she associated her grandmother with Lewis Carroll's Queen of Hearts. We called Queenie 'The Queen of Clubs' behind her back. It was *not* a compliment. She wielded a club as much as other queens wielded an axe.

Queenie's disturbed spirit pottered about the house feeding the brain-cloud she couldn't see with her negativity. There was a time I didn't believe in omens. The events of December made bad luck a sick joke. I ascribed Curse Nineteen to wonky physics. The universe was my true enemy. Queenie was merely its wretched instrument.

My *family doctor* had initially referred me to a traditional bereavement group before Lily's first Christmas, but I was in shock, too weak to fight my corner. Part of me attended without showing up. I didn't deserve to heal.

A year later my *therapist* whose overall policy was to let go of all manner of guilt, anger, and sadness, assured me suffering would end when I stopped punishing myself. She advised me to always accept the truth, however negative, because the truth would set me free.

Two years after ignoring her advice, my exasperated *life-coach* gave me an ultimatum: take control of your life or go away. Her words 'Do or Do Not, there is No Try!' were plagiarized from a wise no nonsense spiritual leader from a galaxy far far away. In other words, stop wasting my time. Face the music or I will abandon you. It was a direct blow leveled at my exposed 'Jagger nerve'. I was in shock speeding towards a total collapse she aptly dubbed 'giving up the ghost'.

2025 – when Lily was six

At my coach's urging I carved out a few precious hours of therapy for myself and hired Nurse Renee to watch Lily. I was no Captain Courageous, but I *was* a devoted father. Someday, I would believe that.

I signed up for three classes. Respectively, a Shakespeare literary appreciation class at the local university, a monthly wilderness survival hike exploring the vast rainforest surrounding my home, and a Tai Chi group that required my full attention in 108 moves.

I still dabbled with writing a first sentence from time to time, knowing from experience that stories were evasive if you tried too hard. I schooled myself by studying the craft of writing fiction. Reading to Lily was playground time. We relied heavily on bedtime stories. 7 p.m. was our special time. We discussed the fantasy I would write one day, so far, an elusive premise with little to recommend it. But Lily was a determined mentor who insisted on knowing what was good for me, and for a while, I wanted to believe her. More than that, I wanted to please her.

That said, protecting Lily from her grandmother and an ethereal jealous sister was a fulltime job. No contest. Goodbye writing.

Lily never gave up. She insisted the book that wanted to be born was about a troubled princess, and either from fear or because she was selfless, Lily suggested the protagonist should be her sibling cloud who possessed her whenever the whim struck. I trounced the idea soundly. Absolutely NO way!

Lily looked especially vulnerable, lost under the expansive

canopy of a fourposter bed surrounded by frothy white bed curtains. She tightened her grip on her Eeyore toy and shut her eyes, anticipating the cloud's wrath, cowering from the shadowy presence that bullied her as harshly as the grandmother who blamed her for her mother's death.

Lily began to shake but she didn't cry. "Will I still be in it?" she asked.

I held her hand, alarmed to feel the extent of her tremors. She was more afraid than I thought. "You will. Not just in it; the whole book will be about you and Eeyore. I promise."

"Can I be a princess?"

I gave Lily and Eeyore a group hug. "What else *could* you be!"

The cloud expanded to the width of the bed replacing its white canopy with a dark veil of loathing. Lily retreated further under the covers. "Yes," the shadow hissed, "you better hide."

I approached Lily warily as I always did when I had to disappoint her. She sat upright, a wise child, dwarfed by her enormous bed, a diminutive spirit with a mind as big as the sky.

There was no point in playing games. "Something's come up," I said. "I'm sorry but tonight's story will have to wait."

The cloud was not best pleased, but neither was Lily when her favorite book, 'The House at Pooh Corner' was hurled across the room in a tantrum.

I stood my ground. "It's the writing, Lily," I said. "A first sentence is begging to be captured on paper. You know how rare that is. We've been over it many times. Since I lost my edge, I am compelled to follow the writing muse when it calls. I've written nothing in a year... so this is a very big deal for me."

The cloud pulsated in disgust. "Well, it never happened before!" Lily whined. "I thought *our* special reading time was a big deal for both of us."

"It still is, Principessa," I cooed to Lily. "I promise to make it up to you. Let's say, two stories tomorrow night and cocoa?"

While the cloud fretted, my lovely Lily whispered to Eeyore and after a short consultation, she held Eeyore out to me for his goodnight kiss. "Eeyore says the three of us are a team and to be a big girl about your writing time," she said. "So, I guess it's okay. Sorry Dad." And then, as an out of character afterthought. "Will there be marshmallows?"

"Thank you," I whispered to Eeyore, tucking him in. "I won't forget this."

The next morning Lily's bedroom door was wedged shut by a rogue book. I forced it open to find the floor littered by dozens of Lily's favorite books, torn apart with evident hostility. I silently placed a wastepaper basket in the center of the destruction and went about my day.

By bedtime, the floor was clear, and Lily had scotch taped 'The House at Pooh Corner' back together as best she could. It waited on her nightstand like an olive branch.

I ignored the gathering storm and loaded Lily's special goodnight music, 'The Magic Forest', into her CD player.

Lily's trembling eased as the room filled with the white noise of forest sounds and flutes that usually pushed the cloud away. But this time it rocketed past my ear and disappeared into the mirror with the sound of shattering glass.

I remained unrattled. "Goodnight Eeyore... goodnight sweet Principessa."

Delta sleep was our only solace. At the end of each day, I was lulled to sleep by my own soundscape of 'Rain and distant thunder', indebted to the binaural technology that permitted me to rest but as my hand touched the doorknob, I heard the cloud stage-whisper *'off with his head!'*

My relaxing Shakespeare appreciation class proved to be an intense wake-up call – an horrific introduction to the corrupt anomalies of Shakespeare's first folio, especially the wholly bogus visual representation of Edward de Vere. The portrait in question was the grotesque 'Droeshout engraving' in the frontispiece –a masked caricature contrived to transfer the literary legacy of Edward de Vere, the seventeenth Earl of Oxford, to an illiterate changeling from Stratford-upon Avon. Edward's fall from grace went from bad to worse. Palace intrigue resulted in a corrupt political coverup destined to obliterate his name from the history books. Who knew!

Happenstance delivered a handy scapegoat, with the surprising name, William Shaksper, the family's eventual hired 'dumb man' – a mercenary actor/wool merchant/hustler – an upstart with an eye to the prize.

Even Puck's sleight of hand puppetry couldn't compete with fate. And so, the mortifying lampoon of an anonymous man without a whit of education, became the official 'bard'.

My new friends, united under the auspices of the 'Shakespeare Follies', commandeered a booth in the local coffee bar, rechristened the Shakespeare Café, where the five of us debated the authorship question, chain-drinking espresso.

Three of us were for Edward de Vere; two sat on the fence until they caved under the smoking guns impossible to dismiss. And then we were five diehards with an axe to grind.

But I couldn't disguise my all-consuming melancholy. Jim, a devotee of Zen meditation and the unofficial leader of the 'Follies' introduced me to Tai Chi that eventually segued into an unscheduled detour from physical meditation to a transcendental retreat with a shaman where hallucinogens would be imbibed for the express purpose of opening my crown chakra to release my stranglehold on suffering. Would I attend? *I'd think about it.*

Jim was against flying into inner space until I could walk. 'Walking before waking', he said. 'If you take it on you will have to prepare. You must begin with an essential sweat lodge cleanse, followed by group meditation, breathing, chanting, and fasting, under the guidance of an experienced shaman. One must retreat to advance. A slow seamless practise leads progressively towards the ultimate intervention therapy of a troubled soul. Approach with humility and respect for the unseen divine forces within nature. It's called dying before you die. Feel intense suffering, relax, and let it go. Resist nothing. Trust what-is. Always.'

The intense suffering came easy, but happily binaural sound therapy enhanced by chanting broke my fight and flight instincts. I surrendered to the present moment. Which is how I embraced the psychedelic jungle vines, hopeful to wake-up the dulled senses that revive the dispirited from self-pity to bliss.

But it wasn't until I attended a live performance of 'A Midsummer Night's Dream' that the fourth shoe dropped. By the time the house lights came on I'd made up my mind to take the psychedelic plunge. I looked forward to dislodging the plaque from my brain by taking a trip into the innermost realm of Fantasyland.

Meanwhile, wilderness survival hikes fanned my childish fears of trees into nightmares. We spent long hours observing black bears from a hide where food was strictly forbidden and hiked off the beaten tracks instructed to sing loudly to offset surprise encounters. I performed an enthusiastic rendition of 'The Teddy Bears Picnic' accompanied by a vigorous thrashing of the underbrush to keep the bears at bay. But the cougars I insisted on calling tigers, kept out of sight in the tree tops ready to pounce. I tried dismissing them as predatory versions of the Cheshire Cat, but my anxiety level remained off the scale.

Several weeks later I found myself raising a paper cup filled with slime in a toast.

Jim tapped his cup to mine. "Into the breech," he said. "See you in the movies."

"Down the rabbit hole," I replied

I remember crushing a paper chalice as the theme from 'Star Wars' played me to the dirt floor where I regained consciousness scrambling in a gore-filled gutter with a vile taste in my mouth.

The stench of London made me retch yet again. Yoda's authoritative wisdom rose above the hysterical shouts of treason. *'Do or do not. There is no try!'* he commanded.

Anthropomorphic changelings filled a forest clearing with mutated characters from 'The House at Pooh Corner' – human bodies with the head of a donkey, a bear, a pig, an owl, a kangaroo, a rabbit, and a tiger that reminded me of Egyptian deities.

The Cheshire Cat transformed into the goddess, Bast; Peter Pan into Sebek the devourer of human hearts; Wonderland Alice into Sekhmet, the goddess of healing and destruction, and Pax into the elephant-headed god, Ganesh.

Edward de Vere, an actor dressed in blue jeans, a white Elizabethan ruff, and a T-shirt emblazoned with the Droeshout portrait, waited for his entrance cue. He emerged from the trees wielding a spear, but Puck blocked his way and bowed gracefully. "It's time to grow up, Edward," he said. "The show can't go on."

So, saying, Puck lifted Edward's head from his shoulders, complete with lace collar and paraded it on a plate. The headless Edward shook his spear at me and vanished into the undergrowth.

I gave chase down a pathway of bluebells that led to a scaffold where I witnessed the grisly execution of a book placed on a block where it was cut in half with an axe. The severed pages of a first edition of 'Shakespeare's Sonnets' flew in a blizzard of paper squares obscuring my view.

I ran blinded by pages, past the tower with heads on spikes, through a city gate, past Bedlam, to Hackney, until I reached a forest where I watched frenzied dancers sidestep frantically scurrying rabbits and fieldmice, earthbound below a swarm of drunken honeybees bumbling into each in a buzzing cloud large enough to obscure the sun.

Absolem atop his mushroom conducted an orchestra of cats the size of brontosauruses. Puck and the Goddess Tinkerbell towered as giants above the diminutive Peter Pan, in raptures watching them dance a lively Volta.

My beloved Hope was there, seated on a gold throne, a queen wearing robes of green velvet and a crown of weeping willow. A dazzling raincloud materialized over her like an umbrella.

The Cheshire Cat called a halt to the merriment by shouting *'It looks like rain!'*

Hope blew me a kiss and then flames engulfed the city of London and I woke with my brain on fire.

Someone placed a cup of tea next to me. I opened one eye and squinted. When the cup said, *'drink me!'* I panicked. Was I still down the rabbit hole? But after a disembodied voice from above asked me the all-important question, I complied without argument.

A finger prodded my shoulder. "You all right, there Tiger?"

"Is that you, Jim? What day is it? How long was I out? What month is it? Where are we?"

Jim chuckled. "It's still June, hot stuff. It's still Friday night. About two hours. Planet Earth."

"But it felt like a lifetime. I remember the trees were talking *tree-son.*"

"Yeah, hallucinogens will do that. Are you hungry, oh, enlightened one?"

"I could murder a plate of buttered toast."

"No problem. A magic toaster and bread await you in the kitchen. Can you walk?"

"I can't feel my feet, but I'll crawl there if I have to."

I took a taxi home, to number 19 Oxford Street and settled into the back seat upholstery of what seemed to be a royal coach pulled by large white mice, counting myself lucky to be awakening so gently from a terrifyingly sublime dream. Jim told me it had been a toss up between making tea or throwing a bucket of cold water in my face.

I headed for the bathroom sanctuary of my wife's forest wallpaper to shake off the last cobwebs of resistance and watched them slip down the drain.

I fasted on bottled glacier water, green tea, and toast for seven days. Miraculously, I had three weeks of writers' camp until Lily came home. She was six but I wasn't about to wait until her nineteenth birthday to liberate my abandoned manuscript from its drawer and wrote like a fiend.

And since writing a novel rarely runs smooth, I gave up the ghost-writing business and entered an imaginary dimension where I rubbed shoulders with Edward de Vere, in a forest scriptorium where tea and chocolate biscuits were served every afternoon at precisely 4 p.m. by a master teacher who rewarded students with chocolate buttons instead of gold stars.

And so, I revisited the precise place in the dark woods where my straight way was lost from December 2019 to the Midsummer solstice, June 24, 2025, and began a new clearheaded life.

My soul was back. Had I known in my darkest hour that it would take six years of dragging my feet before I faced the music and only two hours of derring-do to reclaim my true self, I might never have encountered the Otherworldly dimension of mystical florae and experienced their spiritual properties but that's the perverse way destiny bounces.

I no longer believe in the random nature of human tragedy, mindful now, of being saved through the compassionate intervention of Lily's departed twin. I am eternally grateful for her divine presence after I finally understood the truth about Lily's cloud. It had been there for me.

Once again, I headed for the shower with its floor to ceiling forest mural and surrendered inside a warm waterfall that smelled of soap and shampoo, and without stopping for towels, I fell into bed in a state of peace and dreamed a story for Lily.

— *Henry King* – midsummer solstice, June 24, 2025

THE PROOG'

In **1550**
a boy wonder is born in the English countryside
of Hedingham in Essex who changed the world
but lost his soul.

In **1928**
after a great war in the Shadowlands, a man
living in the Ashdown Forest of East Sussex, England,
created the hundred-acre wood.

In **1963**
twin girls are born across the Atlantic.
One of them was born to rule an enchanted forest.
The other was born to stop her.

PLAYSCHOOL

OTHERWHERE

chapter 2

SOMETHING MAGIC THIS WAY COMES

"Remember tonight
for it is the beginning
of always."

DANTE ALIGHIERI

1968

There was no need to check the corners in our house for demons. Mother's dark shadow crept through the house without her. She told me trees ate naughty children who didn't do as they were told and threatened to leave me in Jabbers Walk if I didn't grow up.

When I was five, no-one knew I could speak, let alone read. But I was fluent in the language of odd ducks. I read pictures, shapes, colors, voices, and faces. My mother's face told me I was a mistake. She secreted me behind closed doors, but one door wasn't enough.

I endured Mother's insults thrust upon me in the world I dubbed the Shadowland where every event foreshadowed inevitable suffering.

But between waking and sleeping I imagined colorful shapes dancing around me out of sight that vanished whenever I dared look, and the sweet music accompanying them stayed, consoling me for hours until I almost believed I was cherished.

One morning, I woke to the first of four events that changed my life. Threatening voices stormed for a long time, followed by a slamming door, and the next day I found a *'tooth fairy'* book under my pillow.

I guarded it all day, and when it was dark I opened the door to 'The House at Pooh Corner'. Inside was a summer's day. A warm breeze heady with pine wafted my hair into a halo. Birdsong drew my attention to the mouth of a green tunnel leading into a comforting forest painted with fingers of sunlight. I ran into it and never looked back.

I would be remiss if I neglected to paint you an accurate mind picture, lest you envisage me left standing alone in a forest clearing of Christopher Robin's Hundred-acre-Wood with a pile of stuffed toys to play with. It was nothing of the sort. Eeyore, Kanga, and Tigger were life-sized animals, but Pooh, Piglet, and Roo remained plush toys which meant Piglet often traveled in my pocket with Pooh bumping along behind us.

I must have stepped into the Hundred-acre Wood when Christopher was away at school because I didn't meet him that first day. A hippopotamus-shaped donkey named Eeyore greeted me – a larger-than-life philosopher king, and wonder of wonders, not the least bit sullen, although his droopy-ears couldn't help but give him a *woe is me* persona.

Pooh Bear was never the brightest bulb on a Christmas tree and his best friend, Piglet was an anxiety attack waiting to happen. But it's less common knowledge that Christopher Robin, the golden boy, became a bit of a dark horse or that Tigger was a tame Bengal Tiger with a twisted sense of humor.

Surprisingly, it turns out, toys can be subject to accidents which explains why Piglet was a nervous wreck. The timid little chap had been mauled by a neighbor's Jack Russel on his first day at Cotchford Farm.

When I met him, forty years later, his sweet little face remained a tad squashed from the incident. And if that wasn't enough, after his friend Roo was lost on a picnic in 1930, Piglet became the unwilling recipient of Kanga's regular doses of strengthening medicine and cold baths.

Kanga, a near-sighted kangaroo earthmother believed fervently in the medicinal benefits of Extract of Malt and never noticed when her son, Roo grew long pink ears.

Piglet had unwittingly been the wrong size to stand up and be counted or even recognized by Mother Kanga and automatically moved up the ranks like a soldier on inspection taking a step sideways, sideling casually and ever so unobtrusively to fill the space of another recruit who had momentarily stepped out of line, to go AWOL – a term I thought referred to Wol, a distinguished owl of letters with a frightful grasp of spelling but a sublime take on life being a moment-to-moment mystery requiring deep thought to resolve. Wol lived in a treehouse – a wise oracle with a shingle hanging outside his front door that read:

Ples Cnoke If An Anser Is Reqrd
Ring The Bell If An AnsR Is Not Reqd

- WOL

Piglet didn't step up to fill Roo's place, the irrepressible Tigger bounced him there in a concerted effort to fabricate the whitest of lies to protect Kanga from the truth that her son was missing after wandering off … perhaps carried off forever.

Wol advised telling porky pies was often the best one could hope for in a tight corner, and he said it so wisely, I believed it was true.

But pork pies being a particularly discomforting thought to a piglet added another fear to Piglet's growing list of dangers. Heffalumps were at the top. Being left alone after a picnic was at the bottom even though Pooh's sixth sense radar often pinpointed Piglet's exact whereabouts.

In any case, I had little to do with what eventually happened. It turns out the 'be careful what you wish for thing' is a double-edged dream. A door had saved my life, but it also set me further apart from children who were considered *normal* ducks.

When I *turned* six, I studied hard, intending to *stay* six forever. I reasoned, not unreasonably, being six years old at the time, that *all* my senses were six-ish. But I remained at sixes and sevens for the most part.

Eeyore taught me to stand firm against all opposing forces that threatened my happiness until eventually, time languishing in the Hundred-acre-Wood with a loving family gave me the confidence to defy my hapless mother.

The fuzzy caterpillar on the tip of my finger smiled and reared up on its front legs to study me. We were busy having a polite conversation when Mother arrived bearing the dreaded daily orange drink pretending to be juice. Being thirsty was not enough incentive to drink the ghastly stuff that always delivered a sugar rush with an aftertaste of what I imagined was hemlock.

I stared into Mother's eyes and tipped it slowly, deliberately, into the grass, crushed the paper cup, and threw it in Mother's face.

The grass screamed, not best pleased from being poisoned, for which I was mortified and later apologized profusely. The traumatized caterpillar fled as fast as its hundred-acre legs could go.

After that, events moved fast. Mother slapped my face, hustled me into a coat, and marched me, soldierly fashion through Jabbers

Walk to a surprisingly benign forest inside the eye of a psychic storm.

I did my best not to grow up anywhere but as the best of intentions rarely applies, and time being a relentless taskmaster, the best thing to do, according to Wol, was to lie. I told a whopper by pretending I was monumentally stupid.

As a six-year-old who refused to age, I was, as you might expect, stubborn as a donkey for survival purposes in an exclusive clubhouse where no adults were allowed. The me who cast a shadow, opted to stay in the Hundred-acre Wood until the sun burned out. I sorted out what was real and what I had imagined that orangey day when I leaped from the cruel frying pan of Mother's child-eating trees to the shelter of a leafy glade where I met a talking tree named Lucy.

Neither event was entirely fictional, but both were mystical.

chapter 3

KIDOLOGY

"But now I am Six, I'm as clever as clever.
So, I think I'll be six now for ever and ever!"

A.A. MILNE

– 'Now We Are Six'

1969 – the second life affirming event

When I was six, I visited 'Tirings' – a care home for unwanted odd ducks. Trust me. If there's anything I know for sure, galumping headaches aside, it's that odd ducks hate surprises.

I'm an uncommonly odd duck, and I thought nothing could surprise me until the day of the bus.

As ever, I carried my magical book, 'The House at Pooh Corner' with me because I could escape inside it whenever I felt anxious – often several times a day.

Since I'd often been hospitalized for routine medical treatments, I entered Tirings for an overnight stay without a fuss – a fragile egg wrapped in a tiger's hide expecting to be examined by yet another stern-faced doctor with cold hands and a lukewarm heart.

My first impression of Tirings' arrived as a spontaneous audible snapshot. The checkered linoleum of its waiting room resembled a giant chessboard swirling with flakes of grey paint collecting in every corner and crevice like fallen leaves.

Brisk footsteps, slamming doors, and tormented human cries

drifted behind the walls painted a color I immediately dubbed *EverGrey*.

But the most telling energy came from the tinny chamber music warbling from a radio that wavered in stops and starts. And when it gave up the ghost, the anguished voices stopped to listen. The building's inhabitants were clearly confused. I held my breath and when the music resumed, the radio's dial had been tuned to a somewhat livelier station by an unseen hand. The agitated souls issued a collective sigh of relief.

But one spiteful voice jeered *you're not supposed to be here* in my ear.

Still, I took comfort that I could open the door of my book should the need arise. The fragrant pine forest of Christopher Robin's childhood on Cotchford Farm awaited me inside.

Mother shook my shoulders hard. The last words she said before she flounced out the door were *'And don't go traipsing about. Look at your bloody book, and mind you do as you're told!'*

While I waited, I became absorbed in the faded pattern of interlocking leaves entwined with grass snakes on the doormat. The snakes hissed. I hissed back and hugged my book close.

My knack of recording extrasensory details with total recall was a calming game I now used while waiting for the doctor, but years later, what I remembered most about Tirings was that threadbare doormat that hissed hello, goodbye, and come back soon at the same time.

Mother hadn't been gone long when an old lady approached me. She stroked my hair and gently informed me that Tirings was to be my permanent home.

Immediately, the sound of a braying donkey burst from my book and a loving voice said, *"Lila, it's time to come home, sweeting. I'm right here, waiting for you."*

I surrendered, blissfully transported to the hundred-acre-wood on a summer day where I rested in an expanse of bluebells with my dearest friend, Eeyore. He nudged me tenderly with his nose. *"You're safe now,"* he said. *"Well done, Goosie."*

I would have stayed in those bluebells forever, but I felt hands taking my book.

I've tried my best to remain docile throughout the endless run-ins with my agitated mother who often locked me in a room for 'a moments peace' but when it came to being separated from my only book, I fought like a Bengal tiger with no sense of humor.

I tightened my grip and awoke with such force that I startled the lady still watching over me and popped the lightbulb hanging above her head.

It was then I realized the inescapable truth. I had not been admitted to 'Tirings' with healing intentions. I was there after being discarded. I'd been thrown away. But had I been thrown clear of a life of certain misery or fallen into a worse trap of my own making? Eeyore was unruffled.

I learned years later that the lady's name was truth. That is to say, it was a name that *meant* truth. Verity Ryder had been dead for years but even so, she was still in charge. She was the one who formally admitted me to a derelict asylum-haven named Tirings the year I joined the voices behind the walls and pretended to be invisible.

When I arrived, Tirings was a crumbling castle keep – a monstrosity inhabited by ghosts, built in dense woodland infused with intense power. At night, I rose out-of-body and wandered happily through its forests free as a moonbeam. It was there I stumbled upon an enchanting clearing – a grassy meadow protected by a magnificent bong tree named Lucy exploding with sweet red apples.

Lucy told me I was in the forest of Silvany and invited me to claim her pocket of peace as my own. Happily, my replica of Christopher Robin's hundred-acre wood fit inside it seamlessly like a missing piece from the center of a jigsaw puzzle. I named it, Otherwhere.

In an odd way, Tirings had been crumbling for a thousand years, long before it had been an outline of pegs and string on a scraggy field of charred tree stumps. Local developers said there was something spooky about the forest which is why old Greenwood got it for a song. The fire that had been set deliberately to clear the land lent the building an atmosphere of defeat. In hindsight it was the perfect place to abandon a peculiar child.

I withdrew into Otherwhere, refusing to engage with anyone, especially the old custodian I named 'The Librarian' who left splendid books at the end of my bed every Saturday morning. I devoured them when no-one was watching. Even so, I didn't trust my librarian the tiniest bit. Lucy said never judge a book by its cover; Eeyore said, always read the last page first. They were both right.

Eeyore guided my first weeks of confinement as an acting coach – a talent he'd perfected to survive his ordeal of being mischaracterized as a stereotypical melancholy mule by the depressed author, A.A. Milne. He taught me the advantages of digesting every word that was said while playacting the simpleton. 'Give people what they expect', he said 'and use your noodle. You are infinitely smarter than they think, and eventually it will be the making of you. And remember Owl's advice. Sometimes being a trickster is the most truthful way to live.'

I was left to myself but never alone, for I was ever off on

Cotchford Farm, spellbound in the heart of East Sussex with my best friend in all the world.

I consumed an entire library of Saturday Books which is how I discovered 'The Owl and the Pussycat', 'Alice in Wonderland', 'The Wind in the Willows', 'Peter Pan', 'Watership Down', the wintry land of 'Narnia', and how to set sail in a wooden shoe.

I was carefree but never careless. Logistically, it was easier to keep track of the stories I loved best if I placed them from left to right in an imaginary bookcase in order of last read. But 'The House at Pooh Corner' had its own shelf.

At first, knowing there were more things in heaven and earth than I could possibly dream of was exciting, but even so, I followed Peter Pan's philosophy to never grow up. It was, therefore, my policy to err on the safe side and reject others before they rejected me. Peter advised me what I already knew; mothers could never be trusted, and all adults were suspect.

I could be as curious as a cat when it suited me, but big adventures were tricky. There was no denying I thrived best on a steady drip-feed of happy endings. For this reason, I continued to consume children's books like sugar.

Words have always fascinated me. I sat down to write once a week in Otherwhere, but nothing came of it. Even Lucy, a poet among trees, was unable save me on that score. But when I stood on the summit of Mt. Shakespeare, dizzy with admiration for words, and words within words, I was infinitely more respectful of Lewis Carroll's whimsical creations: *mimsy, frumious, boojum, chortle, vorpal, burble, galumping, snark,* and *slithy.* But his *'Tugely Wood'* still topped my list of *places I never wanted to be after dark.*

By the time I was twelve my reading had progressed to Shakespeare's sonnets and plays, the Greek stoics, The Tao te Ching,

Ralph Waldo Emerson, and Alan Watts who taught me that nouns were profoundly more meaningful when used as verbs. I wandered into adult fiction late and met Sherlock Holmes who taught me how to sharpen my senses into the super-science of extrasensory perception.

But it was the wisdom of the Roman philosopher, Emperor Marcus Aurelius, who professed that obstacles in life were special gifts to raise the bar of human consciousness, that inspired me the most. Eeyore called Marcus a phenomenon. And I knew well enough to be impressed because, other than me, Eeyore rarely complimented anyone. I was his perfectly timed 'Other-me' and he was mine.

I knew what a ghost was and what enchantment meant but I needed to explain it, so I'd invited characters in books to join me who were the finest companions ever written.

In 1968 there had been six of us: Eeyore, Tigger, Kanga, Pooh, the highly excitable Piglet, and me. But reading the 'librarian's' Saturday Books brought new friends to Otherwhere and soon the population doubled. By 1971, we'd been joined by Wonderland Alice, the Cheshire Cat, Absolem the caterpillar, Neverland Peter, and Tink, who let in the Queen of Hearts by mistake. We were an even dozen.

I was born a wunderkind – a wonder child who instinctively understood Shakespeare's poetry by feeling the spaces between his words. And by the end of 1975, Edward de Vere and Puck made our number fourteen.

I lived in Tirings until I was seventeen, liberated by building inspectors who released me back into the unforgiving physical world of shadows and took Otherwhere with me – the *third* life altering event.

You're only as old as you feel I'd heard one of the ghosts say on their evening rounds. Was this true? I listened between the words and discovered it was.

And since I'd never hoped for the best, I surrendered without a fight. Otherwhere kept me young, so I continued to play mute in the Shadowland for forty-four more years until the fall of 2024.

I'm a hardboiled little egg. In order to survive, I've kept up the pretense of being six years old my entire life, and I thought nothing could ever persuade me to grow up until I heard the disembodied voice on the number 61-bus.

But I never forgot that my dysfunctional homelife had started long before the day of the voice when my name was Lila Swann.

Every day my mother had taunted me. *Don't bother pretending to read that ridiculous book of yours,* she snarked. *You're too damn stupid to go to school.* She called me Cheerless. She was a spouter... my Mum. *Less is more,* she used to spout, so I'd thought cheerless was a compliment for the longest time. I was wrong. She made sure I knew that, too. I was born wrong she'd said, not quite right. An odd duck.

chapter 4

TWO STORIES EVER THE SAME

"If we shadows have offended, think but this, and all is mended,
That you have but slumber'd here while these visions did appear.
And this weak and idle theme, no more yielding but a dream.
Gentles, do not reprehend: if you pardon, we will mend,
And, as I am an honest Puck, if we have unearned luck
Now to 'scape the serpent's tongue, we will make amends ere long;
Else the Puck a liar call, so, good night unto you all.
Give me your hands, if we be friends and Robin shall restore
amends. "

WILLIAM SHAKESPEARE

– 'A Midsummer Night's Dream'

Stay, visitor! Read if thou canst, the paradox of Edward de Vere's *truth that lies,* here.

I tell you plain that sometimes the paths of spirits cross during flashes of kismet and when they do, souls leap across time in joyous recognition. In the same way, stories written many years apart often unite in a shared theme that transcends coincidence.

I know of three definitive ways to wander an enchanted forest. The first is aimlessly, lost in thought. The second is joyously, fully engaged in all six senses. The third, fearfully, is the one I know best because as a child, I was terrified of trees before I learned to cherish forests and allowed them to cherish me.

I remember well, the first time I wandered into the enchanted forest of William Shakespeare's 'A Midsummer Night's Dream'. Something stirred deep within me. Something akin to instinct, the twin sibling of intuition. Edward's story seemed almost to tell my own.

To recap: back when I was six, I'd created an enchanted forest named 'Otherwhere' that suited my need for a safe place to hide. In 1975, when I was still a reclusive twelve-year-old, Shakespeare's Sonnets was one of my Saturday Books. In comparison, when Edward de Vere turned twelve in 1562, his confidence soared over the moon as his title the 17th Earl of Oxford became law.

'Otherwhere' collided with Edward's enchanted Midsummer Forest like a magnet and changed the polarity of both our lives. When he and I met he'd been dead three-hundred and seventy-one years, and I was existing, barely half alive. By happenstance or providence, we met in Silvany, a forest crucible of antediluvian power that forged our bond in fire.

Silvany covers the entire surface of earth as a single lifeform linked by an underground network of sentient roots charged with wick – the lifeblood energy of chlorophyl. Its trees protect the earth from above, below, and within, harboring a multitude of immortal nature spirits that navigate freely in multiple dimensions through myriad revolving doors and portals. And oh, what secrets these portals be – a living maze of tunnels leading to sacred groves strictly barred to the living, reserved for spirits in transition from life-to-life where deeply troubled souls rest in energies older than the pyramids.

For thousands of years, a maze of grassy banks sectioned the landscape into a green map of curious lumps and bumps. Iron Age ditches protect Silvany to the west, and low fences of robbed stone from medieval monasteries mark the edges of the old world.

From the air, the old Roman road, Dere Street, still cuts a straight grey swath through Silvany where Saxons and Normans once traveled as the falcon flies.

Faint traces of prehistoric circles, lines, and squares lay etched into the fields. Phantoms of early Bronze Age ditches encircle mounds and barrows that shimmer to life after the rains, and the hillocks of Iron Age settlements play hide-and-seek in the long nettles. Saxon gold shuffles deep under the earth with Neolithic flint arrowheads, dagger blades made of iron, and mosaic tesserae from Roman villas. And all the while, the tips of abandoned cairns poke their noses from mossy hillocks into the sunlight when no-one is looking.

Stone circles tilt out of kilter in tired fields, straining valiantly to mark the solstices – a gallant reminder of the glory days, while sacred groves reign steadfast under an ancient spell of protection. Puck says it's possible to see a candle burning on the moon, on the solstices, if you put your mind to it.

After every fire and drought and blight and flood and in the wake of slithering human snakes in the grass, the Green Lady, gathers her scattered fairies into colonies and fans their waning magic into sacred fire while the elementals rally weakened whorls of energies into vortices of great power. As ever, comets, falling stars, and solar flares visit the skies above the rumble-grumbles of the earth as it stretches and cracks its skin.

Edward's motto 'VERO NIHIL VERIUS – nothing is truer than truth', served to encapsulate his life as a genius poet. As a champion jouster Edward, ever victorious, shook spears that unseated his opponents with regularity, and later, as a wielder of spear-shaped quills, he shook the literary world by storm. But Edward's pseudonym, William Shakespeare, proved to be a double-edged sword that severed his noble family's ties, cut him from history, and posthumously awarded the lion's share of his fame to an illiterate usurper without a groatsworth of education.

As for me, Peter Pan inadvertently shared his motto with me by accident. Consequently, I repeated 'never grow up' like a mantra – a confounding error that has plagued me ever since.

But before you become muddleheaded trying to make sense of our stories, I fear I must confess something odd about myself that may cause you to think I'm *'not all there'*, as the saying goes. Truth be told, I'm technically never *anywhere*. But I invite you to suspend your disbelief for a few pages.

You see, whenever I read, I view characters as real as you and me. I invite the ones I want to stay to live with me in Otherwhere. If they are agreeable, they manifest perfectly in three-dimensions. In this manner, fourteen friends have joined me in Otherwhere. Edward and Puck were numbers thirteen and fourteen.

Edward caught my eye first, so, as luck would have it, he was number thirteen – a number that lied because it wanted to be famous for being unlucky. Fame being a powerful trap, thirteen's negative claim to fame, stuck. Consequently, humans avoid it at their peril.

But being a precocious child, I refused to follow conformist rules. I can truthfully boast it has been my greatest good fortune to embrace Edward as my friend, and I regard Puck, a nature spirit of the first stripe, to be number fourteen because he is the essential spiritual twin to his master.

Edward is a slave to the truth by way of his noble family's motto– nothing is truer than truth'. I, however, use the term noble lightly – a misnomer if ever there was one. I would be hard pressed to find folk less noble than the aristocratic families of Elizabeth Tudor's reign. For this reason, I feel dutybound to forewarn you that the ruthless story I am about to reveal although odder than odd, is truer than true.

Time being somewhat contrary in Silvany, it's impossible to say in which order our friendship grew. Some days Edward and I were teenagers. On others, Edward was a wise elder, and our friend Peter Pan was a newborn left crying in an abandoned pram on Oxford Street. We rallied in a family of my favorite storybook characters who, in the remains of the day formed a scriptorium of mentors, before Edward taught me to write.

I was born exceptionally gifted but with a crushing feeling of unworthiness; Edward was born exceptionally gifted with aristocratic privilege, invested with high-minded willpower and the high-spirited confidence to champion his extraordinary virtues.

Edward's suffering was meted out one silver spoonful at a time, whereas mine was delivered in one fell swoop of misery the day I was born. Nevertheless, we'd been born in perfect timing to heal each other. My lost *destiny* and Edward's lost *identity* made us worthy allies.

In hindsight, I survived by the skin of my teeth during what I felt was my eleventh hour and Edward died at his own eleventh hour – a broken man of fifty-four. For the longest time I pretended he was my father and that I had a stillborn brother named Henry. But Edward more than made up for a father I'd never known; he was my mentor, and Puck became one of Eeyore's best friends. We were a family of four within the greater family of Otherwhere.

Edward was floundering on the edge of giving up when we chanced to meet.

Gentles, if you are of sound mind, a quickening of alchemy will explain the complexity of such rudimentary metaphysics. If not, I suggest you suspend your reservations and read on. The truth will become self evident all the sooner if you approach life reverently and treat nature with respect. Think but this, we bright spirits document our memories of foggy visions and stillborn dreams by contriving arcane cyphers to tell our truth. But the course of dying never did run smooth, and restoring amends is never easy.

Edward says reincarnation is no place for sissies, but that a deathly quiet forest is the idyllic place to process what was and plan what will come to be or not to be, because if you really want reincarnation badly enough, a little thing like dying won't stop you.

chapter 5

ODDNESS IS AS ODDNESS DOES

*"You've been made by nature
for the purpose of working with others."*

MARCUS AURELIUS

1968 – *the Shadowlands*

Five years of specialists had been my only respite from a woman forever at odds with her odd duckling child. Mother was always cross. *'Once you latch onto a stupid notion, my girl, you are tenacious,'* she'd said, and she was right.

I was born small, and remained smaller on the inside where it didn't count. Doctors with clipboards despaired of my asthmatic panic attacks and a growing list of peculiarities.

The color orange made me nervous with the exception of the fruit that bears its name. I was never comfortable around adults. At some point I was diagnosed with agoraphobia, the fear of being outside, yet closets and attics were equally unbearable which left me in a bit of a conundrum. I was easily startled by loud noises but, most of all, I was desperately afraid of the trees in Jabbers Walk behind our house.

Before Tirings, I drove Mother mad by spending as many waking hours as I could spirited away in the hundred-acre-wood. Doctors came and went. Medicines were swallowed. I had, like Roo, gone AWOL. In hindsight, Mother should have thanked me for setting her free.

Happily, Mother let me keep my book to keep me quiet. I'd

learned tantrums were a vital weapon to get what I wanted. I hadn't wanted Tirings but as it turned out, Tirings wanted me.

Home sweet home – **1969** *– Tirings... Silvany... Otherwhere*

Tirings loomed large after the orange drink incident, but I had Eeyore to protect me. He and I were kindred spirits at first sight. Eeyore is an old dog that abhors new tricks and never hesitates to say so. He's a natural critic. What's more, he encourages me to write and assures me that one day he will edit my 'Edward book' and become my intrepid literary agent. He is an optimist.

Winnie the Pooh never poohpoohed me and happily, Tigger never bounced me as long as I never turned my back on him. Real tiggers lived in the rainforest surrounding my house. Mother called them cougars and they were decidedly *not* playful. A cougar bounce could easily kill a hiker or at least deliver the fright of their life. Pooh's Tigger bounced everywhere which was altogether too disturbing, but he grew on me after Christopher Robin explained he was born an odd headstrong duck just like me.

As a staunch believer in our partnership, Eeyore refuses to hear a word said against me. Besides, he views the world in 360 degrees, is incapable of guise unless it's to save me, and speaks no evil.

In 1970 when I casually disparaged real school as a horrendous thing to inflict on a six-year-old, Eeyore, bless his heart, brayed softly in my ear. "Careful what you wish for, Lila." Moments later, as an afterthought, he gave a delightful little chuckle and serenaded me telepathically in song *'you may grow up to be a mule.'*

Eeyore, stood respectfully in the shadows absorbed in his favorite pastime... deeply pondering. He glanced over at me with his deadpan 'butter wouldn't melt in your mouth' expression, performed a wobbly four-legged soft shoe shuffle, winked, and continued to sing *"and be better off than you are."*

I applauded in slow motion with a straight face. "Of course, I want to be better off than I am," I said. "How could you ever doubt it?"

"I never doubt what *actually* comes to pass," Eeyore said. "As your self-appointed mentor, I only air what may be useful for your higher education. I always thought that there was something positive to be said for throwing caution to the wind loudly enough and with plenty of gusto so as not to be misunderstood. As it happens, I don't happen to care much for gusto, but there it is."

Without a doubt, Eeyore is my second soul. He is essentially my reality check – my *'warning canary'* that literary miners take into middle earth as a safety check for toxic thoughts. At the best of times and the worst of times Eeyore keeps me on my toes. We often rub our noses together for what Eeyore referred to as 'better luck next time'.

Some days, after I fall asleep reading, I startle awake with Eeyore's head in my lap – a lovely woolly pillow of a head with my hand resting upon it. On those sweet occasions, a purring sound emanates from his plush body vibrating life into my arthritic fingers that threaten my writing attempts almost as much as the crushing weight of writers block the size of whatever prevailing elephant was in the room at the time. Such is the life of a geriatric child with the wannabe dreams of a writer.

Breakfast is predictable. Tirings porridge for me; Otherwhere buttercups for my soulful companion. We never obsess about tragic endings but savor the possibilities of brave opening sentences. Case in point, one afternoon after I'd read my latest composition aloud, Eeyore's critique came straight from a donkey's mouth. "That's almost good," he said. "I expect one day, if you keep at it, it will be *almost* brilliant."

I had no such Dickensian great expectations. I hadn't much style to cramp. "How very generous of you," I said.

Eeyore often regressed to his old sad persona to make a point. "Not at all," he replied, ankle deep in a puddle, staring at his reflection. "Delirious to be of service. Think nothing of it... *sniffle*... damp feet always sharpen my perception... *sneeze*... damp feet fairly lighten my mood."

I was good at pretending to be someone else which Eeyore said was a good thing for writers that Edward later affirmed was essential for actors by taking a sweeping bow.

I discovered meditation just in time to navigate the ongoing mid-life crisis of earning my keep. I took to it like an odd duck to water. As a born recluse, solitude suited me. Empty mind was a revelation. It was like living between bookends of peace for a few precious moments each day. Brief respites of calm enclosed me in the loving arms of divine parentheses seven days a week. I daydreamed under dazzling blue skies as much as the transparent blues of watercolor days and stargazed under an umbrella of animated constellations where the Water Carrier kept vigil. Solitude without a breath of wind was my idea of perfect weather. But when rare torrential rains and thunderstorms arrived, I relished them for their gift of deep isolation that bordered on time travel.

Rainy, inside days, were all the better to read by and for the longest time, I was content to be a human homing pigeon. And then I wasn't.

But after I truly woke up, I discovered I'd been mistaken. I hadn't created Otherwhere.

Otherwhere had created me.

chapter 6

TEA FOR TWO

*"Here is the deepest secret nobody knows
here is the root of the root and the bud of the bud
and the sky of the sky of a tree called life which grows
higher than a soul can hope or mind can hide
and this is the wonder that's keeping the stars apart"*

e.e. cummings

1975

I drank my first, *almost,* cup of tea in 1970 when I was seven, still wary of Tirings' maternal custodian. I refused to acknowledge her by continuing to play the dimwitted patient. All mothers, even a kind maternal librarian ghost bearing books, was suspect.

But I'd felt safe when a young ghost named Abigail, resplendent in a starched cap and a servant's pinafore much too big for her, brought me nursery tea and plain arrowroot biscuits on a silver tray. She made me feel quite royal by curtsying to me every afternoon at 4'o-clock.

Eeyore had not been impressed. "You're not a baby," he said. "And you can dismiss any notions of being a princess, too. We established the first day we met there would be no hierarchy of power in the Hundred-acre-Wood. Everyone was to be equal from you to Piglet regardless of stature and intelligence."

I agreed, but Eeyore remained in a disquieting ponder for ten minutes which was a long time for him to sulk.

43

"Ghosts have nothing much to do all day," he finally said. "The least they could do is keep up with the times."

Back in Abigail's day, pampered children my age had afternoon tea with their nannies and were served mock tea made surprisingly without tealeaves. It was pretend grown-up tea that looked appropriately enough like ghost tea – a white drink made with hot water, milk, and sugar served in teacups. Eeyore would have none of it. "I'd rather drink from a puddle," he complained.

I concluded parents in the past were not to be trusted, serving children inferior drinks and dull biscuits as punishments. But Abigail served comfort of a sort. I felt privileged to have refreshments infinitely nicer than the brightly colored sugar water my mother used to give me in paper cups. Abigail made me smile in spite of myself.

I remember the Saturday in 1975 when I was served real tea for the first time because it was also the day that Edward de Vere and Puck came to live in Otherwhere. I was twelve at the time.

The latest offering the librarian left on my bed, Shakespeare's sonnets, had advanced me to poetry. And there he was when I opened his door – a troubled father writing a poem to his son who had been stolen from him. A small boy with elvish ears sat beside him. I watched them both, silent as a mouse while Edward de Vere wrote with a sharpened feather. But he saw me.

"And what ghost child is this, Puck?" he'd said showing no fear, "a friend come to tease me or one to ease my pain?" He looked me up and down. "I sense the latter. If tis so, pray stay little maid. Any sprite of Puck's acquaintance is welcome as long as they're quiet."

Puck held a finger to his lips and nodded.

"I've seen you before, Puck," I whispered.

"Twas not the Puck you see before you," he said in my head.

I looked closer. "Then it was someone very much *like* you. I was newly born. Whoever it was, smiled and peered down at me in my cradle. I thought it was my father."

Puck dismissed me. "It was a dream you weren't supposed to remember," he said.

That afternoon, Edward drank *his* first ever cup of tea, and by evening, I'd brought him and Puck to Otherwhere. Eeyore trotted happy circles around Puck as if they were old friends and showed him our forest. I introduced them to Lucy who summoned Peter and Alice and the others. They fit in. We were fourteen peas in a pod.

And of all things, I was warming to the librarian who had begun a new tradition. Sponge cakes with raspberry jam and cream now accompanied the Saturday books.

Tea leaf reading is more than a parlour game where destiny is reduced to a lark. True divination like any ancient map is tricky to interpret. Life patterns are best deciphered by a conscious master like Puck. "Tealeaves," he said, "contain the alchemy of prophecies yet to be and what dreams may come."

It so transpired that Puck was a natural tealeaf reader. He peered into my cup and prophesied my future as a writer. "A bit like my master," he said, winking cheekily. "But not nearly half as clever." He looked up from the cup and spoke to a lady only he could see and bowed since she was a queen.

"She is royal born, to rule the forests of the world," Puck explained. He smiled, gave me a hug, and predicted I would have a long life, but then her majesty must have shushed him. "Lady Flora bade me keep her secret, and vanished," he said.

1980

Five years later, after I'd been returned to the Shadowland, my fear of trees returned tenfold. Large groups of them threatened suffocation. Deep forests rattled my senses as did the slavering beasts who roamed there. The trees that lined Jabber's Walk, shuffled closer to my house after dark. Trickster demons and sprites hissed spiteful threats from the tree canopy. I avoided fairy circles and for that matter, any round patches of dead grass. The scent of pine invoked intense unease. I often woke feverish from dreams of being a lost babe in the woods.

The patterns of leaves overexcited me. I saw malevolent faces everywhere. The doctors called it normal, but in my case, acute pareidolia was a particularly irksome condition. Taking a bath required blindfolding the water taps and faucet with a washcloth because it resembled the menacing face of an entity I called the watcher. My caretakers despaired of me.

The dilemma of being somewhere or nowhere panicked me, further aggravated by a fear of roads and train tracks that led off into the distance. Mall crowds terrified me. I avoided elevators, and riding a bus gave me palpitations and sweaty palms.

I never hiked other than putting on a fast clip in a hasty beeline from the bus to my front door.

But happily, afternoon tea remained my unchanging ritual. 4 p.m. was decompression time for processing events on a precarious balance beam of work and play.

As a teenager, fully initiated into the workaday conundrum of earning, pardon the expression, a *'living'*, weekdays required strong beginnings with a starting pistol of Builders' tea and a full breakfast. But after the nine-to-five grunt mill set me free, home beckoned with Chai Latte sweetened with condensed milk, and a foot massage with eucalyptus ointment.

Weekends were more relaxed. Saturday mornings, after sleeping in, I read a book sipping lapsang souchong from a special cup that informed me in no uncertain terms that *I see no evil, speak no evil, and hear no evil* – an accolade running inside its rim. And when my favorite cup decorated with the three monkeys was drained, I was rewarded with a message on the bottom that never failed to please me. *'You are a wise monkey'*, it said.

The three monkeys are my wisecracking simian friends, as is Nosey Parker, a curious monkey who drops by often to tease Eeyore. Although I have to say perhaps pulling Eeyore's tail is not the wisest thing to do when he's deep in one of his 'thinks'. As intense as he is, Eeyore takes his pondering seriously. What appears as daydreaming is often an intense conversation with a bluebell or a buttercup.

To cap off the weekend, I spent Sunday afternoons, specifically at the new time of 3 o'clock to take what Piglet called 'EARLY' tea with Edward de Vere, the 17th Earl of Oxford, sipping my tea of choice, Earl Grey.

Indications of my bright future as a wordsmith remained frustratingly unsung but every Sunday, Edward reminded me that having a life that ends well was often the most one could hope for, even though his hadn't. "Words are fleeting shadows that fret on the page – an invisible tale once told to be remembered no more," he said. "Fame is made of gossamer and quicksilver, signifying nothing."

Whenever Edward left, I felt strangely diaphanous, but emboldened enough to scribble a poem I sensed within me. Sadly, it always disintegrated like a cobweb in a storm before I could capture it.

Of course, like everything, Puck made a game of tea and one afternoon I arrived a few minutes late to find the battleground of a sugar war with no survivors – an immature food fight but much stickier. Towers of competing cubes had finally collapsed and being fragile, burst into powdery granules. Tossing cubes in the air and failing to catch them by mouth left the floor crunchy with white crystals and not a few ants.

Tea is customarily served with digestive biscuits. Eeyore assured me they were so dubbed for a reason. "Digestion is profound consummation," he said in one of his authoritative tones. "One never messes with consuming food or grandiose ideas. Being consumed with living a fantasy can upset one's stomach if not taken with a dose of common sense. And what could be more sensible than having a grand time reading a good book eating digestive biscuits coated in milk chocolate."

To this end, I created a philosophy I dubbed 'The Tea-Ching', an ethereal diary of thoughts pronounced 'teaching' aligned to universal truth, premising that imagination is the food of life.

My diverse interests included but were no way limited to discovering brave new words. As a dedicated Oxfordian, my stance regarding the true authorship of the Shakespeare canon resides firmly on the side of my friend Edward de Vere, the 17th Earl of Oxford who, if not the soul of his age, was most certainly its greatest enigma.

I continued to monitor the ongoing controversial debates and penned the beginnings of what I hoped to be a book revealing the absolute truth behind Edward's calamitous sacrifices. I explained all this to Eeyore who is in awe of my speedreading techniques, but then as my second soul he was bound to be.

Peter Pan liked to tease me that levitation couldn't be far behind. *I'll have you flying in the shake of a donkey's tail*, he crowed before streaking off across the sky in gales of laughter shouting back. *Maybe in the shake of a spear.*

chapter 7

RETROGRADE SHADOWS

"Nurture strength of spirit
to shield you in sudden misfortune.
But do not distress yourself with dark imaginings.
Many fears are born of fatigue and loneliness."

MAX EHRMANN

2024

When I was sixty-one, the fourth event that changed my life occurred.

Fifty-five years ago, I created a mind-escape of indescribable beauty in an enchanted forest where my only playmates were characters from children's books. I spoke freely with them, and they, me.

I had been over the moon to discover that the saddest character, famously alien to the concept of fun, had a naturally cheerful side. Eeyore's morose temperament as written in 1928 hid a compassionate philosophical heart. But he couldn't help but behave the way A.A. Milne had created him until he grew up. We have remained steadfast companions ever since.

As a cosseted teenager of seventeen tender years, I'd been delivered from Tirings to the unnerving maw of gainful employment, unprepared for life in the world of shadows where Peter said humans killed trees for fun. Lack of formal education meant my opportunities for work were limited to menial jobs.

Eeyore reassured me my true happiness was portable, and so, we'd taken 'Otherwhere' with us and I kept warm and dry under an umbrella of health and welfare agencies that supported odd ducks like me.

Other than the dreaded daily commute tunneling through miles of forest in a noisy tin can I had a pleasant enough day job sorting books in a public library. Regular off-forest people who left shadows wherever they went, would never have understood my supernatural idiosyncrasies or that fantasy was a safe habitat. The *only* safe habitat for an odd duck.

Once again it was wise to act compliant. "Best not to rock any pea-green boats, if you know what I mean," Eeyore often said. "Be submissive, but never stoop to toadying or fawning. The truth will out with or without you."

Eeyore continued to bolster my spirits with his tongue-in-cheek sense of humor, "Truthfully, you were never born to be toyed with," he joked.

At first, menial tasks allowed me more time to imagine the stories I intended to write that Eeyore insisted were in my future. But the day came when I accepted my dormant literary gene was a permanently lost cause – likely an atrophied muscle memory from a previous life. My writing ventures ground to a halt, which is why I stopped 'venturing' in my thirties, and why, whenever I went to work, I needed a ritual to get out of bed and another to get out the door, and yet another to walk to the bus stop.

Even *on* the bus I was a wallflower. I took the same seat every day with my back to the windows but within view of the driver. There was little comfort from claiming an insignificant place on the sidelines, but I automatically gravitated there. It was my rightful place.

Like Eeyore, I couldn't help but follow the path I was destined to travel. I came into this world heralded by unseen powers under a paradoxical star.

I was exceptionally gifted with a crushing feeling of unworthiness. I didn't belong. But on the day of the book when I was five, a moment of kismet granted Eeyore and I the joy of belonging neither of us had known or believed possible.

For many happy years kinfolk energy promised we could stay in idyllic seclusion until, that is, time got in our way. Correction: old age and depression got in *my* way.

After wasting forty-four years of my life working dead end jobs, I despised the world of shadows so much that Otherwhere could no longer entirely assuage my sense of loss.

I wondered silently if I would die in the Shadowland or Otherwhere. Since Heaven was touted to be an ethereal place, Otherwhere made perfect sense. At least it did on my good days which were becoming less frequent in my sixty-first year.

That's when life intervened in my darkest hour as it's wont to do. I needed a new door.

To paraphrase Marcus Aurelius: one overcomes adversity by ploughing through obstacles full speed ahead.

For a long time, Marcus's teachings continued to sustain me until monkey-mind inevitably arrived throwing excrement into the fantasy world I'd created.

So, in 2024 when I was confronted by a disembodied voice that dared me to grow up, my old habitual fear of being singled out for punishment by a contrary universe, rang true.

It only took a few days of being bullied senseless for monkey-mind to chatter a different tack. What if, I reckoned, an invisible entity who cared enough to kill me with attention was a gift? What if, accepting it as a friend could give me an edge? What if I *was* special. So, when the voice invited me to meet face-to-face, I was lured into a bold experiment. What if Marcus was right.

I have been equally praised and accused of being a perpetual child, but other than having invisible childhood friends all my life, I was never a child. Not a real one. A true child is content to be anywhere there's dogs and cats and ice-cream.

I happen to love cats and dogs as much as anyone, but I'd never felt truly safe unless I was alone in my room reading a book, and besides, I was deathly afraid of ice-cream.

Naturally my worst fears cornered me publicly where I could least escape them, wallowing on board a local bus heading perilously out of control down the slippery slope of old age and dying alone. True to form, I panicked.

Consequently, things became so extraordinary that ice-cream was no longer a detriment to my mental health.

But then, I became infatuated with an old bag lady who appeared on my bus and around Havonford. There was something about her dress and manner that compelled me to follow her and soon I was obsessed with wanting to know more. I stalked the pitiful creature whenever I could, and she started to play a game of cat and mouse with me until one day her innocent presence turned sinister. I couldn't wait to get home to the safety of Otherwhere.

The next morning, I woke with a galumping headache. I left home late for work in a dither, and headed to the bus stop, but the number 61-bus fooled me. It was right on time.

THE REMAINS OF THE DA

HEDINGHAM DETENTION

chapter 8

EXIT STAGE LEFT

The earth can yield me but a common grave,
When you entombed in men's eyes shall lie.
Your monument shall be my gentle verse,
Which eyes not yet created shall o'er-read,
And tongues to be your being shall rehearse,
When all the breathers of this world are dead.
You still shall live, such virtue hath my pen,
Where breath most breathes, even in the mouths of men.

WILLIAM SHAKESPEARE

1604

Edward de Vere woke from the raucous cawing of crows in direct contrast to the soothing ablutions of a warm wet cloth wiping his face. First his brow, then each eyelid in turn, moving slowly down the contours of his nose, blissfully caressing both cheeks, to moisten his lips and smooth his beard.

It was lovingly done. Gently done. Slowly, ritualistically accomplished with steady hands.

Edward detected the scents of lavender and pine resin. He opened his eyes to thank his manservant and beg another hour of sleep but met Puck's mischievous grin instead.

"There you are," Puck said. "'Tis late, master, we must away."

"I must do no such thing, minx," Edward grumbled, "and don't call me that. I'm not your master. If anything, you're mine. Let me sleep yet awhile."

"You have plenty of time to slumber," Puck chided. "Come, while it's raining. You love the sound of rain drumming the forest canopy in the dark. Be quick about it lest it stops."

"It's still dark," Edward noted looking past Puck to the open window. Sure enough, silky threads of white rain fell straight and true in the moonlight. Puck reached the window first, parted the silvery curtain, and drank a handful of threads.

Three events occurred simultaneously. Dawn broke and woke the sun, Edward shielded his eyes from the glare, and a peacock shrieked in the grounds below.

Edward rose, eager to look. "Is it... are its tail feathers..."

"Yes, your Grace, it's showing off as you like it. They're majestically displayed like the queen's most resplendent starched collar. Its feathery eyes twinkle like Elizabeth's pearls. Never a maid, was she, but a proud prince shining amongst white-faced dun-colored females."

The rain returned full force in a grey downpour. Edwards eyes narrowed. "She's dead isn't she."

"Yes, your Grace. For many months."

Edward felt his chin only to find a velvety covering instead of a beard. "I have to say I prefer to be washed once I'm up and about. I'm too tired for one of your adventures."

"You're not tired, you're weary," Puck said. "Tis better we be friends than servant and master. Yet, I serve you, still, as always and as ever. Do you remember how we met? It was raining as it is now. You were four, your skin red from being vigorously scrubbed in a bath of cold water and coarse salt."

"It was a punishment. I don't remember what I'd done."

"You'd given Mistress Allen the slip and run off into the forest splashing mud over your clean shirt. She was too old to catch you and no-one younger dared to. You were a formidable little rakehell even then."

"She was not best pleased. Her words were colder than the water if memory serves. She was the only one not afraid of me."

"I was never afraid of you, Edward. I heard your wild shrieks of laughter before I ever set eyes on you. "In fact, it was your cries that brought me forth into the oak grove where you shivered like a miserable drowned rat."

Edward squinted into Puck's twinkling eyes. "I remember. Once the bright light around you dimmed, I saw we were the same height. Pearl raindrops shone from your budding horns. I thought you were a faun, but your legs were…"

"Spritely made – I was a Dionysian child," Puck interrupted. "Tall for my age. I was barely two thousand years old."

Edward cast aside the counterpane and swung his legs to the floor. "I can see I shall have no rest until I comply. Where are you taking me?"

The landscape below was white as a blank sheet of parchment, silent and still. No sky, no horizon, no hilly terrain, and no trees. Hedingham Castle's forest had been stolen.

Puck proffered a crude wooden cup carved with runes. "Before you think yourself mad, take sup, child. It's honeyed wine. I anticipate your…"

"Every need, as ever, yes yes yes," Edward said. "But this time you have enchanted the forest away. It's a mite chilly for the midsummer solstice, is it not."

Puck tucked a richly embroidered cloak around Edward's shoulders. "Time to go, young sir."

Edward noticed the cloak's hem touched the carpet in folds. "How can it be that I'm still a lad, Puck?"

Puck grinned the truth.

"I'm dead, aren't I."

"Yes."

"And where are we going?"

"The green glade where we met. It's not far. You need its

healing leaves around you." Immediately the forest manifested dense and green as always – a refuge Edward had treasured when beset with the troubled household of his childhood.

The cloak shrank to fit. Bright sunlight dappled the brave grandfather oaks protecting them in a henge of safety from the blue boar known to roam at will.

"Are you…?"

"Staying with you? Yes, as ever, I am yours."

"How does the world?" Edward paused and looked away. Puck always told the truth. "Do any of them mourn me?"

"You died over three hundred years ago. Thousands celebrate you under a false name. Your pseudonym betrayed you as did the queen and her henchmen. Your words are revered, sire."

"So, I am re-Vered yet lost. I grieve to live again that I might have my true say."

"Revenge serves no-one."

"I grieve for the lies that betray history. I grieve from being betrayed. I am undone. Unfinished. Empty. I beg you tell me there is a better life ahead, Puck."

Puck held out one of Edward's boots. "You are weary, Edward. Put these on. It's time to show you something. You will be pleased."

Puck led Edward, a young teenage boy, dressed in a white shirt, doe-skin breeches and matching calf-length boots, to a shady dell with a river of rippling waters where stood a goodly writing desk with quill and ink at the ready. The peacock was in fine fettle, parading around it like a king. Its shriek started Edward's heart.

"I have a tremendous thirst, Puck. Is there anything to drink?"

Puck held out a goblet of Rhenish wine. Welcome home," he said.

KINDERGARTEN

PRESCHOOL

LILA

divine play (pronounced Leela)

*Lila accurately describes the notion
within yogic philosophy that the whole world is the
spontaneous creation of Brahman. It is sportive and playful,
as opposed to self-conscious or volitional in intention.
Lila emphasizes the fact that the world of shadows
is born in freedom and playful creativity, rather than necessity.
In this way, the world is a stage for Lila, or divine play.
It is an illusion to see the actions on life's stage as real,
and those who see them in this way are said to be under
the spell of maya. In other yogic schools and scriptoriums,
Lila is used to denote the divine play
of male and female.*

chapter 9

LOUD & CLEAR

"Speak your truth quietly and clearly;
and listen to others,
even to the dull and the ignorant;
they too have their story."

MAX EHRMANN

2024

I left the house with a worsening galumping headache but two minutes from the door an aura in my left eye signalled the approach of a migraine that would hit in precisely thirty minutes, right on time unless I immediately stalled it with ibuprofen.

I fished in my cavernous purse for my pills. Seeing with one's fingers when in a hurry surrounded by the menacing trees of Jabbers Walk was an exercise in futility. Predictably, in my haste I dropped the first capsule, fumbled for a second, shoved it into my mouth, and proceeded towards the bus stop at a run but the first-aid fiasco had cost me five precious minutes.

As I exited Jabbers' ominous tunnel the blurry image of half a bus pulled away leaving me stranded. I had missed it. And according to the schedule the next one was forty-five minutes away, give or take, if it came at all.

My immediate future was either a full-on migraine or choking to death on a pill stuck in my throat – a bleak start to a long dreary day abandoned between a bus that arrived early and a migraine that arrived too late for a glass of water. I limped to the bench and sat holding a palm over the firework display in my left eye. The hands on my watch disappeared. Left alone with my thoughts I brooded on my bunions, which given my full attention, filled my shoes with razorblades.

The wind picked up and the rain came down. When I say it rained down, I mean it angled itself sideways and hit me full in the face. Partial vision escalated to watery blindness. I shivered deeper into my thin coat and dreamed of my fleece-lined raincoat with its fur trimmed hood and gloves, and my Wellington boots abandoned in the hall closet.

I debated retracing my steps home to call in sick, but it was payday and the cupboards were bare. The deciding factor was not facing the interior of Jabbers Walk again while I was vulnerable. Impaired vision made me an easy target for the unholy terrors that go bump in the forest.

I was alone. Grey rain, a grey coat, and my grey mood made me hard for the driver to see. I moved close to the curb, cold, wet, and hungry with thumping toes, and willed the bus to come.

It must have heard me because it soon lumbered toward me like a drunken beast and came to an abrupt stop that sprayed me with greasy water.

I was not in the best mood. I muttered let's get this disaster over with, under my breath, and hauled myself onto the bus with numb arthritic fingers. If the bag lady wanted to torture me today, she could have me, no contest.

The bus was full.

Someone was in my regular seat.

I barely made it to the nearest handrail before the bus lurched away. I clung to it feet planted apart, braced for sudden movement. And as soon as the bus reached the next stop, I inched myself towards the only empty seat and sat next to a man, who from his countenance, was surely a serial killer.

Once underway, the bus's loudspeaker addressed me like an old friend as if it was expecting me. "Ah, there you are, Cheerless," it said. "I wondered when you would show yourself."

I answered back, in my head. *"Are you speaking to me?"*

"Your name is Cheerless. No doubt you forgot; it's been a long time since we were last acquainted."

"How long?"

"2,300 years give or take."

"And you are?"

"Zeno of Citium."

"No shit, Sherlock" I said, spoiling for a fight.

"Correct," it replied. "Absolutely *no* shit whatsoever."

I took a deep inhale from my puffer and counted to four before I could answer in mind-speak. *"Who asked you, anyway?"*

"Believe it or not, Worthless, *you* did."

I started to wheeze. *"Liar liar... pants on fire."*

"Suit yourself. Your name is Worthless. Literal meaning... unworthy. Since when does the attitude of 'poor me' ever create prosperity? The answer is *never*. So, you can rally or fold, but I assure you it's not entirely your choice... *yet*."

I jutted out my chin and shifted uneasily in my seat, inhaler close at hand, checking the passengers for obvious eye contact. *"So, who's choosing for me, then? Surely not you."* I jerked my head towards the motley passengers and crinkled my nose. *"Surely not one of them."*

"They're not morons, Leela. They're preoccupied with their future. Reach a little higher, Soulless. Madame Universe hasn't got all day. You've been flirting with her unmanifested dimension for a while now. How's that working out?"

I struggled to breath. *"Less than zero, if it's any of your damn business. And my name is not Leela."*

The voice chortled. "Irony is one of the Un-manifested's secret weapons. The more accurate terminology is more than Zeno. Child, is it a war you're after? Coz, that's what's coming."

"I'm NOT a child. The universe would have warned me of war."

"She did, many many times, but your negative thinking drowned her out. Did you know that you think in caps. Perhaps if you stopped shouting at her she'd grace you with her presence. I have to say, you're a topnotch whiner. That lady sitting opposite you... the one you call the bag lady – you'd do well to take an apple from her basket. She loves life which is why she needs you. And if you don't want to be treated like a child, please stop acting like one."

"That old bat needs *Me*?"

"You need each *other* as it happens, so, stop your incessant complaining. No time like the present I always say. But don't overthink it. What would Eeyore do? Use your noodle. Take right action and see what happens."

"Is that a threat?"

"Think, Worthless. What else *could* it be!"

I sat choking in the long silence that followed.

"I'll be in touch... or not," the voice finally said. "I don't choose to waste my consciousness on the hoity-toity mindless stuff. Time's a wasting."

I took short even breaths. *"Thanks for the vote of confidence."*

"I don't believe in politics, Wordless. I only ever speak the truth. Not my personal truth you understand but universal truth. The absolute quintessential truth. And as much as you don't want to admit it, you're a grownup. Sorry, but the art of choosing the high road is one of the toughest aspects of waking up. But if you're serious about making a deal with the universe, you'd better take your vitamins. It's showtime, Leela. And you are *it*."

"My name is LILA."

"No. That's just your pseudonym. Your name is LEELA."

"I don't have a pseudonym. I'm not a proper writer."

"No kidding, Sherlock," the voice said. "There's no need for rudeness, old thing. Why are you so hostile?"

"For a start, I have a blinding headache. I'm old and my feet hurt," I replied. *"Furthermore, I don't like you. You're always late, your breaks squeal like a stuck pig, and you smell."*

"Still… there's no need to disparage my passengers."

"Most of your passengers are complaining, self-centered gossipmongers who stare at their phones every waking moment. They create nothing. They crave mindless entertainment. As such, I label them mindless. I may not be the cheeriest of old ladies, but since you asked, I'm hostile from struggling to survive."

"I mean to help you."

"I didn't ask for your help or advice. You're probably an hallucination like Ebenezer Scrooge's undigested piece of potato. I've read the Sherlock Holmes canon, and you mister Zeno or whatever your name is, are no great detective. Hence, I called you Sherlock to be sarcastic. But perhaps being a bus you're that not well-read."

The number 61 stopped to pick up three zombies – teenage boys with blank expressions, all wearing headphones, staring transfixed at their cellphones.

I was just getting started. My venting took on a life of its own. *"My life has been difficult if you must know. And since you clearly know nothing about me, perhaps your name should be Zero!"*

Zeno chuckled. The bus swerved, narrowly missing a raccoon.

"Is Zeno your real name or is it perchance a pseudonym? We both know I'm never going to write a book. There's no need to rub my nose in it."

The voice paused. "Are you done?"

"I'm done in. Please be more mindful of woodland creatures crossing the road in future. Your road used to be their forest."

"And now if I may," Zeno said. "You may call me *Master* Zeno.

I shall resume pushing your buttons, because, old girl, someone's got to do it. And you may need a pseudonym sooner than you think."

I broke the long silence that followed sounding like a flimflam psychic. *"Hello, is anyone there?"* Silence. I whispered, *are you done, Ducky?* knowing my 'better luck next time' card would likely abandon me like everything else.

"Words are never done," Master Zeno spouted. "Words are everything. Sometimes there are no words to describe the fears of a child. Do you want to be a proper writer or not? *That* is the question, especially since you're suffering from writers' block, Wordless."

"How did you know that?"

"The old bat told me. Have a nice day, Hopeless."

"Same to you with knobs on," I countered wittily between the hackings of a coughing fit.

A moment later, the bus's brakes squealed to a stop and the door opened. For a time that seemed never-ending, the driver drummed his fingers on the steering wheel, never taking his eyes from the road. No one climbed aboard. Then, after his timeout, the driver closed the door and seamlessly resumed driving.

But a presence *had* boarded. I felt its energy quicken inside me. Something was new. The number 61-bus had a pulse. I felt possessed but strangely my fractious breathing normalized.

I still managed to wheeze a shout at the entity which triggered the need for another inhaler puff. *"And by-the-way, the universe is not purely feminine,"* I bellowed. *"It's yin and yang. Commonly defined as duality in the best spiritual circles. Have a nice day."*

"Some days tis rightly so," the entity chided. "Every second Monday, t'isn't. You overthink me, Thoughtless. Did you assume the Universe works without a full Tarot deck, Witless? Life is a house of cards, Mindless."

"And I'll thank you to stop calling me silly names."

The words 'NEXT STOP IS MIDDLE-EARTH' in caps moseyed from left to right across the display banner. "Ditto," the loudspeaker said. "Righty-o. Gird your loins, Wordless. Over and out."

Words escaped me, or rather I wished they had. *"I have no words"* I began, choking on humiliation and the lack of oxygen. Slow strangulation burbled in my throat.

The entity had no such problem. Its voice was positively gleeful. "Cat got your tongue, old girl?" it snarked. The word 'girl' echoed round the bus and bounced me.

I glanced over at Missus Bag Lady. She was smiling in her sleep. I crossed my arms to protect myself from demons, closed my eyes and gasped a long conscious cleansing breath. When I opened them, milady was gone, and my lungs had cleared. "On guard, Breathless," the voice warned. "I am sending you a cloud." Queasiness hit me like a punch of lightning. The threat of adventure had been dropped at my feet. Ready or not, I was *it*.

Eeyore was asleep at the foot of my bed when I woke the next morning. "It's up with the birds, then, is it", he moaned, rolling onto the floor with a thump. "Not my favorite time of the day. Never mind. No rest for the hapless, It's all early birds and worms, then. No porridge I suppose." He was deliberately mimicking his old grouchy self to make a point.

We proceeded to Lucy's field with our eyes trained on the sky which is nigh impossible for a four-legged animal. Eeyore kept up a relentless commentary. "Is that a storm cloud? Or that one? I'm sure that black one *must* be."

"The voice didn't specify," I replied. "So, there's no reason to assume it was sending a hostile cloud. Some clouds are innocent and fluffy."

Eeyore stopped in his tracks and gave me a 'you can't possibly be serious', glare. "Since when did I ever need a reason to expect the worst?" he moaned. "And what precisely do you think 'on guard' means? It means danger lies ahead, that's what it means. But off we go to gather a huffy storm cloud without a care. Hey ho. A pondering we shall go, with ominous clouds dive bombing every which way, ready to attack. Don't mind me. I shall keep my funny little thoughts to myself. No bother. It's a mere walk in the park to Lucy's 'Otherwhere' field."

I resumed my pondering out loud. "Honestly, how many pseudonyms does one odd duck need, anyway," I wheezed, startling a nearby crow. Its squawk made Eeyore jump. He paused to stretch a crick from his neck. "I have no idea. "Stone the crows. Go on, then, surprise me."

"I thought you didn't like surprises," I said. "There's no need to get shirty."

"I appreciate a *good* startle with the best of them," Eeyore said. "My problem is with *loud* startles."

chapter 10

THE HAUNTING TRUTH

"Last night upon the stair
I met a man who wasn't there.
He wasn't there again today.
Oh, how I wish he'd go away."

HUGHES MEARNS

– 'Antigonish'

Eeyore insists stalking is stock and trade for a wannabe writer, he calls it legitimate research. Doing it well is a fine art. To poorly paraphrase Charles Dickens: there were times I did my best and my worst at the same time.

I am a people watcher. Excusable, on the surface, but Otherwhere has strict rules, and the number one rule is to never speak to strangers with shadows. Since when has conversation with a shadow entity ever proven to be light and cheery. Nothing could be stranger than a talking bus that cast a long shadow over my happiness.

When Eeyore heard my plight, he solemnly decreed the bag lady would be the breaking or the making of me and never mentioned it again… for nearly two hours.

Peoplewatching sounds perfectly innocent, but I was becoming 'a glass is completely empty' kind of person. If I continued to wield my increasing old age aches and pains like a 'vorpal sword' there was every chance I'd cut off my whinging to spite my blessings. I may even, perish the thought, become haughtier than Shakespeare's Queen Lizzie or my friend Alice's, Queen of Hearts – a pair of depraved royal terrorists. I was fast becoming a grouchy old woman dictator in an exclusive world of my own creation ever since I'd decreed that ice-cream was dangerous.

I lived between the horrors of writing and writer's block, saving face by the skin of my ego by locking my stillborn pages in a drawer to die a literary death.

But I came to see that secrets in drawers had been the underlying story of my life. I was my mother' secret locked away in a cheerless drawer when I was two months old. And although I never met my father I have been silently shouting 'off with their heads' ever since. I was haunted by a dark rabbit hole inside me. I was no Alice.

I treated meditation like a begging bowl. But I wished too loud. I was no Goldilocks.

I am, according to Max Ehrmann's 'Desiderata', a child of the universe with human rights. To prove my worthiness, Piglet hangs on Winnie the Pooh's every word, Pooh hangs on mine, and William Shakespeare cares what I think.

Feeling sorry for myself had rendered me completely unlovable. I was a spoiled queen bee. I was no Max Ehrmann. Stalking a bag lady wasn't something a wildly unstable child should do. And lately I felt as if I was stalking myself.

The morning after the first voice had been routine. The bus route was routine. The passengers were routine. My personal routine was routine. And after streaming too many hours of Oxfordian truths battling Stratfordian lies I reported my mind hijacked.

I tried explaining my frustration to Pooh who in turn explained it in his simplistic wisdom to Piglet. "Someone wrote something but didn't," he translated.

The Shakespeare controversy was heating up, so my mind should have been on fire, but I sat grimly silent, determined to endure the commute. Such is forced willpower; I gave myself another galumping headache, this time relieved by a bottle of water.

My performance crashed as the Thursday bus hurtled headlong into a tunnel of trees. For the umpteenth time I was heading to a mindless job on threadbare emotions. I had to accept the universe had cut me loose. I was left with the overall impression that the Universe was a tad careless with its budding devotees. Our connection was iffy.

The thought of a haunted house with fitful electrics played in the theatre of my mind. I was mindful of too many empty seats so, technically, I was centerstage in a 'mindless' zone when I saw the word 'WORDLESS' in red caps tap dance across the barren landscape of the bus's digital display board. In Zen, empty mind is considered a high state of awareness, but the number 61-bus had its own rules.

"WORDLESS," the loudspeaker echoed. "MINDLESS ... POINTLESS ... ENDLESS... lend me your donkey's ears."

Ten minutes out of town on a deserted stretch of road where the forest extinguished even the faintest finger of daylight, the bus halted at an unmarked stop and my bag lady climbed on board. She took the seat directly opposite me and acknowledged me with the suggestion of a smile before nodding off to sleep.

A mile later, the bus jammed on its brakes to avoid a deer, causing the old lady to wake with a start and straighten her hat. She sent a second smile from *her* eyes directly into *mine*. Did I see the sly old fox wink? Absolutely. I decided to wait for the right moment when I could say hello properly.

I spaced out and gazed out the window, alarmed to meet milady's reflection staring back at me. I had become the specter of Alice 'beyond the looking glass'. But before I had time to process the vision, the bus lurched to a stop and let on a group of teenagers loaded down with backpacks who jostled noisily past me towards the back of the bus.

The driver pulled out before they reached their seats and knocked them off balance. For a moment they had to right themselves by grabbing onto overhead straps and each other. But they found their bus legs and moved on to reveal the old lady's seat was empty.

Slightly shaken, I looked out my window from what I now regarded as my personal scrying bowl and noticed a distinct disturbance in the treeline as the tail of a sheepdog disappeared into the forest wall.

Muffled barking coming from milady's abandoned seat startled me. I turned sharply as the bus jolted forward. She had left a single red apple behind. Visions of Snow White accepting a poisonous apple from a strange old crone flashed through my mind. The apple and I watched each other without blinking until the bus hit a pothole. It sounded like thunder as it rolled down the aisle where, I assumed it found its way back into the basket from whence it came. I had been spared.

All day, during eight hours of *yes sir, no ma'am, three bags full sir*, I dismissed the creepy event as a mindless waking dream and settled in for my regular mind-numbing two-hour commute home with bitterness subdued into tolerance. Chai Latte would compensate for my ordeal.

Writing is not the stuff of prosperous breadwinners let alone a blocked one. I had to work. And since ageism was a real thing, I had been lucky to snag any job after the library closed. Still, meaningless minimum wage jobs working for unconscious corporations continued to plague me as an odious thorn in my creative side. Every meditation became the determination to manifest financial rescue from a fate worse than death.

Putting it generously, although I was an avid reader, I was never more than a borderline author tilting at wordmills. I was too desperate, too needy, and too hungry to con the universe into sending me a cash windfall or a sensational story premise. Even Lucy rarely delivered a windfall apple out of season. Furthermore, in my steadfast arrogance, I refused to buy lottery tickets.

For the last year, I had calmed my frantic thoughts into submission through meditation. True, my outlook of abject misery was happily reduced to a dull roar, but I had become neutral. Not a thrilling juncture to be sure but an improvement over a constant replay of chronic pessimism and debilitating anxiety attacks that my literary hero Edward Lear dubbed 'the Morbids'.

In desperation, I closed my eyes to separate myself from a busload of disenchanted automatons, thinking to disengage from my running critique of their collective repugnance: their odorific auras and vapid expressions to reconnect with a writer's constructive stream of noble thought.

Perhaps, since I followed the Shakespeare controversy so avidly, I could outline the biography I intended to write about Edward de Vere that would elevate the consciousness of a world gone mad.

As I tuned my internal radio dial for universal guidance, the loudspeaker emitted a recorded announcement. 'This train is for Athens'. I recognized it as the voice of the Vancouver SkyTrain.

I used to be quite the traveler visiting the mainland often, but I was terrified of the wretched SkyTrain with its thunderous dimly lit Banshee screeching tunnels. I didn't drive. At sixty-one my eyesight was dodgy. I could never be sure of plain sight or a misty mirage.

'Train?' Once again, computers could not be trusted. Artificial intelligence had invaded the system and was churning out misinformation.

'Sorry... I meant to say bus', Ms. Sky Train corrected.

I blinked and paid attention. Taped conversations didn't correct mistakes. And besides we weren't *on* a train. Nor were we in Vancouver.

The accompanying digital banner displayed the words 'mind' and 'less'. I watched the red lights flash on and off as they slowly connected into the word mindless.

The screen went blank before spacing out the letters W-O-R-D-L-E-S-S.

I was apparently the only passenger not intent on studying my phone.

Ever the purist, I had promised myself I would never stoop to the lows of phone watching. No texting. No obsessive email checking. No Tetris. No tic tac toe. But in desperation I had ended up stooping to banner watching. More the fool, me.

I scanned the faces of my fellow passengers all eyes down on their phones as if they were high stake Bingo cards. I dismissed them as brain dead, oblivious to the world of imagination. They were quite beneath me, so, why was I here like a hapless sardine trapped with them in a tin can on wheels?

None of them responded to the 'wordless' announcement, but being me, I spoke back as if it was the most natural thing in the world.

What followed was a bizarre conversation that unexpectedly opened the fifth dimension.

The Loudspeaker broke the silence with a question meant, I assumed, for me: do you believe in haunted buses? it shouted over the din of engine fatigue, traffic, and hum drum gossip.

I thought back my answer with my hackles raised. *"Of course not. What do you take me for."*

The loudspeaker lost no time in its follow up announcement: the next stop is ...

I waited, but the truncated message ended in silence. Clearly, we were going nowhere.

I checked the banner linked to the audio. The screen simply spelled HELLO AGAIN.

WHAT IS YOUR NAME?

The old bag lady rematerialized across from me and smiled sweetly.

My reply instantly appeared on the banner. Apparently, we were on Déjà vu time. *"My name is still Lila"*

THAT'S STILL JUST YOUR PSEUDONYM

"I'm STILL not a proper writer. Only proper writers have pseudonyms."

YOUR NAME IS LEELA ... SAME SPELLING as LILA but pronounced with two e's... REPEAT AFTER ME

"Okay."

LEELA

"Leela," I obeyed, warming to the game. But who was playing with me?

EXCELLENT, LEELA ... I WANT YOU TO WRITE A STORY FOR ME. CAN YOU DO THAT?

"I'm not that good but it would be my pleasure to try."

"AH, BUT WOULD IT BE YOUR JOY?"

While I considered a snappy response the loudspeaker resumed the conversation. THIS TRAIN IS FOR ATHENS it announced again.

"No, it bloody well isn't," I shouted back, startling the slovenly passenger about to de-bus in front of me.

A random jumble of Greek letters formed and reformed on the banner in blinking red lights. Μέτρον ἄριστον ... Μηδὲν ἄγαν

"In English please."
MODERATION IS BEST... NOTHING IN EXCESS
"Who are you?"
I AM YOUR SWANSONG ... THIS BUS IS FOR ATHENS

The banner read: WORDLESS ... ENDLESS... MINDLESS followed by three question marks.

"Would you like to have a cup of tea sometime?" I messaged, leaning forward anticipating the affirmative answer I wanted.
SYNERGY RULES... THINKING MAKES IT SO
"I don't understand."
THAT WOULD BE LOVELY
"Where?"
MY PLACE
"And where is that?"

For a moment, the conversation took a more commanding tone, and I was taken aback: THE FOREST PATH ... YOU KNOW THE ONE ... WEAR RUBBER BOOTS.

Of course, trees were the last place I wanted to go, but if it was time to grow up, I'd better go. *"When?"*

There was an impolite urgency underlying the message: NEXT SATURDAY... HIGH NOON ... BRING CAKE!

"I will be there." I couldn't help thinking she should have said please.

WELCOME TO THE FOURTH DIMENSION, LEELA. DON'T -- BE -- LATE!

The screen erased itself and a chorus line of heart emoticons parading from right to left spilled through the wall of the bus into the street. I fancied I heard the shatter of broken glass as they hit the concrete.

chapter 11

AN APPLE FOR YOUR THOUGHTS

"Nothing is either good or bad
But thinking makes it so."

WILLIAM SHAKESPEARE

The first time I saw the bag lady was on the number 61-bus – a genteel old dear carrying a wicker shopping basket. The shawl and bonnet she wore reminded me of Jemima Puddleduck. She carried a rolled-up umbrella that served as a walking stick, and I played with the idea of it having magical properties. I encouraged my imagination to play.

Nagging thoughts are a plague for *almost* authors. Had my dormant literary vibes finally manifested a worthy protagonist? Such was my runaway mind that nothing was too farfetched. She wasn't real. Had she stepped out of my imagination. I considered the possibility that maybe it was *me* who wasn't real but immediately dismissed such a possibility. Wunderkind senses were sometimes off but they never outright lied even when Owl was involved. Milady checked all the witchy boxes. She had the eerie vibes of a person who traversed dimensions and time. I would have to persuade Eeyore to set aside his dislike of loud noises and join me on the bus. I needed his opinions when my decisions waivered. But sadly, there were no earplugs to be had for donkey-sized ears.

After that, I saw the apple lady occasionally around town, but soon she was everywhere: in supermarket aisles and the checkout line; walking a sheepdog in the off-leash park; across the street waiting for a wrong-way bus; and forever disappearing around corners. It was delightfully uncanny. Was she teasing me? It didn't matter, I was hooked. I was on the trail of a story at last.

I didn't have to work at finding her. Milady found me. Everywhere. Just long enough to leave a tantalizing question twitching on the ground that chided "What happens next is up to you, ducky? Do hurry up. You're almost there. Don't *give* up just *grow* up. You know you want to."

But the day came when, accompanied by Eeyore, stalking the bag lady became untenable. I stood on the last sidewalk between a housing development under construction and the wildwoods I avoided, refusing to cross the unpaved street. It was literally the end of the road for me. I reached over to touch Eeyore's ears, but he had already scarpered.

Milady disappeared through a gap in the trees without looking back.

No contest. I turned away. The heady scent of pine followed me home. I called and called but Eeyore was gone. A mad thought occurred he'd been kidnapped by the bag lady.

I would find Eeyore if I faced the old harridan on her increasingly rude terms.

After I followed milady to the children's section of the public library, it was easier to believe a witch had walked out of a fairy tale. It was entirely logical. I'd walked in and out of books most of my life. Eeyore was nowhere in sight, but I heard him whisper *you are a wise monkey* in my ear. *No worries,* I sent back. *I'm coming to save you on Saturday.*

Once milady was sure I was hooked, she moved to an out of the way shelf. She pulled down a book of Shakespeare's sonnets with her eyes locked on mine and left it on the table.

A clear breadcrumb for me to follow. Shades of déjà vu. My librarian in Tirings had left Shakespeare's sonnets on my bed.

I loved Eeyore reading me bedtime stories. It was easy to become hooked on the melodic tone of Eeyore's recitation of 'Alice in Wonderland' that set me dreaming of a land ruled by a heartless queen with a savage temper.

Naturally, I assumed the wicked witch in any story was my mother. So, knowing my love of 'Snow White and the Seven Dwarfs', Eeyore suggested the bag lady represented the old apple seller who gave Snow White a poisoned red apple that turned out to be the lucky charm that not only saved her life but delivered her into the arms of a charming prince. *'Omens come in all sizes,'* he'd said. *'Scary things in dreams are rarely what they seem. They're there to wake you up any way they can. Never assume something in a negative dream is bad.'*

Research confirmed Beatrix Potter in old age was a dead ringer for my bag lady, right down to their threadbare shawls, squashed straw hats, and a sheepdog.

Disturbingly, the lady, now inside my head, juggled my thoughts like apples. "Defenceless," she mocked, "a real writer would have given me a proper name."

I sent her a mental telegram. *"Beatrix. You have my donkey... stop... give him back now! ... stop... LILA Swann."*

"I don't have to read your mind, Spineless, you're an open book," she taunted back.

"There's no need for rudeness," I said. *"I'm not spineless."*

"Spineless is as spineless does," Beatrix mocked.

I treaded softly and played it safe for Eeyore's sake, but I heard his disembodied voice again. *"I taught you to think no evil, Leela. What you don't see is the truth. I never left home."*

The next morning, I was a basket case.

I was the only passenger on the ride home. It was winter dark by 6 o'clock and I lost myself in my reflection from the darkened windows. It had started to snow which put me in mind of Snow White's hapless situation. She'd been a deserted motherless child and had married a handsome prince, so she knew a thing or two about survival. That thought turned the window of the bus into her stepmother's creepy magic mirror.

"Mirror mirror on the bus," I intoned quietly. *"Who is the bravest of all of us?"* My breath fogged the window, and I had to wipe it to see my face.

But I wasn't there. The bag lady's disapproving face stared back at me. She tapped the glass with a bony finger. Her mouth moved and her words rang clearly through my skull.

"You are *it*, Sherlock."

The squeal of breaks alerted me to my stop. I gave the old crone a last look meaning to dispatch the courage I didn't feel, but the window only showed a swirl of freezing black crow feathers that floated skyward rather than down.

I made out the huddled shape of the bag lady waiting in the shelter as my bus skidded to a stop. There she sat, primly on the bench, all smiles, holding her basket of what I now assumed were poisoned apples.

I left hurriedly by the back door and looked over my shoulder. The bench was empty.

Much relieved, I set off at a brisk pace half sliding down the slippery path home through Jabbers Walk. In my mind's eye I saw Eeyore waiting for me at the front door. I picked up speed as new white snowflakes cleared enough to see the back of milady, now walking ahead of me.

There was no place to hide. It was an opportunity to confront her, and surely Eeyore awaited me, returned safe and sound, minutes away at our front door. I took a deep breath from my ever-ready inhaler and sent Eeyore a telepathic message. *I'm nearly home. Two minutes away. Please meet me outside. I need your help.*

I called out "Miss Potter please wait. Hold up," but just then my phone rang, and I fumbled through my purse to answer a missed call. When I looked up the old lady was gone.

I breathed easier but looked around in case she was hiding behind a tree.

Eeyore bounded into me like a runaway toboggan and tumbled me. "Dear girl, whatever is the matter. Is it the Jabberwock?" But the thrill of having Eeyore back was short-lived. My smile froze when he vanished into a flutter of pink snowflakes. Eeyore was a mirage, no doubt manifested from intense wishful thinking. I had been the victim of snow blindness and my own folly of pushing my luck.

Next morning on the bus the old lady was back in her usual seat, facing me, guileless as a child.

I chided myself for ever fearing her and sent her a tentative forgiveness smile.

She returned my pale smile with a wan version of her own. I concluded it was all I was going to get, so, rather than stare at her I read the banner now madly out of control spewing out random letters: S – – D – – L – – N – – E – – S – – E that rearranged themselves into the word, ENDLESS as I watched. The fire alarm went haywire as if I'd won a jackpot on a game show. Apparently, no-one heard it but me.

The bag lady chose a red apple from her basket, and I thought she was going to offer it to me, but her eyes never left mine as she took a bite.

I thought curiosity had always been the making of me, and at sixty-one I was pretty sure I was as 'made' as I could ever be, but I was wrong. Because later, in true fairy godmother physics, I was granted an extraordinarily wild adventure, should I choose to accept it.

chapter 12

DEAD END

"In that book, which is my memory,
On the first page of the chapter
That is the day when I first met you,
Appear the words: here begins a new life"

DANTE ALIGHIERI

—Vita Nuova

When the 'big Saturday' arrived, I awoke with the morning chorus but when I opened the front door to check for rain, the birdsong ceased abruptly. Feeling responsible, I sent a 'sorry to disturb' into the sky and closed the door.

Three things happened to warn me: birdsong immediately resumed, a dog barked from far away, and the hair on the back of my neck and forearms tingled to attention.

The word swansong had worried me all night, so I'd looked it up. According to folklore, swans sing most beautifully before they die. A swansong also refers to resting on one's laurels. Examples given included the final performance of a poet or any creative achievement before retirement. In essence, someone who was leaving in style. Perhaps *dying* in style.

Something in my waters said run. Perhaps it was a message from Eeyore. Beatrix still had him. I resolved he would return home with me by the end of the day and calmed down.

I waived my first cuppa of the day as a mark of respect to Beatrix Potter's good side, considering she seemed to have at least two: polite and rude. Which one of them would greet me was anyone's guess.

I would play to milady's cheery side whether it was present or not and reclaim Eeyore in a few hours. Beatrix was no match for me. I conjured a vision of her choking on my cake as I placed it in a box.

Beatrix's wonky magic may be in the air playing silly buggers, but I was on a rescue mission and my concentration eradicated spells.

But that was before I knew the consequences of tuning out of a surly vibration into a higher one that only dogs and Eeyore could hear.

I dressed for rain and as always, checked my Wellington boots for unwanted intruders. After the all-clear, I set out for 'grandma's house' like red riding hood armed with cake.

Victory was mine. I carried a cake in a wicker basket disguised as a plastic food container. I seemed to be moving underwater against a strong current, but true to my word, I duly arrived at the appointed place and time ready to cross over into the unknown. Hungry trees or no.

Beatrix was waiting for me with an intoxicating nosegay of violets, so sweet I forgot they were out of season. A dog barked closer than before or was it a braying donkey? I remembered seeing Beatrix walking a sheepdog and assumed it was hers and curtsied slightly to disarm her as I accepted the flowers. "I suppose you have a cat too," I said, fishing for clues. "I can feel her."

Silence. I checked behind me. Eeyore was nowhere in sight.

I winked. "Any rabbits or mice?" I raised my eyebrows. "Or perhaps a wee donkey?"

Beatrix gestured to the box I carried. "What kind of cake did thee bring?" she said simply. For the first time I heard her voice. Distinctly north country Yorkshire reflecting my ancestry.

"It's a Victoria sponge," I answered, caught off guard. "I made it myself."

"Splendid... Aye, lass, bloody lovely stuff is raspberry jam and cream."

More awkward silence.

"Her name is Fetch."

"Sorry?" I said.

"Me lodger."

"You don't live alone, then."

"Nay, lass. The cat you can *feel* is *'ow er'* cat, Fetch. Cats don't belong to anyone, do they. She just comes and goes. I call her the lodger for fun. I lead a solitary existence, me."

"But not confined," I replied. "I see you everywhere. Did you just call me nameless?"

She shook her bonnet, no. "What I said was nay, lass."

"Sorry," I said. "I'm an odd duck. Sometimes I mis-hear things."

"I am the very definition of confined, Leela. It can't be helped. Ghosts are forever confined to places they once lived." She inclined her head north. "And I once lived up at yon ruins of Tirings. She paused, leaned on her umbrella, and lowered her voice to a whisper. "I daren't think on it much. I prefer to dwell on the good things that lie ahead, as should you if you don't mind me sayin'."

I was still assessing her, when a large dog barreled from the underbrush. I braced for impact, but it passed through me without a scratch. I could see the vegetation behind it. "That's *'ow er'* Chase. He'll no harm ye. Gentle as a lamb he is, but a right old devil of a guard dog all the same if anyone ventures too close to *'ow er'* cabin."

I stared hard into milady's eyes searching for a joke. She was deadly serious, but her eyes smiled back. "Beatrix, are you teasing me, pretending to be the ghost of Beatrix Potter?"

"Heavens no, child. I *used* to be Beatrix Potter. Well, only for a day or two mind, but she moved on. I'm a different ghost, now. My name is Verity Ryder. Come along wi ye." She chuckled to herself. "This rain, tis coming down like cats n' caterpillars, so it is. Here, Chase, let's be havin' ye, now." And then to me, "I'll have thee dry in no time, lass. Follow me. I'll carry the precious cake, shall I. You hold on to the flowers, eh."

The wind whistled past me screeching the words *'mind yer step, missus'*. A kettle whistled from far away. "Nearly there," Verity sang out cheerfully.

The track narrowed to a shallow impression in the clogged weeds. We came to a crossroads of a sort and veered left. Chase brushed passed us at a tremendous long-legged lope and left us far behind. "He's not a sheepdog," I said, in an attempt to ground myself.

Verity looked puzzled. "Nay, tis a wolfhound, so he is. Chase was born a wolfhound and happy to be one still and forever."

"Only, I saw you walking a sheepdog."

She nodded. "Aye, that was Shep. He belonged to Beatrix. He visits my former form so to speak, from habit. You see, the universe recycles forms. Reincarnation is tricky. It runs in families. So, duplication saves time. Not that we have any shortage of the flaming stuff round 'ere." My confusion must have warranted clarification. "Time," she said. "We have no shortage of time round 'ere."

I automatically levitated a few inches above the ground as we passed through a grove of dryads with trunks sculpted like nubile maidens, pregnant mothers, and matronly crones. They stood rooted proudly in the earth, their arm branches reaching skyward clutching crowns of dead leaves for hair.

A wizened crone with shriveled apples in her hair smiled and turned her head slightly to follow my progress.

Further on, an expanse of brown grass enclosed by a railing of rusted wrought iron spikes separated the tree ladies from an obvious dead zone. The air smelled of decaying plants and rotting fruit.

"Let's not dawdle, Leela. It does no good to pause and reflect on the past. Tis not a cheery spot is the Nozone, but you needed to know it was 'ere. It was designated for restless souls thousands of years ago. Well, we had to put them somewhere so they wouldn't bother the animals. So, we put them nowhere, so to speak. Only sadness and regret dwell therein. Tis a graveyard without graves. We call it the Nozone because it's void of life, but sometimes the residue of a particularly aggressive energy lingers on 'ere. Rest assured; new life is but a season away. If thee listens carefully of a moonless night, you will hear it singing."

As we left the grove my feet touched down lightly and a symphony of birdsong, buzzing, and chattering assailed me. The familiar sound of a dog barking excitedly drew me into the heart of a dense forest. The world of shadows lay a thousand years behind me. "I've been here before," I said out loud. The symphony stopped abruptly.

Verity's hand on the middle of my back guided me forward. "Chase," she called out. "Is the way clear? I don't want any funny business on Leela's first day."

Chase, a grey wolfhound the size of a long-legged colt, guided us forward. I immediately felt a pang of longing for Eeyore. Apart from the length of their legs they were alike in size and color, Chase's eyes were no less bright. Had I deserted my friend? Had my dearest friend deserted me?

"Animals don't abandon us, Leela. I'm sure your Eeyore will be along soon," Verity said. "We left an unmistakable trail of breadcrumbs for him to follow."

Verity's voice was young and musical. I turned eagerly to ask when I would see Eeyore and met the countenance of a beautiful silver-haired woman, tall and graceful wearing a simple shift of dark green wool.

I quickened my pace as Chase escorted us toward what I hoped was the braying of a donkey. The vegetation parted for us. I walked behind Verity, a goddess who carried my cake aloft before her like a treasure.

A broom lay across the path, and I slipped in the leaves trying to sidestep it, but Verity took my arm to steady me. As she led me over it, she let out a tremendous sigh of relief. "C'mon luvvy. Let's put that kettle on. I'll have thee dry in no time."

I heard a loud rustle behind me. I turned in time to see the trees jostle together closing ranks. In turn, a pair of trees before us stepped apart to let us pass. And so, we advanced to a brick wall overgrown with branches where a green curtain of ivy shivered aside to reveal a red door.

A boiling kettle shrieked behind it as if from deep underwater, and the door opened.

ELEMENTARY

SPECIAL EDS CLASS

chapter 13

HOME GREEN HOME

FOREST BATHING
Shinrin Yoku

*Is a therapeutic treatment
To counter mental and spiritual
traumas from chaotic city living.
By exposing one's body and soul
to a wild forest, one soaks up
the healing energies
of sunlight and chlorophyl.*

Eeyore was inside licking cake batter from a mixing bowl. He lifted his head, trying to lick a blob of batter on his nose with his tongue. "Marvellous stuff, cake batter," he said sounding remarkably cheerful for a hostage. "What kept you so long, Ducks?"

"I believe you had a hand in that," I said getting my bearings. "How could you go off with a stranger like that. You had me worried sick. And don't call me Ducks, it's common. Did she tempt you with a carrot?"

Eeyore stood his ground a mite peeved. "Verity isn't a stranger, and she said going with her would help you *find yourself,* which incidentally, made sense. There was no carrot. Ducky is an endearment in Yorkshire, by the way."

"That makes no sense. How is Verity not a stranger?"

We were clearly in the main room of a haunted house that under the present circumstances I was loathe to call a *living* room.

Eeyore shook his shaggy head and changed the subject. "Hands, you say? If I *did* have hands, I assure you they'd be fit to be tied. Fit to be tied is what I used to do best in the old days."

"Sea legs, then."

"Wobbly pins, I calls em."

"Where did Verity go?" I asked. "She was right behind me."

Eeyore nodded to a large squashy armchair pushed close to a toasty fire. "Mark my words, Lass," he said. "You may be losing what's left of your mind. She's sittin' right there, plain as the nose on me face. Can you not see 'er."

I looked hard at the empty chair and saw its seat cushion compress as if a ghost had sat down. "You sounded like Verity just then, Eeyore."

"Aye, lass. I forgot. She's inside me, the now. Just visiting don't ye know. She gave me cake batter. Nice lady. She says I can call her Granny. In't that sweet."

I bent down nose-to-nose and stared into Eeyore's unusually glassy eyes. "Verity, why have you taken possession of my friend? Do you mean us harm? When can I take Eeyore home?"

"Oh, we can never go 'ome," Eeyore continued in a trance. "Sorry, I was distracted by cake batter."

I was alarmed. "Why on earth not. And what has cake batter got to do with anything? Who were you apologizing to just now."

Verity corrected me from the easy chair, manifesting slowly like an image from a polaroid camera. "It's not technically planet earth, Leela. Welcome home." Her voice narrated two feet above the chair from an open book. "Once upon a time there was a girl who woke dead to the world," she read.

Eeyore looked up from licking the bowl, his eyes restored to velvety brown. "Don't tell me. Has something terrible happened or is something terrible *about* to happen?" He hung his head. "There was a time when it was bound to be one or t'other. It was the way of things on Cotchford Farm near the end."

Verity materialized as the elegant lady in the green dress, seated by the fire drinking tea. The open book hovered suspended in mid air above her head like a seagull caught in an updraft. It floated gently towards a familiar doormat of patterned leaves, descending in a lazy spiral. Its title 'Much Ado About Nothing' by anonymous, embossed in gold foil, landed face up.

"That carpet is much brighter than when I first beheld it," I said. "Where are the snakes? The snakes are missing."

"Something quite wonderful is unfolding," Verity said. "I'm on a time-sensitive mission, Leela. I have no time to waste, so sometimes I use my irascible old lady entitlements to cut through the small talk. I earned every one of them the hard way and I intend to use everything in my power to save us from, what did you call it, a fate worse than death?

I will fill you in later, but for now please believe me, I mean you no harm. I apologize for wanting to introduce Eeyore to my forest before you got here but I was that desperate for you to come. I'm under orders to bring you home."

"Whose orders?"

"We're nearly out of time which should be impossible since time is endless here." Her eyes brightened as if remembering something. "What snakes, luvvy?"

"The snakes on the carpet."

"There were never snakes on this carpet."

Eeyore pranced around the room, entirely out of character. "Look Leela, my arthritis is gone. The Sparklies healed me."

It did my heart good to see him so pain-free. I beamed at Verity for her kindness, snakes forgotten.

Eeyore sauntered over to me and lay his head in my lap reminiscent of a unicorn willingly surrendering to the power of pure love. I rubbed his threadbare nose. And when I fondled his droopy ears, he began purring like an extremely large housecat. "I believe you owe Verity an apology," he mumbled.

"Thank you, Verity. You've made me feel at home too," I said, almost meaning every word.

Eeyore lifted his head and looked deep into my eyes. "Can we stay here forever, Leela?"

I came over all teary. "Yes, yes, of course, you silly old Billy goat. As long as you wish."

A persistent doubt crossed my mind but left immediately. I had done what was best. I had found Eeyore, and he was not only well, it seemed he was part of the master plan to bring me to Veratopia, which translated means the land of truth.

Marcus Aurelius's philosophy taught that 'obstacles are the way' and I had inadvertently followed his advice without question to reach Eeyore. Had the broom been an obstacle? Had I been led into a trap? Could Eeyore and I leave?

I was not brave. I had no fight left in me, so, I surrendered. Things being what they were, there was no use crying over spilled beans or lost snakes. But I still had a nagging thought that Eeyore may have been ill used as a scapegoat.

Verity's cabin lay deep within a liminal pocket of rainforest that quickened a faded memory of a past too cruel to revisit. I *had* been here before but the carpet in Verity's living room triggered a feeling of unease. I was on guard on a familiar chessboard. For a heartbeat the cabin floor was littered with grey paint chips before resuming as a classsic Turkish carpet.

In the following days I shrugged off my disquiet, explored Veratopia, and was visited by the miraculous phenomenon of Chrysalis Mundi – the nursery of the world.

A pulsating sphere of light caught my eye, high in an ancient Weeping Willow. On closer inspection it turned out to be a luminescent cloud containing thousands of microscopic eggs suspended in a silvery mist.

I confronted Verity. "I believe I've seen Eeyore's Sparklies," I said.

"Ah, you've met the fairy children," Verity said after I described what I'd seen. Eeyore is a natural born intuitive. He chanced upon a sparkling star."

"Did it heal his arthritis?"

"Yes and no. Eeyore encountered the nursery where human life begins as fairies. The eggs as you call them, quickened Eeyore's instinctive power to heal himself. Each pearl contains the euphoric lifeforce of a single incubating soul – some wait hundreds of years before being called to hasten a human birth."

I soon became delighted to experience the Sparklies' display as zooming pinpoints of light playing like exuberant children that appeared after dark, privileged to feel the joy emanating from tiny shooting stars twinkling through the trees like fireflies. Many nights Eeyore and I go sparkly watching. Once-in-a-while an overexuberant sparkly whizz-banged towards the stars, signalling an imminent return to earth's Shadowland.

I was relieved to discover that the myriad red eyes blinking in the treetops were friendly sprites and that trees are grand storykeepers. I listen to them at night creaking in the wind outside my bedroom window, groaning through the dark and well into the dawn reminiscing about the good old days. Apparently, the bad old days were almost over. "And good riddance," Eeyore commented, "whenever the woodcutter departs for good."

"Who?"

"A sort of bogeyman creature named Greenwood, but no worries, Verity has him under control… that is, she soon will have. "Now then, I must away. I'm off to have a wee Shinrin Yoku before the sun goes down."

chapter 14

EXCHANGE STUDENTS

"What has been said can never be unsaid"

ZENO

Verity's carpet told me I'd been there before.

"Eeyore and I have an understanding beyond physics," I said to Verity, "but I hadn't realized I was so telepathic."

The thought occurred that I may be experiencing forest lag. "I'm not worried. Eeyore says my memories will come back when I'm ready."

Verity hugged her shawl closer. "Your instincts do you proud, Leela, you're a wise monkey."

"That's nice of you to say, but I'm just tagging along with Eeyore, hoping to write a book."

"Nonsense child, you are a storyteller, as you're about to find out. Silkie and I have been waiting for you. Grow young along with me old woman, the best is yet to be."

"And Silkie is?"

"Your... *ahem*, twin sister."

I closed my eyes savoring the scent of sunshine filtered through a canopy of leaves. And when I thought I couldn't be happier a familiar voice wuffled from the trees.

To my delight I heard a boy declare "I'm that hungry, I could eat a horse."

"Pax," I shouted, "is that you?"

"Who wants to know?"

"An old friend. Don't you remember me?"

"Are you tame?"

"I try to be."

"Show yourself." But before I could, a trampling elephant galumping through the underbrush emerged with Pax, the self-anointed elephant king riding on its head. He was jubilant, of course, waving his sceptre, pith helmet slipping over one eye. "Oh, it's you, Leela. I thought it might be. Peter and I have been expecting you."

I shook my head. "You know galumping frightens the bejeezus out of Piglet, Pax. Please show some respect for the hundred-acre wood."

Pax burbled back, shaking his spear. "Restraint is *not* my specialty. And this is *not* the hundred-acre wood," he declared with the authority of a king. He was quick to remind me "Otherwhere is no more; this is Veratopia."

Pax had been the last to arrive in Otherwhere. An unexpected fifteenth friend. Peter invited him because he loved elephants.

There was a time when I wanted to be as tough as Pax, a feisty character from an obscure book, whose desperate need for solitude matched my own. He was pushy, was Pax, although, in truth he was rather a sheepish boy before he read 'Little Red Riding Hood'.

He has an exuberant excess of attitude. More than that, he holds little regard for authority other than his own.

When Verity chastises him for frightening the baby rabbits, Pax responds, no cheek intended, with *'I eat grandmothers for breakfast'* and marches off unruffled.

His headstrong opinions charmed Verity as the 'wolf who cried *boy*' to get his own way (*which he always did*).

Pax remained in control even though the peaceful elephants in his book could, if provoked, rampage and trample and carry on trumpeting fit to raise the dead.

To rule his jungle, Pax wore safari khakis, a white pith helmet, and an expression of absolute confidence. Pax even faced down the Jabberwocky the few times it showed itself. He was one tough kid.

Although I'd come to trust Veratopia's peaceful trees as friends, there were times Pax's baobabs overwhelmed me. It may sound contrary, but I needed to be grounded by the sky. Even so, feeling dwarfed by leaves the size of bedsheets blocking the sun brought back my horror of claustrophobia.

I would have stayed awake all night if the bedposts on my bed sprouted branches as Pax's enchanted bed did. But Pax, whose name means peace, is bewitched by the extreme challenges of scale and like his mammoth elephants, he looms large as their child king despite his small stature.

Eeyore thinks I'm still a bit of a lightweight when it comes to writing hours at a stretch so, I'm planning to follow Pax's example of fortitude under pressure. I have already learned that writing a book is like exploring a jungle armed only with a pen. Sometimes, I'm barely hanging on to a first sentence.

A heffalump sighting was duly reported to Christopher Robin, and I asked Pax if he would please be so kind as to play jungle in his own section of the forest because Piglet was in shock and his nerves were shredding at an alarming rate. Pax continued to burble. "I warned you that restraint wasn't my thing," he shouted steering his pachyderm painted with colorful magic symbols into the trees. His warning "look sharp, elephants coming through," trailed out behind him mutating seamlessly into the hooting of a barn owl. So, Wol was here too.

I purposely lost track of time in Veratopia so I may have been there a day or a week or more when I spied Christopher Robin, Pooh, and

Piglet standing a good way off on a bluff that overlooked Lucy, shining more verdant than ever. Christopher kneeled to Pooh's level. I knew only too well that eye contact was the only way a bear of little brain could retain information. Christopher nodded in my direction where I huddled like a shrimp, arms hugging my legs, my chin resting on my knees. "Let's leave Leela alone today," he whispered. "She needs some space."

"Not too much and not too little but just right," Piglet offered. "Open spaces are a bother, but one needs them to get from my house to Pooh's house."

"Quite right, little Piglet, well spotted," Christopher Robin said.

Even from a fair distance I saw Piglet's ears wiggle and turn bright pink with pride. Like me, he didn't take compliments lightly.

Pooh looked as if he was busy contemplating the way Owl had taught him to appear intelligent. "Hunny calls," he finally said after his think. "Are you coming little Piglet?"

"I'm there," Piglet replied hopping up and down in excitement. "Actually, I *was* there over an hour ago, but I couldn't find you."

"I wasn't lost. I was right here."

Christopher Robin stood up and stretched. "Well, Leela *is* lost."

Pooh waved frantically in my direction. "But I can see her. Shall we go and tell her where she is?"

Christopher Robin bent down again and crossed Pooh's arms. "Listen to me, Pooh. Leela is lost in thought. She can hear our voices like a slight breeze passing by. She's in a trance, here to begin a new story, just like the rest of us."

"I'm here to start a new jar of hunny," Pooh whispered in Piglet's ear. "Or did I just come back?"

"Leela," Piglet squealed excitedly waving his arms to get my attention. "Be on the lookout for Pax's heffalumps. A rabbit told me they passed by not long ago."

Veratopia, although essentially timeless, sometimes keeps the days of the week, literally for old time's sake. But a day could pass in an eye-blink or stretch out to the traditional 24 hours and beyond, if necessary, necessity itself being a rather pointless marker.

By Verity's design, Silkie and I met two sunrises later, give or take. It was almost a Monday morning. Fetch, Chase, and Eeyore joined us gamboling about together, obviously fetching, chasing, and pondering, but also rolling in autumn leaves.

Our unpromising start evolved into an inauspicious afternoon where Silkie and I chatted like robots reading a script.

But I couldn't stay disheartened for long. Eeyore leaped, agile as a young deer in a field of clover, bouncing in delighted circles around me from being pain-free and finding two new friends. We hadn't spied Edward or Puck but Verity told me they were often away working.

Verity had immediate plans for my writing career expressed as 'no time like the present.'

And so, my second childhood began with chocolate cake and strawberries. I am over the moon to admit I am growing up as I grow younger.

Tuesday-ish, Verity gave me my first writing assignment: Create a story premise based on the relevant theme of reincarnation. I chose immortality, the art of staying vs. mortality, the art of leaving.

Lucy's field became my study hall where Eeyore could investigate the buttercup population and his radar sensitive ears could listen to my tutors, Absolem, Lewis Carroll's woozy caterpillar and the Cheshire Cat, if he had a mind to.

Cheshire overheard my story idea and toppled off his branch from laughing so hard but managed to right himself inches before hitting the ground as all cats are encoded to do. He left his toothy grin levitating four feet off the grass, conveniently at my eye level.

Absolem, nearby, hid his face under his back end, his plump jelly-like body pulsating with suppressed mirth. His mind reached mine without the formality of hello. "Biting off more than you can chew is a sore subject, Leela. It was Alice's downfall (quite literally, not to make too fine a point of it) until she righted herself," he said. "Oh, what a tangled web we weave when first we practice to *overachieve*. Nevertheless, I hasten to add your premise was an interesting, albeit mad, choice. Completely on topic but off the scale without a trace of guile to protect you. Whether t'was plucky or foolish tis difficult to say. But then you have the advantage of sidestepping what-was, for what-will-be."

Eeyore jumped to my defense. "I've always protected Leela," he said trotting towards us. "And, by the way, Absolem, guile was one of Leela's finest attributes when we met. I applaud her guile. Indeed, I borrowed a fair amount of it to survive the horrors of the literary lies thrust upon me."

Absolem, wore rose-colored pince-nez that would have hung off his nose if he'd had one. "I never stand corrected for long," he said, vibrating like lime Jello. "As Pax is wont to say, it's not my *thing*."

Cheshire joined Absolem trying to be wise and diplomatic at the same time. "Don't let me rain on your story, young lady. I mean no harm. Guile is in short supply in the real world. So, more power to you. But step back from the old and scrutinize the new, I say. You may only have one chance to overcome your old commitment to misery."

"That's *my* job," Eeyore bragged a little more gruffly than he intended. "The stepping back part. And if you must know, I think it's a magnificently brave start on Leela's first day of school." He faced Lucy's recently deserted branches, and Absolem's swiftly dematerializing toadstool. "You should both be ashamed of yourselves," he called into the ether. "Neither of you ever experienced a nerve-wracking first day of school let alone faced the supernatural origins of your over-sentient minds."

Absolem reappeared as a transparent mirage where his toadstool once stood, pinz-nez levitating in front of his eyes. "Themes are futile," he mumbled, still vibrating with mirth that caused him to choke on hookah smoke. "Sorry," he said giggling. "That went down the wrong *pipe* so to speak."

"You will adjust," Cheshire added, newly returned to the merriment. "Themes are dashed tricky. Do what I do and hang in there."

"You forge on, Leela," Eeyore continued. "If you want to be a writer, and last time I checked, you did, follow your wildest dreams. Hold nothing back and see what unfolds. Be prepared for happy accidents. Any writer worth their salt will tell you they're often the best ideas."

Cheshire, reappeared after he'd regained his composure, was still wiping tears from his eyes with the tip of his tail. "Dear brave girl," he hiccupped, "tis oft said that laughter is the best medicine, and as such Absolem and are grateful to have been healed of such a wanton plague on our extinct species. If we had hats, we would doff them to you and promise to stand *ahem*... solidly behind you through our respective transparent wisdom of 'thickness and thinness'. We have the luxury of being immortalized by an author you highly respect. Lewis Carroll never stifled his need to play with wistful themes. He directly opposed the practical advice of starched nannies, closeminded parents, and academics. We loved him for it. We are honored that he so honored us."

"Live a little, one day at a time or a lot all at once," Eeyore added. "Live it for all the storybook immortals who wished they'd had the pluck to tell their creators how they wanted to behave and what they wanted to say. Mr. Milne wasn't compassionate enough to listen to me off paper. In my case, the traits of kindness and humor were overlooked for literary impact that left my true self shamefully high and dry."

"I can relate," Cheshire said. "Literally speaking, Mr. and Mrs.

Milne manipulated their son by restricting Christopher's choices enslaved to their personal ideals of him becoming a treasured icon of society. Accordingly, Christopher became estranged from his parents as well as distancing himself from his famous toys."

Eeyore shuddered. "I came close to being thrown in the fire more than once, I can tell you. In the end we were saved by an enterprising archivist working for the New York Public Library, no less. Incidentally, not for nothing, I'd rather be here with Leela and you lot than lolling about gathering dust as a famous exhibit in a glass case. I, for one, am wholeheartedly thankful to live in a forest of grass and trees and rain."

"And I am equally grateful to Mr. Carroll for his insight and loving care," Absolem interjected, shamefaced.

"I shouldn't care to become a cliché *or* erased," Cheshire added. "Please forgive us for making fun of a serious issue. Leela, feel free to tell your whole story. Absolem and I are grateful for the opportunity to remember again for the first time, the world beyond our boundaries of immortality. And I can hear what you're thinking, Leela. I assure you; disappearing is not even close to being erased."

"We caterpillars are given short shrift in the real world," Absolem mused. "Fantasy tends to be all about butterflies and fairies. Cats, on the other hand, were once worshipped as gods and as such, have managed to hold on to a semblance of power."

Cheshire preened at his historic celebrity, and blushed until his stripes were scarlet.

"Where's Waldo," Absolem joked.

"I'm right here as you can plainly see," Cheshire replied. "Point well taken, though. I can take a joke… even one of yours, Absolem. Mr. Carroll gave me an artful sense of humor as well as unprecedented perceptive feline wisdom."

"And please don't be late for tea on Sunday," Absolem, called out to me as I was leaving. "I hear Mister Edward is coming. I say, do you think you could bake one of those Victoria sponges of yours. They quite enliven my spirit."

I was best pleased, Edward and Puck had been away for quite some time.

That night, under cover of darkness, in keeping with what Verity called the rules of synergy, she bequeathed her cabin to me, thus granting me the space, if I was brave enough to accept it, to fully embrace the magic of becoming a true writer. I was.

The next morning, I met Pax on the trail to Lucy's meadow. His pack of lovelies cleared the path on their way to bathe in Eeyore's pond. Martha, the lead elephant swayed elegantly, waving a tree branch, like a flag in a parade. "Lovely day, Martha," I said. "You're looming particularly large this fine morning?" Martha tossed her head and counted to three with her foot. She dropped her branch, trumpeted once, and rummaged in my basket.

"I don't mean to question your memories," Pax said, "but I'd like to point out that elephants make outstanding mothers as do housecats and trees. Case in point, Martha our majestic matriarch watches over all eleven of our babies."

"I have no doubts," I said offering Martha one of Lucy's apples.

Pax grinned and put his head to one side. "How fares your … *ahem*… mother librarian?"

"Verity is more of a fairy godmother. Quite a different species. Martha is a star, no question. I'll happily reincarnate as an elephant or a cat or a tree if I have a choice next time around."

"Then it's lucky you won't have to choose. Verity already knows what you'll be next."

A brisk wind blew my hair into my eyes. "Why would she tell you?"

"She didn't. She told Martha, and Martha told Absolem."

A strong gust of wind sent me flying. I grabbed for an overhanging branch and missed but Martha righted me. "Well, Absolem tells Cheshire everything, so I assume the cat's out of the bag."

"Goodness no. It's an uncommonly special secret that you'll only know when it's good and proper." He held down his pith helmet trying to take flight. "I say, it isn't half windy."

"Apples for all," I announced to Martha. "Lucy has prepared a windfall picnic for your family to celebrate a particularly blustery morning."

"Make way," a rabbit called out running ahead of Martha. "Heffalumps coming through. One of you please find Piglet and make sure he's distracted."

chapter 15

DEGREES OF SEPARATION

"To thine own self be true
and it must follow, as the night the day,
thou canst not then be false to any man."

WILLIAM SHAKESPEARE

– 'Hamlet'

Silkie, my self-appointed tour guide, chose to orient me by way of a formal missive.

I sat in the grass with Eeyore's head in my lap to read it aloud, dithering about, shuffling its several closely written pages warily as if they were illustrated with live snakes.

Eeyore was restless, ignoring the bluebells I'd picked for him. "I'm as ready as I'll ever be," he said. "Enlighten me. Is it 'welcome wagon' or a subpoena to appear before Silkie's kangaroo court? Let's get this communiqué over with and have tea. Is it written in Latin or Greek?"

I straightened the threatening pages and fondled Eeyore's ears. "It's in English."

"How thoughtful. Is there no end to her selflessness? Did I say selfless? I apologise, I meant soulless."

"*Shush*… I don't want to drag this out any more than you do."

"Then I shall sit enraptured and pretend you're reading me a riveting story."

At Eeyore's request, I became a storyteller. "Are you ready? Then I shall begin. I shall paraphrase to save boredom. The gist is as follows:

Silkie was raised by Verity, a ghost acting as her adopted grandmother. And in case we weren't bright enough to work things out, Silkie reminded us that having a ghost for a grandmother didn't make *herself* one. But that it *had* set up an uncommonly metaphysical life sheltered from reality.

Eeyore brayed under his breath. "Boo bloody Hoo."

Our impromptu tour guide wanted to, as she so crudely phrased it, *get through* her basic history. Afterwards, if we had questions, we could ask away over tea the following day. Eeyore was welcome to attend if he promised to be quiet. To which he mumbled, fat chance.

Verity is the Latin word for truth. According to Silkie, she had always been Verity's special charge, without question because truth never lies.

The whole truth, as opposed to Silkie's poetic self-serving monologue guff, came straight from a horse's... well, the word mouth will have to suffice. We learned what we already knew that even the whitest lies are ruled by hard physics.

Silkie was keen to impress upon us that all had not been as she had assumed or been told regarding her abandonment and subsequent adoption. She'd been misled – a defenceless child, held hostage for sixty-one years, powerless to withstand the enchanted nature of a forest that operated outside the confines of time and space.

Eeyore chortled, in what Lewis Carroll described as snorting and giggling at the same time. "If Silkie is vulnerable then I'm a monkey's uncle," he said.

The present circumstance in which she and I find ourselves was due to a tactless slip of nonidentical twins – a changeling birth. Consequently, to restore Veratopia's equilibrium we must each be delivered to our respective interrupted destinies. Me here, destined to be a writer. And hers in the Shadowland was anyone's guess.

"I *can* guess but there are young saplings present," Eeyore said.

"Please don't make Cheshire laugh again," Absolem said. "He's already fallen 'out of his tree' too many times for one day."

"Now that Verity's dirty linen is aired, Silkie declares many other whitewashed lies have come to light. No doubt, you and I will find out soon enough, but Silkie emphasizes in capital letters plus an exclamation mark that she's had to suffer for sixty-one years, so we should count ourselves lucky."

Eeyore snorted. "What does little Miss *Sulky* think you've been doing all that time."

Silkie's once debt of gratitude and selfless allegiance to Verity has been drastically altered from a devoted self-sacrificing woman who'd saved her from certain death to an incompetent witch. She says she's hard-pressed to forgive such ineptitude and false pretenses.

I scanned the next few paragraphs for gems. "Ah, here's a good one. Silkie humbly points out she's long overdue for the life she's been deprived of in the real world where Verity's cursory homeschooling is at odds with the standards of social education required to navigate its horrors. She intends to steel herself to the task of retrieving her identity. She notes, we might feel the same about resuming ours. Clearly, we have our work cut out for us.

In her opinion, Veratopia is no Shangri-La. Absolem and Cheshire know, of course, but as they're Verity's creatures, we'd best be careful not to believe anything they say. Ditto with the trees. She warns us to watch our backs. Apparently, Verity's trees report everything they hear or imagine back to her. Her welcome to the 'shattered remnants of your disjointed legacy' speech sounds a tad insincere. She concludes that she wants me to be happy as a ghostwriter.

She reports that Verity asserts all destinies, including mistaken identities are sacred. Silkie has doubts. But she apparently has none when she writes my name as LILA in bold caps. A deliberate gaffe. My name is Leela, as she very well knows."

Eeyore stated the obvious. "I believe that girl's pants are on fire."

"She refers to Peter as *my sad little friend* and whines she will have to prepare for a life attached to a restless shadow like he did."

"What a whiner."

"Master Zeno, a Greek philosopher is to instruct Silkie in the psychic martial arts to avenge Verity, (her *bogus* grandmother) whose been stalked and bullied for a hundred years by the angry spirit of Veratopia's resident woodcutter from 'Snow White'.

Furthermore, Greenwood's reign of terror will never end until you and I make it so. Lovely. And so, she goes on and the gauntlet bounces."

Eeyore nudged me hard. "I do believe there be dragons here," he said. "We'll have to watch our backs."

"Finally, she believes telling us a few things about herself may help us fit in. She brags that she could read before she could walk, but the Shakespeare canon never interested her as much as comic-books. She adds that Verity makes learning a game and will no doubt do the same for me if I do what I'm told and play my tarot cards right.

Ah, here's what she *really* wants us to know. When Verity found her, she was a newborn abandoned in a rusted-out bookmobile."

"Oh, boo hoo," Cheshire catcalled. "I saw the whole thing. She was alone for ten minutes, tops. Are Absolem and I her creatures? I think not."

"Silkie says, quite poetically, that when she was old enough to ask questions, Verity called her an unwritten child and promised to create a story for her because "Certain events have restless souls and circumstances must align themselves to birth one's best life."

Cheshire coughed up a hairball. "I'll *tell* that girl a story if she's not careful."

"And sometimes," I said aside to Eeyore, "one's best life takes several directions before heading true north where, one was supposed to be all along."

"And more often than not," Eeyore added. "Everyone must contend with starting over several times before they get it right."

Silkie isn't sure how much higher Verity's plan for my higher education can reach. She describes Verity's exhaustive curriculum as ever a mystery. But now it's up to us to find a way to integrate what was with what will be.

"And the best of British luck to you," Cheshire joined in, hanging in mid-air like a huge painted seagull.

With our arrival, the time draws near for Silkie to board a bus that will take her to 'big' school. There's no chance it will be an ordinary school bus because everything Verity does is outrageously mystical.

"I call it 'too big for her boots school,' Cheshire said, turning brighter with pride.

Eeyore and I nodded in complete agreement. "How could it not," Eeyore said.

I folded the letter. "That's it. The end. We have been summoned."

Eeyore shook himself alert. "Okay, tea break, chocolate or plain, he said. "And in case you are unable to understand my simple English, I'm speaking of digestive biscuits. I'm guessing the good stuff is warranted."

As usual, Eeyore read my mind. "I heartily agree," I said. "For it must follow, as the night follows the day, thou canst not then be false to any old cup of tea."

"Chocolate it is," Eeyore said.

After my one-sided paper conversation with Silkie, I was at sixes and sevens (or at least 'sixty-ones) about my situation being more perilous than I'd been given to believe.

The clearing around the cabin became oppressive. Spiky leaves prickled good riddance inside my head. The claustrophobic beating of insect wings, crow laughter, and all manner of gossiping, chirping, nattering, and stinging nettles pushed me towards the Shadowlands and my old bus stop.

Could I jump the broom of no return? Could Eeyore? Would he?

The trees shuffled too close, invasive eavesdroppers hoping to catch me out. I listened my way through them, a blind bat caught between sending and receiving. Branches that had once reached out to say hello poked my eyes and scratched my face. Invisible roots tripped me up. Silkie had turned them against me. I felt panicky, giggly... feverish. I suppressed a wild urge to run out-of-body and never be seen again but picked up my pace trying to escape the voices in my head clamouring for my expulsion, and to my horror I saw my old shadow approaching through the underbrush trying to catch me up. My ordeal might soon be over. If I still cast a shadow, I didn't belong.

And then it rained and by rain, I mean I was drenched with a cold bracing deluge – as if raining on my parade was anything less than a 'get out of town and don't come back' sign.

My hysterical laughter unnerved Eeyore. He padded after me with the most assuring words he could muster. "Leela, there's no use pretending Silkie wasn't grossly out of order," he said, "but she doesn't control the weather. Forests need rain plain and simple. And please don't use that *Sherlock* remark."

"It isn't funny, Eeyore," I said, helplessly grinning like Cheshire.

"Atta girl," he replied. "You see, laughter *is* the best medicine. Especially in Silkie's case, if taken with a large dose of Kanga's extract of malt."

"Pooh Sticks," I shouted. "In case you hadn't noticed, Silkie towers above me in more than just confidence. Compared to her so-called extensive education I'm academically deficient. I feel a little underwhelmed to put it mildly."

Eeyore trotted around to face me. "Leela," he said gently, "listen to me. You were born a wonderchild, and as such you outrank her. Your problem isn't mathematics. A phony math proof is Silkie's way of cheating. She's pushing your buttons. Don't forget she's been a spoiled princess for a long time. She had no competition until you showed up."

"I didn't show up. I was headhunted."

"Settle down, Gretel, that's a tad harsh," he replied, chuckling. "Verity isn't some evil witch at the end of a trail of breadcrumbs holding open an oven door. Keep calm and boil the kettle for tea. We can handle this."

"A cup of Lapsang Souchong isn't going to make me feel better."

"Of course it will. Hasn't it always."

"When Silkie asked me, I calculated the degrees of separation between us as one, and that the distance was closing fast because according to Verity, there are no degrees of separation between identical twins, hence my low calculation."

"Leela, you're *not* identical; you're...*ahem*... a smidgen *biological* is all, hence your miscalculation. You calculated a number; Silkie is just plain calculating."

"She said, we were a team, so I thought we were equals. She hooted like an owl and corrected me."

"Okay fine. She's a piece of work. Let's move on."

"I can't. Her degrading remarks have turned the trees against me. Now, I'm looking over my shoulder worrying about hostile trees. I've only recently began to trust them. Silkie is trying to alienate me before she goes. But why?"

"Because Leela, you pose a threat. And by the way, it wasn't flippant. That girl rehearses her lines."

"Well guessing isn't good enough. We must ask someone who'll know for sure."

Eeyore stared into the sky. "*Hmmmnn...* let me have a ponder. Do we know any brainiacs in this forest nosey enough to see and hear everything that goes on?" He yawned. "Please take your time..."

I closed my eyes and pretended to chew my lip.

"*Ding ding ding,*" Eeyore said. "Time's up. I need an answer."

I laughed out loud. "Could it be Absolem and Cheshire?"

"And, we have a winner. Huzzah! – a couple of tricksters on a forest lark held together with sleight of hand tricks, magic words, and fairy dust. Who could ask for more. Listen, kiddo, we've both got to toughen up. Keep on our toes. As ironic as it sounds this forest has as many sinister shadows as the world we just came from. Verity's little welcome to Oz speech dazzled me at first, but illusions wear off. Don't get me wrong, Verity means well but she's in some kind of trouble. We need to know a lot more. Oh, and for the record, one-sided conversations leave *everyone* confused."

We rubbed noses. "Better luck next time," he whispered.

"Took the words right out of my mouth, Sweetpea."

"Happy to oblige," Eeyore said. "They weren't doing either of us any good in there. Now, let's prioritize our questions, shall we. The best thing to remember is that neither of us is alone. It's of prime importance. I'm here wanting a few answers on a need-to-know basis myself, and I believe Lucy will sort us out. She usually does." He trotted off, assuming I would follow. "Last one there is a rotten Flappers Pie," he called out. "Try to keep up."

He was chuckling to himself when I caught up to him a few feet on. "I suppose you want me to heel," he said barking a pretty good impression of a dog twice his size.

The magnificent Lucy bowed to us in greeting, and while I meditated beneath her branches Eeyore sniffed through the ferns at the edge of the pond. "Sometimes Absolem's mushroom materializes in here," he called out. "No insult intended Luce, but we could use a higher mind, today."

I closed my eyes and sent an S.O.S. to Cheshire or Absolem… whichever one opted to answer first if at all.

Eeyore returned to my side. His ruling was curt. "Caterpillars. Never there when you need one."

I shrugged. He was right, relying on a wily cat or a drugged caterpillar were not the most reliable of helpers. "Never mind," I said. "One thing I *do* understand is that one can't hurry magic." I settled myself back into a meditative pose before I spoke to a cloud that wasn't there. "I've asked Verity to explain my situation," I said into the blue, "but I still don't fully understand. Please will one of you talk to me. I need your perspective. Your collective wisdom."

Lucy's crown rustled like a giant green windchime caught in a supernatural blast of wind. *Whoosh!* I looked up expecting to see a grin materializing in her foliage. "Cheshire's not there," Eeyore announced. "But then if you ask me, Cheshire's never really *all there*, if you know what I mean, but there it is. Cats are contrary at the best of times. I don't trust a cat that never meows."

Cheshire read my mind from wherever he was, but his voice preceded him. "A wise choice, Leela," he announced. "You can always count on me to tell you the truth. I'm on my way. Almost there," he said. "Sorry to be late for an important date."

"Sooner or later," Eeyore muttered to himself. "Whatever."

Finally, Cheshire's familiar apparition waivered into view. Eeyore winked at me and looked up. "Lovely to see you, your cattiness."

Cheshire made up for lost time. "What's a Flapper Pie?" he said. Eeyore switched from sarcasm to his diplomatic ambassador voice. "Always a pleasure. It's vanilla custard topped with meringue in a graham cracker pie shell."

I didn't waste any time either. "Cheshire," I said. "Is this heaven? Am I dead?"

"Not entirely on both counts... a little of one and not so much of the other."

"Am I hallucinating?"

"Yes, the good kind."

"So then, I'm *almost* dead?"

Cheshire giggled and performed an accidental semi-vanishing act with an involuntary swish of his tail. "Sorry, about that, my tail sometimes has a life of its own," he explained.

Absolem, newly materialized, at eye level on a transparent three-foot high mushroom at my side, chimed in. "No but you're almost right which is infinitely better. Tell me, Leela, do you remember jumping a broom on your way to Veratopia?"

"I didn't jump it; I *stepped* over it. So, where exactly *is* Veratopia?"

"It's not on any map if that's what you're asking," he replied quickly. "But the entrance is always on the furthest edge of the town on a street where the construction ends, and the forest begins. Its exit is a hidden portal in the trees opposite your bus stop. You've been staring at it for years." *Ahem...* "As for being dead... 'not entirely' is partially correct. You're more alive than you've ever been but your old life is dying. That is to say, you're forgetting it. Officially, and by that, I mean existentially, you're in a timeless pocket of liminal territory as a tentative new life force."

Eeyore brayed his contempt. "Well, la dee la. Very hoity-toity for a green slug."

Absolem continued, momentarily peeved. "The *when* of it shifts. And it's Mister Hoity-Toity to you, Eeyore. Theoretically speaking, Veratopia's timeline is on par with the world of shadows you just left... give or take a year or two."

"That said," Cheshire added, "Veratopia is a paradox. Timelessness takes time. Let's just say the number 61- bus's schedule has never been an exact science."

Absolem's answering chortle made him cough and he accidentally blew smoke in Eeyore's face. "As I recall, it usually arrives on its own sweet time."

While Eeyore caught his breath, I got in the question he was never going to ask.

"Can we ever go home?"

"Silly girl," Absolem said between puffs of his hookah. "Verity already told you. You *are* home. Technically, you never left."

Cheshire joined in. "Please remember, Leela. You did *not* create Otherwhere. Verity did. She sent you a working copy. Think of a holodeck program and you'll get the general idea."

"And while we're not on the subject, which we weren't," Absolem said. "Your body is resetting itself. And as there are no mirrors here other than wavery reflections in mud puddles, you can't quite see how you've reverted to being six years old. So, let's be clear. You've lost fifty-five years as the crow flies. A new life doesn't lie ahead of you, it's right here and now. It's yours to do with as you will, pardon the phrase."

I covered my ears. "And why, pray tell, did no-one feel the need to ask me what *I* wanted!"

Absolem pulled a hurt expression from his bag of magic tricks. "No need to get huffy, Leela. You clearly asked to be saved. The transcripts of your conversations with Zeno's bus are on file if you require verification. Your transition will take work. And by work, I mean play, obviously. Consider this as playschool if it helps. Verity is your teacher, as are Cheshire and I."

"Absolem is a little put out," Eeyore said. "Greenwood had a go at him yesterday."

Cheshire smirked. "I was there. He called him a pudgy little worm."

Absolem huffed and tried to cross a few of his legs without toppling over. "What he *actually* said was that I reminded him of a miniature Jabba the Hut. Well really, I ask you."

"Absolem is determined to have the last word and possibly one other," Cheshire said. "But before he does, remember…if you want to graduate from writing school never listen to Owl's advice. He can't even spell 'owl'. And keep as clear of the woodcutter as you can."

"Why? Is he getting worse?"

Absolem shook his head, no. "Sorry, question period is over, Leela. Brace yourself for your first term of school." His form faded until his last words floated like the ghost of a stoned butterfly in an updraft.

"Glad that ordeal is over," Eeyore said, shaking his ears and tail at the same time. "Trust me, Lee, we've heard the worst from those two. Their best is yet to come."

I gave his ears a scratch. "I'm way ahead of you, Eeyore. I will always trust a donkey that can bark."

Cheshire's farewell was pithy. "The feeling's mutual, I'm sure," he said. "Must dash."

"Curiouser and curiouser," Lucy commented. "Alice is always right." Cheshire left as usual, in a theatrical sweep of blurry stripes. Eeyore toddled off towards his damp glen humming the Donkey Serenade. "I have never been pudgy," Absolem called out from the ether, his indignant voice fading into a puff of smoke. "And Eeyore, if a mushroom is not available, I can sit on a toadstool. Either one is a suitable seat from which to offer wisdom." I went in search of sugar.

chapter 16

MOTHERBLIND

Repeat No Evil

"From hence your memory death cannot take,
Although in me each part will be forgotten.
Your name from hence immortal life shall have,
Though I, once gone, to all the world must die."

WILLIAM SHAKESPEARE

— sonnet 81

The morning was overcast. Eeyore seemed listless, and I dragged the tip of my umbrella in the dirt like a sulky kid. I carried Verity's old basket with our makeshift continental breakfast – a thermos of scalding hot Builder's tea, dinner rolls, cold porridge, a jar of marmalade, a runcible spoon, and chocolate shortcake biscuits. We had been summoned by Cheshire to meet under Lucy.

A bitter wind picked up as we walked in silence. We hunkered down facing its wrath together, so, it was a shock when Eeyore bolted without a word and broke out in a run.

He was no calmer when I arrived at the meadow. Lucy had a dark raincloud caught in her branches and from within it the stripes of a large wet cat tumbled in a blur of pink and blue splotches. Pent up emotion churned everywhere in danger of unwinding too fast.

The bluebells had disappeared, and rain clouds hung low enough to cast a purple shadow over the grass. To say the mood was damp was an understatement. Several miniature cyclones, a few inches in diameter, touched down, spiralling over the field in fierce whirlpools of blue petals.

Eeyore was still in a frenzy, severely out of sorts, trotting the perimeter kicking out his back legs every few feet, braying like a donkey. He frightened me. I'd never seen him so agitated.

"I'm not agitated" he replied in my head. *"I'm terrified."*

"Well, now I am, too," I returned. *"Can you please settle down. I brought tea and biscuits."*

His gate slowed but he continued to amble with his head low against the wind.

"They're chocolate ones," I shouted.

I spread two blankets under Lucy and pinned them with square stones, commonly known by the tree sprites as Tirings' bricks, and laid out the thermos, cups, marmalade, a container of stale dinner rolls spread with butter, sliced porridge, and two packets of Hobnobs. Lucy had arranged her lower branches to form a windbreak, and Absolem, sheltered under a large leaf, puffed happily atop his mushroom without a care in the world.

I'd drunk two cups of tea by the time Eeyore crash-landed onto his blanket.

Cheshire, obscured from view inside a mist, gave a cheery shout "I think there's a chance of rain." from within Lucy's wind tossed foliage. I didn't need a crystal ball to know we were in for a deluge, and I was in for a serious lecture.

Cheshire got right into it as the first raindrops pitter-pattered my umbrella. "Silkie has been Motherblind since birth," she announced. "Verity has been Daughterblind for the same amount of time. Leela, it is vital you understand that your strangely *estranged* long-lost sister is seriously Sisterblind. But this dynamic will only work in your favor if you stand up for yourself."

An ominous cloud of thick black smoke obliterated Absolem from view but his voice rang out clearly, filled with hookah power. "It's quite simple," he said. "Your hindsight has deteriorated so much you can't see the trees for the forest. You are in a precarious situation, my girl. You will have to grow into your newfound power, and fast.

Silkie is overconfident. *Puff puff*... And not a little arrogant. She has no intention of being your ally let alone a loving sister. *Puff puff*... Personally, I hate it when someone waggles a finger in my face. It's not something done in acceptable company. So rude."

"And you let Silkie get away with it," Cheshire accused. "Think back a few yesterdays and look in her eyes. What did you see?"

"They were blank. She wouldn't make eye contact with me."

"Look again."

"They're full of hate."

"And why do you think *that* was?"

"She doesn't like me."

"Oh, my dearest girl," Cheshire fumed. "That simply won't do at all. That's no answer."

I heard Eeyore's worries inside me. *I fear I may have coddled you. I should have done a better job. Oh, dear girl, I should have shown you how to let go of feeling unworthy.*

"I couldn't possibly pose a threat to her," I replied. I'm just, you know, me."

Eeyore continued to blame himself. *You will have to ride it out. True to form, Silkie is overreacting. I'm sensing she feels blindsided by your presence, Goosie.*

The session began in earnest as the storm cloud released its payload of freezing rain.

The lecture was delivered from a hindsight point of view, no doubt about to become a tsunami of unforgiving insight.

Cheshire swooped down like a master of ceremonies. "Twenty-four-ish hours ago," he said, "give or take a sunset or two, Silkie stood before the imaginary podium in her unbalanced mind, speaking to a spot way over your head, Leela, addressing a distant horizon behind you in a narcissistic stage performance. Be of no doubt, her intention was to tear you to shreds."

"Silkie had entered a state of unconsciousness," Eeyore said, which means she wasn't taking Leela seriously. She was phoning it in. I blame myself."

Absolem picked up the gauntlet. "As Silkie droned on, you learned what you already knew, that Verity's cabin had begun as a crude shack before it was a wildlife blind in the heart of bear country and that it was called a hide for a reason and sentient enough to grow with age until it became a luxurious accommodation with three fireplaces and three armchairs laid in front of each." He gasped, short of breath.

"I have to say, Silkie segues fast," Cheshire returned. "She launched her first covert little barb disguised as a backhanded compliment, so you missed *and* dismissed it. But then, it came back like an echo to haunt you. Still, you said nothing. Why?"

"I was speechless."

"In case you've forgotten, here's what Silkie said. *When I was small, I kept an open packet of chocolate creams at the ready in case Goldilocks should visit at any hour. Funny, she hasn't visited since you came, Ms. Lila-la di da. I hope the truth is finally sinking in that you're not supposed to be here.*

Silkie's historical diatribe had barely begun when the gloves came off which made Eeyore more determined to protect you. He tried to make a joke of it."

Eeyore looked innocent. "I recall mumbling 'what a splendid story, I think I'm going to be sick,' in your head, Leela."

Cheshire's fur bristled. "No, you didn't. You gave a hilarious impersonation of a cat choking up a hairball, and I should know, I've had a fair few. But Eeyore, it wasn't in Leela's head. You forgot to guard your inner voice, and Silkie heard you. In Eeyore's defense," Cheshire went on, "he immediately launched into, what I have to say, was a magnificent improv performance, feigning an insensitivity worthy of a master dullard to cover his faux pas."

Cheshire waved his tail over the invisible microphone like a wand. "Master Eeyore, will you please take a rather wet spotlight and do the honor of repeating your disastrous diatribe."

Eeyore was only too happy to speak. "Well, Silkie was so determined to freak out Leela, my response came out like, well... very much like a sort of bark. And then I launched into a memory to illustrate a point I no longer remember. I said something about Mr. Alan Milne being a prolific storyteller and that I was often privy to observing him in his study. He used to borrow Christopher's toys and arrange us on a table for inspiration with Pooh centerstage – a shrine to Saint Bear of Little Brain.

He made copious notes staring into Pooh's mind. It wasn't as if he channelled him or anything close to it. But a look would come into Alan's eyes, and he was off scribbling. I sat, lumped in with Kanga, Tigger, Roo and Piglet while the presence of Pooh inspired Alan to jot down ideas. Maybe some of the ideas *did* come from Pooh. Once in a blue moon Pooh's brain appeared to eclipse his simpleminded nature and bordered on brilliant. Although, when I queried him later, and being obsessed with *hunny* cravings he 'barely' understood a word I said.

A few of the complex plots were good. But then Mr. M's editor would storm in, invading his writing space with a red pencil and attack. Loose papers flew as he circled the stories he approved. The rest were thrown in the fire but before they were destroyed, I kept them stored in my noggin to be delivered to you." He took a cheesy bow. "You're very welcome."

Silkie had checked her watch and folded her arms – an imposing gesture that clearly said she would tolerate no more delays. The tension in the room snapped like a frozen tree branch. Silkie's patience was at breaking point. "Okay," she'd said. "If Eeyore is quite done. I'd like to continue *my* story which, if you remember, was the entire purpose of this meeting.

Imagine, if you will," she blurted, "that I am Verity as I speak, so you and Eeyore might feel the full effect of such a momentous occasion."

Eeyore cut Silkie off mid-preamble. "Being rescued after abandonment is no small event," he piped up. He nudged me in the ribs and raised his voice. "Is it, Leela? We've been there, done that and survived. Given the chance, Silkie, Leela would love to tell her side of the story at some point."

Silkie stopped tapping her foot and resumed her superior attitude. "As I was about to say, Verity always painted a vivid scene before she began my story. She loved to set it up like a mystery. You know, with lots of atmosphere and sound effects. She knew how to tell a story."

Sensing another ramble from Eeyore, Silkie dived into a whopper of a lie. "Like all closely linked twins, you and I are somewhat telepathic," she said. "And like all children, I repeatedly asked my grandmother for my favorite story about my birth."

Barely a second later, her attitude dived further south.

To my everlasting shame I recall begging Silkie to tell me more. Even to my own ears I sounded desperate. I felt as breathless and pink as Piglet.

For a heartbeat, the life came back into Silkie's narrowed eyes. "Aren't you too old for fairy tales," she sneered.

No less than you, I thought. *We are twins after all.*

Eeyore messaged me immediately. *Leela, you have every right to be here. Meet Silkie on your high ground. Imagine Lucy is behind you. Feel the soil. Take strength from her roots. Silkie is toying with you.*

But I heard myself bleat like a whining automaton. *Never. No-one ever read to me.*

Eeyore flinched and sprang into action as if he'd received an electric shock. *Ahem... scuze me. I beg to differ,* he said in my head, giving me the hairy eyeball. *No-one except for ME. Strictly speaking, Leela, I rarely read to you at bedtime. I narrated stories from memory until you fell asleep.* I had ignored him at my peril.

The out-of-season hail stopped, and a flock of blackbirds swarmed Lucy's branches until a giant feline face materialized and hissed them away with a giant paw.

"Okay okay," I said to my lecturers. "I surrender. I want to be heard. I want to shout from Lucy's treetop. Years of being dismissed and stifled in Tirings will be suppressed no longer. I am weary of feeling gutted. I recall only too well the humiliating treatment I endured from a certain, and I use the term loosely, *nursemaid.* If it hadn't been for Eeyore and the books that appeared on my bed once a week, I might have wasted clean away."

Cheshire's stripes rippled as if they were on fire. "Excellent. Now, what do you intend to do about it."

"Before you answer, Leela, may I just add that surrender is often the best response to take," Absolem suggested. "Accepting your rights would be more... well, advantageous."

I hesitated. Eeyore averted his eyes and sent me a telepathic message. *Let it all out, girl. It's time.* Cheshire's colors intensified. He was just getting started. "Leela, tell me what you *feel* like doing. Go with your first thought. Hold nothing back."

"I'd like to throw a drink in Silkie's arrogant little face."

"Atta girl," Cheshire hissed. "Then what?"

"I haven't thought that far," I said shamefaced.

"Okay, take a minute. We can wait."

I drew a blank which meant I had no choice but to suffer through the entire replayed fiasco of my shame because Cheshire took his lectures seriously and if any part of them were edited or truncated, I'd rather meet the Jabberwock on a dark night in Tugely Wood than face his wrath.

I observed Cheshire and Absolem as we once more replayed

yesterday's ordeal in our linked minds. Cheshire grimaced several times and hid his face behind a paw. Finally, he coughed what sounded like an overtly serious hairball. "Is anyone else embarrassed by this?" he said.

Absolem laid down his pipe and crossed two of his legs in disgust. "I can't stand by and say nothing."

"A chance would be a fine thing," Cheshire retorted. "Now see what I just did there, Leela? That was sarcasm. Absolem and I use it to insult each other all the time. But we're friends. It's even more effective when confronting an enemy. And by the way, a snappy comeback is something you must keep at the ready in your back pocket. Ready to launch without a second thought. One must respond ...*snap*... at the right moment, without blinking. Knock Silkie off her high horse. She's not expecting it."

"Furthermore," Absolem droned lazily. "You have an edge. Silkie's confidence is almost as fake as your humility."

"Can either of you see me? I'm standing right here. You do know that I can hear you, right?"

"Hearing is not the same as believing," Cheshire said.

Not to be outdone, Absolem responded one better. "Believing in yourself requires intense silence. You are a child of..."

"Quote the Desiderata at your peril," I snapped. Then I faced Cheshire without blinking. "How was that, Cheshire, snappy enough for you?"

"Not bad. Your response time was perfect." He sighed and curled into a catnap position. "The penny drops, Absolem, but will it ever land, I ask myself. Will it *ever* land."

"Where is this Everland? Is it far?" I said tongue in cheek hoping to get a rise out of Cheshire.

It worked. "There is *no* Everland," Cheshire said, rolling his eyes. "But at least you're listening between the lies."

Absolem responded as if he'd just awakened from a dream.

"You carry on, Leela dear. Many a falsehood is revealed in the truth."

"A diet of crumbs has given you an appetite for power," Eeyore said to me. "I didn't know how much until now."

The next day, I reconvened Silkie's meeting with an apology for having had a headache the previous day. Silkie proceeded to begin where she'd left off, but before she could speak, I figuratively jumped on stage. "I feel I must apologize, Silkie. Please let me get this out before I lose my nerve. I'm that ashamed. I don't know what came over me yesterday," I said, pretending to cower. "You were being so helpful, and I was rude. The truth is, Silkie, you intimidate me." And then I went all out for pathetic. "I'm in awe of your superior education. I can't possibly replace you."

Eeyore recoiled but said nothing.

Silkie couldn't resist upstaging me. She took the bait and milked her peevish act for spite. "You know, Leela, I called yesterday's meeting specifically to help you. I even invited Eeyore along to make you feel comfortable, but I really think you might have restrained him a little."

Eeyore used telepathy to answer me. *Well played old girl. Your sainted sister may be clever enough to outfox Pooh, but who isn't. She's not smart enough to outfox me or Absolem. Cheshire won't give Silkie the time of day. Piglet nearly wets himself if she so much as looks at him.*

"He's a highly strung little piglet," I replied out loud which must have sounded strange, but Silkie ignored it as if she hadn't been listening.

Eeyore countered aloud in his inevitable droll wit for my benefit. *"Well, he's much higher, now."* Cheshire howled with laughter, in my head.

"Silkie responded to my *'and then what happened* by sharing the most horrific nightmare of all. Causing Cheshire to comment "Nice over-acting, Leela. You almost had *me* fooled for a second. I thought maybe you'd thrown in the towel."

An ominous tone had crept into Silkie's voice. "Verity tells me you have no birth story worth mentioning, Lila, so you and she will no doubt create one. For a woman whose name means truth she's rather savvy at telling lies."

"I've tried to imagine my birth several times," I said. "But I never got very far."

Silkie smoothed back the hair that had fallen into her eyes. "Then you'll have to make up something juicy," she said. "Verity loves making things up. Sometimes she actually believes them. Some of them are truly chilling." Silkie's smirk contrasted with her indifferent shrug.

"Have you ever seen a ghost, Leela? You're bound to see them around here. The woodcutter is the worst. He has sockets where his eyes used to be. You must stop your ears when he shows up. It's impossible to make eye contact with him but you could fall into his eye sockets if you get too close. And make sure Eeyore stays clear of the axe blade. Old woodcutter likes to swing it like a tennis racket. He threatens to chop down young trees for fun, but he never does. At least… he hasn't so far."

"That girl is even more spiteful than I thought," Cheshire grumbled. "Never mind. As Absolem is wont to shout when he's in a particularly philosophical mood, 'Poo happens!' I've always said that Pooh is more of a happening than a deep thinker. Now get on and please change the conversation."

Eeyore brayed louder than a wolf at a full moon. "If Silkie bothers you again, I swear I'll get the Jabberwock to bite off her head, so I will. He owes me a favor."

Absolem's hookah emitted a final gasp of smoke as he drifted off to sleep, awake enough to burble a final profound thought. "There's more than one way to decapitate a traitor," he said.

A TIRING 'HOUSE'

*A curtained off area
on a Shakespearian stage
housing props and costumes
where actors dressed
and awaited their cues.*

chapter 17

THE BACK OF BEYOND

"The man who lies asleep will never waken fame,
and his desire and all his life drift past him like a dream,
and the traces of his memory fade from time
like smoke in air, or ripples on a stream"

DANTE ALIGHIERI

Silkie heard Greenwood more times than she cared to remember, tap tapping, scritchity scratching, at the door of a moonless night until he scuttled away.

When a lone wolf howled from the direction of Tirings, he was gone.

Squirrels chattered the all-clear and a heady perfume of pine and honeysuckle wafted from the forest floor. The wings of birds and insects flapped away the residue of negative human energy. Blue sky pushed through the forest canopy like a finger of joy. Bees buzzed their old business with new spirit. A gentle cleansing rain fell. The Green Man momentarily reappeared in the bark of trees and a peace that surpassed all understanding settled briefly over the land.

Fetch shook frazzled psychic energy from her fur and Chase rolled onto his back, thumpity thumping his tail on the floor like an angry heartbeat.

Verity's first instinct was to load her shopping basket with a treasure trove of delicacies: fig jam, sharp cheese, gingerbread, chocolate buttons, marzipan mice, potted fish paste, and Devonshire cream. The second was to set the kettle to boiling and charge flames to leap in the grate.

According to the food chain, Eeyore and I had arrived at a particularly fractious time for ghostly activity. Eeyore grimly noted they were coming out of the woodwork.

He made a derisive gagging sound when Silkie left. "The little cow," he grumbled. "I hope you tell her in no uncertain terms that we are thrilled and delighted to stay."

"I already did. She didn't look impressed. Anyway, we still need some background about old Greenwood. Apparently, he's taken a shine to understudying the role of Snow White's woodcutter. I'll ask Cheshire. Snow White's step mama wanted her killed but the real woodcutter faked her death because he had a smidgen of compassion."

"There are trees," Eeyore mused "who swear Greenwood doesn't have a conscience let alone a soul, so a smidgen of compassion is out of the question."

I told Silkie we were quite resilient and there was no need to soften the facts on our account.

A chance would be a fine thing," Eeyore sniffed. "I say, can you smell something odd?"

"I believe it's happiness," Cheshire called down from his aerie.

Eeyore shook his head. "There's no point in gloating over broken promises," he remarked, trying to smile mid-chew with a mouthful of oat straw.

"Not to worry, Leela," Absolem said. "As piglet in the middle, you may have to pay the price for a while. Just remember, Cheshire and I have your back."

Eeyore shook his mane as if dislodging a hornet. "Greenwood was a worthless multi-millionaire. Isn't that an oxy something or other?"

"It's a paradox," Absolem said. "A paradoxical oxymoron."

"Huzzah! As I thought. A moron by any name is just as worthless."

I hadn't heard the disembodied voice for a while. "You're off the hook, Blameless," Zeno declared as clear as if he were in the room. "Castle Featureless was Greenwood's Waterloo. You'll have to deal with Greenwood. But not to worry, compared to Elizabeth Tudor, Greenwood's presence is a puff of Absolem's hookah smoke."

I waited demurely, teacup held high, pinky finger extended to make a good impression while Silkie's lectures droned Eeyore and I into a coma. Eeyore impatiently thwacked his tail, catlike, against my leg.

There was no preamble. No welcome-wagon smile. The diatribe turned into a horror story. Greenwood was a paranoid psychopath who became increasingly deranged the more besotted he became with Sherlock Holmes. But more than Conan Doyle's books, Greenwood was obsessed with his fame. He copycatted the model of Sherlock Holmes as a template for his lame mysteries financed by selling stately homes upgraded to palatial estates.

Landscape architect, Lancelot (Capability) Brown died eighty years before Greenwood was born. Sadly, Capability's fame inspired Greenwood, a greedy entrepreneur, to become a landscape enthusiast.

Greenwood mistakenly thought to honor Brown's memory by basing his protagonist sleuth, Jackson Greene, as an homage. But memories of the dead run deep, and the consequences ran high.

Greenwood grew ever more deranged with time, coercing, begging, and finally blackmailing Verity into domestic servitude. He was too neurotic to live, the trees said, and it would have been a great service if he'd *stayed* dead after he died. The contract he forced Verity to sign was non-negotiable."

By the time Seneca Aurelius Greenwood's ill begotten funds overshot his wildest business expectations, he was certifiably insane. He strongarmed Verity into accepting humiliating positions of increasing servitude until essentially, she hit bottom and dug her way towards China.

Essentially quarantined with no books to edit, Verity was downgraded to Greenwood's care nurse – a housekeeper without pay, no doubt inspired by Sherlock's maternal housekeeper, Mrs. Hudson.

Verity, the ghostly gatekeeper of Greenwood's *literary* flame, inherited his forest and the mock castle she was compelled to haunt after Greenwood's death until she set it aflame and watched the main building burn to the ground.

After the smoke cleared, Verity promptly renamed the surviving keep, Tirings at Edward's suggestion, and transformed it into an asylum for her displaced lodgers, the infirm, and abandoned motley odd ducks.

Greenwood's protagonist, Jackson Greene, was hardly subtle. But Greenwood truly overstepped literary etiquette when he blatantly pirated Sir Arthur's good name by referring to his realty empire as Sherlock Homes Ltd. His lead protagonist and architectural landscape designs were likewise 'acquired'.

"One might correctly say *abducted*," Eeyore said in a stage whisper. "There's nothing pseudo about stealing another man's creative life force."

Greenwood's plan for celebrity disintegrated into several lawsuits citing plagiarism. He escaped like a thief in the night, beetling away under cover of darkness with bags of cash and two tickets for passage on an ocean liner headed to Canada where he trekked its west coast covertly for three days using Verity as a pack animal.

Intending to build an unwelcoming estate but not being the slightest bit *capable* of designing one, Greenwood built a forbidding Norman keep, loosely based on an old 1831 engraving of Hedingham Castle, the remains of Edward de Vere's family seat.

Greenwood's crew hastily assembled a commanding mountain of undressed stone into an austere tower – a severe, menacing vertical tunnel of a castle.

Edward recognized his former home at once. In an homage to Verity who had dubbed it her 'Retiring Home' for homeless odd ducks, and his fond memory of the theatre, Edward renamed it 'Tirings' for the curtained-off area on stage called the Tiring room where actors changed costumes and stored props.

But more apropos, actors changing clothes to match their multiple performance roles was a perfect metaphor for reincarnation. And if nothing else, Silvany was ground zero for rebirth.

A photograph of Hedingham Castle, Tirings' Spartan architectural mother, showed a tall featureless tower, stark as a prison but then it had been a fortress in it's first incarnation and in turn, Greenwood's reincarnated monstrosity served as a prison for Verity after her death.

Greenwood's blight on the landscape that had polluted Silvany's sacred groves, was reduced to a blackened heap in the fire of 1925. As a traumatized child of six, I knew it as a crumbling tower surrounded by a forest, both Haven and Hell – a sanctuary for the ghosts who once served the homeless, one of whom was me.

I was six years old then and I'm six years old, now.

I was 34 the day Tirings burned to the ground in 1997, liberating its inmates and ghosts, and I'd wondered if my generous librarian still haunted its ashes.

I'd been returning from work, stuck in the ensuing traffic jam, a mile from home, while the sirens of the fire engines wailed around the number 61- bus like banshees. Eeyore messaged me that Tirings was on fire and that sympathetic clouds of acrid yellow smoke had penetrated Otherwhere. The fire damage in Otherwhere persisted as a disturbing echo for many years. Long after the danger passed, the smell of smoke lingered in the trees, grey from toxic ashes.

Verity's revenge inadvertently played into Greenwood's hand. The vegetation charged with her newly-acquired supernatural powers gave his spectre the perfect refuge of invisibility.

Capability's unique concept of an expansive landscape seamlessly unspoiled by man yet altered by formal designs where Greenwood could be the observer of his thoughts rather than be observed – the secluded environment of a stalwart recluse.

But privacy wasn't enough. Greenwood demanded total obscurity – a 'Brigadoon' where he could rule as Oz inside the experiment upwind of us.

I made a derogatory face. "No wonder it fell into ruin," I said.

"Abandonment is a regular phenomenon around here," Cheshire said.

Silkie's tea party took an ominous tone. "Reincarnation isn't as tidy as one would think," Eeyore said.

But even Eeyore couldn't have predicted how low Silkie's insults could go. I thought I'd misheard when she announced that Greenwood had thrown Verity *under the bus* as soon as she perjured herself by signing a confession as party to plagiarism – a statement hitting too close to home to be coincidental.

Silkie grudgingly hinted an apology but tactlessly summed up her poisonous dissertation as Verity's disgusting 'game of lies in a nutshell', and a lame, sorry but you had to know.

Eeyore rose like a dignified poet at a recital and delivered a scathing eulogy. "And in Greenwood's happy *never after* his malignant legacy devolved into a pretentious library of musty unpublished compositions that *decomposed* in a parallel dimension.

Absolem filled his cheeks with smoke and expelled it in a furious jet stream. "Verity says Tirings *fell* into ruin by accident, and *that*, Leela, was the only time to my knowledge Verity ever told a lie. The fire was set on purpose by Verity's ghost to celebrate Greenwood's demise. The dictator was dead. She was effectively dancing on his grave. And apart from some extraneous damage for which she was punished, in my opinion, Verity deserved a medal.

Not even Verity has come up with a reasonable explanation why Greenwood's demonic spirit is so intent on staying here."

Eeyore gave a guilty cough. "Excuse me, but I may be able to shed some light on that. Lucy hinted the 'albatross' Greenwood made Verity sign is still hidden somewhere in the forest and Verity will remain a victim until it's destroyed. It's partly the reason the woodcutter is still here."

I was about to ask what other reason *could* there be, but Eeyore grimaced and nosed the field flowers at his feet disrupting a cloud of bees. "Eventually, time always tells," he mumbled with his mouth full of buttercups.

Silkie had waffled on in a malevolent gush noting Greenwood favored the Stratford usurper in the disputed Shakespeare identity question – a spiteful ploy to rub Verity the wrong way, fully aware that Edward, had been thrust into obscurity by shameless Elizabethan powermongers and plagiarists who made Greenwood look an amateur. She delivered the axe blow she'd been saving for last, inclining her head towards me before declaring she was happy to leave 'Bedlam' in my *capable* hands since my arrival had *inflamed* matters. Her smirk put Cheshire to shame.

Absolem was that startled he swallowed a puff of green smoke. "That little hussy," he sputtered. "Why, the little baggage."

"Little is too small a word to describe a greedy monster," Cheshire hissed.

I felt microscopic, left behind to deal with the future Silkie promised me. Eeyore's ears went haywire. "First let me assure you, Silkie *promised* nothing; she *threatened* you. She's jealous of you. And as much as she loathes Verity, she's dead keen on keeping her feelings of entitlement. She'll be a social climber in her next life if Zeno doesn't sort her out.

Neither of you are on trial but at the end of the day, after Verity qualifies for reincarnation, only one successor can rule Veratopia. And when that happens ..." Eeyore's words trailed out, lost in a patch of clover. "I've said too much already. And I shouldn't be speaking with my mouth full." But I heard his thoughts. *According to Cheshire, the King of Scuttlebutt, Verity's grooming you for the job. Rumor has it bequeathing you the cabin may be in the works."*

"Verity already did," I said aloud. "But she stipulated it was to be a writing space, nothing more."

Eeyore lifted his head dislodging a determined bee. "I have to say, for a writer you don't read between the lines much," he said.

MASTER 'CAPABILITY' BROWN

1716 - 1783

Lancelot (Capability) Brown
was a famous landscape architect.
His success sprouted from the 'ground up',
as a lowly gardener's assistant.
But his genius designs with lavish
formal gardens, water features,
and follies transformed stately homes
into flamboyant estates that trebled their price.

chapter 18

HAVE BOOKS WILL TRAVEL

"Stay Passenger, why goest thou by so fast?
Read if thou canst, whom envious Death hath placed
Within this monument Shakspeare: with whom
Quick nature died: whose name doth deck this tomb
Far more than cost: sith [since] all that he hath writ
Leaves living art, but page to serve his wit."

— BEN JONSON c.1623

Inscription on the monument to William Shakespeare
- Trinity Church, Stratford-Upon-Avon

Verity sat with me by the fire pretending to read a book while I blew on a mug of cocoa too hot to drink. Her alert posture and faraway eyes told me she was paying attention to something in the past that was about to happen.

I braced myself for a sharp knock at the door and held my breath.

Verity visibly relaxed. She settled deeper into her armchair and motioned for me to tend the dying fire. I poked the flames releasing a shower of red sparks and added another pine log, but it was green and damp from the rain and released a lazy cloud of pungent smoke. Mesmerized, I rode its back up the chimney.

I followed it into the night sky and stared at the moon without leaving Verity's side, but a paper-thin memory arrived that pulled me back to the fireside.

Verity was sitting with her eyes closed and I thought she was dreaming. "Ask me, child," she said without opening her eyes.

"I've been here before, haven't I? Did you forget me? Did you make a mistake?"

She leaned forward warming her hands on a new generation of flames. "Greenwood outlived me by one year," she said. "I passed in 1924 but that's all I remember. I had no place to go. No *other where* to go, so I created 'Otherwhere in the forest."

I set my cocoa aside. "I thought I'd created it. I had delusions of grandeur when I was six."

Verity chuckled. "Goodness, yes, you most certainly did. You had to for survival." Her eyes flashed open, and she tapped my nose with her finger "Never apologize for creativity, Leela. There's too little of it in the world outside Veratopia."

"Tell me."

Verity's eyes clouded over, and a tear escaped down her cheek. I wiped it away with a fingertip and held her hand. "I remember the day you and I met," she said. It was a day I made a great mistake for which I hope you will someday forgive me."

I squeezed her hand. "I'm just going to put the kettle on," I said. "You could use a cup of tea. Keep talking, I can still hear you."

She spoke as if to herself while I rattled away in the kitchen, but her voice still rose above the whistling kettle. I was soon back at her side pressing a cup into her hands.

"I consider this period my second childhood or was it the first childhood of someone I'd forgotten. No matter, I knew all about children's books and toyed with populating Otherwhere with a storyland of harmless characters who loved children.

The tremble in her voice reminded me how imperfect things can be in times of transition.

"A knock at the door called me away from Silkie," she said, "and I was eager to get back to her. I was far too focused on Silkie in those days, and I'm afraid I rather spared the rod and spoiled her."

"I noticed."

"There *you* were, a timid child, or so I thought, and I had to break the news to you that Tirings was your new home. You did not take it well. You disappeared inside yourself, and I had to wait a long time for you to come back, which I might add, you did with a vengeance when I tried to pry your book from your hands."

She chuckled at the memory but suddenly teared up again.

I kept her tea steady and let her cry. I finished my cocoa, set aside my mug, and waited.

Verity had read a busload of ghostly tomes forgotten inside the derelict books-on-wheels bus parked off-road, abandoned on a vacant lot behind the old Havonford Library.

It was the habitat of rabbits (she called a rabbitat), and white-tailed deer and off-leash dogs, and because of our dual worlds, Verity had dubbed it 'Parallel Park'. Verity's cup stopped shaking; she took a sip and spoke clearly. "The abandoned bookmobile rusted away in a graveyard of trees on a vacant lot behind the old library. Its rusted frame was dangerously sharp, and off limits to kids poking around after one of them, Nathaniel Sloane, cut his leg and never told his mother.

The way of shadows is a sad one. I know because..." she suddenly appeared lost. "Little Nate sickened and died of sepsis, thus becoming the youngest ghost in Tirings. After that folk were afraid to go there. Only a few teenage boys dared each other to explore the bus after dark. Mind you, teenage bravado only goes so far. Those same boys were terrified after I got through with them. I placed a spell of protection over the bus. Dogs let off their leashes howled bloody murder and ran in circles when a rabbit or a squirrel made sport with them (*and they always did because I'd charged them with courage beyond instinctive animal understanding*).

Dog owners eventually got the idea and hastened their pets to the beach. And after frightening their children and themselves with a lame ghost story, the land was left to itself as was proper."

Verity read my mind swimming with the questions I'd been loath to ask.

"Very well, Leela. If you're going to reclaim your destiny there are things you should know. I erased a lot of my memories from the middle of my life that were too difficult to keep, and I don't remember a great deal of the end. But sometimes there are regrets that flap on the ceiling like bats. On those occasions I escape into a book until it's safe to come out.

I picked up my cocoa which had replenished itself complete with marshmallows. "Now *that*, I *can* relate to," I said. "Destiny recovery is a mystery. Although, Eeyore hints at things. He's a sly old horse in the guise of a sly old donkey."

"Never mind, that's his memory not yours," Verity said. And then she forgot everything.

We sat in silence during which time I ate the marshmallows with a spoon.

At last, Verity spoke in a faraway voice filled with unshed tears. "Most mornings I left Tirings to gather some much-needed books. Little Nathaniel needed children's books. The residents, poor souls, had been more restless than usual, drifting through walls and wailing piteously. Some days trying to be solid was overwhelming, even for me. Their easy chairs had long since been removed, leaving the presence of ethereal chairs, and the frustration from no longer having bodies to sit comfortably in the memories of chairs to watch a television no longer there, was often too much to bear.

So, I did the only thing I could. I seated them in a circle and encouraged them to tell each other stories they remembered from childhood, until I could bring them a new supply of reading material.

I remember it was a Friday. I took a basket and left the grounds in broad daylight heading for the bookmobile. Folks were used to seeing me. Perhaps they thought me hard of hearing because they called me an old bag lady behind my back loud enough for me to hear. No matter, it was what I wanted them to think. It was also the truth. I usually felt old, and I always carried a basket to collect the books and groceries." She clasped and unclasped her hands, fitfully, staring into the distance. "Or was it apples?"

Greenwood bequeathed me the wildlife blind he used as a hideaway when his fears came calling. So many terrible fears came calling in those days," she said, searching the lengthening shadows. "Has someone seen my Alice? I can't find her anywhere."

Verity had many duties during her time at the castle. They started out as a literary calling and after several variations, by lessening degrees, she ended up in abject servitude to her employer. But only after he'd sapped her energy and destroyed her sanity.

As a literary agent she drifted into a semi-retirement of sorts which was appropriate as the castle was turned into a 'Retiring' Home to replace the local poorhouse. Technically, she was the first inmate and the last to leave.

Near the end, Verity no longer knew what tasks were written in her contract. She was too confused to put up a fight. But like she said, she had nowhere else to go. It was before Edward arrived in Veratopia with Puck. And even so he was at his wits end.

Verity accepted the thankless position of voluntary work serving the sad tenants who were abandoned or had drifted in after Greenwood's death as an extension of a punishment she deserved. She assumed the words contractual obligation in the legal document she'd signed bound her, body and soul, to the castle. But that's what happens with words in a living contract. A lawyer must use strange words to make sense of fiction and senseless words to tell the truth.

No matter, the land protected its own. The spirit of the librarian in the bookmobile was its friend and the abandoned books in the old bus, its children. And as impossible as it sounds, the stories inside it were a lifeline to the ghosts up at the castle. It remained their personal lending library that harmed no one. Verity couldn't have borrowed books from the local library without stirring up trouble. Her final duty as a force of nature, forged from force of habit, was cheering the troubled souls abandoned by their families and left to die and haunt a heartless building.

I thought Verity was asleep, so she startled me when she began to speak. "When I found Silkie, a new lifeforce quickened within me and for a moment death seemed reasonable, and Edward rallied to my aid.

I served them to the last soul – a madwoman at death's door refusing to cross over, and a living child released as a young adult. Seventeen she was. Put to menial work as a disabled person by the powers that be. I watched the car that took her away until it drove onto the main road. It was the end of an era. Tiring's gates were locked behind her and I returned to my life as a wannabe grandmother."

I pressed a fresh cup of tea in her hands. Her eyes were closed. "Did you ever think of that girl... the last one?" I asked her.

Her eyes opened, brimming with tears. "Oh, Leela. I'd like to say that I did," she said. "I was only half alive myself then, which also meant half dead. Of course, I wished her well. She was a sweet little thing. A distant lonely child. Innocent and afraid. Sometimes I imagine she's still here. I've seen her in the woods talking to Eeyore.

The castle ghosts rallied around her as aunts and uncles as best they could, but she never responded to any of them but one. For a while I took on the role of her fairy godmother.

I left a stack of illustrated books for her to 'read' on Saturdays. I am pleased to say that the books I chose for her made her smile. She always hugged her favorite book during the day, taking it with her to the garden and slept with it like a teddy bear before drifting off to sleep.

I came to think of the books I laid out on her bed as a raft. The story of Winken, Blinken, and Nod sailing off in a wooden shoe was one of her favorites.

I don't remember her name, now. She remains anonymous, isolated in a virtual playground populated by imaginary friends she met in the books I gave her. She may not have been happy, but I believe she was content there. I felt heartened whenever she smiled."

Verity scrutinized me. "I forget things these days, but you look familiar."

Since the characters in books are immortal, the lifeblood of their adventures became spiritual food for the odd girl. She survived on vicarious nourishment from the lifeblood of their adventures. I never tried to reach the true child behind her fear. Silkie took all my energy.

But now you're here, child, and I can offer you the schooling that child could have had. What is your name, again? Sorry, I forget things. I never meant to be cruel. Goodness knows she had far too much of that from her mother."

That's when I had a quiet little cry. *Oh, Verity, please come back and remember. You are the one I called my librarian. I'm right here and you have nothing to forgive.*

Days later, I learned the truth of Silkie's rescue through the power of Verity's restored memories.

The bookmobile was there in the shade as usual but the rotted tarp that covered it had been tossed aside. The gaping door on its hinges was open wider than usual and a holy light flickered from deep within its murk.

It was the light Silkie liked to declare was her soul and Verity had agreed in order to nip an argument in the bud.

So many facts made their way into Silkie's fertile imagination. "Silkie told me you found her on a bed of leaves," I said.

Verity smiled as she corrected Silkie's poetic cradle image to a crude makeshift mattress made from the leaves of a wet book. Specifically, the musty pages torn from an old atlas.

"And Paddington Bear?" I asked.

Verity shivered and pulled her shawl close around her. She smiled, closed her eyes, grimaced as a terrifying memory surfaced. "When Chase was asleep, I used to tell Silkie he was dead to the world. Of course, I explained it was a joke. But I was never sure she believed me. That girl has a powerful sense of the tragic about her."

"Did Silkie's plot *thicken* the way she said it did?"

Verity beamed. "I think it might have. The front cover of Paddington Bear had been pinned to her nightgown by her mother. The woman (also *your* mother by the way) Silkie always referred to her as 'the traveler."

Verity leaned towards me as if divulging a secret. "There's many secret truths hidden in Shakespeare, right enough," she whispered as if we might be overheard. "Much ado about fiction is the art of telling lies." She looked over her shoulder shook and returned to her story. "The traveler had had the presence of mind to cross out the word 'bear' on the cover illustration of Paddington's luggage tag that read *please look after this bear* and written *baby*."

"Is that why you told Silkie she was born to travel?"

"Oh, lor, I never said such a thing, that little scamp. I placed Silkie in my basket instead of the books. And that night while she slept alive to the world in my cabin, the 'jungle drums' gossiped her arrival, and I spoke far into the night with Zeno and my friend Edward. A plan was hatched then and there, but it required divine timing. And after a few years…"

Verity paused as if falling deeper asleep, so I didn't press her. I took the empty cup from her hand and tucked a blanket around her. Later, Verity confirmed that Christopher Robin, Pooh, and Piglet visited Silkie on the night she was found and presented her with an illustration of a kitten and a puppy by Christopher's godfather, Mr.

Shepard. She chuckled "And with a little help from me they grew into Fetch and Chase. A little magic makes a world of difference, wouldn't you say. Just ask Alice." A bewildered look crossed her face. "I've looked for Alice everywhere. Have you seen her. She's a few months old. She was here a moment ago. Did I lose her?" Verity honored the classic folk tale opening *'once upon a time'*. "Anything less would have been a waste of story," she said. "Where is that girl? Alice traipses off every day. Sometimes I see her lingering about in the Nozone. Why on middle-earth would she do such a hopeless thing."

GROUND ROOTS

THE FOREST STOA

chapter 19

I AM AN IDEA

"I AM BORN. Whether I shall turn out
to be the hero of my own life,
or whether that station
will be held by anybody else,
these pages must show."

CHARLES DICKENS

– 'David Copperfield'

I am infinitely more at ease with the lovely woman in the green dress who showed herself to me the day she led me to sanctuary. I led with an elephant-in-the-room question, "Is this heaven?"

Verity nodded at first. "I thought you'd never ask," she said, but then she raised her eyebrows and shook her head. "Well, it is, and it isn't. I'm not permitted to disclose more than that, but I will say it's close enough to the heaven average humans dream of. Essentially, we are happily ensconced in a pocket of natural peace, separated but unavoidably connected to the physical world by a threadbare shadow. Think Peter Pan's rogue shadow and you will have grasped the matter... pun intended."

Admiration shone in my eyes. "Oh, my stars, you're a writer" I gushed.

Verity bowed and smiled. "At your service. I was once a literary agent. Now I am an editor who writes from time to time. Timeless, being the operative word."

"Well, I wish I'd written that little speech of yours."

"You did. I merely paraphrased a memory of yours."

"Then, you're a mind reader."

"That's pretty much what an editor is. But I truly appreciate you not calling me a plagiarist. That would have been too close to the bone."

"Sorry?"

"The bone I have to pick with you."

"What did I ever do to you?"

"You were a calm sweet infant. Had you been fussy, your sainted mother may have abandoned you instead and we wouldn't be here righting a mistake. As such, changeling, my happiness is delayed and yours must be saved. Neither of us is to blame."

A clear image of a devastated teenager flickered and was gone. Verity was hiding something, but I didn't press her. My immediate concern was connecting Havonford with Heaven and determining my future. "I've seen the disturbing shadow of an old woodcutter lurking in the trees," I said. "Does it have a name?"

"Seneca Aurelius Greenwood."

"I've seen that name on the spines of books in your library."

"He wrote spineless stories… pointless stories, basically pale regurgitations of the spine-chilling stories of Conan Doyle's Sherlock Holmes."

"Jackson Greene was the pathetic hero of his wimpy sleuth mysteries. Precisely what happens when copycat stories are translated into other languages, or otherwise reincarnated as flavorless ghosts of their inspirational counterparts. Greenwood crammed his churned-out rubbish between books of Sir Arthur's creative genius in the hopes a little fairy dust would rub off on them without a lawsuit."

"I don't see what that's got to do with me?"

The glamorous lady faded, defaulting to the wizened librarian who had given me shelter from a heartless storm. Verity let out a huge sigh and stared at my shoes. "My dear, Colorless. You carry a special 'quality' that entitles my mistress, the Lady Flora of Silvany, who recently granted you sanctuary, to a modicum of gratitude for turning back the clock against absolute cosmic orders.

"Oh, my stars."

Her eyes lifted to mine. "No kidding, Sherlock."

I panicked, stuffing my belongings into a plastic garbage bag. "What's going to happen to me if Eeyore and I can't go home. Is that woodcutter fellow dangerous?"

"I don't know yet. I only have a preliminary glimpse of your new life at the moment. You're still forming. But no worries, Greenwood is only a danger to himself. Best ignore him. The past is over. Well, mostly over. Leela, you are an idea."

"So, I'm a story waiting to happen?"

"Weren't you always?"

"Can I start tomorrow?"

"No worries, Greensleeves. You started the day we met in the Havonford library. You look confused. Don't try to remember. Some things must be remembered before they happen."

The next morning my formal classes with Vera, Verity's younger counterpart, began.

Vera had created a leafy corner with a comfy sofa and armchairs upholstered in pink cabbage roses, and a coffee table laden with a pot of tea and a plate of chocolate Bourbon biscuits. This brand of confectionary had long since been discontinued so I eyed the plate with interest and minded my manners waiting for an invitation to dig in that never came.

Vera, the schoolmarm, opened a satchel of papers and laid a pile of them on the ground using a moss covered Tirings brick as a paperweight. The morning chill had not yet been burned off by the sun, so I snuggled deeper into my fleece hoodie and waited. I concentrated on the corner of a piece of paper that periodically lifted in the wind, easily lulled into its sense of playfulness, until Vera's voice startled me.

It was much softer and more innocent than Verity's and so I relaxed immediately. I'd heard all about the terrors of regular school, which I'd never attended, but this was being homeschooled in every sense of the word, home. Soon it would be all tea and chocolate biscuits.

Vera's voice may have sounded meek, but her opening words dived into the heart of life itself. I sat up straight and paid attention. A butterfly landed on the tea tray and stilled its wings as if it too was listening. Presumably a fellow student. I sent it my best encouraging smile from one teacher's pet to another.

Our teacher stood without a lectern; eyes closed to ground herself. She looked like a preacher about to enthral her flock. "Everyone begins life as a creative thought," she said as if to herself, and took a long pause. "But it's important to understand that every writing lesson you will take here will be informed by the three Rs: Reading, Righting, and Reincarnation."

Vera's eyes flashed open and stared piercingly into mine, and we were off. "Every living thing including inventions begins its existence as an energetic impulse, indistinguishable from any design that takes up physical, mental, or astral space," she said in one prolonged breath. "But for a while we humans float in a warm jelly-like medium, absorbing, adapting, and hopefully, perfecting ourselves."

The butterfly fanned its wings in a frenzy and flew off. I sensed its panic.

Vera looked at me over an old-fashioned pair of wirerimmed glasses that suddenly manifested on the tip her nose and sighed wearily. "However," she said watching the butterfly disappear, "*Some* of us never make it to dry land. Please stay focused."

She sat down heavily, drained of energy, but immediately

brightened. "Shall I be mother?" she said cheerfully, lifting the teapot.

"I never had a mother. Not a real one," I said.

"The past is gone, little one," Vera said pouring me a strong cup of tea with three sugar cubes and a long dollop of cream. "Lesson one. Sip that and tell me what the creative idea of tea is. First, close your eyes. Listen to the tea. Feel its essence. Please allow it to fully steep in your mind before answering."

I savored the steam warming my face as I drank in the scent of bergamot and floated away. "Ah," I said, "is scent the creative idea of tea?"

Vera drained her own cup and clattered it onto its saucer. "Think again. Look around you. Here we are in the heart of flora and fauna. Does that spark any ideas? Your tea was a sensation was it not. You look lost, girl."

The word girl hit a nerve. I looked at my young hands. My senior years had melted away. I *was* a girl. A second childhood girl. A fairy tale child.

Vera's expression followed my revelation. "Don't get distracted, Leela. Just accept what's happening and delight in your new life. And never mind not knowing all the answers. Questions are never meant to distance you from a true teacher. So, I will get you started. Tea is a nourishing sensory plant. Its properties of scent, color, taste and prophecy are sealed. Think on that before you answer again."

I savored the aromatic liquid, almost too hot to drink which is the way I preferred it and stirred it dreamily, savoring the anticipation of morning tea. I was soon lost in thoughts of white porcelain cups, Blue Denmark teapots, and cubes of brown sugar.

When I heard the delicate clink of the saucer and the chime of a silver teaspoon against the inside of the cup, I envisioned myself as a fairy princess drinking from a bell. Soon my tea was an experience that evoked happy memories. "Is tea a story?"

Vera beamed. "In a very real sense, you're correct," she said.

"The tealeaves stuck to the inside of your cup are chapters of your life yet to be or long since gone. She reached out and patted my hand. "Well done. Yes, tea *is* an idea. But its essence is something more."

I felt engulfed by the heady thrill of being understood by a grownup. I *was* in heaven. 'Otherwhere' was within me and somewhere the shadows of Havonford skulked on without me. I experienced a peak moment in a grove of trees, and I wasn't frightened. Their friendly branches waved like the motion of a loving green sea – an audience applauding me. I was so over the moon being celebrated for who I was, I almost missed Vera's absolute truth.

"The *first* idea of tea is thirst," she said.

I sat through the rest of the lesson in a trance. Vera explained that every lifeform has a story. "Some stories never make it to the page," she said. "But it's never too late to write your own opening sentence. This is why Verity brought you here. She's more than a fairy godmother granting your wish to be a writer. You are here to complete your story that never made it to the page." She broke off eye contact and shuffled her papers distractedly. "Now, you'll need a working title, of course. 'The Life and Times of Leela the Wunderkind' is appropriate as a placeholder. True titles arrive *much* later. Trust me."

For a moment I felt like David Copperfield. Who would I turn out to be?

chapter 20

OTHER ME

"Who are YOU?" said the Caterpillar.
This was not an encouraging opening for a conversation.
Alice replied, rather shyly,
"I—I hardly know, sir, just at present—
at least I know who I WAS when I got up this morning,
but I think I must have been changed several times since then."

LEWIS CARROLL

I'm inside an uneasy memory, dreaming I'm another Leela standing behind a window of frosted glass. "All the better to see you by, Grandmama," her reflection says in a breathless voice, husky with pain.

"I'm not your grandmother, I tell her. But I know a story about one and a girl wearing a cloak with a red hood."

"Tell me."

"What's your name?" I ask. "Mine used to be Cheerless."

"I don't remember. My physician didn't care to ask. He insisted I remain nameless."

And then I'm beside her building a sandcastle on a white beach on a jewel of an island that smells of lemons. She's a pale girl with stringy black hair and dark circles under her eyes. Her breath comes in short gasps interspersed with a shuddering cough. Her voice falters through a white mouth surrounded by blisters.

"Don't go, Cheerless. Please stay," she begs.

The sun is too bright in her world. The sea is too blue, and the air, hot with the scent of lemons, makes my eyes water. Then I am inside her looking out and a pair of blue eyes hands me a cup of water and says goodbye. "I'm sorry," the eyes say. "I have to go. I am so very very sorry."

The girl places her hand against the glass. I can't see you, Cheerless," she rasps. "I'm blind."

The last thing I see is her tap tapping her way through a ward of hospital beds with a tree branch painted white.

I stand alone on a white beach, listening to the surf, looking for the girl who couldn't stay. The sun glints off the frosted glass and hurts my eyes. A salty breeze blows my hair into my eyes. The girl appears out of nowhere and gallops past me on a black mare, and I wake up crying with Eeyore licking my tears and Cheshire yowling to beat the devil.

Beatrice is an angry ghost. She says I'm an odd duck and to sit still while she ties my hair ribbon. "You've been metaphorically blind all your pathetic life," she hisses.

I asked Wonderland Alice what metaphorical meant, and she said it meant she had wished for a dog companion ever since she overheard Owl telling Pooh he could have a pet when he was more responsible. "I've always been responsible," she says.

That night I have another dream. How many children am I? This time I'm in a large nursery with rows of beds all the same with itchy green blankets tucked tight with hospital corners. The prone children lay as statues under shallow grass-colored mounds like buried corpses.

I overhear the ghosts whispering in the hall. "Leela believes she has a real donkey named Eeyore. Just play along, it makes her happy."

"Good on her," another says. "She's an imaginative little thing.

I'm glad a stuffed toy brings the poor child comfort. Her eyesight is much worse."

"What does invisible mean?" I ask at bedtime.

"It means special," a sad voice replied. "Now close your eyes. Verity will be here soon to deliver a new book, and we will change your bandages. I reach for her hand, but it isn't there. "Please stay. Beatrice, is that you?" I withdraw my hand immediately in case it was. Beatrice likes to pinch.

I feel a gentle hand placed over my lazy eyelids to help them close. I cuddle my Eeyore doll and my Pooh Corner book tight hoping I will be allowed to keep it all night. "Are my eyes closed?" There is no answer. "Who's there? What does tenacious mean?"

Eeyore licks the tears from my cheek. "Don't you worry, little one," he says. "Verity has come and gone but you're not alone. Invisible donkeys live a long time, and we are endlessly faithful."

"Cats too," Cheshire meows. "And we are endlessly fearless."

"Don't fidget, and don't stray," Beatrice hisses. "Sit still on the bench. The bus driver will be on a tight schedule. He won't tolerate shenanigans from slowpokes like you. Understand!"

"Yes, ma'am," I say out loud, saluting her like a soldier. Do I have to go to school?"

Beatrice is unhappy. "If you ask me the living have too many rules," she spouts.

"Good," Eeyore says, beside me. "You're all set. Now then, what does a bus look like?"

Piglet's ears twitch nervously. "Owl says its like a heffalump with wheels and squeaky brakes." He shivers and his voice squeaks higher. "Miss Beatrice, do I have to go to school too?"

Beatrice grabs Piglet from my arms, tosses him on my bed without looking, so, he bounces off and falls to the floor. She continues to brush my hair with rough brisk strokes. "Your toys must stay here, Leela. You know that, stupid girl!"

"Can Eeyore and Piglet sit on my bed while I'm gone?"

"They're safe enough," Beatrice answers. "No-one wants you or your toys."

Eeyore nuzzles his nose into my hand. "Not to worry," he whispers. "It's only Tirings having a bad dream."

I know this to be true because I've never taken toys with me into Tirings, I've never gone to school, and Eeyore was always waiting for me whenever I came home.

chapter 21

NOW I AM SIX... AGAIN

"If you can keep your head when all about you
Are losing theirs and blaming it on you.
If you can trust yourself when all men doubt you.
"Yours is the Earth and everything that's in it!"

selected lines from 'IF'
by RUDYARD KIPLING

Vera collected her papers and stashed them in her backpack – a subtle hint that today's class was over. "You look troubled," she said. "Is there anything you need me to re-explain?"

"No, but I *am* troubled."

"I'm all ears."

"I'm certain a new woodcutter startles me on purpose. Soundless as the ghost he is, he appears without warning, a silent intrusive presence from the ether 'where' he belongs.

He startles Eeyore which I didn't think possible, so I'd like to banish him somehow. He's a sour note in the forest, and now he's taken to wearing army camouflage which makes him all the more disturbing when he suddenly manifests at my elbow. I wish he would go away."

"The restless dead are more apt to be indiscreet. Shadows make no sound. And to be honest they probably want to go away but can't," Vera said. "I think he may be a soldier who lost his way. Troubled souls regularly wander in Lady Flora's Silvany looking for a way home. I expect he's come here for a reason. None of us are clear what that could be but, in the meantime, we aren't here to judge. I doubt he was a woodcutter in life. An axe is a symbol of separation and violence which would explain much if he'd died in battle."

"Why have I never met Lady Flora? Are we in Veratopia or Silvany or Otherwhere?"

Vera looked as lost as I felt. "Our forest... *this* forest, is always Silvany, ruled by the Green Lady and Pan. I met Lady Flora, the current Green Queen, much the same way as you found the forest surrounding Tirings those many years ago. She found me wandering like Greenwood. I was in a quandry, a 'witch' recently passed, and she adopted me as her apprentice. I'm here in the Queen's place while she's away. I call my part of Silvany, Veratopia. It's complicated as well as simple. For now, you are here with me for your own healing. So, to answer your question you exist in all three forests at the same time but essentially there is only *one* forest... Silvany. You will meet Lady Flora soon. No-one meets her until the time is right."

"I'm sorry for the woodcutter's troubles but I have a duty to protect Eeyore from needless suffering. He's as loyal as any dog and he's becoming the hero of his own story, as well as mine, no longer a sidekick thrown in for color to throw the adventurous exploits of Pooh and Piglet into the forefront. No longer a ploy for comic relief or a reason to mock. Eeyore may be tenacious, but he has the soul of an innocent child."

"As Leela's namesake, you are your friends' north star. Their new Christopher Robin. Their spirit of adventure has never stopped but they aren't dead creatures doomed to repeat their one and only story in a book. Leela, they're beginning to think. They're reincarnating. They're playing.

"Eeyore loves you. He is exactly where he wants to be, and he's tougher than you give him credit for."

Vera zipped her backpack closed with one deft movement. She lifted my chin and patted my cheek. "Now then, let's have no more worries about things that won't happen. We're expecting a visitor tomorrow, an old friend of yours who will no doubt cheer you up."

I groaned inwardly as an anxious memory resurfaced. Vera reminded me of my harried mother at her wits end tempting me with a new flavor of ice cream. "I may not know *who* I am, but I do know *where* I am."

"Me too," a voice said behind me. It was my friend, Peter Pan, a precocious eleven-year-old lost boy. "Tinkerbell made me come," he said, his arms crossed in his favorite stance of *you can't make me*. "She thinks creative writing will give me something to grow up for."

"A chance would be a fine thing," Cheshire said swooping in. "You're as stubborn as a donkey, Peter. I suggest you follow Eeyore's lead. He's accepted his new life. Not that life is the best word to describe a Veratopian."

I did what I often did when confused. I visited Lucy, sat silently beneath her shady branches, leaned against her, and listened. "It's time to visit Owl," she said. "He hides his wisdom under an eccentric sense of humor but he's more serious than you imagine. He's a watcher, is Owl. He keeps his deepest revelations under his wing.

He's partial to plain arrowroot biscuits and herbal tea, and he often comments wistfully that *a cuttlebone wouldn't go amiss if anyone is listening*. One tends to underestimate Owl at first meeting which is his intention. There's nothing frivolous about Owl. He glides soundlessly over Silvany, ever vigilant. We should all take a page from his book and listen closely to the trees."

chapter 22

BIRDS OF A FEATHER

"The Owl and the Pussycat went to sea
In a beautiful pea-green boat.
They took some honey, and plenty of money,
Wrapped up in a five-pound note.

EDWARD LEAR

"The thing you have to remember," Owl said, "is that what is left unsaid is what you most need to hear." He scrutinized the arrowroot biscuits I'd brought him and selected one, crunching it without delay in an explosion of crumbs.

"It boils down to witches and woodcutters," he said, polishing off two more biscuits.

Owl closed one eye and opened it slowly until I received the full disconcerting impact of his penetrating stare. "As an oracle it's not my duty to give orders," he began. "It's my privilege to dispense help whenever a true seeker knocks on my door. Is it any wonder we owls go about calling who who Who? But *hoo hoo* are we calling? That is the question. Hooey indeed!

Ask your question without guile, my dear, and I shall endeavor to answer it with the insight bequeathed to me by the Green Lady, Queen of Silvany. Please take your time. Thanks to you I've plenty of biscuits to keep me occupied and may I express my thanks for bringing me my favorite plain ones and a cuttlebone. Most appreciated."

I remained silent until I could barely make out Owl inside a flurry of crumbs.

He stared at me with his owly expression, sensing my frustration.

I took a breath and cleared my throat. "My question is this, how do I stop the woodcutter from pestering Eeyore?"

Owl closed both his eyes and ruffled his feathers, dislodging a fine covering of arrowroot dust. "Leela, your real question is what does Eeyore most need to hear? Which woodcutter and what...."

"There's more than one woodcutter?"

"My dear girl, there are thousands in Silvany and a dozen in Veratopia at any one time. You see them as one because they look identical. That is to say, anonymous, without their identities. Each one is a deceased troubled man or boy wandering in a private nightmare."

"Are there female woodcutters? I've had nightmares too."

"Yes and no. Women woodcutters are called witches," Owl said, cleaning one of his talons with his beak.

I startled. "Verity called herself a witch, so, am I ..."

"You needn't look so put out, Leela, witches in fairytales aren't real." He switched to his other talon. "True witches are wise-women, gatherers, healers, and nurturers who became lost after giving their power away. In your case, it was *given* away *for* you without permission. Perhaps then, you're really here to ask who *you* are? And... yes, you are indeed, a witch of sorts. All women and girls are. However, I *will* say this: Your bedevilled mother used the fear of trees not so much to torment you but to punish herself. As such, it is her challenge, *not* yours."

I poured more nettle tea. "And Eeyore?"

"Your fears may be correct. I presently detect three woodcutters at large in Veratopia."

I dipped a biscuit in my tea, nibbled another, and refreshed my cup while Owl searched his brain.

After a silent ponder, Owl gave a sharp screech. "Ah, yes, it's clear, now. I'm able to confirm Eeyore is selectively being stalked by a significant woodcutter," he said. "Eeyore's no different than a haunted human in that regard, having been created by a superhuman writer. Often, the victims being stalked are afraid to know the truth because it forces them to confront their counterpart pain."

"What is it? Perhaps I can help."

"A name is a meeting place. Hearing a name spoken in distress allows a nature spirit to intervene. The frequency of Eeyore's sightings tells me his woodcutter is ready to transmute Eeyore's innermost suffering into freedom." Owl shivered involuntarily releasing a few silver feathers. "Silence is a devastating obstacle for both of them," he said in a dither. "Immediate intervention is required. Please ask Puck to come and see me."

Owl's eyes blinked shut. "Thank you, Wol," I said. "I'll find my own way out," but his yellow eyes flashed opened. "Stay, Leela. I'm ready to answer *your* question now. If I'm not mistaken, you have one."

Much to my surprise I relaxed. "Why am I here?"

"Well, that's rather a long story. Not so much long as complicated. And one I'm not at liberty to divulge completely but a few insights are allowed. Suffice to say, despite Silkie's prickly opinions, you *are* supposed to be here. In fact, your presence is critical. As such, I believe reinforcements are called for. Perhaps you can rustle up some lunch in my kitchen. Verity keeps my larder stocked with delicacies. She quite spoils me."

The patter of rain on leaves automatically ignited a fire in Owl's grate – the same delightful spell Verity cast over our own cabin. I rummaged in Owl's kitchen to make a fresh pot of tea and found a French baguette, freshly churned butter, a ham, a large green tomato, blue cheese, and fig jam.

Owl and I sat in contented silence sipping builder's tea and ate a delicious lunch. When it was over I cleared away the plates, and Owl gave his wings a flap to fluff up his feathers and presumably, his thoughts.

"Ah, good company, good food, and a cozy fire. I haven't had such a pleasant visit in donkey's years. Now, if you will indulge me, I will begin with a brief history of Silvany.

Silvany is an enchanted forest containing, among other things, many sacred groves reserved for spirits in transition. Human suffering accumulates until the only place to go is a wild place that forces revelations and interventions as Eeyore will soon discover.

During the scattering time when trees first began to flourish, Druids planted round henges of living trees on raised embankments surrounded by ditches to honor their ancestors. Living trees progressed to cut trees planted in deep potholes, then stone circles. Standing stones precisely aligned to the stars time the solstices from seasons of springtime birth to midwinter death.

As humans evolved, they built forests of stone called cathedrals with carved stone pillars and arches reaching to canopies of stone skies. Each fairy ring and soaring cathedral marks the entrance to a primeval tunnel that connects the twin dimensions of spiritual and physical."

He closed his eyes to reflect.

"Each of us is a story, Leela," he began. "Most humans are faded fairy rings; only a rare few are cathedrals. Fairy tales can be 'Grimm' stories painted with maelstroms and night terrors, and enchanted forests filled with sunshine and chlorophyl, from Robin Hood's Sherwood Forest to Christopher Robin's Hundred-Acre-Wood.

This much you know for sure and certain: You are here in Veratopia to write a beginning, a middle, and an exciting conclusion of the story of your new life and play awhile. It's your turn to help Eeyore, now.

Trees are the keepers of stories. If obstacles are a stoic way through challenges, then forests are surely the way out. Verity had to make up for a mistake and return to Havonford to leave breadcrumbs for you to follow home. Zeno helped."

I breathed a sigh of relief. "So then, Veratopia *is* home."

"Silvany is your *true* home. Think of Veratopia as a neighborhood. Shinrin Yoku, the therapy of the sun is a tonic for rejuvenating the earth's lifeforces like the Sparkly that healed Eeyore's arthritis.

Being lost in the woods is a metaphor for depression. Disturbing fairy tales abound of possessed trees and poisoned apples where nightmarish thorns and brambles cover doomed castles, stifling the terrors of sleeping princesses, to ultimately vanquish the misrule of royalty drunk with power.

Master Carroll's Queen of Hearts is a humorous parody of the cruel monarch who tragically ruled Edward from childhood to death. Edward had been instilled with a blind allegiance to power. Is it any wonder he wandered for centuries trapped in his afterlife forest with Puck– a nature spirit charged with teaching a noble child how to cry.

I saw what was going on then and I see it now, a reflection of an old story ever the same. Edward is a woodcutter stalking himself. Verity is a witchy twitchy girl who gave her power away. You are a witch destined to lead others after your natural powers are restored. Your cycle must complete.

Mr. Carroll, Mr. Milne, and Edward are woodcutters haunted by toxic memories, forever young boys dreaming of power and vulnerable princesses bowing to it. In Edward's case, a spear to shake or a sword to brandish in order to serve the Tudor Virgin Queen and escape her witch's axe. For Mr. Carroll it was a pen to document his imagination built on wishes and dreams and a Bandersnatch to keep children on their toes. To this day, it presides over Silvany to keep out the hunters and keep in the gatherers, hence the trespassers sign that so transfixed Piglet who craved a family history. What was I to tell him but several white lies. Piglet is a perpetual child in need of comfort, and I am one of his guardians as well as one of yours."

chapter 23

THE DONKEY'S TALE
repeat no gossip

"And by the way, if you choose to be a fighter,
You may grow up to be a writer."

Before Vera's class, Eeyore and I had a heart-to-heart about the place he best loved to be – his secluded meadow beside his private pond. Cheshire hovered above us like a striped cloud doing aeronautical rolls singing *'nothing but blues skies from now on'* or words to that effect.

Absolem, who invariably accompanied him, sat nearby, enthroned on a giant mushroom looking extremely regal. "You called this meeting," he said dreamily in my direction. "What's up Tigerleela?"

Eeyore stared mesmerized into the concentric ripples of water from an invisible apple thrown by an invisible source. "That's life, that is," he said. "A single splash and there we are, expanding from every big or little bang that comes along. "Yes, please get to what you want to say quickly, Leela. I'm all ears."

If they didn't want small talk, it was fine with me. I dove in with my mind wide open. "Ever since I was six, I've wanted to be a writer of stories," I said. "I don't know why but it has been the one thing that has kept me going. It even tops the loss of my parent's affection which, I must admit, may only be a figment of my imagination. You know how I escalate things."

Eeyore looked up from his reflection in the water. "Your figments are truly legion."

"I don't know why I'm so obsessed with writing."

Eeyore's ears rotated excitedly. He was clearly upset but he regained his composure before looking me straight in the eye. "I know why. I've known it all your life. There. I've said it. I promised never to broach the subject but now you've asked I have no choice. It's time you knew the truth. Remember, I was there."

"Then please enlighten us," Absolem said.

Eeyore shook his mane to clear his head. "As understudy for the stubborn quality of Pooh's brain, which seems to fit sometimes, I'd like to state that stubborn is as stubborn does. I prefer to think of myself as determined."

Absolem's reply, *well, aren't you the dark horse*, from the thick grass gave me goosebumps.

Eeyore's ears resumed their forward direction, straining to listen, twitching erratically. "If you must know, the woodcutter has been stalking me. I find myself startling at every snapping twig. I sense him behind me but when I look, he's not there."

I leaned my forehead against Eeyore's. "Talk to him even if you can't see him. Ask him what he wants."

Eeyore shook his ears. "Cheshire says he's a lost soul. I think he wants to tell me something."

"Lucy said something yesterday that I didn't expect. She told me to visit Owl. She calls him a misunderstood oracle an underestimated shaman. She wasn't joking. Do you feel up to a 'reading'?"

"I wish, but I am a uniquely *determined*. I've never liked the term *stubborn*. I am a grey donkey with newly awakened emotions." He brayed proudly. "I earned every single one of them the hard way." Eeyore bowed his shaggy head and toppled over in his enthusiasm. "Please excuse my loss of dignity," he said, looking up from the mud. "I meant only to offer you a heartfelt compliment."

I stifled a laugh but grinned my thanks. "Please enlighten me."

A rousing chorus of "US, US, US" from the Cheshire Cat and Absolem shattered the stillness.

"I can tell it now." Eeyore deferred to me with an incline of his head. "Sorry, Leela, the rules of kismet forbade it until you showed a definitive sign of maturity."

"How flattering."

Eeyore trotted once around the pond to limber up. "Very well, if you insist. Are all of you seated comfortably?"

"We are," Cheshire said," high above us, drifting on a playful wind.

"As am I," a familiar voice declared in the cultured British accent of an aristocrat that stunned the circle into a respectful silence.

Edward de Vere materialized from a backdrop of trees, an actor entering stage left, and promptly sat cross legged on an elegantly embroidered black velvet cushion sporting the words 'tempus fugit' in gold thread that he'd brought with him, having anticipated a lack of chairs in a forest setting.

Puck, who had accompanied his courtly master, backed away with averted eyes as was politically correct.

For a moment, I was my old Wordless persona. Edward usually appeared at teatime when we were all feeling casual and peckish, but his youthful appearance caught me off guard. Edward had always visited me as the older man I met writing an early sonnet. It was like meeting a new person for the first time.

Eeyore was unimpressed and resumed his speech. "I must warn you the telling is a long story since my own sad tale is unavoidably written between the lines. So, please be patient."

"Get on with it, then," squeaked Piglet who had appeared by mistake thinking the gathering was a picnic. Seconds after he recovered from the silence, he wiggled his way to Puck. "Come with me," he said bravely. "Pooh has shown me the best hiding places for a smackering of something if you're feeling peckish.

Seventeenth century England is a goodly journey from here. You must be starving. Do you like honey? It's not far. Right this way." And with his pink ears fairly spinning, he scurried into the trees as fast as his piggy legs could carry him. "Goodbye all," he shouted barely above the whisper of a distant cricket. "*Busy backson.* Lovely to see you Mr. Edward, Sir," he called over his shoulder. "I mean your worthy earlness, Lord Shakespeare, your majesty. Sorry to have disturbed."

Puck's advise floated back to us. "Always hold onto your ears little Piglet. Ears can be dashed tricky and don't I know it."

Eeyore dolefully shook his head and cleared his throat which sounded like he'd swallowed a sheet of #6 coarse sandpaper. He glanced up at the Cheshire Cat as if he might be holding a cue card with the words he was searching for, but his branch was empty.

While he dithered, Edward sighed deeply. "First, thank you everyone. As you are aware. I came to this class, specifically called by my dear friend, Verity to mentor Leela, a novice writer, and tutor Peter, a lad often beset by pirates who could benefit from some fencing lessons."

Peter beamed and sat up straighter. This Edward was a more formidable presence. No longer an older brother but a wise uncle who would never tolerate nonsense.

Edward tried to put us at ease by removing his sword. "Verity thought of me because I too have experienced a catastrophic encounter with pirates. Secondly, and more important to me, I'd like to remind you that my name William Shakespeare is a pseudonym, necessitated during a time of strict Elizabethan control over literary matters. I could shake a spear at you if that helps you to remember. A pseudonym was never a blatant lie. I was proud to be a writer, but as the earl of a noble family I was honor bound to obey.

According to Queen Elizabeth, writing in secret was a necessary convention that preserved her majesty's dignity. By her command, it was decreed that nobles of her court remain distanced from the commonplace lowbrow theatricals of the day.

I chose the pseudonym Shakespeare after the goddess Athena, patron saint of writers. She carried a spear and waved it as a symbol of power. It was never meant to take my place. It can never be me. So, please, if you will, dispense with the title and call me Edward."

"It's customary to warm up your voice before you begin a story, Eeyore," Cheshire said, reappearing on a lower branch. "But that exercise can be tiresome, so without further delay, on behalf of Vera and her writing students we are honored to welcome you Edward, the most noble 17th Earl of Oxford, to our special needs group, again."

Eeyore gave an embarrassed cough. "Yes, quite so. Thank you, my catty friend. I could never have thought of that without you." He addressed Edward and bowed his head so low to the ground he lost his balance, toppled over in a soft grey heap, and hurriedly righted himself.

"Edward, since you are comfortable in our humble surroundings I shall begin. *Ahem*... Once upon a time, say fifty-five years ago."

"Stop stop, I've heard this one before," Absolem interrupted in a peevish voice. "Owl almost saw it coming. But I will still *pretend* to be surprised if it's boldly told." He took a long draw of medicinal smoke from his pipe and sent it billowing around the circle in an atmospheric net of intoxicating fog, curled into a lime green blob, and closed his eyes. He waved his pipe at the gathering. "You may continue. Don't mind me."

Eeyore brayed loud as a wolf howling at a full moon. "Continue? I have not begun."

"Start at the beginning. Go right through to the end, then stop," Absolem suggested.

"The thing of it is..." Eeyore paused to wheeze through a deep breath of second-hand smoke... "The thing is, I very nearly didn't happen. I can't fully describe how inadequate that made me feel.

But the truth of it is if someone hadn't chosen me as a Christmas present for Christopher Robin... well, there it is. No more Eeyore."

Edward examined his immaculate manicure, incompatible with ink-stained fingers. "But surely you could celebrate your good fortune, being as you were hand picked, put in a lovely box lined with tissue and wrapped in paper sprinkled with robins and sprigs of holly. Surely magic was present, was it not? Were you not presented as such, before a prince?"

Eeyore shook the water from his mane. "You make it sound almost poetic, your earlship. But I *was* there, and it wasn't. Christopher Robin was in some ways, a chosen prince. But that's the thing about history as you no doubt will attest, Edward."

Eeyore stared at the ground. "Are you sure you don't mind me calling you by your first name?

Edward clapped his hands in delight. "By all means, if I may call you Bottom. I've immortalized your form in 'A Midsummer Night's Dream' and I am honored to share this stage with you. I too, am all ears to hear a mad tale told by a donkey who is a prince among horses." He doffed his cap adorned with a pearl brooch and a single curvaceous swan feather.

"Nothing or no-one less than truth itself would have summoned me here. Verity is an old friend of mine from... well let's just say the past. I am as indebted to her as no doubt she will one day enlighten you when she returns."

Eeyore gazed enraptured, and for a while I thought his voice may have left the forest with Piglet, but he shook himself and proceeded as if there was nothing amazing about telling William Shakespeare a story about toys who sprang to life from the mind of a troubled writer.

"On you go, Eeyore," Cheshire prompted. "You have the forest floor or are you speechless, which in my memory, would be a first."

Eeyore cast his eye to me for help. "*Um*... where was I?"

That's when Pooh pushed in and surprised us all. "Eeyore, you were saying that Edward sounded almost poetic and that you were there, and it wasn't."

I covered my mouth lest I laugh and spoil Pooh's breakthrough moment. I nodded to Eeyore and mouthed the words 'Go on'.

"Yes, yes of course. Thank you, Pooh," Eeyore began. "Well, indeed, there was nothing poetic about my, pardon the term, birth. And by birth, I mean being purchased in the crush of last-minute Christmas shopping in a famous London toy store. A lady's maid of one of Christopher Robin's disagreeable great aunts chose me. The old lady couldn't have cared a fig, shopping for children being a disagreeable imposition.

But I must say, Mr. Milne was no slouch when it came to celebrating his son's birth name. He had an affinity for Robin Hood, and he honored Sherwood Forest as much as Ashdown Forest as inspiration for his famous 100-acre wood.

Robin of Loxley, a.k.a. Alan of East Essex, searched out whimsical robins for obvious reasons. Thankfully, he wasn't big on donkeys else Christopher may have been named Christopher the scapegoat."

Edward grinned and crossed his arms, loving the performance.

"You see, Christopher Robin once explained that his father used sound effects when he read bedtime stories. Donkeys bray. The closest thing to that is a ghastly sound between a screech and a parrot choking on dry toast."

Cheshire covered his eyes with his splendiferous tail. "Eeyore, dear boy, I do hope you're not wishing with your head in the stars, again."

"Sorry to disappoint but I can't help thinking that had my designer been more generous, I might have been a jolly fellow but my legs and neck were a tad weak from lack of sufficient stuffing and so I appeared droopy and forlorn. Mr. Milne was hard put *not* to give me a personality to match."

I wasn't about to let Eeyore become droll. "But that's how your great heart came into being," I said.

Eeyore sent me a nod of gratitude. "Kind of you to say so, Leela, but the truth of it is, unlike Pooh and Piglet and the others, I'd been written without a soul. I was an afterthought, tossed off as a cliché – a foil, if you will, to be pitied. I have been celebrated, immortalized as the animal among the Group Soul of Christopher Robin's special toys to symbolize gloom in all its forms of whinging and morosity. The butt of bad jokes. *Ahem...*" he bowed to Edward. "The *'bottom'* of a list as it were."

Edward threw back his head and laughed. "Well done, noble steed."

"Oh dear, that's torn it. Now Eeyore's going to ham it up," Cheshire said.

"My rope tail was singled out for disaster after being criticized for not being attached securely," Eeyore said "and so, it fell off, never to be seen for weeks, lost in the somewhere enroute from Cotchwood's farmhouse to the 100-acre wood.

Christopher Robin was so upset his father had to settle him down by memorializing the event into a chapter with a happy ending. Naturally, Pooh was declared the dimwitted hero who found my tail after it had been turned into a bell pull for Owl's front door."

The word 'hero' eclipsed any possible negative reference of having fluff for brains, and Pooh took a bow.

Eeyore let Pooh have his moment before continuing. "Mr. Milne deliberately wrote me accident prone and a bit of a headcase to enrich the escapades of Pooh and his merry band of followers. I was never a follower. I stayed in a damp boggy field waiting to be the lord of misrule for comic relief. That did nothing for my image or self worth, I can tell you." He nodded to Edward. "Well, you'd know all about that from your own experience, your wordsmith.

Eeyore episodes had to be invented. I was invariably left out in the rain as often as the adventures. After the grand *expotitions* it was all pots of honey and tea and chocolate biscuits until nanny asked, moments before bedtime, where is Eeyore?" 'Oh Christopher,' she'd say, 'you haven't left him in the woods again, have you?' But he had and there I'd been, alone and damp the entire time.

Sometimes it rained for days when I was left outside. I was a new toy, but I suffered enough weather to condense my stuffing into small clumps the consistency of rubbery pebbles. From that time on I was, pardon the expression, spineless.

I might have been a noble horse had the toy shop sold such an animal. As it happened, I was braced upright between several species of colorful teddy bears and, of all things, a large yellow duck.

Ironically, I stood out in a grey sort of way and was trundled off to join the main event, Edward Bear, better known as Winnie the Pooh – a special bear dragged from pillar to post, dangled by a paw, bumping up and down the stairs. How amusing. No wonder I settled into the gloomy disposition that made me a famous laughingstock."

"Nevertheless, fate decreed there was an extraordinary upside to your existence," Edward mused. "Indeed, according to Verity, I too, may be so honored."

Absolem's breathless voice wafted from the shade. "One that if I'm not mistaken was an intervention of a spiritual nature. Fate works in mysterious ways." He winked. "Doesn't it Eeyore."

"Absolem-utely right," I said. "Righter than right." For someone who had recently declared they were an idea the conversation was lost on me. "Anything good is good, if that's not too absurd a remark," I said. "I concur with you Caterpillar, please continue."

Eeyore raised his head as high as his stuffing would allow. "It's like this," he said. "*Exactly* like this. Mr. Milne wrote some notes for my character. He used the word cheerless as, what he called, my defining characteristic. In fact, he wrote it in bold capital letters with a red pencil and underlined it twice.

It acted like a beacon that flashed whenever Leela's mother called out *'Cheerless, where the bloody hell are you?'* The name Cheerless drew me to you and you to me. Leela, we were allies battling a dreary emotional storm our entire lives. It was fate. We were twins.

The name Cheerless was an unkind insult. So powerful, it transfixed us. Our happy ending was that I was chosen for your totem animal, and I was happy to comply. The one thing that made me happy was you."

He sniffed back the emotional tears that threatened to spill, and coughed until he could continue. I wiped a tear from my eye and smiled bravely.

"That said, Mr. Milne eventually wrote me into a few upbeat gratuitous chapters to teach Christopher Robin compassion for the underdog." Eeyore gave a lame *woof.* "An underdog was born," he said. "And I am here to tell the truth of it. I call it pinning the tail on a donkey. I watched Leela become enamored of Mr. Milne's career."

"So, I have A.A. Milne to thank after all," I said, much recovered. "In hindsight his oversight was a magnificent opportunity for you and me to turn our lives around."

Pooh scratched his head. "I'll explain later," Vera whispered in his ear.

I, on the other hand, was emboldened. "Eeyore, Milne's stories about you inspired me to be a writer. Much later, when I read how Sir Arthur wrote Sherlock Holmes's partner Watson into an amateur reporter it sealed the deal. I may have been out of Sherlock's league, but I thought if I tried hard enough, I could pull off writing a simple newspaper article like Dr. Watson. But alas, I could not. I was reading from the peanut gallery where the only thing I could do was watch Sherlock think. I became the watcher of his thought processes and vowed to master them. I read endless books about the craft of writing intending to dazzle my readers with words."

I turned to marvel at our guest. "And hats off to you, Edward Wordsmith for being the, pardon the term, God, of my expanding idolatry. And oh, the feeling of inner power from your glorious words that delighted me the same way as Mr. Lear's invented language.

And now you're here, not only as a guest for tea, but as a fellow. What could we possibly do to show you how honored we are."

"Accept him as he comes," Caterpillar said so all could hear. "Treat Edward as a humble human being. In his heart of hearts, that's what he wants. It's what he never had."

"Fair enough. Nothing is truer than the truth," Edward mused to himself.

"Mr. Edward de Vere (not to be confused with Edward Bear) is here to save his legacy canon because, pardon the pun, he forgot to reVere himself," Absolem said, giggling.

"But that's what self-sacrifice does," Eeyore said. "That's what happened to Verity. Ask her sometime. It's better not to ask Silkie although she understands more than she lets on. Leela, I believe the reason we're all assembled here is to help Verity. This forest is all about setting oneself free."

"Absolem-utely," I repeated. "And reaching one's new goals."

Eeyore dithered about in a circle. "Now, where's that Peter chappie got to? He's a key member of our special needs group."

Tinkerbell fluttered by, circled us three times, hovered over Eeyore's head, and lightly touched down between his ears. She crossed her arms with a stern expression – a miniature version of Peter Pan. "Peter's not overly fond of doing what he's told," she said, "but he will be along later if Vera insists. And she will."

Eeyore shook her off and smiled weakly. "I prefer to envisage this writing business as a long bumpy road with Christmas at the end," he said.

"Imagine that my little imaginative donkey. ITBFTW," Absolem chimed in.

"What, pray tell does that mean?"

"Imagining The Best From The Worst," Cheshire translated. "The best of times and the worst of times? Very Dickensian – the best and the worst in a single pitch."

"I've mastered a lot of new dog tricks in the ninety-seven years since I was *ahem*... published," Eeyore mused. "I'm not just a pretty face, you know."

I gave him a skwudge. "Ninety-seven years is no time at all between friends. Birds of a feather stick together."

"My dear Leela. Things have a perverse way of happening in perfect timing. Happy endings from ghastly plot twists, grow. It's one of the golden rules of fiction. Anxiety, (your old specialty) and mine (sadness) happen to be the primary components of a cracking story."

"So", Cheshire said. "To sum up. Mr. Edward must perse<u>vere</u>; Peter must find something to grow up for, and you, dearest girl, must awaken the truth of ultimate worthiness in the world of shadows. And Owl has a few vital secrets in his beak. Now then, Leela, did you bring an apple for the teacher?"

"I most certainly did not." I cited the *coals to Newcastle* rule as my reason. "I brought her wine gums."

Cheshire yawned and casually licked his front paws. "I thought you would connect Verity's bag lady disguise with the apple-seller who poisoned Snow White."

"Ah! Sometimes I forget."

Cheshire flashed his polished claws. "No matter *'all's well that end's well'*, right Edward? Verity is brilliant at borrowing personas from Children's stories to make a point. She created this enchanted place. But I wouldn't mention the art of borrowing personas. Life might be a vast lending library, but Verity has a particular aversion to plagiarism as you have no doubt heard. Put your jealousy aside and ignore Silkie."

Cheshire dissolved slowly, tail first. "Time for a cat nap or is it catnip? Either one will suffice."

"Silkie Ryder 'the brilliant child wonder, I *don't* think', doesn't always see the forest for the trees, so I advise keeping an open mind," Eeyore said.

I blew Eeyore a kiss. "This is why I want you as my critique partner."

"I thought you'd never ask," Eeyore said. "It's not only my pleasure; it's my duty. As such, I advise you to never compare yourself to Silkie again. To honor you, I shall bow to your wisdom without falling down. I've been practicing."

"Oddly enough, Domesday isn't about doom or gloom," Edward announced to Absolem.

"You're preaching to the choir," Absolem replied, bowing his head. "But please keep on doing it. Cheshire needs to be on board, too. He can be so catatonic about details. He can't always see in the dark, if you get my meaning."

Cheshire burst back into focus, his stripes pulsating with outrage. "As you well know, Leela, I'm above being a copycat. Please tell Edward that I see plenty and keep quiet for a reason."

Out of the mouths of pampered cats and drugged caterpillars, I reminded myself.

"Despite the fact you two always double-dazzle me," I said. "Metaphorically speaking, I'm pinning the resolution to Edward's tale on Eeyore." I turned to face him, but Eeyore was gone. "Speaking of Eeyore, when did he leave?"

"I believe it was when Absolem mentioned Owl having secrets," Cheshire mused to himself.

"I wonder," Absolem said. "Who chose Eeyore as your companion, Leela? Eeyore never said, but it couldn't have been you. You were ironically, a 'closed book' as he recalled. Funny, I was about to ask him, but he left in somewhat of a hurry."

chapter 24

THE TRUTH 'WILL' OUT

Lizzie Tudor took an axe
And killed her friends
With just one whack

The hesitant 'soul of the age', William Shakespeare, sat to my right in class. Peter Pan sat on my left. Their familiars, Puck and Tinkerbell hovered nearby. Eeyore kept both of them honest until he started to go magic on me. Absolem and Cheshire ruled from above and below. Every now and then Pooh dropped by for elevenses and where Pooh went, Piglet followed. It was a writing class like no other... and I'm delighted to say it was mine.

Our curriculum based on the essential chronological stages of outlining fiction became hopelessly random in short order. "No worries," Eeyore brayed when classes got out of control. "You'll get a smidgen of everything you need. We don't live according to the real world so why would we learn that way."

Eeyore sat me down for a chat before Vera rang the bluebell. "Listen closely," he said. "I've had a pondering."

I was all ears. Eeyore was famous for his ponderings.

"Between you and me and a plethora of fence posts there's a good reason why mapmakers painted dragons at the corners of maps," he said. My expression was quizzical. But that never daunted my champion.

"You know," he went on, "those blurry edges at the drop-off where ships disappear over the horizon to the open sea. It's where nature spirits play games with clouds and weather that perfectly describes the emotional spaces, where terrifying memories fade into fiction. You've been there and so, have I."

Edward nodded pushing back from the table. "No need to remind *me*," he said. "Please, I must take my leave. I need to be alone for a moment."

The class was all a dither not trying to bow or curtsey or otherwise cause a fuss as Edward exited stage left without another word, surprisingly without Puck.

"Danger zones strike fear into the hearts of dreamers and writers on all sorts of maps," Eeyore said. "In Edward's time it was a map of London and the maps of several prominent European cities in Italy and France."

I felt reprieved of a heavy burden. "I have to say, any existing map of Stratford Upon-Avon would have been nothing short of useless – it was less than a 'hamlet'(pardon the expression) of ramshackle houses and lacklustre streets," I said.

Eeyore concurred and changed the subject. "Verity's death is shrouded in dark dealings," he said. "Mind you, I don't fault her. A violent death is not something one wants to *relive*."

"Why would you assume Verity's death was violent?"

Eeyore's ears twitched madly and after a long ponder he begged me sit quietly and listen.

"Verity's been hinting she wants her past revealed. So, as her apprentice I believe it's time you had a heart-to-heart with her," he said, "but the situation is extremely difficult."

"How so?"

"Verity admitted to me she's completely forgotten everything about her death. All attempts to retrieve her memory have failed. She's blocking out a terrible truth, Leela. She's terrified."

"How can we help her?"

"I'm certain the manner of Verity's death holds the key to her future happiness and until that truth is out in the open, leaving Veratopia is not only impossible for her; it effectively delays *your* progress. Moving forward as a writer is your key to attaining the life you missed – the whole reason you were awarded a second chance to live life over."

"How can you know such a thing? As far as I'm concerned writing class is purely a perk fulfilling a long-lost dream."

"Trust me, I know different. Sadly, I'm forbidden to explain."

The penny dropped. "So, I was *right*. Something big *has* been bothering you."

"Yes, but bother is too small a word. I may have already said too much. I promised to keep you safe; your new life is worth our combined weight in gold."

My shock turned to fears for Eeyore's peace of mind. Eeyore tried valiantly to assuage them. "I am compelled to follow Lady Flora's wishes. I haven't liked keeping you in the dark, Leela. That's not how it is between us, but confidences must be honored until the owner decides, and so I have waited. Some relevant details were best left unsaid until now."

Eeyore's words ricocheted from tree-to-tree until the forest rustled with excitement. The tension I'd felt visibly relaxed. The trees had kept Verity's secret too long.

"While Verity's away, the cat will play," Cheshire joked. And that was all it took. Verity's truth loomed as a priority that required spilling out. Even so, Eeyore's secret continued to grow like a mushroom in the dark. What wasn't he allowed to tell me? And by whose orders? Who chose him to guard me?

Eeyore shook his ears like an urgent bell. "Leela, I hope you will listen while I explain what I can."

"It's time for you to be all ears," Cheshire volunteered. "I am here to clear the way. Verity met Lady Flora, in the aftermath of her setting fire to Greenwood's castle and was led, somewhat in disgrace to 'Poet's Corner' – a secluded spot in a cathedral of the oldest trees. She had inadvertently destroyed a grove of sacred trees."

"Please tell me more about the Green Goddess."

"We can't," Eeyore said, staring at the ground. "At least, not yet. One day you will understand. I'm so sorry I can't explain further without violating a significant secret."

Cheshire was more forthcoming in as much as his revelations were couched slyly in metaphor. "Verity's *friendship* with Edward began in 1925 when Puck took matters into his own hands," he began, settling into the pose and manner of a storyteller with his tail curled over his paws. "Puck led Edward to Silvany in a drastic intervention after Edward had been brooding over the betrayals of his past life for 320 years. As a native spirit, Puck had a free pass to Silvany and an audience with Lady Flora. And as luck would have it, Lady Flora was experiencing her own dilemma concerning what to do with the ghost of Verity.

She had to punish Verity for her transgression against Silvany; Edward had to be snapped out of wallowing overlong in the forest surrounding the castle of his childhood – the very place he'd chosen to spend his afterlife."

Absolem joined in. "Edward de Vere was ever a force to be reckoned with – a wild child, compelled to be unruly to defy and survive the violent competitive nature of the nobility in which he was born," he revealed, puffing out great mind-altering clouds of hookah smoke.

Eeyore, still clearly at odds with a secret he'd kept from me that no longer required wheedling out. All was well. Surely perfect timing would be revealed at the right moment. I had faith that it would be so,

The Green Lady had been hard put to punish Verity for a

mistake that relieved Silvany of a burdensome cloud of negative energy.

Puck and Lady Flora formulated a plan that would resolve two disturbed souls in pain. Verity found a solution. In exchange for initiation to magic she would govern Silvany under the forest's new name, Veratopia, for a hundred years from her death in 1924.

"And so it was," Cheshire intoned theatrically, "Edward de Vere, an earl, and Verity Ryder, a commoner, bonded as kindred spirits of sound mind with a firm resolve to move on."

Creating Tirings proved to be a fortuitous opportunity to heal karmic wounds that culminated in a pledge to reincarnate together at the right time.

Sadly, breaking a divine oath with a goddess carried a severe penalty so, due to Verity's punishment, reincarnation meant a long wait while she atoned for her blunder. But happily, compensation was at hand.

Verity's inbred gift for supernatural horticulture and her green thumbs blossomed seamlessly into the mystical ability to manipulate time and space that eventually served her extraordinarily well.

Eeyore gave a short announcement. "Verity has asked me to express her fervent wish that soon her predicament will be over and invites everyone to please use her folly to appreciate your worthiness to shine in the sunlight that ever follows one's darkest nights." At that, he bowed and departed for his field.

Cheshire, Absolem, and I continued a tight-lipped discussion about the truth and lies of Queen Elizabeth's reign. Absolem refused to make eye contact with me until I put his absentmindedness down to his hookah's smokey haze smarting his eyes.

We agreed that after being coddled by conspiracy theories and bogus death threats, Elizabeth 1st would have believed anything her chief administrator, Lord Burghley, told her except the truth that a common, illiterate, disreputable money lender who hoarded grain, money, and lies manipulated the history plays she adored, including the ones she feared.

By Edward's descriptions, Elizabeth 1st resembled Snow White's stepmother – a queen obsessed with vanity, forever needing to be reassured by her magic mirror's reply *yes, your majesty, you are the most beautiful of all*. Which perhaps accounts for Elizabeth's outrageous collars that grew ever larger and more ridiculous by the day until they required an ingenious contraption of supportive wires and straps, and a courtier at each elbow to keep the queen upright when she needed to appear steady in control, and elegant. She came off even more stiff and haughty, blissfully shielded from uneasy truths, kept ignorantly unaware of being seen as a buffoon.

I stared gobsmacked as the wind sighed contentedly through the trees taming their excited leaves. Verity is deeper than I thought. She has a romantic attachment to Edward, the author of the Shakespeare canon, no less – a much darker horse to watch out for.

"Go easy on Edward when he returns," Absolem advised. "He's as touchy about the grim circumstances surrounding his last years on earth as ever. The Essex Rebellion in 1601 was swift and bloody. Ask him when he gets back but expect him to clam up. It was an especially rough time for him. But I sense the time draws near for resolution, hence a partial exposure of the truth is necessary to all parties involved."

I protested my innocence. "But I'm *not* involved."

Cheshire sent me an exasperated upside-down smile. "Of course, you are. You are so incredibly involved. We'll say no more for now, but the time is fast approaching for your own truth to will out. And by that, I mean the hidden truths that even *you* don't know."

"Should I be worried?"

"No-one should be worried about the truth coming to light," he said. "But go ahead if you must."

In the end, I had no choice but to worry in silence and trust Eeyore knew best. If one can't count on their best friend, then nothing makes sense.

Inevitably, Edward and Verity discovered the same enchanted peace I found when I was six.

chapter 25

THE FOURTH MONKEY
Whoop No Evil

"Enough of this miserable, whining life.
Stop monkeying around!"

MARCUS AURELIUS

When Wonderland Alice keenly observed, yet again, that Parker was becoming curiouser and curiouser every day, Lucy was processing photosynthesis in her sleep, dreaming of sunlight and rain.

An exhilarating rush of super-charged chlorophyl surged up her backbone and into her limbs. Not fully awake, Lucy, giddy from the bracing sensation, concentrated on the spinetingling miracle, animating her trunk.

It was precisely at this moment that Nosey Parker chose to swing by looking for his friend Hattie who always wore a yellow bonnet. He'd observed the old woodcutter, creeping stealthily amongst the trees searching for Verity, and wisely kept out of his way. In that regard he was a fourth monkey wiser than was previously believed.

The woodcutter was no friend to man or beast. The morning mist cleared, and Parker was delighted to climb as high as he could. The vista of an endless forest spread before him. A yellow bonnet could be seen for miles at this height, but all was green with a few bluebells scattered below.

"Excuse me, Lucy," he chattered to Lucy's leaves. "I'm looking for a yellow bonnet. "Have you seen one lately?"

Cheshire materialized in a blur of golden fur draped over a branch. "I saw a shiny yellow rain slicker passing through the forest not five minutes ago," he said still dreaming. "It was attached to a yellow hood. Or was it the other way around? Perhaps the hood was attached to the yellow slicker. Perhaps it hasn't happened yet." He yawned and resettled his tail over his nose.

"Was my friend Hattie under it?" Parker asked, but before Cheshire could answer, Parker was distracted by a snake that flashed in the tall grass by the pond. *Oh, what's that*, he chattered to himself moving to take a closer look.

The leaves slowly absorbed Cheshire's stripes. "Long thin tube-like things are rarely snakes in this neck of the woods," Cheshire said within a peaceful snore. "However, that particular tube belongs to Absolem's hookah pipe. Leave it alone. It's not a snake and it's not a toy, and Absolem won't thank you breaking it."

Surely enough, a thin wisp of foul-smelling purple smoke drifted lazily from the ferns, shortly followed by Absolem's slow dreamy voice wafting from the tall ferns at the water's edge. "Lucy can't answer you little monkey," he said. "She's asleep. I suggest you check her leaves for Cheshire, he's usually hanging around up there seeing how he treats Lucy like his personal hammock. Anyway, he's bound to see more than I because he gads about a great deal. I keep telling him his gadding will get him in trouble one day, but does he listen?"

An answering smoke ring with the word 'no' inside it evaporated in Parker's face.

"As for me," Absolem went on. "I'm stationary and by that I don't mean writing paper. I leave that to the writers in Vera's class. Mushroom life suits me. I'm delighted that my hookah keeps me in a state of permanent twilight where yellow bonnets, I'm happy to say, rarely venture."

Cheshire's eyes snapped open, fully conscious. "I do *not* gad, Absolem! I Never have nor ever will, and as it happens I highly respect Lucy's branches. They're a dashed comfortable place to hang out as you correctly noted. Sorry, Parks I couldn't see a face inside the hood for the downpour. Except I could when I looked a second time and it was Silkie's face set in a grim determined sort of 'I have to go even if I want to stay', look. She was not a happy camper."

Absolem's smoke rings spiraled and paused mid-air, bumping into each other. "Oh, hello, I didn't see you up there, my little sourpuss."

"As it happens, that's the whole point of invisibility," Cheshire replied testily. "Nosey Parker, I might have known it was you causing such a racket!"

Cheshire yawned and rolled over to find a comfier spot. "Monkeys are always frantic. It's a crying shame they like trees so much," he hissed.

Parker investigated the tube, parting the fronds to expose Absolem seated in full regal splendor with a distant look in his glassy eyes. "I saw Verity earlier," he spluttered at the intrusion. "She was filling the bird feeder with nuts. If you hurry, there may be some left unless a squirrel has scoffed the lot. By the by, Parks, Verity weighted the nuts down with a banana. You might like to try that first. I know every bird in the forest, and I assure you none of them will stoop to eating a banana. It's impossible to make a nest with a banana. Even the bears, well barring Pooh of course, won't give bananas a second look. One sniff and they're off in search of porridge."

Parker celebrated his good fortune, Hattie forgotten, leaping madly from branch to branch shrieking the word banana as he went. The word banana echoed in a loud stream that woke Lucy. "Goodness is that the time! Cheshire you might have woken me."

"Didn't have to," Cheshire smirked. "Parker here, beat me to it."

Lucy chuckled. "Goodness, Parks, there's no need to shriek, so. Keep you fur on. You'll straighten your tail if you keep doing that."

Parker didn't hear her, having already found the birdfeeder.

Lucy stretched her branches and shook her leaves, nearly unseating Cheshire who had slipped back into a cat nap during the lull in the conversation. "It's a big day," Lucy said. "Silkie's leaving for school. I can see her waiting at the Poets Corner bus stop. Fetch and Chase have gone with her."

Parker returned with the banana and popped it in his mouth, peel and all. "Chase ignores me," he said his cheeks bulging, "but Fetch always chases me."

"Those two have it backwards," Absolem mused. "I wonder why."

"It's about time that girl left," Cheshire said drifting off in a desperately 'clinging to a tiny twig' sort of way. "Parks, you really shouldn't jabber with your mouth full. It's not very attractive."

Parker nattered something rude to Cheshire in monkey-speak, promptly grabbed his tail, and smoothed its tip into a perfect spiral for spite and stuck out his tongue.

Absolem closed his eyes and swayed from side-to-side. "Zeno's on his way," he announced, blowing a lazy cloud of pink smoke rings. "It's Leela's forest now!"

Chesire had the last word as he surrendered to sleep. "Bananas are yellow," he said and promptly disappeared.

THE TEACUP CHRONICLES

TURNING OVER A NEW LEAF

chapter 26

UNDER THE WEATHER

"So, rested he by the Tumtum tree
And stood awhile in thought.
And, as in uffish thought he stood,
The Jabberwock, with eyes of flame,
Came whiffling through the tulgey wood,
And burbled as it came!"

LEWIS CARROLL

— 'Jabberwocky'

It was raining heavily when Silkie left the cabin with Fetch and Chase. The bright yellow presence of her Wellingtons and matching rain slicker transformed her into a bright flag trekking through the dripping forest. I observed her from the hide. To be more precise, I observed her in the natural scrying bowl of the puddle that seeped through a hole in the hide's roof.

To my right, Winnie the Pooh's latest *'expotition'* to the North Pole marched boldly through the underbrush. Their adventures took place on a semi-regular basis every second Wednesday. Thursdays in a pinch.

The forest chattered to itself as three focused travelers moved at a slick pace. The trees tugged at Silkie's sleeves as she headed for the bus stop. She was their child too. Their branches reached to grab her scarf. "Don't go," they rustled. "Stay, traveler's child. Beyond the forest lies a world of shadows. We can't protect you there. Shadowland's trees aren't like us."

Silkie glared daggers at them and shrugged them off.

The path leading from Verity's cabin was a squelchy sponge of wet leaves pressed into a slick carpet through a green tunnel alive with a million wriggling insects.

Silkie wielded her umbrella rolled into a walking stick and waved it ahead of her like a machete pretending to cut her way through dense jungle. Being overly aggressive, this was entirely normal.

Verity had prepped Silkie on bus lore. *'Buses arrive early and are gone in a trice or never show up at all. It's best to be waiting fifteen minutes ahead of schedule and remain calm when they're late – a regular occurrence due to adverse weather conditions, mechanical breakdowns, or accidents'*, Verity cautioned. *'Flow with the system and expect disappointments with grace.'*

I had no desire to retrace my steps that Silkie now took towards the sound of a downpour as she left the warm hugs of her old babysitter trees.

A thunderstorm was in progress. Lightning illuminated the bus shelter on the other side of the grey snake called the West Coast Road. Thunder crackled. Silkie's umbrella startled and dutifully opened on its own steam. The aperture in the forest wall regularly opened and closed like a hungry mouth. Matriarch pine trees stood sentinel on either side of it swaying goodbye.

Silkie stood grim-faced, sandwiched between her companions. She looked left then right then left again, and quick-marched across the road. Chase bounded across. Fetch was more of a slinker. The weight of the shadow world took its toll. Silkie looked too old to play splashing games. I suspected she hadn't noticed her changes because she still made a conscious effort to splash through every puddle the way Christopher Robin had taught her. I picked up Silkie's thoughts more easily than I expected. So, there she was, on the other side of reality where inhabitants cast shadows, standing in a bluster of serious weather. She felt different. She had changed, no longer the confident bossy britches. She was an old woman leaning on an umbrella for stability.

I felt her aches and pains where there had been none. She had aged in accordance with earth's shadowy timeline. It was a rude awakening for starting the first day of school.

It was clear to me more than ever why the world outside our sanctuary was called the world of shadows. Not long ago I'd been a shadow too. And here was Silkie, trembling, confidence gone. In the space of an hour, she'd become a vulnerable shadow of the rude excited girl I had seen earlier that morning. *She would fit in or be eaten by a warrior tree*, I thought.

Fetch and Chase have always been real. In shadow-world terminology, they were Silkie's invisible childhood friends. Christopher Robin may have donated them, but it was Verity who gave them power. Or rather they borrowed their power from *her*.

It is perfectly normal. They are meant to guard Silkie on whatever this *expotition* turns out to be. Not likely a home away from home. She's in for a severe dressing down.

Although Verity taught her to accept whatever shows up, her advice went in one ear and out the other with no thought of staying. Fetch and Chase will be her teachers as much as the professor she's about to meet.

Zeno is his name. Verity has known him forever and then some, so she says, and I believe her.

Zeno is to be Silkie's tutor while Verity becomes a shadow of her former self – a wiry young go-getter who prefers to be called Vera, busy putting finishing touches on a classroom for me.

"The castle ghosts are getting out of hand," Verity explained as she donned her bag lady hat. "It's up to me to put a few things to rights. I won't be gone long but I don't want your studies to lapse. Your education is coming along great strides. I'm proud of you. I planned this. Well... actually *you* planned this.

Both you and Silkie were born with the same plan and it's wise to enjoy it now that it's deconstructing and reconstructing itself. Consider it a second birthday cake without candles."

I couldn't leave well enough alone and begged Verity for details. "Can I see those plans? Is there a map? I love lists. Is there a list? Are there directions?" I faltered remembering how tiresome questions derail enthusiasm.

I replayed our last meeting. Silkie hadn't cared for details, all she wanted was an answer to a question she had no intention of asking. "Fetch and Chase are coming with me," she'd stated in no uncertain terms. "Of course, they will," Verity assured her. "They're your heart and soul. You wouldn't get far without those. The cabin is Veratopia's rock. It will be here, waiting." She crooked a finger at me. I reluctantly stepped forward. "Leela and Christopher Robin will see to that, won't you Leela."

My lying words tumbled out, directed towards my shoes. "Of course."

Verity also stared at my shoes. "That's my girl," she said, even though she knew I'd lied.

Silkie's eyes narrowed. Her brazen smile folded into a hard straight line.

Verity shook her head, smiling bravely. "The forest takes care of Christopher Robin. And Christopher Robin takes care of you two. Your plans are not printed on paper, they are imprinted inside you."

"I prefer things printed on paper. They smell magical," I said.

"Books can only be as magical as the reader, Leela," Silkie snarked. She sidled towards Verity. "Since this is my last bedtime, Gran," she crooned. "I wonder if you might tell me how you found me one last time before I leave for *LILA'S* benefit."

Verity nodded obediently. "It's worth retelling. A baby in a basket story is a fine thing. Especially when it's true and you know what I think of the truth."

I was quick to reply. "You don't think it; You *know* it," I said, freezing Silkie's pathetic imitation of a smile into a grimace.

Christopher Robin waylaid me as I left the hide. "I wonder if I might have a quick word," he said. I was flattered, Christopher rarely addressed me when he was alone. "I want to set something straight," he said. "People always get me wrong. I wasn't the happy entitled child my father portrayed me. We are alike, you and I, so I'd like to share… and by that, I mean confess something that may help you and Eeyore.

You see me as a perpetual six-year-old." He nodded to the forest's exit, "but I grew up out there, Leela. I had no choice. Everyone assumed I was happy to have lived the enchanted fantasy life of a spoiled boy. It was fun until I turned seven. After that, all I remember is a waking nightmare. There is no-one better than you who will understand this. I was frozen in time like an exhibit in a museum. No one allowed me to be an adult or make a decision until it was too late. The older I got, the more I resented my father for stealing my childhood imagination and turning it into a story template for other children to cherish.

I detested being a famous child, forever considered the luckiest boy in the world. I lived it differently. I was shunned and ridiculed at school by boys who never let me forget what a precocious spoiled prissy I was. Children can be cruel at the best of times, but jealous boys are cruel with a vengeance. Strangers habitually invaded my public life. So insensitive. They discussed my Pooh adventures as if we were family.

Eventually I distanced myself from my parents. My mother had already disowned me for not marrying the girl she'd groomed for me. I hadn't cooperated. I was a bad, selfish son. Oddly enough, I almost made a living from Pooh. I bought a bookshop that became the mecca for adult children everywhere to come and stare, expecting a child wearing a smock and Wellingtons not an aging man in a cardigan with elbow patches. I was no longer an inspiration; I was a destination. I'm happy for you." I turned to go but Christopher stayed me with his hand on my arm. "It won't stay that way," he said.

chapter 27

SIXTY-ONE NO LONGER

"Grow old along with me, the best is yet to be."

ROBERT BROWNING

I beetled off home. My inner clock always reminded me when 4 o'clock teatime approached. Eeyore was waiting, thumping his tail like an angry cat, staring lovingly at a plate of biscuits. I must have looked deep in thought because Christopher's confession had saddened me, it had been insensitive of me to take him for granted.

"What's up, Leela. Cheshire got your tongue?"

"I wish. Christopher Robin unsettled me."

Eeyore brushed off my concern a little too quickly. "Verity left a message that she would join us for tea, so something must be up," he said crunching a chocolate cream. "It will be good to see her. Maybe she's missing Silkie. She hasn't been gone more than a few hours. Will you take Earl Grey or..." Eeyore anxiously eyed the clock. "I think we should start without her," he said. "It's 4:15. Teatime waits for neither man nor bear."

"I could murder a cup of tea. Shall I be mother?"

Eeyore bowed graciously. "Since Verity isn't here, the role of mother is yours."

I drank my tea without taking a breath. Something moved at the bottom of the cup. It was a face. Verity's face. "Hello Sweeting," she said. "I hope I didn't startle you."

Eeyore stared into his empty cup and answered her. "Seeing's that you aren't at the bottom of *my* cup, I remain blissfully unstartled. And Leela's nerves have calmed since she came here, so no worries milady, we're fine."

Verity spoke quietly so as not to be overheard. "I want to keep you both informed of Silkie's progress. It's imperative she does well, so I followed her. She doesn't know I'm here sequestered in an empty corner of her mind. Her future and mine depend on it. And more to the point, Leela, yours is even more critical."

"Is this to be a regular visit?" I asked.

"Oh, aye. The same time each day is best. I know your teatime is punctual, so it seemed a perfect solution."

"I saw Silkie from the hide, today."

"That's fine for now but Zeno is on the move, and I have no idea if he's time jumping or slowing down to smell the roses. He's erratic. I'm guessing he's not best pleased with being a bus. Well, can you blame him. He had to fall a long way from his former incarnation as a master philosopher. He bore it well but he's as anxious as I am for it to be over."

"How does Zeno's class affect *me* so much?"

"One of his students, who he refers to as Ruthless, for good reason, is the greater part of the group soul that gives you power. Greenwood is a spin-off from Ruthless. Calm yourself. He is more of an influence than an ancestor. Remember me telling you were linked? I'm sorry, to be the bearer of disturbing news that confirms you are Greenwood's distant astral descendent – a cousin several hundred times removed. But his influence has been and remains potentially annoying. No worries, dearest. Zeno is more powerful. He will protect you.

Under Zeno's direct influence Greenwood's mental abnormalities are temporarily nullified which is why you will be able to write in his absence. Zeno must render this situation permanent for you and...*ahem*... a few others to go free. Ruthless must become Harmless, do you see?"

"So, if Greenwood returns, you and I suffer?"

"Yes, but much more than that. If Greenwood returns the earth will suffer."

Eeyore let out a terrifying primal bray that nearly stopped my heart.

"Eeyore is telling you that he has been aware of this long before he was created as a depressed toy. Psychopaths like Greenwood exist outside the influence of divine power – a rogue energy humans call evil."

"Then as my twin, isn't Silkie also Greenwood's victim?"

"*Um...* not so much. It will be clear later. Twins are often precocious opposites."

"Foremost, please believe there are no victims in life. Sometimes it's a difficult concept to wholly embrace, but in the end, there is only love.

However, there *are* evil entities that exist outside of love. Notice I didn't use the word live. They aren't alive. They're abominations of negative energy that must be eradicated from the world, especially from Veratopia and the immediate Shadowlands pressed against its boundaries. Their behavior calls for permanent death. An action I assure you that is never taken lightly. But the trees may save them... again, an explanation best left for later. Eleventh hour reprieves don't exist but there is a way to start again, if perpetrators are repentant.

All souls have work to do. Often luck is the corresponding cause and effect of astral influences. Usually, it's selfless but in the case of a psychopath its bally destructive.

While you and Silkie have the same biological DNA, you have individual souls. Greenwood is not a flukey uncle. He's a rogue entity that attaches itself to weak humans from time to time. I was such a woman. As such, I was responsible for allowing Greenwood to absorb my energy. I was rendered soulless for a time. But this is also how I became the initiate of the Green Lady Flora who once reigned here. As day follows night, a new lady will take my place after I'm gone else evil will surely proliferate. You, my girl, are a powerful force who could answer that call if you've a mind to."

"But I was a powerless child."

Eeyore made an anguished cry of protest that scared me. "No, Leela. It was your mother who was powerless," he said. "But an infant, even one as powerful as you remains at the mercy of its parents. It takes an extreme effort to find your true power, and even more to hold on to it, but it is always with you."

"And Silkie?" Verity sighed. "Silkie is willful due to being damaged by my influence for which I will have to answer for. I thought being a mother, albeit her grandmother, was warranted. I was wrong. I was selfish. The powers that be say it bordered on child abuse. I used Silkie opposite to the way your mother deserted you. As such, I have to make amends, but while I'm under Greenwood's power I cannot. I had to release Silkie into Zeno's control. It is the only way to set us both free. She was fast becoming cruel on her own. And one more thing, I will go into later, Mr. de Vere is also involved."

"Right, and Zeno is a bus."

"*Almost* a bus. Of course he isn't a *real* bus. Zeno has sacrificed greatly, so, reincarnation has allowed him to be temporarily possessed by a machine as a great service to mankind.

As a master soul philosopher, he has accepted his role selflessly and with great courage. Goodness knows he will have his hands full with Silkie, but he brought forward the students who were involved as Ruthless's classmates. Great harm was unleashed two thousand years ago. It is time to end the ensuing reign of terror."

"So... the woodcutter?"

"The woodcutter is, in some ways, an innocent storybook character who happens to resonate to axes and murder. But sometimes he is also a convenient ghost possessed by Greenwood for his own purposes.

"How can a ghost be possessed by another ghost?"

"It's rare, but it can. Ruthless was born without a soul – a perfect vehicle for an entity to hide. Being soulless, the child had no defenses. The universe is doing everything possible to save that child and bestow it new life. If all goes as planned, it will reincarnate under special circumstances with the help it requires to grow past its misfortunes. As such, a noble soul worthy of extreme compassion will be its guardian."

"Did I have such a guardian?"

Eeyore brayed an embarrassed cough. "Ah, that would be *me*, Leela."

I stared at Eeyore unable to speak, tears streaming down my cheeks. He licked them away. Our foreheads touched. "There there, Goosie, don't take on, so. It's going to be all right. We've come this far, haven't we?"

I hiccupped in the affirmative.

Verity tried not to cry, but she failed. Tears are catching the same way a yawn will trigger someone else to yawn in response. "My next report will cover the events immediately prior to Silkie boarding the bus," she said, "but until then you have your own transition to make. Nothing too strenuous. Nothing you can't handle. Stay strong dearest girl. Christopher Robin told me he spoke with you. He's a good lad. He and Peter Pan understand your predicament more than you know. They both think the world of you."

"As do I," Eeyore said. "And to prove it I will put the kettle on. We could all do with a fresh pot of messenger tea."

I checked my Eight Ball. Will Silkie find what she's looking for? I gave it a long hard shake for good luck. *Unlikely, better luck next life!* it predicted.

chapter 28

BEYOND THE SCRYING BOWL

"Ah, but a man's reach should exceed his grasp,
Or what's a heaven for?"

ROBERT BROWNING

Veratopia called and I didn't have to sail away for a year and a day in a pea green boat to get there. I only had to cross a quiet street and jump a witchy broom left on a forest green floor.

I handled the transition Verity spoke of with Eeyore's help. She was my 'swansong' reliving the moment I encountered the broom on my first day. Because I had to transcend properly, of course. There was no sense denying it. The offer of a second childhood inevitably comes with caveats and a special acetylene torch for burning any bridges one leaves behind. But burning bridges aside, when you deserve something for long enough, a little thing like almost dying isn't an issue.

Mixed feelings had once surged through me when a door was offered to me in the rain forest a few blocks from where I never grew up, but whenever Eeyore nosed me forward, I balked like a stubborn mule.

And when I finally took the plunge, I accepted my second childhood without a care. An ugly duckling blossoming into an odd Swann diving into muddy water.

Life can be a load of nonsense to the parents of a precocious child. Imagine if you will what my mother would have made of me had she been sane. Nothing as it happened, she abandoned me in a singularly unimaginative plan. When I was six, she left me in the custody of a ghost in charge of a haunted building infamous for its quirky patients and never looked back. If she had, she would have seen a donkey the size of a mama bear taking a dump on her front porch.

I grew up in a single heartbeat. I call second death by its true name, reincarnation. Reincarnation was a small, gentle half-death. Dying twice was well worth finding the life I'd never had.

According to the Universe's strict rules of citizenship, one's first name is written in permanent ink, but I was allowed to keep mine. All that was required was a profoundly new pronunciation, Leela, for the divine energy representing the illusion of freedom and playful creativity, sacrosanct under the spell of maya. Cheerless remains a melancholy pseudonym locked in a dark cupboard. It's still there. If I remain vigilant it will be there until the sun burns out.

My troubled mother didn't have a last name. I assumed she gave me the name Swann in a moment of lucidity inspired by the illustration of a swan on the cover of her only book 'Shakespeare's sonnets'. But I was wrong. Later I discovered she never cared a whit for Shakespeare, but she did care passionately for someone on the street who cared about him a great deal. That teenage boy was my father. He gave Mother the book of sonnets. She clung to it as if the boy lived inside it. After all his name William was on the front cover.

William Jonson learned of my birth after Mother abandoned Silkie. He met me long enough to bond with me quickly and leave just as quickly. It was William who bequeathed me the name Swann.

But I write my backstory ahead of myself. Verity would be the first to congratulate me on such a noble paradox. Like Silkie, I was not privy to the details of my life leading up to and through my captivity.

However, I must have learned books were alive from Mother because she spoke to William hiding inside her book and slept with it under her pillow. So, in that regard, I am grateful for her unsettling beliefs about life and death. I met Eeyore in a book after listening to her conversations with William. Had I not found the hundred-acre-wood Eeyore could never have rescued me from the Shadowlands and I couldn't have rescued Eeyore from his sad memories.

Then… I recognized with lurching hindsight it was the very book the bag lady led me to see in the library.

Such is the metaphysical world for which I was born to serve. I was unaware at the time that an otherworldly point of view was an invitation to shine which was why I didn't recognize it at first.

I'd never anticipated a happy ending. I'm not now nor ever have been conventionally sunny. Nor was I well-situated for success. Up until delivering a Victorian sponge cake to an unlisted forest address, I'd led a wretched limbo existence of fail until you succeed. Sounds ominous but the average human brain functions differently from mine − outside the box of logic and inside a quagmire of mathematical chaos. The succeed part of the equation never happened. Or did it!

My thoughts had been butterflies fluttering without a destination. I hadn't believed in treasure maps. I might have known I would follow magic breadcrumbs left by a witch, albeit a nice one. As I think back, the abduction of Hansel and Gretel was an early influence, and one that no doubt reinforced my fear of trees.

Eeyore nudged me with his nose. "Didn't I once tell you that the gift of fear leads one to great achievements."

I suddenly remembered that he had. "Once upon a time, you did," I replied. "Why didn't you remind me?"

"There was no need," Eeyore said. "It was inevitable. Lost memories only arrive at the perfect moment if they've been forgotten."

"And so?"

"Ironically, your memories weren't forgotten. I don't like to discuss it because it makes me angry. What a stupid boy! Tampering with memories is not a small thing."

"Who? What boy? The disembodied voice who dared me to grow wings was not a boy."

Eeyore whispered an aside in my ear. "Not so much wings but an urge to fly."

And then it came to me. My friend Peter Pan had a particularly fractious running quarrel with happy rainbows, and so he'd taken me by the hand and flown me safely *over* the River Styx to protect my memories and advised me what I already knew, that mothers could never be trusted.

Eeyore had been fit to be tied when he found out. "Christopher Robin and Peter Pan are a pair of stupid boys. I'd arranged a clear slate for you which meant no disturbing memories to... oh, dearie me. Now you'll freak out remembering the hateful look in your mother's eyes. How will that help? It won't, that's what." His voice got louder. "Two wrongs never make a right. Three are even worse. From now on check with me before you do *anything*. And I mean ANYTHING. Are we clear?"

I was silent.

"I need a proper yes, Leela."

"YES!"

Eeyore was angrier than I'd ever seen him. "Less attitude if you don't mind," he brayed. "There's no need to get huffy."

But there was.

chapter 29

D - DAY

the Departure

"Whatever your labors and aspirations,
in the noisy confusion of life, keep peace in your soul.
With all its sham, drudgery
and broken dreams, it is still a beautiful world.
Be cheerful. Strive to be happy."

MAX EHRMANN

Somewhere in the Shadowland the words 61- SORRY NOT IN SERVICE appeared above the bookmobile's windshield and woke Zeno. The headlights of the bus flashed its brights into the early morning downpour. Raindrops beaded the windshield with transparent pearls. "Silkie's on her way, Sir," the driver called out. "Look sharp," he said. "She has two rather large creatures with her."

"Please don't let one of them be Tigger!"

"No, sir. It's a much more subdued beastie, a canine named Chase."

"Not to worry. Chase is a guard dog that avoids chasing anything. Silkie's cat, Fetch will accompany Chase, she does all the hunting and chasing. Her size is formidable, but a sprig of catnip will render her harmless. Is the front door ready?"

"It will be in half a tick. Judging the forest scuttlebutt, no-one describes Silkie as harmless."

The ghostly engines roared to something akin to life. "Did Verity's supplies arrive?"

"They did, Sir. And a fine repast of foodstuffs it is, too."

The surrounding trees shivered as Zeno pushed onto the road. "Our other half will be with us soon... right on time for once. Be on your guard. Silkie's a handful. I have it on good authority from a boy named Pax, she's a wild thing."

"They're waiting at the stop on Poets Corner," Cumulus said. "All three – an old woman and two animals. I see what you mean about Fetch's formidable size. I thought you said Silkie was a child... *was* being the operative word."

"She's both at the moment. If our luck holds, by the time we set sail, Silkie will be six."

A heartbeat away, Cheshire opened one eye and surveyed the forest. "Zeno's on his way," he announced to the morning chorus. It's pelting down cats and caterpillars out there. Silkie isn't going to be happy about getting wet. But then, she's never happy these days."

chapter 30

THE BUS STOP AT POETS CORNER

Two signs were nailed high up
On the tree trunk closest to the bus shelter.
They flanked the small red door of Owl's house.
The first one read:
Ples Cnoke If An Anser Is Reqrd
The second read:
Ring The Bell If An AnsR Is Not Reqd
- WOL

reverently paraphrased from

'THE HOUSE AT POOH CORNER'
– by A.A. MILNE

Verity surfaced right on teatime. She spared no time for niceties and got right down to the essential information I would understand from what she saw. Remote viewing was second nature to her.

The bus shelter of wood and steel stood at the bend in the road Verity occasionally referred to as Silkie's corner, but its name Poets Corner had its own mad pseudonym, the Wiffinspit.

No-one had explained to Silkie precisely what a bus looked like. She heard what I knew to be passing traffic and that a bus driver would collect her from the bench.

It was quite extraordinary. Verity hadn't known what to expect either. Zeno the philosopher, always had a few tricks up his sleeve. But then, a bus has no sleeves.

The word incoming ran around the inside lip of my teacup. I felt it shudder.

My telepathic connection linked with Silkie.

Silkie disliked being kept waiting for anything. She was in a confusion of excitement and bravado with Verity inside her head as a tour guide or referee whichever became necessary.

I could tell she was twitchy because she poked the tip of her umbrella into everything, giving it a violent stab for good measure. When she stopped, exhausted from her outburst, she leaned heavily on it as a cane. She had withered considerably as she moved further from our cabin. Her back was bent forward from a sudden loss of bone density.

She was famished having dismissed the breakfast I offered to make her with a rude gesture of her middle finger. I'd seen it too many times of late to bother. A few feet from the door, pain enveloped her toes rising to her knees and swollen fingers and settled in her lower back.

Her head felt like a teapot full of bees. She rubbed her thumping forehead at one point and screamed at the trees as if they could help. "Get them out!" she screamed but they were under Verity's strict orders not to interfere.

As a true empath, I felt the agony of Silkie's corns and bunions trapped in the unforgiving vise of wellington boots when she shifted her weight from foot to foot.

Fetch and Chase paced restlessly, unsure of what to expect under Zeno's charge.

Silkie unleased a flood of unsavory words meant for me, knowing I would hear them wherever I was.

A gathering of waxwork humans, locked in depressing thoughts of the menial work that awaited them, fretted in the shelter. Sleepwalkers. Day-trippers carved in alabaster. I pitied them as the lifelong enslaved employees they were, ensnared in a corporate earth that used them abominably.

Verity had warned Silkie not to look in their eyes, but she did. The trees linked arms while she sulked, and the forest aperture slammed shut in a mighty gust of wind startling an upstart crow warily eyeing Fetch. She'd had him in her sights long before he landed temptingly close to her nose, but she paid no notice. "He's small pickings," she said. "I have bigger fish to fry."

Cheshire interrupted from Veratopia. "You go, girl," he shouted. "And don't come back!"

The crow unruffled by a ginger housecat as large as a horse hopped closer to Fetch. She stared it down and hissed while Chase sniffed the coats of the passengers who snapped to attention whenever they checked their wristwatches. *It's late*, one of them declared. *Isn't it always,* moaned another. Clearly, as I'd long since suspected, their smart phones far outsmarted their intelligence.

It was the first time Silkie had been allowed to associate with the shadow folk. She would only have toyed with them had they been able to see her; they were far better off suffering alone yet together, huddled in gloomy thoughts.

Verity stood with Silkie, silent and invisible, acting as her ancient eyes now blind from cataracts, staring into a curtain of rain straining to make out the bus. Naturally, I saw it before Silkie did. The illuminated sign on the bus penetrated the weather:

SORRY NOT IN SERVICE.

Fetch had a hissy fit as only an entitled feline can. "That bus is not for Athens," she hissed, "Yours should be right behind it, Silkie."

The bus lied. It *was* in service and to prove it, it slid sideways, sending a spray of puddle water over the shoes of the passengers before screeching to a wet stop a foot from the curb.

The waxworks soaked with greasy water, cursed under their breath as they jostled to be first in a line of push and shove, and entered the bus.

The bus shed its skin like a snake and pulled away in a stream of water continuing on its mission, bound for paychecks and doom, leaving its astral form behind – a grey tunnel of rain with wheels. The illuminated sign 61 ATHENS BLINK shone within it.

Chase, fur bristling, growled at a pulsating ball of energy clinging to its roof like a stubborn tumbleweed. He instinctively howled blue murder despite the fact he recognized it as a common willow-the-wisp, the likes of which he'd met countless times before in the wildwood.

In light of Silkie's diminished eyesight, I saw the shape of a door carved from tree bark and the sign beside it that read *'ples cnoke if an anser is reqrd. Ring the bell if AnsR Is Not Reqd - Wol.*

Being well versed in 'Winnie the Pooh' I recognized Owl's message to the animals of the hundred-acre wood and the ratty looking bell pull as Eeyore's lost tail.

Silkie's umbrella sneezed and immediately closed by itself. She rapped the door smartly with the tip of it. "Owl? it's me, Silkie Ryder. Can we come in?"

The door opened with a loud mechanical groan.

Chase whined through his nose, thumped his tail, and sniffed the wheels. "It smells like a tree," he declared, lifting his leg.

Silkie stopped him in time. "I don't care if you do that later," she said, "but for now, let's try and make a semi-good impression, shall we." Chase slunk behind the bus shelter and doused it good and proper.

A fuzzy ribbon of carpet unrolled slowly from the door and touched the toes of Silkie's wellington boots as a cheery voice emanated from the empty driver's seat. "Ahoy baby bear, welcome aboard."

Silkie was not best pleased. She was old, infirm, exhausted, and not in the mood for a joke, something foreign to her. An Owl, who was clearly not there, who couldn't tell the difference between a dog, a cat, and a human being was hardly a flawless start.

"I am *not* a bear," she replied curtly, clearly miffed."

"Duly noted," replied the disembodied voice, now manifesting as a cloud with human arms. "But according to the poster behind you, Havonford is bear country and it pays to be careful who or what gets on my bus."

Silkie brandished her umbrella like a Jedi knight. "I appear to have become selectively blind. I may not have seen it."

"You don't have to open your eyes to read signs," the driver said, coming into focus with a head and legs. My name's not Owl it's Cumulus. Horatio Cumulus McCloud. We've met before. It'll all come back to you. Watch your step, now."

Silkie touched her face; happy her eyes were open but upset that her life had manifested inside dense fog. "Very funny, Mr. Mc*Clown*. No-one could see a crow in a bowl of milk in this pea soup."

Cumulus gave a kindly chuckle. "I expect that's how you read the sign on my door. Is that a bear with you?"

"That's Chase," Silkie snapped. "He's a special dog."

Chase panted and nudged Silkie forward with a purposeful bark. "We're on our way," he said. "First day of obedience school. I expect to be put through my paces... I wonder if there will be breakfast."

"Are you starving for knowledge?" Cumulus asked. "Or drowning in regret? One must be at least one or the other to ride the old 61." He patted his steering wheel. "Both are recommended."

Silkie was most put out, but she remained polite. "I'm not hungry but thank you for asking, she said."

Chase had no need for small talk. "Well, I'm hungry if it matters to anyone," he said. "Is that bacon I smell?"

Silkie patted Chase's neck. "Well, perhaps on second thought, Mr... *um*... Cloud, some bacon wouldn't go amiss."

"That's my girl," Chase whined.

Cumulus was having none of Silkie's cheek. "If you can't see, how do you know I'm a cloud, young lady?" he said, grinning.

At this, Silkie's regular whinging turned ugly. "My field of vision is entirely cloudy. And I'm well aware of the term cumulus. I've studied weather patterns. As for being a young lady, I seem to have aged quite a lot by crossing one little road."

"You don't look old to me. And my vision is 20/20. That's how I got my licence."

Silkie's anger flared but her energy was flagging. She forgot what Verity had taught her about social behavior and yawned without putting her hand in front of her mouth. "This shadow world is only just swimming into focus," she said. "I expect my sight will improve inside."

"Ah! Then you *can* swim. Did I mention my name is Cumulus? Sometimes I repeat myself. A hazard of aging, don't you know. Please call me Horatio – chef, chauffeur, and editorial lifeguard at your service. Zeno will address you shortly, once we're underway. Make yourself comfortable. I'd keep your umbrella close to hand if I were you, Miss. There will be times you'll need it to navigate Master Zeno's philosophical maze. It's brain teasing at its finest, but it can be a tad aggravating at times. This bus is for Athens. Please hop on, we haven't got all day."

ZENO of CITIUM
Greek philosopher

Near the end of the 4th century B.C.
Zeno of Citium, the founder of stoicism,
discussed philosophy with his followers in the
The Stoa Poikile or 'painted porch'
(Ancient Greek: ἡ ποικίλη στοά)
– a colonnade of open-air classrooms
situated on the north side of the Agora in Athens.
It was a large building that housed
government offices and merchant vendors.
The walkway of its open marketplace
was handy for public lectures and debates
in a series of covered porticos
decorated with colorful mythic scenes
ideal for teaching and discussing new ideas
within a protective shelter of doric columns
– the ancient prototype for our present-day
shopping malls with floors of offices.

GROUND ZENO

THE BOTTOM LINE

chapter 31

ENDLESS IN ATHENS

"Good friend, for Jesus' sake forbear,
to dig the dust enclosed here.
Blessed be the man that spares these stones,
And cursed be he that moves my bones."

Inscription on the false grave of William Shakespeare

- Trinity Church – Stratford-on-Avon

September 1, 2024, on board the Havonford bookmobile bound for Athens

My real name doesn't matter. For the purposes of Zeno's quest, my pseudonym is Endless. He gave all his students 'Zeno names'. How I came to be here on the number 61-bus of Havonford in the year 2024 hasn't yet been explained to me. But Master Zeno rarely explains. Instead, he prefers to forge on until the truth dawns in a student's eyes. I am such a student. In the most simplistic terms, I have arrived, and to prove it I shouldn't be here.

I answered Zeno's call from affection and loyalty, dragging my name, Endless, with me – a potent pseudonym both blessing and curse.

Zeno's pseudonyms always ended in the word less to teach us the value of more. He explained the axiom 'less is more': Less and more can cancel each other out or fan each other into a maelstrom of unbelievable chaos.

There were three of us in Master Zeno's special class culled from his conventional soul-searching followers. Apparently, our presence contaminated them because our triumvirate signified more conflict, more anger, and more despair.

Our Zeno names were: Endless, Ruthless, and Childless. Within days of meeting each other our conflicting destinies became intrinsically fused through Zeno's spiritual teachings.

But sadly, we needed to be sequestered from the herd. Nipped in the bud. Zeno was resolute we should be quarantined for the greater good. And so, it was. He cited some nonsense about heaven and such so, at first, I dismissed it.

But now a memory, once banned from my mind, is resurfacing in the shadows, veiled, as I once believed for my own safety. I was wrong. I've come to realize that many a true lesson must be read between the lines of magic and commonsense and the far-reaching effect of human suffering is far more dangerous than one would first believe.

I for one do not relish the reunion of our disturbed clan. There was only one among us who could have brought down such devastating ruination upon the world. And so, 2000 years on, we must summon the best of who we failed to be and silence the worst.

Only Master Zeno can finally purge our resident psychopath – a malefic degenerate, allowed to run riot for 2000 years who fanned revenge and black magic into humanity's two greatest flaws, guilt and shame.

In my forty-seventh year, circa 2,300 BC, I dropped out as a 'failure-to-thrive' perpetual child. It was in this way I discovered I had died several times, and that my life persisted building layer upon layer on the memories of predecessors who were not my biological ancestors.

I recall filing the event under the universal law of existence dictating 'the less stratums the merrier'.

Today, eons later, I find myself with Zeno in a hot windowless room hurtling across a barren landscape where a delightfully cool breeze flows from a spinning discus. He holds a finger over his lips, begs me to listen without interrupting, and opens a door I hadn't noticed.

Zeno leads a sullen young girl into the room and seats her in a hardback chair across from me. The pair of strange animals accompanying her take their place either side of her like sentinels guarding a throne.

The girl avoids making eye contact with me. She is there and not there, phasing in and out of physical form as if unsure of the age she should be or what dimension was best to house her. I assumed she was a soul in transition waiting for Zeno to choose for her.

"Endless," Zeno announced. "I'd like you to meet Silkie. She's an old acquaintance of yours. But you haven't met her yet."

I appraised the girl's delicate features and silver hair, but I couldn't see her eyes to determine her enthusiasm or indifference. "I've never seen her before," I said. "And why are there two statues guarding her?"

Zeno strode about the room, his white toga swishing as his pace quickened. "Silkie has two guardians. The feline's name is Fetch for a specific reason."

"Which is?"

"A fetch is an entity come to lead a soul across the River Styx."

"Is Silkie going to die?"

"Everyone dies a few times. Do not stress yourself. The dog's name is Chase. The two together form a compassionate circle of power that... there's no use staring, Endless. You won't recognize Silkie, nor she you, until I give the two of you leave."

"I gather we had a meaningful experience together."

"It was an event that sadly, as it turned out, was quite pointless. But times have changed. The tide is turning."

"Can she hear us in that state?"

"When you knew her, she was an infant. She must decide on

which of three ghosts to pursue who will help her most. You, her great grandmother, or her birth mother."

As we watched, the girl alternated between a squalling red-faced newborn in swaddling clothes, an old crone, and a fair-haired child of six.

I suddenly felt a tug of connection. "Her mother? Was she a friend of mine? Oh my God. Was I her father? Is she in trouble? How can I help?"

"Wonderful. Your compassionate instincts do you proud," Zeno mused. "Better late than never. Let's give your lost child a moment. Occasionally she's reasonably clever. She may choose rightly. All in good time. It's actually her twin sister who matters most of all, but we shall leave that for now."

"I have two children! Not possible. I would have remembered."

"You were rarely in a state to remember anything at all as I recall. Neither was Silkie's teenage mother. Curiosity and lust ruled the day. Love was never part of the equation."

"Not many things have more meaning than a powerful pseudonym," I said warily, fishing for proof of any wrongdoing on my part. "I have certainly lived up to mine. What was her mother's name?"

"Her mother's name was Beatrice."

I faced Zeno of Citium, my possible accuser, unflinchingly although it pained me lest I had once again neglected my duty. As a physician I had pledged a solemn oath to do no harm. "You bequeathed me the honorary title, 'Endless' over two thousand years ago. Your reason, so you once elaborated, was that my excuses and challenges were endless. Apparently, such decisions are as legally binding now as they ever were. I beg you to enlighten me. Am I in trouble?"

Zeno turned away from me and addressed the closed door. "Always in trouble but impeccably blameless," he said. "The final outcome is for Silkie to decide. If you have gained sufficient wisdom, you can help yourself by helping her.

Master Zeno would never have recalled us together unless it was to undo the harmful consequences we unwittingly unleashed on the world, related as it now seems, to the child Silkie. I dread to think how she connects us, but I was born dreading almost everything, so facing the past is infinitely more difficult than facing a doomed future.

The day of my Zeno name had dawned in Athens under a brilliant blue sky as I hid unsuccessfully in the mauve shadows of the stoa. It was my second week of attendance in Zeno's outdoor classroom.

Zeno knew things. My silences filled his mind with details even I didn't know. He spied me trying to hide and called me out. "You there, Endless, sit closer to me. I've been saving a place for you. I thought you would never come."

All eyes were on me, including my own because I left my physical body and watched the scene from above. Zeno culled me from his herd and accordingly 'seated me at his table' and placed a philosophical banquet before me. "Partake Endless, you're starving, child."

I protested. "I…"

But Zeno wouldn't let me speak. "And please do not feign denial of what is. Your truth will out. Isn't that what you're here for. The truth!"

"I…"

"No need to answer a rhetorical question when both of us know the answer. Of course it is. Now be wise for once, Endless, and listen until I give you permission to speak."

"Or not," a voice beside me whispered. "Master Zeno has taken a fancy to you so be prepared for war."

"War?" I whispered back. "I came here for peace of mind."

"Zeno claims each of us is here to win a war with the inner voice that berates us all day long. You're up for execution or martyrdom. But it's inevitably your choice."

Zeno glared at us and placed a finger over his lips for silence and continued. "There's a reason you're squeamish about bloodshed and violence, Endless." He threw open his arms as an invitation. "You may speak now but make no mistake, this is your only chance. Pretend I'm a child, and you're telling me a story to excite me and calm my nerves at the same time. Please begin from your earliest memory. Take your time."

Memories rushed in jostling to be aired first. I took a deep breath and chose one. "I was born with a desire to heal, Sir. Especially after my mother's early death when I was six. It started with injured birds with broken wings and evolved to dogs and horses and oddly enough, bees."

I took another breath and noted Zeno's serene expression. He seemed miles away with his eyes closed. "Don't stop. Endless," he said without opening his eyes. "You haven't excited me yet."

Words spilled from my lips that I heard as if for the first time. "I've been miserable despite my undeniable success as a surgeon. People seek out my skills from far away, which I see now, was part of the problem. An endless stream of patients with endless complaints... endless pressure. Why did some die and some live? What separated fate from folly? And why was I unable to harness a counter energy to foil death?"

"You refer to the plague child?"

I thought of playing ignorant, but I wanted Zeno to know the truth. "I never knew the plague girl's name. I couldn't save her. She died." My voice became barely audible. "How do you know of her?"

Zeno's eyes flashed opened to reveal the color of the sea. "Ah. There it is. The excitement. What will Endless do next, I wonder?"

The last time I died, Master Zeno declared it wasn't the end. He was a venerable man of sixty-one when he watched me slip away. We are not blood relations, yet we share time as the synergized energy of teacher/student as much as Zeno's magic and my guilt allows.

I also knew the venerable Zeno in 300 B.C. (when BC meant Before Christ). Zeno and I passed each other as strangers on the street a few more lifetimes before I latched onto his energy trail in 1962, drawn to a new vibration of B.C. that refers to British Columbia and leaves 'Before Christ' in the dust.

After Master Zeno of Citium had been my long-suffering mentor, my go-to therapist, philosopher god, and my surrogate grandfather, he became my dearest friend. If he hadn't, I wouldn't be here today. Which brings me to reveal I'm not *exactly here* today. I am a *gone tomorrow* sort of person.

By gone tomorrow I mean adrift after deliberately abandoning my soul. I don't seem to have a replacement soul worth searching for. I'm inexplicably drawn to running away. Whenever I stay it's only to fume over past mistakes and worry about the future.

"The last vestiges of ego must die, Endless. It's time to let go," Zeno said. "Regret nothing!"

Zeno taught that certain places on earth have *atmosphere*. There are haunted houses with temperamental electrics, dogs with attitude… and most certainly finicky cats but the number 61- bus of Vancouver Island is wholly sentient.

But I return now to the déjà vu of my naming, after I'd grown disheartened – weary of the relentless blood and gore from staunching and stitching battle wounds both domestic and military.

Zeno's benign blue eyes had approached me stealthily, pinning me like a moth to the mauve shadows where I once again sought to go unnoticed. "Endless," he said gently, "I thought you'd gone for good. Please come forward. He gestured to a row of students sitting cross-legged at his feet and nudged two of them apart. "I saved your place."

I complied reluctantly. I had thought only to observe one last time and slip away.

"What good can be done," Zeno announced sprightly, "through endless meandering in sadness and regret?"

My tongue was in my cheek when I boldly replied. "I came here to find out" with a conviction I didn't feel.

Zeno gave a deep throaty chuckle. "Quite. We'll make a late start, then, shall we? We've no time to waste."

Like it or not, this Havonford bus ride is for mastering spiritual road rage.

There's no chance I'm the only one of my kind, but for a year I stood apart from the world of shadows for a reason (at least I *think* it was a year) though *which* year out of all the hundreds of years there has been between us, is impossible to say.

Time-sensitive has never been a more relevant catchphrase than in 2024. And as catchy as it is, I'm not an insufferable psychic wielding a 'the end is near' sign... except that maybe as a time-traveller, I am! Zeno named me Endless for a reason.

On my second day of Zeno's classroom, he was far from gentle. "Look sharp, Endless," he barked heading straight for my jugular. He took a step back from his podium. "Please enlighten us, Endless. What does a great soul do with stifled *chutzpah*?" Zeno's shrill tone defined his strange new word as a disaster.

I answered instantly with military cheek "One gets on with it, sir!"

Zeno wasn't about to let me get away with a glib response. "And without enthusiasm for life," he said in the tone of a disgruntled wet bear "what could possibly go wrong I wonder?"

The stoa evaporated, swooning into the stifling room in 2024, now airless with the discus stilled, and Silkie's companions stretched sleeping, dead to the world.

Zeno rubbed his hands together. "Well, Endless, old friend, we had better get on with changing the past." He placed a hand on Silkie's shoulder. It's time to wake up and join the party young lady."

Before I leave you, I'd like to say something encouraging about earth's future, but, in all honesty, I cannot, yet I feel compelled to share my truth with anyone troubled enough or aware enough to realize they're standing directly in the path of an erratically swinging demolition ball – a rogue asteroid of energy trained on a fallen world on the brink of self-destruction.

I say to you. Do what I failed to do many times. Feel your emotions fully and then let them go. Accept what is. Listen to everything three times. Wait in silence and dare to respond with borrowed Jois de vivre. Find it anywhere you can. It won't stay long if you don't use it.

chapter 32

GRADE ONE — GNOTH SEAUTON

"That which is an impediment to action
is turned to advance action.
The obstacle on the path
Becomes the way."

MARCUS AURELIUS

The loudspeaker burst into an announcement. "Nothing is realer than real," Zeno said. "Know that you are a human with mortal limits. You are not a goddess, Silkie. Pax of the forest glade said you were a wild animal. Make no mistake. You *will* be tamed. Grandmothers tend to ignore their grandchildren's bad behavior. I will not.

Be forewarned. For those who fail my class, soul death can be arranged. Gnoth Seauton 'know thyself' is prominently displayed at the entrance to the temple of Apollo in Delphi. It would be wise if you commit it to memory!"

Silkie sat primly perched like an angel on a mission with one hand entwined in Chase's collar. His tail thumped the ground like a bass drum.

"Take charge but don't stake your own claim until I give you permission," Zeno said. "You are now part of a group young lady, one quarter of my allotted teaching time. These are your classmates, Endless, Ruthless, and Childless. I suggest you stay clear of Ruthless. He's an old acquaintance of your grandmother's."

Silkie's temper snapped. "How many times must I tell you that Verity is absolutely *not* my grandmoth…"

"Sorry... *Great* grandmother," Zeno said, "who may care for you, but has *absolutely* no jurisdiction concerning my classroom and very little influence outside Veratopia."

Endless, hoping to rescue Silkie, diverted Zeno's attention. "Does Silkie have a Zeno name?"

"Yes," Zeno said calmly. "It's Powerless."

Silkie choked on a rude word stuck in her throat and thrust out her chin. "I refuse to answer to it."

Zeno chuckled. "Suit yourself. Endless, please tell Silkie how many eons of time we can wait until she learns her manners."

"I believe the word in Silkie's world is oodles," Endless said.

Ruthless smirked hello. "Little girl, I assure you, Zeno's reserve is never broken."

"Then let him show himself. I personally count invisibility as extremely rude."

"Zeno is quite visible to the rest of us," Ruthless continued, "including your pets. You won't be able to see him until you show some respect."

Endless circled Silkie, examining her from every angle and when Fetch purred loudly, he paused to pet her. Chase, in turn, thumped his tail and raised a paw for Endless to shake.

Leela, asleep in Veratopia, suddenly sat up in bed, eyes closed and shouted SHAKES-PAW into the dark. "It's only a dream, Goosie," Eeyore said, settling her back under the covers. "Go back to sleep," and proceeded to recite: "*Winken, Blinken, and Nod, one night, sailed off in a wooden shoe.*"

Puck looked puzzled. "Not another pseudonym. I thought we were finally out of the woods."

Eeyore giggled. "Nice pun," he said, and waggled his ears. "Leela has never grown out of bedtime stories. She still insists on her favorites. The 'Wooden Shoe' always does the trick."

"What mules these humans be," Puck said to make Eeyore laugh.

VERITY'S REPORT:

Zeno introduced himself while Catch and Fetch were asleep. That alone sent off alarm bells.

Zeno was as invisible as a god, regaling Silkie from his loudspeaker on high. I looked for a camera, found one on the ceiling, and gave Zeno a wave.

I believe there was a singular moment when Silkie's audacious spirit amused him, but Zeno's voice was austere. "My dear young lady. I'm sure you have questions. But for my teaching to be effective, I ask that you hold your questions until I open the floor. For now, please listen carefully to my ceiling. First, be advised our meeting has been ordained at the highest level of divine wisdom.

Now, with regards to your origin as a species brought to my particular attention; you were neither an accident, nor were you chosen. You and I have been an event waiting to happen for many years. Essentially, although you're a quickening of genetic material I like to think of as random space fluff, you are a specific conscious energy connected here in a time-sensitive moment. That is to say, our meeting is timeless in the overall 'Wei' of things – a moment of intensive precision.

A single heartbeat either way and our connection could not have occurred. We are the *'to be or not to be'* of conscious meeting. That is how important you are, and how vital consciously participating in Leela's divine game is.

That said, there *are* 'happy accidents for those aware enough to see. Utilize these super-gifts with gratitude for therein lie the miracles of the unmanifested dimension – a realm of *endless* creative expansion when you embrace it with your true heart.

You will come to know I use the term endless as a catchword for spiritual growth, and although you're only dimly aware of the extreme importance of the Universe's *endless* games, I urge you to remember there are no princesses in chess. However, there *is* a Queen of Trees. Verity has been a placeholder for one such goddess who will come after she has been liberated. But we'll discuss that in detail, later."

Zeno's digital blackboard flickered erratically. "I see you fidgeting, child. Please ask your question before you burst."

Silkie deliberately stared out the window, determined not to cooperate by accepting the cheek of a master hiding behind an electronic banner. She was full of the precocious confidence instilled in her by me, her doting grandmother. "Are you taking me from A to Z like a good bus?" she asked. Her body language told me she was ready for a fight.

Zeno raised his voice without shouting. "Let's get one thing straight before we begin," he typed. "I don't drive this bus. Cumulus does that. I AM the bus!"

Silkie immediately adjusted her posture, fixing her back poker straight as if tied against the trunk of a thinking tree and gave her best impression of a drooling wunderkind.

Against all odds, Zeno, relaxed his stern lecture. Silkie fell for it. I saw the images flutter behind her eyes. She stupidly imagined Zeno as a kindly Santa Claus bouncing her on his knee, smiling at her as if she was the most important little girl in the world.

Zeno interrupted her musing. "A journey from A to Z would be futile, dear one. We travel to the end of the line which is infinitely further than the 26th letter of the alphabet. And to be perverse, *you* are a passenger. Are we clear, Miss bossy britches?"

Apparently, she wasn't. "How long before we reach 'B' then? … A ballpark number is fine if you have one."

"You've been made aware of the bookmobile in Parallel Park."

"I have. And I'm *not* your little one."

"Then by all the calculating of calculus, the distant *endless* past where time stands still is our destination."

The letters on the display sent off sparks and fizzled into a row of explanation marks. "BALLPARK," he added in capital letters. "You were not born in the bookmobile; you were placed there, and due to the exemplary timing of your twin birth, your soul migrated there of its own accord. Your mother simply followed it. Your sister landed elsewhere in a nearby hospice for unwed mothers. Leela's birth was registered as a single child. By the way, the bookmobile was never intended as a nursery for a newborn, even one as miraculous as you think you are."

His answer disgusted her.

"Why on earth, not!"

"A pair of powerful earth spirits would have been impossible to contain in a single forest clearing regardless of its magical nature. It was all Verity could do to manage you."

"She often remarked *it's not easy being green*. Does that mean I'm a powerful earth spirit?"

"It was only a pun to make a point."

"Lila and I don't get along."

"To be more accurate, it's *you* who doesn't want to get along. And her name is Leela. You were powerless then and you're Powerless, now – a wannabe princess to be eclipsed until the moon is ready to comply."

"So, I've been demoted, then?"

"Quite the contrary, what eventually awaits you after graduation, *if* you graduate, which seems most unlikely, is the divine gift of reincarnation. My class is not a pissing contest. So, pay attention and apply yourself. I am not a pushover like your grandmother."

Well, that riled Silkie up out of all proportions, I can tell you.

She double-dog dared Zeno without blinking while quaking in her wellington boots. "I hope you're kidding your majesty," she said, cool as a cucumber but her stomach, as empty as it was, churned with acid reflux.

"You can hope, wish, and pray... whatever shows up. I care not for puny games," Zeno said. I honestly couldn't see any trace of the Zeno I knew. He had swallowed a pill of such bitterness, he spat his words like poison darts.

Silkie recoiled with an expression I knew only too well. It was a dare that said *if you want a war bring it on old man.*

It was a red flag to a bull moment, and I had no idea where the axe would fall. I almost rooted for Silkie but when Zeno countered with, *I don't fight silly little girls,* I admit I cheered.

"Let me be perfectly clear," Zeno barked. "There will be no princesses in this class. No whining, no talking back, no speaking before you're spoken to. Your pets will sleep through it all, out of sight. No theatrical outbursts will aid in your favor. If you thought Verity trapped you, this bus will be an emotional torture chamber the like of which no grandmother, biological or theoretical, would ever dream of inflicting.

Consider this your finishing school, Silkie. But remember, another word for finishing is ending. Where it ends no-one knows. What you do is up to you. Your destination, and please note that the word destiny inside it is *not* an accident. Your passing or failing grade, is entirely up to me. I suggest you act accordingly.

You have landed in a Special Ed class for a group soul intervention. Survival is recommended. I am not an ogre, little girl. Neither am I a namby-pamby philosopher. My curriculum is simple – I teach the three Rs simultaneously: Reading, Righting, and Reincarnation!

chapter 33

INSIDE THE EIGHT BALL

"And would it have been worth it, after all?
After the cups, the marmalade, the tea,
Among the porcelain,
Among some talk of you and me,
Would it have been worthwhile,
To have bitten off the matter with a smile,
To have squeezed the universe into a ball?"

T.S. ELIOT

The Love-Song of J. Alfred Prufrock

Yesterday afternoon at 4 p.m. sharp Verity appeared in my teacup and delivered an agitated report with an admission that sounded a lot like guilt. What happened next was mindboggling. Her report preceded my first cup of tea and was so longwinded, there was no time for a second lukewarm cup.

VERITY's REPORT:

"I decided to accompany Silkie covertly to help her and ease my mind," Verity said. "She has never been alone. She needed me. I believe what I say in these transmissions will help you proceed with your own lessons. I am, in essence, Silkie's grandmother and more fittingly, your fairy godmother as far as such titles go.

I'm not accustomed to being overwhelmed but the goddess Athena greeted us in the bus terminal. She stood smiling brightly, an owl perched on her shoulder, a spear in one hand, and a clipboard in the other. She wore a white robe with sweeping windblown draperies. "Tickets please," she asked sweetly, waving a ticket punch over Silkie's head, tapping her forehead with it like a magic wand.

There were two curtains to the left and right.

Silkie kept her cool and stared the owl down. Her past dealings with Wol gave her confidence. She looked daggers at Athena and in her iciest blast shouted, "I wasn't *issued* a ticket! Ask Zeno if you don't believe me."

I must admit Silkie's arrogance made me proud. She acted fearlessly. I was almost convinced she was having a good time; except she was terrified. She held her ground, a six-year-old mini-goddess and looked down her nose at Athena's towering presence above her. "Are you an air hostess?" she asked as unflappable as you please. That girl is an actress plain and simple.

"It would have been an ethereal ticket came the calm reply. Do you have one of those?"

"NO!"

"It is also our custom to ask if you have anything to declare."

"I have two animals and an umbrella."

"Yes, I can see that. What is your formal declaration?"

"I don't understand the question."

"Your intention," Cumulus called out. "Athena requires your intention. State your purpose and destination."

Silkie folded her arms and replied disdainfully. "My intention, which is none of your damn business, is to make up for lost time. My destination is independence. I am here to attend my first class with master Zeno."

"Ah," Athena said. "Why didn't you say so, my dear. In that case, you're seated in first class." She pointed to the right. "Behind that curtain."

"Zeno was in full form. My old friend's subtle metaphor of

going beyond the proverbial 'veil' was perfect. I'd forgotten how theatrical he was. What better person to engage Silkie than the daughter of Zeus born without a mother, emerging fully-grown from Zeus's forehead. Athena never had to grow up.

But that's what makes Zeno a master teacher. He is the only person I know who can tame Silkie. His methods appear gentle but he's cutthroat, as is the way of all genuine cunning."

Athena smiled. The owl hooted. "That's the ticket," Athena said demurely. "However, your animals are too large to enter a public forum." Out came a ticket punch and Fetch and Chase were transformed into a mouse-sized transparent kitten and a squirming puppy that fit into a small basket.

Her next instructions were pure Zeno. "Your pets and the chip on your shoulder will be stowed in the baggage compartment under the bus. I assure you it's quite safe there. Your attitude can be left with Cumulus, baby bear. A vinyl umbrella is quite useless here. Tomorrow, you will be issued a standard Greek parasol."

Silkie's haughtiness suddenly made me squirm. "Para as in above... Sol for the sun?" she bragged. She has no social filters. My fault of course.

Athena was gracious. "You speak Latin," she said.

Silkie's reply... "Lady, I could speak Latin before I could walk. And I am not a damn bear" was cringeworthy.

Athena calmly told her to *please take your assigned seat before you get too old*. "There are no wheelchair facilities on this bus."

The back of Silkie's hands recently covered in age spots had faded into smooth youthful skin. Was she being punished, or was I? It was hard to say.

Zeno has detected my presence. My mission is no longer covert. It had been wrong of me to come, but here I am, and I expect Zeno will speak as he finds. He never lies. And when he's confronted, he welcomes every situation as serendipitous to save time.

There's no denying I'm in for it. There's no reason to fake a coolness I don't possess. I've landed myself in the hot spot of unconditional awareness. Which is undoubtedly what I need. Two birds... one stone, appropriately hanging motionless on an upwind of lofty expectations.

Sorry to digress. What I want to describe before I go is the stunning vista behind the veil. We were met with a white temple on a hill overlooking an amphitheatre. Beyond it lay a pristine expanse of white beach and a dazzling turquoise sea. The amphitheatre will serve as our stoa. The stands will be empty. It's not booked for entertainment. It's a class meant to bring out the worst in each of us, including me. I assume to set it and us, free.

Silkie heard me gasp and knew I was a stowaway in her head. She made no protest. She saw me as an unexpected escape card. Escape being uppermost in her mind.

Zeno's colonnade seating is built of white marble on a slight incline in sixty-one tiers. The stage far below displays a digital sign on an arch over the stage that mimics the bus's display panel. It appears to be made of alabaster with the letters carved intaglio, and once read, they vanish like chalk from a blackboard. The words, *what has been said can never be unsaid,* runs in a loop, disappearing behind the stone arch before returning again, repeating a phrase I'd heard Zeno use many times: It's *better to trip with the feet than with the tongue.*

A heady lemon scented breeze jolted me from bus lag. The horizon shone like a slick of gold paint where it met the flash of blue beneath it.

Dominating the cliffs is the headless statue of a Nike about to touch down – the original of the famous iconic figure, the Nike of Samothrace, housed in the Louvre Museum.

The sound of birds greeted us. Their white wings hanging on an updraft fanned Nike's draperies into a snowy landscape of undulating creases and folds.

She serves as a reminder of our pending defeat or victory – a goddess messenger high above us on a tall cliff, silhouetted against a cloudless blue sky. Her head and arms were already missing but the trumpet she once held floated as if held to her lips. A sound of fluttering wings emanated from it until the words *Hello Silkie* greeted us.

The loudspeaker's voice was stronger, now that it identified itself as a goddess. Zeno is using Nike as he once used the loudspeaker on his bus. Her simple hello echoed the call of the road. I think, knowing the circumstances of Zeno's present responsibility and his sense of humor, it is a call to arms, pun intended.

Silkie heard me, surprised I was still in her head. She had thought to be rid of me. *"Why are you still here,"* she said. *"Have you been a naughty grandmama?"*

Nike answered for me. *"The truth stands alone, child."*

Silkie sniffed. *"Well, Granny, is this the school you had in mind? I thought there'd be less sand and more desks. Where on earth is that Zeno chap? Let's get this, whatever it is, over with.* She checked the rows of empty bookcases behind a row of columns high 'in the gods'. *For a bookmobile there appears to be no books."*

"This is a thought library," Nike said.

I almost said penny for your thoughts, but Silkie beat me to it.

"Zeno will remain a disembodied voice," Nike said. "You won't see him, but he will make you see more than you ever thought possible."

Silkie was quick with a comeback. "Well, lucky for me that we're in a thought library, then," she said. Silkie closed her eyes and addressed me. *"There's no need to stay on my account. I can see where I'm supposed to sit."* She referred to a goblet of water and a bunch of purple grapes on one of the steps.

Silkie thinks she's some sort of guest of honor. She's in for a surprise!

The stage is set with a Corinthian pedestal centerstage – a podium of sorts, its speaker being a ball of light that flickers like a lantern whenever Zeno speaks.

"Well, here we are, granny... a bit of an anticlimax, wouldn't you say."

A stunning landscape couldn't be further from the truth. *"I plan to monitor your progress every day,"* I said. *"I promise not to get in your way."*

"No worries, I plan to get expelled by the end of the week."

I countered, not to be outdone. *"As in ex-spelled?"*

"I doubt your spells are any match for a living sculpture with no arms or a mouth who plays the trumpet."

The pain in Verity's voice surprised me. I had no idea how much she hated me.

"Neither did I," Silkie said. *"I think you might have told me to pack sunscreen."*

Without warning Silkie shouted. "Zeno, if you can hear me, I demand that my pets be restored to their full size immediately!"

Amazingly, Zeno complied. For an instant Fetch nattered at Athena's owl. Chase whimpered and twitched his paws. *"There must be rabbits in Athens,"* Silkie remarked. *"He won't chase them here either. He's stubborn as a stupid donkey."*

And that was all – a swift game of hide and seek. Fetch and Chase were hidden once more, and it's unlikely Silkie will become a tamed seeker.

A pen and paper are provided at four places. There's a single bottle of water. Silkie assumed it was her seat considering she'd been notified in advance that her missing classmates weren't alive enough to warrant food or drink. She haughtily assumed her seat was the place of honor reserved for the star pupil.

The teacup went silent. Verity's sobs rippled the contents of the tea still in my cup, swirling. A tempest in a teacup. Her voice quivered into hiccups. "She - - - hated - - - me."

"She's acting out right now," I said. "She's putting on a show for Zeno. She's challenging him. Surely, she's being watched. Can you see Zeno?"

"I can. Silkie cannot. His arms are folded and he's frowning at Silkie. Not an impressive start."

"All's well that ends well," I replied. "Sorry, that slipped out. I see Edward every day now and, well, he says things like that all the time to tease Eeyore. Tink and Puck are a pair of monkeys. Tink is teaching Puck some of her magic and Puck is teaching Eeyore some of his old party tricks. Edward, Peter, and I are fast friends. It's all very exhausting but exciting."

The tea in the bottom of my cup crystalized into salt as Verity wept. "I doted on that girl," she said. "I was a fool. She was never my daughter. I see that now."

A sharp intake of breath told me something untoward had happened.

"The lantern just flickered with white light, Verity said. "Zeno said Ver and then it went dark. He may have been addressing me or Edward, it's hard to say."

I heard a male voice say 'Verity, your true daughter is here. Forgiveness takes time,' in the background.

"What just happened?" I asked. "Who was that?"

Verity laughed weakly. "Zeno's lips moved that time, and he blew me a kiss. That's my cue to stay. I was mistaken, our teacher is going to be visible after all. 'Gnoth Seauton – know thyself' is about to become my biggest challenge.

Meet me tomorrow when I will no doubt be wiser. Over and out."

chapter 34

ZENOPHOBIA

"I have seen the moment of my greatness flicker,
And I have seen the eternal Footman
hold my coat, and snicker,
And in short, I was afraid."

T.S. ELIOT

I awoke with Eeyore standing over me his ears pinned back in fright. "You've had a bad dream, Leela. You were calling for me. I tried to wake you but when you started screaming, I sent Puck to fetch Vera. Tell me about it, if you've a mind to."

I swung my legs out of bed and steadied myself against Eeyore. "I will be fine if you help me to the kitchen."

I swooned and Eeyore guided me to a chair, his ears wild again. "Sit here, little one. Puck's put the kettle on, and I've told him to make the tea extra strong and nightmare sweet. Vera is on her way."

I heard my voice thank him as if it belonged to a stranger. A stranger, who by all accounts was as small as a sparrow floating near the ceiling. It was worse than bad. I thought my nightmares were long gone. I assumed the forest would be a haven after Silkie left. "Eeyore, I should talk to Vera as soon as she arrives. Maybe she can throw some light on what's going on. I'm not myself."

"Of course you are," Vera said, entering the bedroom as business-like as Mary Poppins on a mission. "Now, where's that tea?"

"It's here milady," Puck said from the doorway, laden with a tray.

Vera pressed a mug of tea into my hands and cupped her hands around mine to stop it spilling.

Puck, true to his word, had made the tea as sweet as syrup. "Do you think Leela can eat something?" he said looking more serious than I'd ever seen him. "I've made buttered toast, and I can easily fetch the marmalade."

"Sweet tea is best for trauma," Vera said. "We learned that in the London blitz. Maybe Leela can manage a slice of dry toast if you would be so kind. It's too soon for breakfast but I'm most grateful for the buttered toast. I expect you're hungry too, dear boy."

Puck, never overly fond of being called a boy, grimaced and left without a word to make more toast.

"Is it all right if I stay," Eeyore asked Vera. "I don't want to tire her."

"Of course, you are Leela's person."

I sipped and nodded in agreement. I croaked out a feeble yes, delighted to find my voice was returning. I reached out for Eeyore. "Oh, Eeyore you never have to ask. Your place is always by my side."

Vera let go of my hands and ate some toast with Eeyore. Puck returned with dry toast for me. He must have used some of his magic because after one bite I was ravenous and ate four slices.

Vera waited while I finished my toast and poured me a second cup of tea before speaking.

"Not to worry, my dear. I know what's happened," she said. "I felt the same disturbance an hour ago. In fact, I was putting on my coat to come here before Puck knocked on my door."

Puck settled himself in the corner with a pot of marmalade and a runcible spoon. Eeyore plunked down beside him eating buttered toast, his ears finally calm enough to listen to Vera without interrupting her.

"It will come as no surprise that I'm in contact with, well, with my older self," she began. "So, I understand what's happened. I'm afraid you'll have to sit this out for a little while, Leela, but rest assured the worst is over. Silkie is disrupting our thoughts. Verity is with her and is experiencing one of Silkie's full-on tantrums. Let me explain."

I got back into bed and sent Eeyore a cheery thumbs up before I closed my eyes.

"Silkie has been blocking your telepathic link ever since you two met. It was the only way she could feel superior. She isn't, of course, but she's used to being queen of the castle. She didn't expect to feel so jealous. And quite frankly, neither did Verity."

"She's a selfish little madame and no mistake," Eeyore said to Puck.

"You'll get no argument from me," Vera said, "but for now the only way to process this little *episode* is to accept that Silkie is going through some challenges that have knocked her for a loop."

"A loop that had Leela screaming in her sleep," Eeyore sassed back.

Vera took my hand. "That was the worst of it, Leela. Waking up in someone else's nightmare is far worse than experiencing one of your own."

I opened my eyes and shushed Eeyore with a finger over my lips. "We're listening, Vera. Please continue."

Eeyore grunted and dropped his head onto his forelegs in a sulk.

"Leela, dear. You will share some of Silkie's thoughts as if they were your own. As uncomfortable as that will be, just go along. It will seem as if you *are* Silkie for a while."

Eeyore lifted his head and twitched his ears. "How extremely ghastly."

"But it will pass, Eeyore. Remember it *will* pass. All is well even though it doesn't feel like it just now. As Leela's guardian you're understandably concerned. Let it go. Leela will feel better soon. Holding a grudge against Silkie won't help her."

And then it was my turn to let things go. Silkie used my vocal cords to speak, and I forced myself to accept her without resistance.

"The open road unhinged me," Silkie said. "As soon as the bus pulled away, I felt queasy. Even now, icy-cold travel sickness rises in my throat. There's a hate-fest buzzing inside my body. I need to be sick. Stoicism is a namby-pamby approach to goody-two-shoes life. I simply don't hold with it."

"Verity does," Zeno replied. It would be wise to listen to your grandmother."

"She is NOT my grandmother. Verity was badgered into spirituality from circumstances beyond her control."

"And how did you manage to escape that?"

"The same way I'm going to break out of here. I have no love for condescending kindness. I must thank you for revealing a timely loophole that will permit me to say goodbye forever. Leela is welcome to take my place. Verity only needs one of us to satisfy her neediness for motherhood. So Leela can be that someone." There was a pause while Silkie addressed the me of me. "No need to thank me, sister dear," she called out.

"Remember Bilbo Baggins' travel song we used to sing?" Eeyore said to ease the tension. *'The road goes ever on and on down from the door where it began. Now the road has gone far ahead, and we must follow, if we can,'* he sang.

Eeyore laid his head on my arm. "I'm certain many slippery patches lie ahead on Silkie's open road. I just don't see why you should be the one to fortify her nerves. When it comes to 'we' it's just you and me, Leela. Silkie has Fetch and Catch, and Verity to face the difficult future she's determined to make for herself."

I covered my ears and screamed "I want to go home. Stop this bus and let me out or I will do myself an injury. I want my mother! Right now!"

Eeyore was clearly rattled.

"Illness is just plain laziness," Vera said offhandedly. Which of us she was addressing wasn't clear. My sainted sister was a wild child stinging everyone in sight. Spiritually clumsy when she wasn't being outright rude. Stinging was Silkie's forte. She knew how to zing and run.

Eeyore's eyes showed concern. "It'll pass," Vera told him. "It's only emotion sickness."

"Says you," he replied, "Like negative emotions are nothing to worry about when a young girl is about to begin a new life."

"Oh, Eeyore, Silkie is terrified," Vera said. "Verity has never seen her so out of control. Her crying jags are making Zeno angry which judging from Verity's reaction, she didn't think possible. Even Fetch and Chase are cowering in a corner out of her way."

Silkie screamed "Leela, help me!"

"Ignore her, Leela," Eeyore said. "You can't help her. You aren't *supposed* to help her. You are here, safe in Veratopia with me. But isn't it just like Silkie to ask you. The selfish creature knows full well it will unsettle your mind. It's time to come back, Goosie. Follow my voice and come back."

I took a deep breath, and the shaking stopped. "She's gone, now," I said relieved. "I'm not in her head anymore. I'm in Zeno's."

Zeno pushed Silkie from my mind and spoke through me. "Verity never saw this outburst coming but then neither did I, and I can see farther than most mortals or at least I used to. Just remember it's essential to watch Silkie's back without keeping score."

The tree canopy winked like the aperture of a camera. Individual trees snapped their branches like starting pistols. Zeno's gears ground like a herd of squealing banshees as he pulled directly into the jam of morning rush-hour traffic, and Silkie was back inside my head.

A Sasquatch ran alongside the bus, dodging oncoming bears and the occasional darting, electrically charged, fireball.

Silkie felt queasy and grabbed a handrail. "Help me, I'm going to faint."

"Report to the school nurse," the loudspeaker said.

"That'll be me," Cumulus answered from the driver's seat. "I multitask anything that requires hands-on assistance. He took a bottle of pills from his pocket that chimed like a bell when he shook them.

He broke one capsule in half. "Take this with a grain of salt," he chuckled. "No worries, you just left your sea legs back there on the corner, that's all. Corners do that to reluctant legs. As we speak, they're running behind us lickety-split, as fast as the poor wee things can.

Look out the window and see for yourself.

Take a few deep breaths and focus on a spot on the horizon until they catch you up. Once you've found it let it pull you inside. Resist nothing. It's only the first of a hundred such horizons. You'll get used to it."

"This train is for Athens," the overhead speaker announced.

I gasped for air, remembering my own conversations with the regular 61 bus. "I thought this was a school-bus," Silkie sniped."

"Correction," the voice continued. "This bookmobile is for Athens."

It was then I discovered that Master Zeno of Citium entered one's bloodstream one drop at a time before bursting into psychic flames.

A hitchhiking, slack-jawed, Big Foot stood on the left shoulder the road absentmindedly scanning a mobile phone, his hairy thumb extended. Spider webs from his elbows to his toes attested he'd had no takers for quite some time. Once the Green Man stepped from his bark matrix, bowed reverently and saluted.

Silkie tried to locate her equilibrium, and I felt my body floating in space.

"Help me, I'm going to be sick," she wailed. "I want my grandmother. Right now!"

At long last a pleasant vibration as if a cat was purring in my solar plexus indicated the first level of returning to my body – I felt like a soul waking up without an alarm clock. Eeyore nudged my hand with his nose wet with tears. "Leela, it's me. I have you. You're safe now," he said. "You're home."

Zeno's final words to Silkie fuzzed in my ears like radio static. "You'll get used to being out of body after you do a little growing up," he said. "Motion sickness is a perk of time travel."

PRIVATE TUDOR'ING

THE SCHOOL OF HARD KNOCKS

chapter 35

TOP OF HIS CLASS

*"Our plans for the future
descend from the past."*

SENECA

1554

Four-year-old Edward de Vere ran barefoot through the forest outside Hedingham Castle, sloshing through a slurry of slick leaves and mud blinded by needle-sharp rain, towards the terrifying cries of a creature in pain.

The cries changed direction and when Edward spun around to listen, he found himself in a clearing where a dozen peacocks penned in by fallen trees, shrieked like lost souls. A peacock is a formidable bird for an adult to confront, so, Edward being shorter than beak high, was justifiably alarmed. Their fanned tails brushed his face. The tip of each feather, painted with an all-seeing eye, paused to glare at him.

Edward shielded his eyes from pecking beaks with his arm and plunged through a gap in the trees. Branches whipped his face, twigs caught in his hair, and tree roots grabbed his ankles dragging him headlong into a grotto dripping with water. Edward collapsed into a miserable ball, drenched and shivering, clad only in a sodden shirt. "Mimsy," he called out. "I am here in the forest, please come!" He settled down waiting for the rescue sure to be obeyed, credulous, even at age four, that he'd uttered the word please when addressing a servant.

"What's all the fuss," Puck's voice whispered in his ear. "What's your name, child?"

"I'm lost," Edward sniffled. "I'm Lord of Hedingham Castle."

"Not yet, you're not. There are servants looking for you. If I were you, I'd fake a limp for sympathy. Mimsy is that angry she's ready to skin you alive. And, by the by, that creature you heard crying, was you. Close your eyes. Edward."

Edward woke safe in bed, feverish with Mimsy dabbing his scratches and bruises with witch hazel. She muttered *You'll be the death of me young master* under her breath as she ministered her herbs and simples. Life changed. It was a time of reckoning. Edward missed being called *a bloody little rakehell* – Mimsy's loving endearment. Sir was a cold reprimand.

Years later, Edward wandered in a strange forest consumed by memories that seemed to belong to someone else. The air was heady with the scent of awakened pine and damp earth. Rain still thundered from a grey sky as he stumbled towards home.

For the first time in his life, Edward was at odds with his surroundings – the perfect place Puck said he needed to be. He vaguely recollected writing this forest that now seemed to be writing him.

The recurring nightmare of being stalked by a woodcutter wielding an axe returned to haunt him. He tried breathing through mounting panic the way he'd been taught. Puck should have been back by now. He dropped to the forest floor clawing his way through the bracken on all fours, panting with fear. Fallen branches snapped with footsteps. An owl hooted *look out*.

"I'm here, Edward," Puck said. "You were dreaming again. Although why you choose to dream of sad times is not to be borne."

"Where are you? I can't see you."

"I'm right here. Take deep breaths."

"You promised never to go far," Edward ranted.

"I'm always close by, Edward. You dream by yourself, like everyone else."

"How long have I been here?"

"By human reckoning, this dream makes it four hundred years all told, give or take."

"What other reckoning could there be?"

Puck quickened his pace. "Your imagination. Your endless stream of stories."

"I don't imagine anymore."

"You do. You just don't care to remember the good things. Do you recall how we met? It was a fine wet day. I was drawn to you. I'd never heard laughter so completely devoid of mirth."

"I wasn't laughing. I wasn't allowed to cry."

Puck, grinned. "Yes, it was quite unnerving."

Edward studied Puck's eyes, nose, and mouth as if seeing his face for the first time.

Puck danced around him. "I'm in raptures to see you again, Edward. You haven't looked at me that way for donkey's years. I thought you might never come back."

"One thing I do recall, Puck, is that you magic a lot of impossible things."

"I'm magicking one now as we speak. I've found an afterlife better suited to us. We need to move forward. As I recall you used to be keen on your future."

"The past, being a massive confusion of sadness and regret, is never over."

"Do you remember anything of happiness?"

"You task me, Puck. Life ended with painful shadows, but I have a hankering for variation – a distraction of some kind. I refuse to follow another peacock. Let's have done with pomp and flattery."

"Birds don't flatter. It's their nature to lure a mate, nothing more."

"I used to be a human peacock."

Puck gave Edward's shoulder a friendly punch. "Oh, but you were a swan, too."

Edward brushed him away. "Stop, your blathering Puck, you tire me with your riddles."

"You are weary, master, not tired. My friend, Moonspin, says you're fit to be tied."

"I don't recall this friend of yours."

"You met him a long time ago in a sweet dream of midsummer."

"How quaint."

Puck punched Edward again, hard enough to knock him off balance. "You do Moonspin a great disservice by dismissing him so lightly. He has made mistakes to be sure but he's a fine fellow with a selfless proposition for you. He and I have been searching for meaning in all your mindless troubles if you would but listen."

Edward regained his poise and raised his arms in surrender. "Enough of your blows. I am chastened by the pain in my arm and the look on your face. I will listen.

Puck gestured with his head. "Moonspin is but a short way off through yon trees follow me and as we go, we'll spin your best memories into a splendid cloak to warm your spirit. What say you?"

"It has been chilly of late."

"It has been *frozen*, Edward. Sunlight beckons. Do you dare follow it."

Edward stopped suddenly, looking baffled. "Puck, who is Mimsy?"

Puck frowned. "Mimsy was your wet nurse, Mistress Allen, your first teacher, utterly unaware of your importance, unafraid to punish any impudent child who refused to do as they were told. She had no qualms about smacking you when you had the cheek to stick your tongue out at her."

Edward winced rubbing his sore arm. "So, you remind me."

"What you choose *not* to remember is that Mimsy encouraged you to cry."

She was never sorry for giving me a sound thrashing for being rude.

She was ruthless," Puck said. "I hope you thanked her."

Edward shrugged. "I regret, I did not. Earls rarely apologize."

"False titles need never bother you again where we're going."

"And the peacocks in my dream? They tried to peck out my eyes."

"Well, there's a clue. Did you not recognize the proud nobles and hangers-on of Queen Elizabeth's court clamouring for attention. Now then, what else do you remember?"

"The queen was a consummate actor, as well you know, Puck. Eliza had a wandering eye for the lads and lords. Speaking of which, where is that friend of yours?"

The sound of twittering birdsong grew more joyous as they crossed the borders of Hedingham and Silvany. A surge of white light serenaded them with sweet music.

"He comes, hither, Edward, with his own fair queen, the Lady Flora of Silvany."

The Lady Flora, resplendent in robes of green embroidered with wildflowers smiled and stepped forward. A crown of grapevines adorned her head. Vines entwined in her silver hair formed thick braids and the Celtic torc coiled about her neck. An offshoot meandered slowly, inching down her shoulders into a pair of clasping armbands. Another caressed her wrists descending into a slender tendril twisted around her index finger that raised its head to appraise Edward.

"You are welcome, Edward, Puck has petitioned me on your behalf, citing your dire circumstances. I too, have a troubled maligned soul under my care.

I have conspired with Puck and Moonspin that the two of you shall meet for the purpose of mutual kinship."

Moonspin, too dignified for the moment to scamper like Puck, waited, mindful to stand apart from the queen in respectful silence. As her appointed shaman of hallucinogenic dreaming, he assessed humans with his divine powers of perception. Humans were entering a new world of spiritual consciousness where mystical insights initiated by primordial plant forms that had survived for millennia, kept sacred by the descendants of jungle shamans in accord with the laws of Pan.

He bowed formally to Puck's impish wink. "What further hallucinations does this fellow require, friend Puck?"

Edward stirred as if to answer but Puck stayed his arm. "Hush, Edward, please listen to Moonspin as he has listened to *you* all your life. He is the source of your imagination."

Lady Flora ushered them to a meadow where Lucy, an ancient mother tree, grew resplendent with apples in her hair.

A comely maiden waited; eyes closed in wakeful sleep beneath Lucy's shade. A striped cat lounging on a branch above her smiled and blinked out as soon as Edward made eye contact. "Well met, stranger," Cheshire said, his sarcastic voice trailing away in the wind. "Verity, dearest. Awake, I believe your prince is here."

Lady Flora gestured towards Verity with a raised hand. "Edward, may I introduce you to my apprentice, Verity Ryder. I believe you fully appreciate the meaning of her name."

The tip of a languishing vine wound its way from the queen's finger and tapped Verity's forehead. Her eyes fluttered open.

Edward bowed, a commoner, prompted by Puck, with nothing to serve him but his newly engaged goodwill. "Madame, I am here, newly arrived. Pray show me the charms of these woods else I fear I may wander back to the unhappy wilderness from whence I came."

A SECONDARY EDUCATION

THE SCRIPTORIUM

chapter 36

THE EXCITING ACCIDENT

"Monday's child is fair of face,
Tuesday's child is full of grace.
Wednesday's child is full of woe,
Thursday's child has nowhere to go. "

Vera was busy sharpening a box of pencils, particular to lay them in a neat row reminding we students more than once that sharp orderly pencils keep one's mind sharp. It was her teaching ritual as important as afternoon tea was mine and elevenses were Pooh's.

I tried my best to look like a real writer, shuffling my notes with Eeyore when Pooh stopped by with Piglet.

"Morning, Miss Vera," Pooh said in a casual *'I wonder how things are going'* way. "Am I too late?"

Eeyore sighed deeply. "Please don't tell me our class is to be canceled on account of honey."

I paused my shuffling. "Sorry?" Vera said without looking up, "Late for what?"

"For the exciting accident," Pooh said in an *'of course I mean that'* kind of way.

Vera chuckled and continued creating the finest lead point possible. "Did you mean the *inciting* incident?"

Piglet fidgeted himself into a twitchy state. "Did you, Pooh? What does inciting mean? Will it be dangerous?"

"I mean," Pooh replied, "The smackeral of a story that excites one to go on reading."

Vera blew the shavings from her last pencil and readjusted her glasses. "A smackeral is not the true beginning of a story. A story begins with a hero called a protagonist."

Like me," Pooh interrupted, "the hunny hunter or Piglet the intrepid explorer of disturbing beasts. And the story is about a pot of hunny somewhere it can't be found except that it can, and it is?"

"Yes, but why tell the story in the first place?"

"Because I was hungry, and Piglet loves a good fright."

"Fair enough, but what's good about fear?"

"Without fear there is no hunny. Which reminds me," Piglet said. "Isn't it about time for elevenses?"

"The thing one has to understand about hunny," Pooh volunteered, "Is that it's either eaten or lost, and here's the exciting part, will it be found or will there be an *expotition* to search for more. Where is it and is it coming back? That's what I want to know. If I'm not *x'cited* I simply wander off and make up a song."

Peter and Edward emerged from the trees and Vera waved them forward to join us.

"Strangely, Pooh," Vera began, "the inciting incident, which is what you *meant* to say, is precisely where a story begins. And more often than not it's sorted out by a first thought called a premise. A protagonist thinking to themself is known as exposition that often turns into an expedition."

Piglet folded his arms which meant he was undecided. "Am I one of those pro propper tagging along people, and will we be going on an *expotition* today?"

Pooh gave him a knowing nudge. "Yes, you are and no we can't because were already having one," he whispered.

Vera set her lesson aside under a flat stone. The trees bent closer to listen. A curious bee stopped buzzing. Vera steepled her fingers and sighed. The lesson veered left. "Pooh is correct," she began. "But bear in mind, Piglet…" she stopped. "Sorry, what I *meant* to say, Piglet, is *keep* in mind, a story is a journey where a protagonist could meet a heffalump or a grand idea. Gather round everyone, the story circle is about to begin. And Piglet, do please *try* to keep still."

"He's over *x'cited*," Pooh said. "Heffalump sightings do that. But Piglet loves to be scared when we're all together." He paused and scratched his head. "Now that I think about it, so do I."

Piglet's ears turned hot pink and wiggled uncontrollably. "Will the heffalump be joining us?" he squealed, "if it isn't hungry. And is the bear in my mind, Pooh?"

"Now, this is why I don't bring hunny to story circles," Pooh said. "It's all right little Piglet. Today is a Mundy and Owl always says nothing *s'nifficant* ever happens on Mundys."

Piglet lifted his snout high and sniffed the air. "What do heffalumps smell like," he said.

"The problem is," Pooh said after a think. "Mundys turn into Toosdays, don't they Leela?"

Piglet wriggled down into an intense pink ball, trembling slightly. "Is a Toosday a happy ever after sort of day, Leela?"

And that was it. The day's lesson, as Vera later told me, that was going to be a discussion about genres and their specific promises turned into a lively debate about a pot of honey (also known as a MacGuffin) and heffalumps (an antagonistic imaginary creature that constantly unsettled Piglet's shaky peace of mind).

This in turn, led to how a story can be about several unrelated elements and still answer the initial story questions in the set-up. Where was the honey? And would there be heffalumps before teatime? Indeed, one would have to have a more thorough ponder about the details.

That left out the more important story question that needed to be written between the lines to pique a reader's curiosity enough to turn the pages until the end could be delivered in a satisfying and hopefully surprising, resolution. To set a story in motion," Vera advised, "seek the incident that caused it, and the mystery will take care of itself."

Absolem puffed excitedly. "And never forget the first business of an author is to spin a *what-if* into an *'and that's what happened'*, and have fun while doing it," he said.

And so, I learned a vital storytelling lesson about setting up at least two distinct parallel questions that inspired the reason for a story in the first place.

"Without a compelling reason, a non-story is as useful as a blue balloon without air," Eeyore reminded us. He winked at me. "Unless, of course, one has an empty *hunny* jar to keep it in."

I knew without a doubt my present assignment was to discover the inner truths haunting the protagonist I'd not yet chosen in a story I hadn't yet imagined.

"All stories are true," Vera said at last. "At least they contain the essence of truth."

I didn't like to contradict her, but books lie all the time.

"In any case," she went on. "It was my job when I was an editor to scan for snippets. Snippets are easier to believe because they *sound* true, she said. They reveal secrets and clues and pretty pictures and make one hungry for the main course. The settings can be moody. Even the happy-ever-after ones.

In the early stages of writing a novel it can be helpful to jot down snippets. I often analyzed a manuscript on the strength of a few choice snippets. I recall my early days as an editor negotiating truncated snippets."

Luckily, Pooh and Piglet had wandered off, so neither were present to ask the meaning of snippets let alone truncated ones. But what became clear to me was that Verity had deliberately left a few significant snippets out. The main course of Silkie's birth, abandonment, and subsequent supernatural adoption, and me hanging on to my kite tail story of a changeling birth were epic tales, surely worthy of several substantial snippets.

"Personally, I measure my past lives in unhappy snippets," Vera said. "Of you, Leela, I remember nothing at all. But then you have no memories of me either. Verity says sometimes people are like two lost ships sailing towards the end of the world."

"And into the dragon's mouth we go," Eeyore announced. "The last one to be consumed is a sour rhubarb pie."

"Can paradoxes be far behind," Cheshire mused aloud.

"All rhubarb pies are sour," I commented.

Vera looked up, pleased. "Ah, yes, consummation – a subject much too large to be discussed in snippets" She made a notation in her calendar. "Definitely a topic worthy of a separate class."

She wrote something in her notes and circled a date on the calendar.

She answered my puzzled expression by tapping a square on the calendar with the eraser on a freshly sharpened pencil. "We must think of something that will distract Pooh and Piglet by Friday, else we shall never finish a rough draft." She checked the position of the sun. "Goodness is that the time?"

Vera swept her hand over us dismissively like a magic wand. "Now then, I am away to my tea, dear ones," she said packing to go. "Tomorrow, we do battle with hiding in plain sight."

chapter 37

PSEUDONYMS ABOUND

"What's in a name?
That which we call a rose,
by any other name would smell as sweet."

WILLIAM SHAKESPEARE

There was a class, not so long ago, that had begun with the words *open your books to page 101* and ended with a writing lesson when Piglet arrived at the stoa agitated to the point of falling over and tugged at Vera's hem. "Please Miss, do I... that is... am I... I mean, do I have... oh bother. Am I a soda?"

Vera, used to odd questions, set Piglet on her desk between Edward and me. "Calm yourself," she said. "Now then Piglet, please slow down and start from the beginning. Leela will help you, won't you Leela? Because I have to sort out a few papers before today's lesson can begin."

Piglet sidled closer to me; his eyes wide with expectation. "Owl says we have soda names. And Pooh has three sodas. So, I was wondering."

"Owl is notorious for getting names wrong," I said. "For instance, Trespassers Will is not your grandfather's true name." I gasped and tried to cover my blunder. Piglet's eyes were round as saucers, and he hiccupped uncontrollably. "What I meant to say was, Trespassers Will is... it's a... well, it's a ... soda."

I should have been more careful. Piglet gasped for air, and I thought he might explode, which in a way he did because he burst out several questions at once. It was like the time he tried to tell

Pooh about a heffalump when he was out of breath and could only manage the sentence 'heff heff a hol a huff a hollerable'. Holl - a hoffable hellerump, and other combinations of letters to that effect.

"Am I still a piglet, Leela?"

Relief flooded through me. "You are a very *special* piglet whose name is Piglet. And Pooh was an Edward before he was a Winnie and later, he was a Winnie the Pooh and now just a Pooh. Well, not *just*. Being Pooh is quite something. Winnie the Pooh is a grand title. The same way 'Uncle' Edward, here, is the Earl of Oxford. At which time I handed the Eight Ball to Edward who was sitting back stifling a laugh and making extraordinary sounds of spluttering and coughing.

After I punched Edward's arm, he managed to splutter in somewhat teachery tones. "You see, Piglet, in my time I was called Oxford, although I signed my name Oxenford, but that is a whole other pseudonym called a portmanteau that I didn't understand fully at the time. I had several teachers who were very odd. Not at all like Miss Vera. Anyway... I was Oxford in order to..."

"To save time?" Piglet said hopefully, beginning to return to his natural shade of pale pink. It was a shortcake, wasn't it. Pooh and I often take those when we visit Owl." He scratched his ear. "I don't suppose we will be doing that any time soon if we need a proper answer to something. We will ask Leela or Miss Vera or," he faced Edward, dipping into a strange bow more like a curtsy, in front of him, "you, Sir Uncle Edward Oxford, that is, if we aren't in a hurry."

By now Edward was determined to sort Piglet out in terms he could understand. He rubbed his hands together and took a deep breath. "Almost, but not quite, my little porkchop. It was a complicated time for names and titles and much ado, that is *to-doing*' about everything."

"Oh, my word."

"Quite."

And that's how a history lesson with a little fantasy and a plate of chocolate biscuits thrown in for good measure, began.

Vera put on her *let's begin* face and addressed her class. "Well, happen we should discuss pseudonyms or non de plumes or pen names that authors sometimes hide behind or laude to become known. Names can be tricky if you're writing something dangerous or secret and you want to remain anonymous. If, for instance," she looked at Edward. "You write plays about real people and royal affairs and don't want to anger a queen."

Hyphenated names work wonders. Hence Shake-speare – simply means one who shakes a spear, also known as swords and lances, a dead, pardon the expression, giveaways for spear."

She started with me. "Leela is Lila's pseudonym or vice versa which means... never mind, we'll put a pin in that for later."

Piglet started to tremble. "I don't like pins," he said to himself. "I found a safety pin once and it wasn't safe at all. It was jolly *un*safe to put a point on it."

William Shakespeare is known as 'The Soul of the Age' which could be construed, along with 'The Bard' as pseudonym-titles," Vera went on. "Can you help me out here, Edward."

"I named Oberon's attendant in 'Midsummer Night's Dream' Robin Goodfellow," Edward volunteered, "but after a few lines, he was a goblin named Puck – a name that stuck ever since."

Piglet emitted a faint squeak only I could hear. "Stuck with a p p pin! Poor Puck."

Edward continued enthusiastically, his pseudonym being the crux of his ongoing identity dilemma. "Puck is a name that has since come to represent the essence of mischief. My own pseudonym, Shake-speare, likewise symbolises the ancient truth of the goddess Athena who carried a spear that she shook at people when she wanted to make a point. But nothing sharp, he hastened to add seeing Piglet's fear.

"Not a nasty pin."

"I won't lie to you, Piglet. A spear is sharp. So sharp that it's threatening to have one waved in one's face. The best pseudonyms are a play on words. Hidden in plain sight. And if I'm honest, Puck was a parody of me. I was a bit of a 'rakehell' to put it mildly. So, in a sense, Puck is one of *my* pseudonyms, commonly referred to these days as handles, multiple personalities abandoned in the shadows for old time's sake. Not always a simile for posterity.

In fact, it's time I told the whole truth about my pseudonyms. There were so many, I often lost track of them.

I expect you had a lot to say.

"I did, Piglet, but more to the point, I had nothing to answer for. You see, my status as an earl was without question so, I didn't worry about something as common as an identity."

"Until now," Absolem said drily.

Edward gasped and turned a color that eclipsed Piglet's pink. "You're right, Absolem. I'm mortified for my shameful display of arrogance. Please forgive me."

"And you have the Puck to make sense of it all," Puck interrupted quickly. "Your energy is returning, Edward, so a new identity might be forthcoming. Edward wrote letters and lists, Piglet."

"I wrote to express my most volatile opinions, to introduce an opinion, to dismiss other's opinions, to air all manner of good and bad opinions, to clear the air," Edward continued.

Piglet wrinkled his snout. "Phew. That's too many onions for me. No wonder the air needed cleaning. One onion goes a long way if anyone cares to ask my... *um..* my..."

"Opinion," Edward said, "which means what you think. For instance, would you prefer to look for a heffalump or read a book?"

"READ," Piglet shouted louder than he intended. "What's a *frinstance?*"

Edward looked defeated but didn't give up. "A 'for instance' is a little story that explains the what of something. Mostly, my reason for explaining things was to feel free."

Vera reclaimed the reins in case Piglet might ask what a reason was but was somehow sidetracked to Christopher Robin who was nicknamed Billy Moon by his father because he couldn't pronounce the name Milne. "One might say his nickname is a pseudonym for a pseudonym," she said, losing me entirely. "His legal name was Christopher Robin Milne known when he was a soldier as plain, Milne. Even his father had a private pseudonym: 'Blue'.

For my sake, Vera segued into Capability Brown, the pseudonym of the gifted gardener, Lancelot Brown who Greenwood plagiarized for the protagonist in his books named Capability Greene. Greenwood himself, whose real name was Frank Barren, appropriated the names of two sages with impeccable reputations so technically Seneca Aurelius Greenwood was a pseudonym."

I couldn't help but blurt out 'Shocker'. Frank Barren was hardly a name that could be compared to a lush forest.

Puns are usually a dead giveaway as in the author L.E. Fantasy – an obvious pseudonym for elephant (L. E. phant). And as a fantasy is an imagined story, one is made aware of an immediate play on words. A joke. A funny name is often but not always a 'soda' name. Do you see?"

"Like Pooh, who smells lovely? And he has a silly smile."

"Whatever made you think of that?"

Piglet smiled to make a point. "You were going to tell us about silly smiles and a poster, but you were carried away by Billy Moon."

"The Simile and posterity," Vera whispered to Edward's puzzled expression.

"Quite so, well spotted, Piglet. Although Pooh is more of a paradox."

Vera swiftly proceeded allonyms, surnames, maiden names, epitaphs, and misnomers.

It was like watching an accident in slow motion when Vera deconstructed the meaning of Madonna, my lady, signora, signorina, Mrs., Miss, Monna, mona, and the 'Mona Lisa' the anglicized nickname for the already abbreviated Monna Lisa Giocon*do*, that had in the truest sense become a title because the word Giocon*da* meant laughter in Italian and Leonardo had caught 'Lisa's' enigmatic expression somewhere between amusement and a secret.

In France, 'The Mona Lisa' was 'La Gioconde', an icon of art in her hometown of Paris – where her pseudonym was in essence 'The Smiling Woman'.

Piglet put his paws over his ears to drown out the unstoppable Vera. Peter had long since left the forest to a daydream where he flew less dizzying circles around Big Ben.

Piglet suffered as best he could through nicknames and surnames but was asleep by the time Vera said 'Gioconda' so, he missed the incorrect attributes of Tigger who as a tiger did not bounce but instead, true to a tiger's nature, pounced.

Let Vera have a go at explaining Queen Elizabeth's pseudonym 'virgin queen' I thought, rather hoping that Piglet would ask. But in the end, I didn't have to because Vera was soon reduced to burbling that too much knowledge was a dangerous thing for a piglet.

I'm not sure Piglet left any the wiser after we woke him with a cup of nursery tea.

But after Edward reassured Piglet that his pseudonym wasn't porkchop, he was happier, comforted that his grandfather was a great explorer, once again.

Edward left me a note: *I'll explain more later, why I needed more than a dozen pseudonyms to debate and criticize in secret during the pamphlet wars. I often had to debate myself to cover my tracks and defend ideas I wasn't allowed to discuss. But once I started writing as several people I couldn't stop.*

Pooh and Piglet wandered by the next day in case there were any smackerals going for a late breakfast. Pooh acted casual. "I was having a wonder," he said. "How's school in the meadow proceed-caking?"

"Leela is teacher's pet." Eeyore declared. "Hardly surprising as Peter is off with Tink, and she only has one student now that Mr. Edward has gone AWOL."

Piglet's eyes bulged round as saucers. "Has Mr. Edward turned into an owl?"

"No, Piglet. AWOL is a sort of pseudonym for going somewhere without permission."

"What's a supernim?"

"It's a nym that's extraspecial," Pooh said. "You and I are supernims."

Piglet inevitably agreed. "Yes, I quite understand," he said, breaking into a husky chorus of his favorite song: 'Sing ho for Piglet. Piglet Ho!' and hid behind a tree that wasn't there.

"Speaking of metaphors, which we weren't. I'm the apple of Lucy's eye," Cheshire bragged. He glared at Piglet. "And don't ask."

Eeyore noticed Piglet's snout trembling from holding back tears. "Edward's disappearance was foreshadowed, Piglet so you shouldn't be surprised or alarmed."

Piglet sniffed and wiped his eyes with one of his ears. "I d.. d... don't like shadows in the forest," he stuttered. "Speshly not ones that make friends disappear."

"Not forest shadows," Eeyore said. "Calm yourself, Piglet. A foreshadow is only a hint that something will happen."

Piglet promptly sat down in a tither. "Yes, and then it always does."

"Well, yes, Edward has gone away to think," Eeyore said. "We all do that don't we. Pooh does that, don't you, Pooh."

"*Proceedcakes* happen all the time, Piglet," Pooh said. "Tell him, Edward."

Piglet jumped up and down. "But Pooh, Edward isn't here."

Pooh scratched his head. "Then, I expect he won't be long."

"Has anyone else noticed that Vera is more stressed?" Puck asked. "Somewhat dithery? Like a sleepwalker? She reminds me of Verity's bag lady persona."

"Precisely," I said. "She wore a crumpled straw bonnet to class this morning. And she was limping. I had to help her to her chair."

"While we're on the subject. I'd like to point out that an apple doesn't fall far from the tree," Absolem noted. "Zeno was only saying last week ..."

"Well, then it couldn't have referred to Vera. Vera hasn't met Zeno yet. She's advancing or retreating. Either way she's not her old self. She's forgetting that '*I before e but not after c*' thing, and her commas are a disgrace."

"These days it's a toss up who will arrive at the classroom to ring the bluebell."

Puck dropped down from a low branch. "The trees have been talking amongst themselves. I overheard them and got the gist of their conversation."

"Interrupting a grove of trees discussing the identity of Shakespeare is tantamount to tree-son," Absolem said.

I attempted to inject a sense of calm. "The sprites are saying Verity's no longer spritely, and she's taken to wearing reading spectacles."

Absolem coughed inside a haze of green smoke. "Who's a spectacle?"

"You are," Cheshire said. "Your future wings have been following you everywhere trying to catch up. It's a sorry state of affairs when one's almost wings are forced to hop after their owner."

Absolem continued to worm his way over a low hanging twig.

"Oh, is *that* what those things were. I saw them out the corner of my eye. I thought I was having an hallucination."

"Dear Absolem," Cheshire said. "I do believe the transition from wriggling towards flight is making you lightheaded." His fur suddenly spiked with static electricity. "Do you know, I just noticed caterpillar is spelled with a cat followed by a pillar," he said. "What do you suppose that could mean?"

"It means you can spell," Piglet said.

Eeyore winked at me. "Piglet has anyone ever told you you're a MacGuffin?"

Piglet shuffled his feet and looked at the sky. "Loads of times. At least I *think* they did. I'm quite fond of muffins. Speshly blueberry ones."

chapter 38

VISIBILITY CLOUDY

"How do I love thee? Let me count the ways.
I love thee to the depth and breadth and height
My soul can reach, when feeling out of sight
For the ends of being and ideal grace.

I shall but love thee better after death."

Sonnets from the Portuguese
ELIZABETH BARRETT BROWNING

When I was fifty-four, I woke with the joy of a loss so great that I wrote down the date and made a big to-do about it to Eeyore. "A weight has been lifted," I said. "And I am still haunted by the strange lightness of being that has never left me. But I need rhymes and reasons."

"Ah," Eeyore said pondering. "The dreaded annus horribilus. What was that date again?"

"April twelfth, 2011. Thirteen years before we came here."

"I'll have an extra long ponder and get back to you. But I know what it was."

"Then tell me. Put me out of my misery."

"You said this date brought you joy. Don't be too hasty. Joy is worth holding onto for a while. Joy tends to dissipate."

"Do you always have to be so correct. Never mind, I know your answer is, yes."

"Please understand, some things are wise to keep under your hat

277

until you're forced to throw it into some good for nothing ring and let it play out as it should. Timing is ..."

"Yes, I know, everything."

"... worth savoring. For an epiphany to be of any value, you must discover the answer yourself. The dreaded twins of unnecessary details, rhyme and reason, are a distraction. Toys may live forever but things and people come and go."

"Are you trying to depress me."

Eeyore lifted his head and brayed with gusto. "I guess I need to try harder, then. Leela, at this moment all is well. Don't poke it with a stick. Leave well enough alone my dear, and like one of Bo Peep's sheep it will come home wagging its tail behind it. Which reminds me, my tail is close to separation point again, so if you would please be so kind as to sew it on again, I would appreciate it. Gadding about the woods with Puck is not a tail-safe 'expotition', as Piglet often reminds me. The little chap dwells on the 'door pull incident' and heffalumps in general far too much."

I pulled out my emergency sewing kit for toys with seams that I carried in my pocket and waved it at Eeyore like a magic wand. One or two stitches later, Eeyore craned his neck to check my seamstress skills and brought home his timing metaphor with a smug bow. "Now that's what I call a stitch in time saving nine. One doesn't want to be, excuse the pun, the butt of every pin-the-tail-on-the-donkey joke."

"Well, there can't be many of those."

"You wouldn't say that if you spent more time with Puck. He's not called a trickster for nothing and Tink is the very embodiment of a scheming wily fox."

"Perhaps they're a bad influence on you. Should I be worried."

"You know how rhetorical remarks make me crazy. Please think before you speak nonsense. You're no Edward Lear."

"Well, thank you for reminding me. I am aware. I guess my old confidence issues are far behind me, or you wouldn't be so blunt.

So, that's something to celebrate." I shivered off my inexplicable rush of joy and left April 12, 2011, to ruminate on itself. Much later when all was revealed, I had cause to marvel at the amazing synchronicity of the universe to astonish me.

I sat before Vera with several dogeared pages of notes about William Shakespeare, ready to be praised or at least be supported in my story outline. "First things first," Vera said. "A genre is a category. Is Shakespeare's identity the subject you want to write about? If so, we're looking at the historical fiction genre. Lucky for you, Edward's available for research right under your nose. Ask him whatever you wish. Don't be shy. Feel free to embellish although it's unlikely you'll need to. Edward's story is juicier than most. Scandals usually are. Tragedies even more so. Make your first question a good one. Don't waffle. Get to the heart of his story."

I stammered gamely, tongue-tied in front of the class. My notes read: tall, distinguished manners, formal, guarded, trimmed beard, elegant, dashing, with an alarming impression of lace garnishing John the Baptist's head on a platter.

"I eyed the starched lace ruff around Edward's neck. "Is that collar as uncomfortable as it looks?"

Edward visibly relaxed. "Excruciating. More than you can imagine," he said. "Tis the bane of Elizabethan discomfort, as if serving a tyrant wasn't bad enough."

"Did you hate her?"

For a moment, Edward blanched. "I was afraid of her. She was a queen with a cruel heart."

I thought of our heartless Queen of Hearts. "Yet you charmed your way into Elizabeth's good graces... how apropos, your *ahem*... Grace."

"That woman was graceless. And please call me Edward, we've been friends for quite some time now. She'd have eaten me alive along with the rest of her courtiers. My obvious disinterest led to her majesty seeing me as a challenge. In Elizabeth's voraciously twisted mind I was a dish worth craving and she was ever starved for attention. I learned early on to feign affection. I played into her weakness for flattery, and she turned me into a monster for power – a vain popinjay famished for praise. Thankfully academic studies were heaped on me fit to suffocate a boy who might otherwise have wandered a delightful forest dreaming of love."

"But you admired her, and she loved you."

"She admired herself. I *thought* she loved me, but she was using me. I was in love with... let's just call it a possibility and I was astute enough to submit to her whims for fear of death. Her executioner was never far from her pen itching to sign a death warrant. Elizabeth was giddy on ancestry. She inherited the fear of death more than most from her mother, Anne Boleyn. That alone made her commit atrocities of unnecessary punishment including but not limited to the crime of serving her with loyalty. She preferred to play with her victims before swallowing them whole, like a cat. No offense, Cheshire."

Cheshire bristled from out of nowhere. "None taken, I'm sure. Catching is much harder than the game of hunting."

Vera leaned forward. "Leela, circle that last remark in red pen. It is the core of Edward's story."

I was thankful when we were distracted by the screeching advice of Wonderland Alice's Queen of Hearts that burbled *off with his head* in a speech bubble floating through the woods. It popped on impact with my pen leaving a dark cloud of foul-smelling ash raining on my papers.

Edward brushed some off his sleeve with a disdainful glare.

Lucy shivered. "Ash was everywhere after the fire of 1666. I thrived, growing out of the carpet of deep grey matter – a reincarnation of new growth following the death of an acre of trees. See that your writing thrives also. There are no shortcuts. A writer must tend seedling words with care so that others will grow."

Edward chuckled, picked at a bunch of grapes while sipping a bottle of ginger beer with a kick of carbonated energy – an energy drink that never failed to surprise him by painfully assaulting the inside of his nose. "Let's make learning fun, shall we," he said. "My tutors were relentless, being equally in fear for their heads. Terror keeps one focused. All play makes Greenwood a dull boy. Confront him. Dare him. He'll turn tail and beetle off. Bullies always do sooner or later."

Edward tossed a purple grape at a passing bee that doubled back with a vengeance until Vera shooed it away. "No motive like a terrorizing one," he said. "It transformed me into the overachiever I was born to be. We writers banded together in a scriptorium, an exclusive writing class comprised of men orphaned from their pride, serving a mistress muse that made the queen seem like a nagging wind."

"You weren't a lone writer?"

"No writer is, Leela. I hope you'll come to discover that soon before your soul is eaten alive by greedy publishers."

His next comment was immediate and final. "If your book is about me, I'd rather it wasn't."

"Not even after 400 years?" I asked.

"Not even after a thousand. If you need clarification Puck will help you understand. He appointed himself my ambassador for questions I'd rather not field myself."

I found Puck hanging upside down from a low branch deep in discussion with Quizzick, a grey squirrel named for his question mark shaped tail who asked endless questions, over what appeared to be an abandoned game board set on the ground. On closer inspection I recognized it as a hide and seek gaming board with three walnut shells spaced equidistant apart in a row. One shell hid a nut. Guessing which shell offered Quizzick a juicy reward, an illusion best not played with a fairy with Puck's inborn sleight of hand. Clearly, the heated disagreement in progress was Quizzick demanding a rematch. He scampered off swearing when he saw me approach.

Puck crowed his victory without a hint of humility. "Hail Leela," he called out. "I won."

"What a shock."

"Do you happen to know the whereabouts of my good friend, Eeyore. I've searched everywhere and can only conclude he still wants to be alone."

I could not. "Sorry, Puck. I believe Eeyore is experiencing a change of heart that naturally comes from reaching the ripe old age of ninety-seven. Perhaps he's finding it difficult to relate to me as a teenager. Eeyore grows older as I grow wiser. We are at odds over my writing class. I've become obsessed and Eeyore was never keen on an unbalanced lifestyle."

"That saddens me, Leela. Eeyore is in dire need of your companionship."

"Dire? Eeyore has been my unselfish babysitter for so long, I feel dutybound to honor his need for private time as he honors my writing time. I love him."

Puck made a triple somersault in mid-air and landed on his feet, planted either side of the game board. "Then do you happen to know the whereabouts of the shell with the nut?"

I offhandedly pointed to the middle shell. "There."

Puck squinted at me. "You seem so sure of your choice."

"I'm sure because I'm not choosing one of the shells that are empty."

Puck's expression was puzzled. "May I suggest you rethink your assessment of Eeyore's hiding out of sight with the same attitude."

"I promise to reexamine Eeyore's state of mind. But I came here to ask why your master has no wish to be the subject of my first novel. His abrupt 'no' shocked me. I was all set for a *yes please, I would be honored.* I feel a bit left high and dry."

"Quite so. All I ask is that you consider that's exactly how Eeyore feels. Loving him to death is a lame excuse."

chapter 39

WE ARE A MIDDLE-GRADE
PARANORMAL ROMANCE

*"There are more things
in heaven and Earth, Horatio,
than are dreamt of in your philosophy"*

WILLIAM SHAKESPEARE

Every morning that I sit down to write my stomach churns with emptiness. "It's no use, Eeyore," I whined. "I can't do this."

Eeyore nodded knowingly. "Ah, yes the dreaded collywobbles," he said. "An upset tummy can stop a runaway bus, so it can."

I sipped a cup of lukewarm builder's tea and stared blankly at a slice of burned toast.

"Now then, imagine yourself back on the 61-bus and strain to hear the loudspeaker. It will be faint at first but stick with it. Zeno will be along when he can."

I spread the toast with butter, took a bite, and counted to ten. "I like things, but I don't *love* them. I'm no Pollyanna."

"Did you think the words would write themselves," Zeno said from out of the blue. "Writing is a natural part of you that has been sleeping. Wake up, girl. The business of writing a play was just as confusing for Edward as riding a bus during rush hour but with more bloodshed."

I nodded, my mouth full of toast.

"I venture to guess it was no happy hour tea party."

I swallowed. "Perhaps that's why I reserve that particular hour for the art of tea."

"You're far *too* particular if you ask me, Leela," Cheshire interrupted. But after receiving no thanks for his timely observation, he faded to a branch further away. "You carry on," he stage-whispered. "I'll be over here out of earshot so I can hear you properly."

Zeno's voice came in louder. "If you're truly artful, tea is a solution every time at any hour. It's your choice, Leela. But if you've decided that 4 o'clock holds some special magic then you've lost all the other times relaxation was calling and you've become smaller because of it."

"Small won the day for Wonderland Alice," I said.

"Alice won the day by accepting whatever showed up. An infinitely small door led to where she was supposed to go."

"Are you saying I need to find a bottle with a label that says drink me?"

"I'm saying, conjure the experience of feeling larger than life. Think of the sound of tea pouring into a cup. Smell the fragrance and find its door."

"I'm no Alice."

Cheshire's colors brightened. He stretched to his full length and flexed his claws one at a time. "A word of advice if I may, Leela dear. Meditate. Clear your head. You used to do that quite well as I recall." He rolled upside down to make a point. "Then write whatever shows up."

As ghosts, Peter, Edward, and I roam freely disturbing the living for a lark as part of the writing process. The three of us can't help causing optimistic optical shifts within the overall illusion of time.

Often a person will do a double take, sensing a peripheral movement in a clear line of sight. We don't set out to freak them out, but some have such low thresholds of fear they sensed our presence in a room but imagined us in the wrong corners.

We were there on a high school field trip to research how far behind the times we were. Two minutes into our mission, we knew. We needed new clothes and a new set of rude etiquette if we ever wanted to make a difference and fit in. We needed to be free of tight restricting fabrics and strict rules and voted unanimously to let the chips fall where they already lay, regarding making a difference. The teenage students were on *their* own. We were on *our* own. Some of their wayward paths crossed ours in an embarrassment of riches. But most proved spiritually poor. Compassion barely moves the needle in the 21st century unless a violent board game is involved.

Large breeds of dogs and cars ruled in 2024 the way falcons and horses had in Edward's time. But bullying was still the sport of arrogant princes. If children were cruel, and they were, sullen teenagers were evil. They used handheld devices as servants, and the 61-bus driver who delivered us to the local high school never stood a chance of enforcing the rules of bus etiquette.

Edward pointed out, a tad too flippantly, that he knew from experience that accidental murder was ruled as suicide if a nobleman's sword was in play. Rules changed but one-upmanship had not.

It was the word, or rather the *concept* of 'romance', that blew entitled boys out of the water. Chivalry was so dead it was an embarrassment to even hope for a glimmer of resuscitation.

We never once crossed paths with a modern ghost other than once, in the library when Nate Sloane tailed us through the stacks and escorted us to the exit. He clearly regarded us as some form of rival. I imagined him calling from the ether when he slammed the door violently behind us. "Don't let the library doors hit you on the way out."

Edward is the only true ghost between us. But all three of us are in search of reincarnation. Peter's literary persona is transforming bodily into flesh. And I'm exploring the gift of second childhood, in spirit form, under the supervision of a ghost within an enchanted forest who has finally come to terms with unbearable guilt.

chapter 40

I AM A NEW ADULT

"You've been made by nature
for the purpose of working with others."

MARCUS AURELIUS

This I declare to be my highest truth... I can only be a 'new adult' after 'I've been a new teenager.

To this end, Peter, Edward, and I are a trilogy – three stories linked together intent on moving on by moving backwards. We formed our clique and a plan by accidental design in the cabin at half past teatime three weeks ago. But the location was happenstance. It came down to camaraderie of the moment. And since the hands of the clock had pointed to mid-afternoon, chocolate cake and tea came to mind.

That, and the cabin being in plain sight of the classroom, decided our destination. We meandered, and by that, I mean we gravitated towards it like hypnotized automatons.

But the cabin was not our true meeting place.

While I put the kettle on, Peter set out the pastries, and Edward suggested we synchronize our ages to better relate to each other for an intellectual debate. He said he was overdue. Would we oblige? We would.

Despite Edward becoming the 17th Earl of Oxford at twelve years old, his first age of choice was twenty-two, the pivotal year he made a questionable decision that not only changed history, but one that led him to a life of devastating servitude.

But after a brief discussion we settled on age seventeen as being mutually beneficial, since I had recently turned seventeen. And so it was that our teenage years became our true meeting of the minds place – a come-as-you-were tea party, and since then we have flowed into a single-minded river of something Edward calls *confidens triumphus.*

I remember reaching over and squeezing Edward's hand after he announced it. "And I feel *confident* in seconding that, Edward because I bow to your knowledge of Latin," I said. "It makes me feel smarter. And 'tri' clearly represents the three of us."

"It means positive thinking that leads to victory," Edward said a tad dismissively. "Better to bow down to my knowledge of Latin. But let us speak plainly. In my time I created many English words we can now share."

"I feel smarter already," I said mid-smile, but a wave of nausea hit me without warning.

A shadow crept across the sun. Edward wasn't listening. He'd shut down. He withdrew, trembling violently and slumped into a chair, babbling incoherently to someone who wasn't there.

"They came as words will on the tail of a muse," he said to himself. He looked into my eyes without seeing me – a creature in pain. "There came a time I couldn't have stopped them if I tried." Just as suddenly, the sun came out. Edward took a deep breath. "Don't mind me," he said. "I get maudlin when I least expect it. It comes and goes. No worries."

I patted Edward's cheek and did what I always did when I got scared. I made a fresh pot of tea.

Peter and I have Edward's creative genius to thank for the mind-blowing confessional that followed because showing up for traditional tea and cakes on a stifling Indian Summer Wednesday jumpstarted a stunning new perspective on life.

There was Edward, 40-ish, in effeminate Elizabethan costume, clearly red-faced and uncomfortable in a starched lace collar, a black velvet cap bejewelled with pearls and feathers, and tight silk hose; twelve year old Peter, puttered about the kitchen barefoot in short green pants; and me in floppy house-frau bedroom slippers and an old lady's shapeless dress that had morphed into the size fitting, but not *befitting*, a flirtatious girl.

Our aha moment called for a concerted pledge to grow up or out of whatever held us back from reincarnation. I taught them how to pinky-swear, and we were on.

All we had to do was show up and we'd already done that. The hard part was over. Recreation was in the air. After that, all that mattered was a concerted triple shift in age and attitude.

Reincarnation can be physical, emotional, theoretical, or a mindset. In the end it took commonsense and vanity as much as bravery or sheer drive to arrive at a grand plan, although courage and willpower were definitely factors. It was *'an all for one and one for all'* thing – a *'now or never'* thing. It was a spiritual *'conscious alignment to the universe'* thing. And we three were on board with bells on. Everything old is new again!

As soon as I declared myself seventeen, I felt like a great lady who owned the world. Peter felt free, growing up without the constant pressure of needy boys pestering him for direction. "I can lead my life on my own terms," he crowed. "Tink was right. She wanted me to be independent."

Edward was more practical. "I could teach you two swordsmanship," he said. "But that might induce you to act as mindlessly as the woodcutter and we don't need that. Falconry would be my choice of a life well spent if I had to do it over again. Working with nature is the *summus exemplare* of Veratopia."

Peter chuckled. "Of course it is, everyone knows *that*."

"The highest ideal," Edward said in answer to my raised eyebrows. "Without violence."

Neither of us had intentions of delving deep into the realms of death-defying, life affirming changes. As teenagers, we three had been deeply aligned to growing up the hard way on battlefields of our own making. Fighting for survival had backfired. Surrender was similarly pointless. Our worst enemies, simultaneously real and imagined, were the reasons we failed to beat the systems based on fear, cruelty, and greed. Blaming one's parentage or in Edward's case, citing it as an entitlement caused no end of suffering.

I reminded them of Verity's policy. "One is born as they are," she always said, "rich or poor, clever or dimwitted, exactly where they belonged." Thinking otherwise, or in my case 'Otherwhere', pretty much guaranteed chaos.

Our plan called for leadership and so, we agreed that we would take turns at the helm. Peter had ruled an island of lost boys with a newly attached shadow and a willpower of iron; I had commandeered a hideaway to withstand the terrors of loneliness, and Edward, had been the captain of a surprise military attack, the only one of us who had experienced physical combat.

A call to arms, Edward called it, where less is more. Where had I heard *that* little gem before. I kept silent about my mother's less than positive observations regarding my personality.

Edward continued. "It's the strategy of yielding rather than fighting."

"Quite," Peter replied. "I'd prefer to avoid pirates if you don't mind."

"Hear hear, Edward said. "I experienced an alternative form of combat as the art of alchemy and numerology courtesy of John Dee, the queen's 'don't argue with me' astrologer who acted as if he was personally acquainted with God." In the end it fanned the queen's natural affinity for violence into a divine right.

Peter and I were in transitional modes, respectively from Neverland and Otherwhere to Veratopia. Both of us had been brought up under the grim shadow of unworthiness. Edward was brought up with an overabundance of self-worth. Quicksand thinking would never work.

After that, it was all about three musketeers without swords facing a modern world of busses and traffic signals. Crossing roads could have no ill effects of us being injured but it turned out we were far more vulnerable from mental injuries sustained watching local teenagers act as if they owned the world. We were jealous of their power and angry at their lack of appreciating it.

That's why, when it was my turn to lead, I took my 'moving buddies' to the local high school on the number 61-bus.

In short order we three changed our appearance and levels of comfort. From then on, we dressed in faded blue jeans, trendy T-shirts, and sneakers. It was sad we were invisible because we looked rather natty, but most of all we grew younger and happier. Limbo felt better.

Surprisingly, Edward chose to wear a T-shirt featuring an image of the infamous 'Droughsout portrait'. "Not to celebrate it," he said "but to proclaim my disgust with an act so callously vulgar from my 'nothing-is-truer-than-the-truth' kinsmen and a brotherhood of playwrights who professed loving friendship for me. They collectively banded together to invalidate my very existence.

I despise the nagging disquiet of any who sanctioned this false icon, or those who said nothing," he said puffing out his chest to the portrait's full advantage. "They were cowards. But when it came to Lord Burghley, I have to admit, I'd have been better off if I'd cowered once in a while."

The following day, Edward arrived in class looking extra dapper in a trendy doublet that eclipsed the quilted nylon vests of twenty-first century fashion that had come full circle. Boys in 2024 still favored the romantic buccaneer look of pirates and starship pilots due to

Star Wars, dragons and dungeons, and hobbits. For this reason, Edward's doublet, accentuated his T-shirt emblazoned with a faux caricature of Shakespeare, and caused Alice to give a shrill wolf whistle that sent Puck running for cover.

Minus thirty years of grief, a scratchy starched collar and cuffs, and with shoulder-length hair, Edward was the image of a romantic swashbuckler. An ideal actor who'd taken fencing lessons and shed the buffoonery of clown pants and effeminate slippers with silver buckles.

And therein lies the problem with the term romantic. On one hand it designates an intimate human love match and on the other, an idealized version of history under a fairy glamour, made more desirable minus the stink of realities, especially rotten teeth, and yellow plague-pocked skin.

Edward appeared in our next class, down in the mouth, but looking handsome as a Cinderella prince. Vera's lesson, a follow up to killing one's literary darlings, began with a summary reminding us that the arts of crafting evocative settings, punchy dialogue, and showing instead of telling can best evoke an effective mood without killing it with purple prose. "Syrup is best served occasionally in small doses."

I hastened my opinion that purple prose was not always poison and not necessarily a darling worth killing. Vera countered with "killing your darlings is an act of literary kindness."

Edward spoke defensively without putting up his hand. "Poetry relies on *keeping* one's darlings."

A heated debate followed. "Writers develop a style that sometimes relies on savoring the finer arts of purple prose," I said for Edward's benefit. "Whereas writing a history play of political intrigue requires dramatic effects of murder and chaos. Killing one's characters may be necessary to make a creative point."

"I will give you that narration is essentially telling," Vera admitted. "But it can do much more. It can be deeper than facts. It can evoke questions, hint, explain, and create tension."

Peter, our self-elected master of cheek, spoke out. "I sense Edward wants to *tell* us a chocolate covered story. Perhaps even an embarrassing confession." He winked at Edward. "The Elizabethan court was literally a *hot bed* of secrets. I've gotten to know Edward well since we became 'teenage brothers' and I know he needs to purge a few troubling memories and kill at least one serious darling."

Edward wasted no time. "Peter is right. I do have a story to tell."

Vera looked delighted. "By all means, Edward, we are here in Veratopia to prepare ourselves for future lives." She turned her smile on me. "Wherever they may be." At that, she produced a packet of chocolate buttons from her schoolbag and handed them around like badges of approval. "Leela's writing class is meant to inspire everyone. Secrets may be interesting but, in our situation, as actual ghosts or ghosts of our former selves, desirous of reincarnation, many emotional obstacles delay us from that goal. One of them is harbouring secrets."

Edward proceeded to unburden himself in an emotional command performance:

"From a distance, Queen Elizabeth was a handsome middle-aged woman when I was seventeen, but much of her glamour was an overabundance of red wigs and voluminous collars the size of a startled peacock's tail. I won't lie that I wasn't impressed by her. She was an audacious caricature. I couldn't take my eyes off her. No-one else dared to. There was a lot she wanted everyone to see. Her insatiable appetite for attention sucked up all the greed in the room.

But then, she was, by reputation, larger than life. I was told of her legendary academic accomplishments when I was four. Indeed, they were meant to encourage my own exhaustive studies. Perhaps they did because in a few years I developed an inbred passion for words from rare translations of ancient texts available to me.

I became an orphan and an earl the same day. I was twelve when I entered Burghley House as William Cecil's ward.

Initially, I confused ward with word and cared nothing for her majesty's favors. When I was seventeen, I attended Gray's Inn to study law."

"That isn't a confession," I said.

Edward sighed and continued. "It's an observation. My confession is that I succumbed to the queen's powers of seduction when I was mature enough to become a lawyer. She had a way of fixing her eyes on me that ferreted out my very soul until I was dizzy under her spell. Her profound ugliness was strangely compelling. I was under the spell of my own vanity. The most powerful spell of all for an untried ego such as mine.

The queen's powers of persuasion were unrivaled at court, and she found pleasure in confusing me. She invited me to sit beside her, so our thighs touched, fondling my knees until I was quite lightheaded. I hasten to add this reflected the giddy urges of puberty. I was as easily aroused from an exposed ankle or a flash of girlish eyelashes.

In hindsight, I was young enough not to know how to dismiss urges but old enough to want to keep them as a prized possession no-one else had. Please understand, it wasn't all vanity. My body was coming alive. The court was filled with lovely lasses my age who flirted openly with me until the queen made it clear there were negative consequences should I respond in kind.

I discovered later that I was not particularly special. I was simply one of a hundred of the queen's sporting amusements. The fact that I showed no sexual interest in her inadvertently raised me to the topmost notch on her bedpost. I'd come face to face with irony – a dangerous bedfellow.

I had been too young to realize playing with a fiery redheaded monarch was over the top dangerous. But the court was also a school, and by emulating a few obvious flamboyant rules of courtship evident all around me, I discovered my natural affinity for acting.

As with fencing and jousting, I played to win. I was in love with besting the best. The most admired. The smartest. Centerstage taking a bow. The brightest star of the sky.

Sadly, as such inclinations often are, acting was my undoing before it became the making of me.

Surprisingly, Elizabeth's interest in me turned from entertainment to lust and a passionate obsession for being the first to 'tame' me.

Play acting was a powerful drug that sparked a game with a powerful lady who appeared to favor me over the suitors vying for her hand. But my talent for mimicking emotions served me ill. I won without competing.

But I had *wanted* to lose. A new sensation for me. I could do nothing but play out Elizabeth's folly to its conclusion and hope for a distraction that a more wholesome boy would arrive to displace me.

Despite my noble rank, Elizabeth had no intention of sharing her power with anyone, let alone a child. She was playacting too. Her starring role was the Virgin Mary. And play it she did, burying her last remnant of humility in the part.

I continued to churn out enchanting songs and love poems stories that held her in raptures. I had Eliza in the palm of my hand. It was too easy. And by the time I realized being top dog was something I didn't want; it was too late. Girls my age avoided me. It never occurred to me they did so out of fear."

Peter, impressed as all get out, clapped enthusiastically.

But I sensed there was more Edward wasn't telling us. Pleasing everyone eventually backfires.

Edward and I were becoming more telepathic because I felt his energy retreat as he sighed inwardly with relief. *Something is terribly wrong*, I thought. *Put your money where your mouth is, Edward. So much for nothing's truer than truth. Help me understand.*

He heard me. Edward's involuntary facial tics couldn't lie.

I leaned forward and took both of Edward's hands in mine. "What is it that's really holding you back from reincarnation, Edward, we're all friends here. We're the three musketeers, remember? Complete this sentence, please. When I was seventeen I …"

Edward's eyes blinked erratically but they stayed fixed on mine. "When I was seventeen, I killed a man," he said.

After a moment of reflection, Edward released his supressed emotions with unqualified courage. "When I said my words came on the tail of a muse, I meant to say a royal muse with a sting in its tail! Did I say, *it*? I meant '*her*'. Did you hear me say, *sting*? I meant *poison*. Did I say I came over maudlin from time-to-time? I meant to say every hour."

Peter and I linked arms with Edward. Peter spoke first. "A gauntlet was dropped. And who better than a talented nobleman like yourself to pick it up and honor a suggestion to serve your country."

"Elizabeth never *ever* suggested anything," Edward said, "but when she wanted something she had a way of disguising her commands with flirtation and flattery. I believed her. How could I not. She was a superb actress."

I finally understood. "Are you familiar with the saying in for a penny, in for a pound," I said.

Edward's relief was tangible. I hoped he would break down and cry, but he needed to suffer. I heard his tortured thoughts. He had something unbelievably terrible to confess. He would play it out and I would wait to forgive him.

"Leela, you've grasped the situation perfectly. As the highest-ranking earl of the land, pennies were beneath me. I was surrounded by constant grovelling, and in the face of unctuous servility, I failed to recognize myself as prey. The trap closed sweetly like a golden cage.

The queen stressed it was my god given duty to use my literary abilities to raise England from what was rapidly becoming a cultural laughingstock. Of course, she didn't paint her request quite so succinctly. Elizabeth used flattery and her special promise to keep me enslaved.

England's reputation, rapidly degrading into farce, was correctly branded as a notoriously unstable realm plagued by impulsive rulers with a thirsty axe culminating in a fecklessly vain queen, thinly disguised as a saint with a preposterous claim of divine virginity.

Thin rumors of power based on frivolous palace intrigue and hearsay receded into – a Tudor inspired heresy in a bloodthirsty police state of selfish errors overseen by a select star chamber of greedy powermongers and a spy network too corrupt to save itself. I accepted, naiveté being my youthful specialty.

"I had something to win. Something to prove. Something too absurdly thrilling to ignore. From then on, writing became the driving force of my existence. I was drunk with power.

The queen, a spendthrift at best, bequeathed me an uncharacteristically generous settlement of a thousand pounds a year for life.

I eventually controlled a scriptorium of the best writers I could find and bade them sing Elizabeth's praises that would heal her withering legacy resting as it did on the laurels of copycat literacy, into an historic triumph to rival, nay eclipse, Italy, France, and the philosophers of ancient Greece.

All were achieved through blind devotion, gruelling painstaking work on the queen's blood money. Irony advanced from lust to a life of creative purpose. 'Pride goeth before a fall' should be added to the de Vere coat of arms."

That's when Edward broke and fell into my arms, sobbing. I could barely make out his words.

"I was so close, everything in my grasp for a stupid single heartbeat, rebuffed instantly and completely without seeing the victory in Elizabeth's eyes. And later, to my everlasting shame, my exposed victory was snuffed out – a human candle extinguished by arrogance.

I was insane but I hadn't yet written the line *Take physic, pomp!*

But the sad thing is, the full extent of Elizabeth's transparency didn't completely sink in until the Essex rebellion. I had my suspicions, but it had taken thirty years to advance from a starstruck wunderkind to a village idiot. I loathed myself. I welcomed my death by humiliation that quickly followed. I am thankful Puck was there at the end."

When the dust finally cleared, I'm proud to say Edward had stepped out of fancy dress – a pauper in prince's clothing.

chapter 41

SPRITEWOOD

Come to the edge, he said.
We can't, we're afraid!
Come to the edge.
We can't, we'll fall!
Come to the edge.
And so they came
And he pushed them
And they flew.

CHRISTOPHER LOGUE

'Spritewood' began as a story spark that burst into flame, burning through pages like wildfire.

My fire on paper was a fiery story of a displaced tree sprite named Chlora whose job was to care for the eggs and fledglings in her home tree's nests. Chlora was rendered homeless in the line of duty by a raging forest fire until an unlikely friend arrived as a helpmate to enable her to reclaim her identity, find a new home, and move on to live her best life after learning the greater lesson of trust.

"*Hmmm*," Eeyore mused. "Where have I heard *that* story before?"

"Because you noodle, it's about me. *I'm* Chlora."

"And who am I again?"

"You are Wick the dog."

Eeyore paused to reflect. "I see. Am I a wonder dog? A heroic noble beast? A creature who saves the day until Chlora faces her new best life without training wheels? Coz, if I'm not, I refuse to be in it. For one thing it would mean me taking an enormous step down. A donkey reduced to a tree sprite is quite a drop in status. Heroism isn't the same with two legs – not quite as *surefooted* as a creature with four, if you know what I mean."

"Tree sprites make up for stability in agility," I said.

"True, I'll give them that," Eeyore said. "But as Absolem says there's a certain mental agility required for standing firm. Upright being the moral of our, or any, positive story. So, please write on. I always said I would edit your first Edward book. I expect there's no harm in writing two books."

"A book about Edward requires his approval."

"That may be true but *hearing* his story also requires trust and exceptionally sensitive ears."

"And," Cheshire volunteered, "maybe editing what Puck says with a ton of salt. He tends to elaborate."

Absolem's voice arrived without his form. "Leela, you cut me deeply," he said from the ether. "I am aware tricksters rely on sleights of hand as well as words. I duly informed Eeyore when I first met the Puckster."

Cheshire's words manifested alongside Absolem's. "Absolem wants to keep Puck honest."

"Right," I said, "because Absolem never varnishes the truth for effect or applause."

Eeyore coughed knowingly. "My dear Leela, if a story lacks effect and no-one applauses one may as well be illiterate."

Cheshire popped in like a fully inflated balloon. "Curiosity happens to be one of my fields of expertise," he said. "Nosey Parker is a child. An adorable monkey but when has an adorable child ever solved a murder."

"I take it you have."

Cheshire's stripes flashed on and off. "I am solving one as we speak. I've gathered the evidence and when the timing is right, I will reveal all." He yowled to make his point.

"I'm all ears."

"Oh, donkey," Cheshire said. "That's not *all* you are, but that's another story." He winked out of sight with a real wink.

Lucy giggled. "That loveable scamp. Cheshire is more fun than a barrel of monkeys... more than a dozen tree sprites."

This is how my writing happens. I wait in silence until the voice of Chlora arrives, and then I scribble down what she says in a fever without stopping for punctuation. Vera calls it entering the literary slipstream, but it feels more like riding rapids. Vera said it would come but until I experienced it firsthand, I hadn't believed it possible. I have a story in my head and it's telling me to pay attention. She warned me against run on sentences but when an excited tree sprite demands one's attention one doesn't stop for commas and line breaks, especially if the aforementioned tree-sprite is as wise as a monkey. I am pleased to report that Chlora and I get along like a house on fire.

Excerpt from 'SPRITEWOOD' by Leela Swann
'A Fiery Start' for young readers

Snowflakes gathered clouds of woodsmoke into slush that hissed the glowing embers into a harmless grey fizzle. The lack of wind and a natural break in the trees broke the flames progress but not before my treehouse was lost.

I mourned the loss of the baby birds I was unable to save and returned to my friend Rufus's rabbit warren where many recued fledglings had been given refuge.

After racing off to calm the ruffled feathers of several anxious bird parents, it was time to find myself a bed for the night. Although the number of rabbits and rabbit children had increased in the last few hours, somehow Rufus made room for me. Rabbits of every size filled alcoves and corners in piles of cozy fur. I snuggled into one using an entire family as pillows and a blanket.

They were content to shift and accommodate me but as I was a third the size of the smallest rabbit I fit in quite well.

Three medium sized rabbits had linked together in a circle of heads-to-tails forming a wreath-like nest. The rescued baby birds were cuddled together inside. It would be my job to find them homes and reunite them with their parents. But for now, I closed my eyes and dreamed of green foliage.

Reforesting takes time. I would have to seek further afield to resettle them.

As it happened, the very next day, I fell into an unlikely companionship with a sleek black and white Dalmatian of the dog persuasion. I'd been chasing pesky firebrands without looking where I was going, putting out the sparks they were feeding to the dying embers when a terrifying woof stopped me cold.

A large black nose had seen the firebrands and was snuffling them senseless. Wick's nose had led him off the beaten track when he caught sent of a fox guarding her burrow of kits. She stood her ground and bared her teeth which surprised Wick into a hasty retreat. He was lost and I was numb from shock, so we made a perfect pair.

He offered me a ride on his back, and I accepted. It made my job easier to travel the long distances between devastation and freedom. In return I showed him an abandoned cache of nuts and berries.

Did I mention that I'm deathly afraid of dogs.

chapter 42

MOTHER'S DAY BLUES

"Beyond a wholesome discipline,
be gentle with yourself.
You are a child of the universe
no less than the trees and the stars;
you have a right to be here."

MAX EHRMANN

Vera built a campfire at midday for the weekly story circle. The forest classroom was relatively quiet after a squabble of *'my childhood was worse than your childhood'* thought instigated by Peter Pan that quickly escalated to a lively *'my mother was worse than your mother'* debate. I could have easily won had I not been concentrating on writing an opening sentence.

First sentences are difficult to begin with and nigh impossible to hear during a kafuffle, so, when Edward showed up with Puck in tow, I put the cap on my pen and took a break.

Eeyore tossed his head. "Welcome, Uncle Edward," he called out.

"Relative being the operative word," Absolem mused.

Cheshire couldn't help but be drawn into so noteworthy a subject. "Not much of a mystery regarding monkeys, considering their attention span," he said. "It's pretty much a 'monkey see; monkey do' situation, and there's an end to it."

The forest went quiet as we all stared up at him, preening on a low branch.

Cheshire's stripes blushed. "Sorry, did I wander off topic? I put it down to too much monkey business of late. I can barely hear myself think, let alone believe anything I hear anymore. Monkey mind is relentless."

Vera's mind drifted after startling at the word relentless, Parker had traced in the dirt.

I had been deep in my blocked writing assignment as snippets of conversation filtered down onto my paper from a private discussion meant to be unobtrusive. Each point of view raised the stakes and their voices.

It had begun, simply enough when Peter casually mentioned how he'd once been a lost boy and why he might be destined to remain one. "My mother was strict, too," Peter Rabbit, added. "Where I lived it was commonplace for one's siblings to be eaten. Mrs. MacGregor baked my father into a pie, once. I've had nightmares ever since. Thumper had the same problem with his family. Real forests aren't like this one. They're dangerous. More dangerous than a hundred woodcutters."

It was meant to be a casual discussion – a meeting of minds. One confused angry mind and several sleepy placeholders conversing like speed chess.

'Having no mother is better than a terrible one.'

'Having no mother is depressing.'

'Growing up twice is dashed awkward. Far worse than depression.'

'Growing up twice without a mother is just plain careless.'

'Careless is not a pseudonym for Cheerless.'

'And cheerless is not a pseudonym for carefree.'

Eeyore called the discussion, a meeting of the mindless rethinking the mind.

Peter harped on about lost boys being motherless until a spasm of pain crossed Vera's face. She stood suddenly. "Sometimes it works the other way around. There are times losing a child has nothing to do with being careless or distracted or witless or even absentminded. Sometimes a child dies."

Peter blushed. "Sorry, I forgot. I almost lost Tink that way, once."

"Just be aware there are little rabbits with long ears within hearing," Vera said, "who don't need to be bothered about pies."

Peter stood up defiantly, legs apart with his arms crossed. "Tink came back to life from the power of children believing in fairies. I wasn't impressed. I trained them during years of pantomimes. Bullied them every Christmas. Leela can begin her story on a slate wiped clean of anger and grief, but it may be too late for me."

Absolem interrupted with a dream of his own. "I've had a premonition, if you will, that when I die, I will fly off to Neverland on diaphanous blue wings and tell Peter Pan, who still maintains a presence there, unequivocally, I might add, *not* related to the Green Man, never to judge a mother by his fears. There's a reason Mr. Barrie named it *Never*land. But why oh why do I waste my puff."

Peter looked incredulous at Absolem. "What are you talking about. I'm Peter Pan! I live here now. You won't find me in a book anymore."

"I thought Wendy became your mother," Cheshire said to change the subject.

"That was a game to make the littluns feel better," Peter said. "Wendy could *never* have been a mother to the lost boys. She was a lost girl."

"Exactly," Absolem said, a tad put out. "That was the *reason* Mr. Barrie named it *never* land. Never a dry eye in the house. Pathos unplugged."

I'd drifted into musing about the word never for ten minutes and much to my surprise I blurted out "You don't hear me blubbing about never having a father."

Cheshire disappeared like a popped balloon.

"Nonsense, child," Absolem said without missing a beat. "Who do you think gave you the book when you were five?"

"I found it under my pillow."

Absolem took a long inhale of smoke. "Fancy," he said. He must have been an elf. Elves do all sorts of odd jobs at night in fairy tales."

"Absolem hold your tongue," Cheshire chided, stern as a headmaster.

"Then on the exhale, Absolem closed his eyes dreamily. "In that case, Leela, I believe you'd best thank Peter, here for your first flying lesson. You look puzzled my dear."

"Because I don't understand."

"Peter made sure you kept all your memories. One of which was missing your father."

Eeyore pushed in. "Yes, Peter, I never *did* thank you for flying Leela so high above the River Styx that her memories remained untouched. I'd wanted to give her a lovely blank slate."

"I was helping her," Peter said pouting. "I'd overheard Leela telling Absolem that she'd jumped the broom. And we all know what *that* means."

Eeyore kicked out his back legs. "It means, thanks to your meddling, Leela hasn't been able to burn the bridges necessary for her to fly free. Negotiating transitions from the Shadowland is tricky business.

I can't tell you how many times I've had to pick up the pieces at the eleventh hour to prevent the nightmares I sensed on her horizon. It has given me a few of my own, I can tell you. But I've said enough. What was done is done. Much bigger mistakes have been made in Veratopia and I've already said too much." He shook his shaggy head. "Now, who's for cake. I don't like being reminded what a gloomy Gus I used to be in my own past life."

Christopher Robin who'd arrived during the heat of the argument, seated himself, and helped himself to a piece of sponge cake. Suddenly, all eyes greeted him with an 'at last someone is here who can resolve this argument', expression. Christopher squirmed uneasily.

"How about *your* mother, Christopher," Cheshire said, slyly. Wasn't she rather *special*?"

Pooh answered for him. "I only saw Mrs. Moon... I mean Mrs. Milne, once or twice, but I don't remember her," he said. "Christopher couldn't pronounce the name Milne, so he called himself Billy Moon."

Cheshire covered his eyes with his tail and scoffed. "Billy? How common."

"I believe it's short for William," Pooh replied. "But in Christopher's case it wasn't." Then, "Oh dear oh dear. Oh, bother and nonsense."

Christopher's face turned scarlet. He checked his watch. "Goodness," he said. "Is that the time" and beetled away without touching his cake.

"What's got into him," I said.

"It certainly wasn't cake," Cheshire replied cattily.

"I'll eat it, shall I," Piglet, offered. "I've only had three slices."

Eeyore, somewhat recovered, coughed for attention. "Listen up the lot of you, mothers don't always know what's best. Christopher's mother was an awfully odd duck. Christopher had a playmate named Alice (a different one than ours). And it so happened that Mrs. Milne came to think of her as the daughter she never had and fixated on Alice and Christopher Robin growing up and getting married."

A knowing murmur of *ooooh* swept through the animals not understanding a word.

"But it was much worse than that," Eeyore said. "After Christopher grew up and married someone else, his mother disowned him outright. Even on her deathbed she refused to see him. And Christopher carried a grudge against his father for turning him into an iconic boy who was never allowed to grow up. He was constantly ribbed and bullied at school for his smock, girly hairstyle, and, of course, his namby-pamby Mary Jane shoes. Growing up or not is a tricky business as Leela will attest."

Eeyore shivered. "Strangely, all things considered, Christopher's desire to burn his past along with his toys meant I came perilously close to the flames once, but I was saved by a stranger."

"I know this one," Piglet squeaked. "Tell them, Eeyore."

"As a disturbed grown-up, Christopher purchased a bookshop that, due to him being its famous owner, couldn't help but become a magnet for parents expecting him to be the childhood hero they remembered. Christopher was mercilessly hounded by their endless memories how he featured in their childhoods, constantly being measured against a full-grown man and found wanting. Christopher Robin had changed. Pooh had not." He turned to Pooh. "And, happily, you never will."

"Like I said, *never*-land," Absolem sent in an echo of smoke rings linked together in a chain.

Cheshire yawned. "Listen to *you* lot, chattering like monkeys over nothing."

Eeyore nodded solemnly. "Quite right, Cheshire, I thank my lucky stars we were rescued by a stranger who donated the rest of us, minus Roo, to the New York Public Library where our doppelgangers, if you will, remain to this day displayed dustless under glass, for everyone to ogle."

Verity poked the campfire until new flames shot up and stirred up Eeyore's memories. "Poor Kanga was always a little beside herself, but she would have been devastated had she realized Roo was missing. It was lucky Piglet was afraid of speaking up in those days because near-sighted Kanga took him for Roo. It was 1930 as I recall."

Vera warmed her hands. "The woodcutter was doing his worst in Veratopia at that time. The trees were, quite rightly, afraid of him, and Verity was distracted as Lady Flora's apprentice.

After a long awkward silence, Piglet felt brave enough to continue where he'd been rehearsing what he planned to say earlier in a much taller voice. "Mr. Edward. I've been wanting... I mean *waiting* to tell you..."

"Come to think of it," Pooh interrupted, "Once upon a time *my* name was Edward. I don't know why."

"It was taller," Cheshire remarked looking pained. "Tell us what happened next, Pooh."

Pooh scratched his ears. "Funny thing about not remembering is that one goes on not remembering long after something happened, they can't remember."

"Let me be of assistance," Absolem said gently. "Toys are named several times until a child is satisfied."

Eeyore nodded in agreement. "Tis so, right enough, Pooh. Mr. Milne, a stickler for upper class attention, named you, Edward, because it was a fine upstanding name, grand enough to distinguish a commonly manufactured teddy bear for greatness."

"Manufactured?"

Eeyore sighed. "Once upon a time, in a grand shop named Harrods, there were shelves filled with potential Edwards and Poohs. You were a popular toy at Christmas, Pooh. And as a serious journalist, Mr. Milne was keen that the seemingly frivolous children's book he was writing outside his professional career, should have panache, otherwise known as credibility or charm depending on your preference. He was marketing a book not knowing a toy bear would catapult him to the highest realm of literary fame. Indeed, years later he was rather depressed about the whole thing. But Edward Bear couldn't compete with Winnie the Pooh. Pooh wasn't the least bit hoity-toity but it worked."

Piglet stood up again in case it was his time to be heard. "Well, I think Pooh is wonderfully hoity. And I would think it a lot more if I knew what hoity meant."

"As for Winnie," Cheshire continued. "It was borrowed."

"We *were* in a book, Pooh," Piglet said. "I remember."

Pooh looked thoughtful. "I'd like to be in a book with '*pancakes*'."

"Panache," Eeyore corrected. "Dear me, I didn't mean to cause a commotion."

"You are several books," I said to Piglet, trying to get back to my own. "But here's something to consider before I dismiss you all and close the door for some peace and quiet."

"There are no doors in the forest, Leela," Eeyore whispered. "I'm just saying."

"Pooh dear, you had a matching bear – a real one in a city called Winnipeg."

"That's in Canada," Absolem, volunteered. "I think I may have been there once."

Piglet held up his hand and waved it hard to get Vera's attention. "Please Miss. Are there books in Winnerpig?"

Eeyore banged his forehead on the table and let out a prolonged bray that sounded like a pair of bagpipes being strangled under water.

Absolem choked on his hookah smoke and managed to splutter the words, "dearie me, yes, there *are* books in Canada, Piglet, even in Winnipeg. What has become of us? I do believe we live in a cultural abyss." He took a few deep breaths before adding. "Abyss as in abysmal."

Edward, the playwright, stood up to stretch his muscles and flex his fingers. "I need to be alone for a while," he said. "It's all been fascinating, but I require peace and quiet to write, as does Leela."

Piglet counted to three which would have been his best

opportunity to once again address Mr. 'Please don't call me Shakespeare'. "Your authorship, I was about to tell you for the *'levnth* time that I am related to you. My grandfather was an explorer named Trespassers William.... Trespassers Will for short."

"I hadn't finished the point I was sorely trying to make about the long and the short of things," Cheshire whined. "Bear with me, pardon the expression." He was brief. The Winnipeg bear had been taken to London Zoo where, as fate would have it, Mr. Milne was visiting with Christopher or Billy, depending on the weather, and Edward Bear. Christopher renamed Edward, Winnie, on the spot. And not long after, father and son came across a swan named Pooh while they were on holiday.

"I have no idea what the swan smelled like," Cheshire added, "but I assume as with all wet birds it wasn't roses. As for your family tree, Piglet..."

Piglet was so excited having his family mentioned in a forest where trees stood for intelligent life, a little to the north of Owl, but not quite as north as the North Pole, he didn't notice Edward had gone.

"I hasten to add little piglet, that this information does not mean you or any of your relatives were once, nor ever will be trees," Cheshire continued.

Piglet tugged at Vera's ankle. "What's a roly-poly moth, please Miss?"

"I expect you heard me talking with our Edward who is a polymath which means an extremely clever person."

"Like Owl?"

"*Um*... not exactly. Owl likes to think he's a polymath but he's only an owl of little brain."

"A birdbrain?"

"Exactly."

"But," he snorted with anxiety, "Owl discovered my grandfather, Trespassers Will."

"Of course he did. Sometimes even an owl can get lucky."

Peter singled out a large black sea pebble hiding in the grass and sent it flying with his toe. His eyes squinted with anger. "Christopher Robin is like a brother to me. And it's about time I shared his tortured confession about his so-called *'golden'* childhood – a conviction that not only echoes my negative opinion of mothers but also reinforces my decision to stay young. Christopher flat out admitted that growing up was the ruin of him. As for me," he shouted, "I don't care what anybody says, a proper mother doesn't lose her child. They don't just walk away and forget where they put them!" And with that, he trailed after Edward and forgot the conversation until the subject came up again, ten minutes later.

chapter 43

THE META FOUR

*"Better to trip with the feet
than with the tongue."*

ZENO

By half past elevenses, Pooh and Piglet lay stretched out on a blanket with their eyes closed as they often did to digest their elevenses.

Vera says our personal beginnings, middles, and endings are hidden inside metaphors and make-believe. All stories have a backstory although writers are urged not to make a point of beleaguering this. Some births are a mistake and accordingly, some stories must begin at the end and work backwards. Such is the way certain mysteries unfold as they should.

"This is true of Leela's abandonment as well as Edward's betrayal," Vera said. "It's also clear to me, Edward, that your gallantry and heroic nature came near to destroying your heart and soul and not a few careers of your literary colleagues along with them."

Eeyore pointed out later, that due to Verity making a colossal mistake, my heart and soul had to languish for forty-four years in a dead-end job. "There's no accounting for some beginnings and endings," he said. "But now amends can be made so, it's best not to blame Verity and move on.

I have two *Edwardian* friends: Edward Bear and Edward de Vere. The first is a slave to honey. The other was enslaved by treacherous lies. But one thing is curiouser, Edward de Vere's presence is becoming stronger by the day.

Absolem offered an explanation that naturally featured himself centerstage. "Edward de Vere visits his hideaway often," he said, puffed up with hookah smoke and self-importance, "He visits *me* expressly to discuss the secrets embedded in his sonnets far into the night, divulging the truth how Shakespeare came to be and not to be. But his secrets are not mine to tell. I must remain *silent* on the matter."

"*Hear hear*," Cheshire said, warming to the diversion. "And there's no need for history to repeat itself when it's already truer than truth."

"Precisely. Done and dusted."

Cheshire purred with a cunning gleam in his eye. "There's nothing like a paradox to stir up a certain pair of animals I know. Shall we have some sport with Pooh and Piglet?"

Absolem took the bait. "I believe we shall, my scholarly friend. Piglet, did you know you're a wee paradox," he said.

Pooh tried to sit up but failed. "Well, I've always thought so," he agreed.

"Have you, Pooh? Am I? Am I a pair of ducks?"

"It means you're brave."

"But I'm never brave."

Edward watched, shaking his head. "Piglet, my dear fellow, you're like Cheshire during a thunderstorm – a fearless fraidy-cat. A shy show off like Absolem."

"Nothing is impossible," Pooh said. "Impossible is not a word I ever use."

Piglet scratched his head. "But Pooh, you just said…"

"I think you must be mistaken, Piglet. Saying that would be impossible."

Vera caught Edward's bemused smile. "Well spotted, Piglet. Edward, my dear de Vere, can you please help Piglet understand. You write paradoxes better than any writer I know."

Edward unfurled his lanky pop-star blue-jeans and stood center stage at the head of the class, out staging Vera. He took a sweeping theatrical bow and addressed Piglet who was, by now, more in the dark than over the moon. "We shall die, we shall spill... we shall resume," he called out.

"Try not to ham it up," Peter catcalled. "Remember Piglet is not an Elizabethan pig."

"My dear little chap," Edward began. He stopped and made a great to-do of clearing his throat and projected his voice all the way to Lucy's meadow. He stopped and focused on Peter. "Young man, can you hear me from the cheap seats?"

"Almost," Peter sent back. "A little more rehearsal wouldn't go amiss. Methinks you must be out of practice."

Edward bowed towards Piglet. "I do declare, my princeling, that I see you as a tiger's heart in a Piglet's hide."

"Bravo. And there you have it, Piglet – a paradox," Peter said.

"Do I?" Piglet stammered. "*Do* I have it?" He looked at his feet. "Where is it?"

Peter stamped his feet and Vera applauded, much to Piglet's delight.

Eeyore and Puck made a display of gamboling about. Tink did a midair spiralling somersault, and a pair of crows divebombed Pooh.

"I see a triad of *very* odd ducks indeed if you include Pooh," Eeyore said.

Piglet bounced, happy to understand at last. "I always 'clude Pooh. It would be impossible not to '*clude*' him."

Suddenly, for no reason other than it was fun, Cheshire and Absolem continued to play ping pong with dares and innuendos. It was interesting to hear, but sadly less fascinating to watch a couple of livewires bored enough to spar themselves silly.

Cheshire started with: "To coin an apropos pseudonym for feeling feisty, I'm feeling rather Puckish, not to be mistaken for peckish although I could eat your words if you're game for a game, Absolem, dear."

Absolem countered by puffing harder until he was obliterated by a purple cloud. "Do you care to make the bet sweet," he wheezed. "Say, the winner supplies sweets for the offending sourpuss for a month."

"But who can judge the invincible?"

"Nigh impossible."

And so, it went until the sun set on two exhausted happy campers.

Cheshire finally caved. He fairly shrieked his last hurrah "Rabble-rouser," and disappeared.

"Firebrand," Absolem shouted, and declared himself the winner. "When Cheshire's away the caterpillar will play," he said pleased as puff.

"Who won," Pooh asked a passing rabbit.

"A cat can eat a caterpillar," came the answer.

Vera held our next lesson in the meadow Eeyore shared with Lucy. I put up my hand as soon as Vera announced class was in session. "Excuse me for interrupting, but I have an urgent question if you would be so kind."

Vera graciously stepped aside. "By all means, ask away."

"I think I may be writing about myself when I write about Chlora."

Vera looked as if she were about to cry. I'd either said something brilliant or she was in despair of me. "How wonderful," she said.

"If Chlora told you that it must be true," Edward remarked. "I always make a point to discuss my plays with the characters in them. Sometimes they try to get away with murder, but I always find out. In fact, they're often real people in my life who need a sound thrashing. Only verbal, of course. There's no point in being bloodthirsty. I give them all pseudonyms to protect myself."

Down in the buttercups, Eeyore lifted his head as if he'd heard our conversation. I waved and he commenced to nibbling yellow flowers and taking time to smell the magnificent red roses that cropped up as they chose which were sometimes bluebells.

Absolem threw caution to the wind first. "Leela, you're missing the whole point of Vera's scriptorium stoa. Vera will never tie you to a place and time. You are free to find your best thinking place or the best writing time. Don't limit yourself. Find both. If you listen hard enough, I promise you will be visited by a voice you can tryst."

"You mean trust?"

"What is a tryst but a meeting of kindred souls exchanging vital confidences," Edward said. "But if trust works for you, so be it. You're the boss. You've always been the boss but now you have a sign on a tiny door that says 'Leela Swann department head of story development', which, I have to say is not easy to write on a door three inches wide."

I sat cross-legged under Lucy wrapped in a cozy shawl despite the day being excessively warm, armed with a thermos of Lapsang souchong and a packet of chocolate biscuits. Pooh was visiting owl; Piglet hung about trying not to stare at the biscuits.

"Comfort food," Cheshire commented. "Good plan. I prefer cream myself. Funny thing, cream. It must be in a saucer to taste right."

Eeyore messaged me. He spoke gently with disdain. "Why do you always wear that old thing?"

I fingered my shawl's blue cable knit pattern. "I didn't choose it.

I found it in a trunk in the attic, before I met you. It appears whenever I feel lost."

"Nice metaphor," Absolem mentioned casually.

"Oh hello, Absolem. Pardon... a what for?" I asked.

Eeyore hung his head in shame and mumbled. "An *empty* what-for, as it happens."

Absolem suddenly became engulfed in smoke. From deep within a cloud of lime green wisdom and after a bout of coughing, his voice righted itself. "Sorry. My bad. That's lesson twenty-two," he burbled. "Ignore me. Sorry to disturb. I was getting ahead of *yourself.*"

Eeyore continued, never missing a delicious yellow morsel. "Seeing as its out, we may as well get something sorted. Leela, your mother's shawl is a metaphor. Your instinctive need for care attracted it to you. What Absolem is saying is that certain words and phrases mean something more significant than their face value."

Edward helped himself to one of Lucy's apples and joined in. "An attic represents a storage place for memories as well as abandoned things you call junk. Finding something significant hidden away sight out of mind is not to be taken lightly. Your mother's shawl holds her troubled imprint – a few threads of her vanishing soul as it were. Well, at least one of them. Perhaps one that was hoping to be maternal before she succumbed to depression. Naturally, as a sensitive child you instinctively reached for your mother's love however evasive it was."

Eeyore paused to make eye contact with Cheshire. "Correct me if I'm wrong, dear wise kittycat, that trunks in stories always contain a surprise ingredient from one's subconscious which is to say, the attic of one's mind. Sometimes they're metaphors but sometimes they're MacGuffins, objects in a movie or a book that serve as a trigger for the plot. Pooh tried to explain what they were to little Piglet once. In his befuddled way he was correct. '*a*

MacGuffin is an object mentioned in a story like a pot of hunny that doesn't need it to be there in the first place, but it is."

"I hereby irrevocably confirm my absolute agreement," Cheshire said with a flick of his proud tail. "Consider them linked to backstory, history, foreshadows, signposts, and lucky or malevolent touchstones. In a movie they're props to alert a vigilant watcher of an impending challenge. In a word, they're anonymous clues dropped without ceremony."

I closed my eyes and made a list. "So, my mother's old shawl is a backstory, a metaphor, *and* a MacGuffin. Who knew. Well, besides you."

Even from a distance I saw Eeyore shuffling his feet trying his best to appear humble. "Most welcome," he sent back. "Your shawl is also a plot point. Plus," he mumbled in a stage whisper. "In an etcetera sort of way."

"Are you saying my shawl is a backstory, a metaphor, a MacGuffin, *and* a plot point."

"And that isn't the end of it, I'm afraid. It's a motive, a memory, a clue, and a few other things besides. So, at the end of the day, I'd have to revise what I said earlier. Your shawl is *not* a MacGuffin because it's too important to leave out."

Piglet, now eating a chocolate disc as big as his head, took a bite and spoke with his mouth full. "Pooh says, one should never leave a pot of hunny out alone in case a heffalump smells it. Heffalumps can smell hunny from miles away." He suddenly spluttered crumbs everywhere. "Can they smell chocolate, Leela?"

"No worries, Piglet," I said patting his back. "Today is Tuesday and heffalumps can't smell chocolate on Tuesdays." Piglet's cough stopped immediately. I had a question for Edward. "And a plot point is?"

Eeyore answered instead. "A plot point is where a story changes direction. It's a placeholder, like turning down the corner of a page when you don't have a bookmark, which you really shouldn't do."

Eeyore didn't usually waffle. I suspected he was spending too much time with Pooh and Piglet, and Puck.

I blew him a kiss. "That sounds *exactly* like one of your deep ponderings."

Eeyore gave a satisfied bray. His nose blushed pinker. "Truer words were never spoken. Now then, listen to the silence Lucy brings. I will be close by, just down here in the meadow, pondering and eating buttercups if you need me. But don't get soft and take my previous blathering as a permanent invitation for me to jump at your beck and call. I'm not your muse. Neither, which is more to the point, is a moth-eaten shawl. I won't write your story for you. No-one can. The best I can do is cheer you on."

"This scriptorium never ceases to amaze me," Edward said.

"Well done, you two," Cheshire said. Go to the top of the class."

Piglet stared hard at Edward blinking a question.

"A scriptorium is a classroom," he said, "like this one where students like us discuss hunny and MacGuffins, and days of the week."

Piglet ran off and returned carrying a massive bluebell like an umbrella. Vera pretended to ring it, Eeyore bellowed ding-a-ling in a loud voice, and I applauded. Piglet blushed scarlet and raced off, no doubt to tell Pooh of his triumph, but circled back to take a seat behind a nearby tree.

It was then we heard Zeno loud and clear from the blue, addressing his class of four dropout students. I saw him in my mind's eye, singling out Silkie with the formidable glare Verity had ascribed him. "Loose the chatter," he said. "Please open your minds to page one."

"And there's another metaphor," Cheshire said. "The forest is on fire today, knock on wood."

Piglet gave a hiccup of fear. "Is it? Are we on fire?"

"A mind and a book are two different things," Cheshire said. "But if you compare an open mind with a book, you're saying they're related."

"Also," Eeyore added. "You aren't *really* on fire, as you well know, Piglet. Your thoughts are running out of control the way flames engulf a forest. *Frinstance*, Piglet, I can see whenever you're tickled pink."

Piglet, clearly pink but not tickled, looked about for help and dived straight into one of Pooh's hums, but Eeyore shushed him. "Listen, Piglet. You're already pink. Correct?"

'Mmm hmm'.

"And you're confused about what some things mean which is serious, but tickled means you think it's funny.

"Precisely," Piglet shouted, bursting into his standby song, *'Sing ho for Piglet Piglet ho!'*

I scooped up a trembling Piglet, kissed his nose, and settled him down with a new chocolate biscuit broken into small pieces. "After one opens a door, metaphors are everywhere." I paused to rethink my remark, "Was that one, too?"

Piglet nibbled his biscuit nervously looking over his shoulder for approaching metaphors.

Eeyore nodded. "A story shouldn't have too many. It would seem contrived."

"If I'm not mistaken, and I never am *entirely* wrong," Cheshire said, "I believe we may have inadvertently invented the *mega*phor."

Eeyore pondered for a second and nodded "I believe I know what you mean, Cheshire. Mega means a much bigger, a more extraordinary metaphor."

Not missing out, Absolem felt it necessary to offer yet another demonstration of his hobby collecting unusually pithy words (including the word pithy) yet again. "As luck would have it, Leela, the number four, as in *four* students, means something to the rabbits in your story. Richard Adams told me. Rabbits can only count to four, so they have a particular word that means more than four. That word is Hrair. Sounds like hare. It can mean a hundred or a thousand or a million."

"Meanwhile, to lighten the moment and grab the spotlight, Eeyore narrated in his best melodramatic stay-tuned mystery voice. "Meanwhile, back in the forest, a story is fit to be borne. Thinking caps on, straighten your spines, pens at the ready, and adjust your attitude." He glared at me. "I'm looking at *you*, Wordless."

I wasn't about to let him win. "Sometimes too many teachers spoil the ... Oh, never mind."

"Correct," he said. "Learning to write a novel is nothing like making soup. Or is it?"

chapter 44

THE SNOWMAN COMETH

"Now is the winter of our discontent
Made glorious summer by this sun of York;
And all the clouds that lour'd upon our house
In the deep bosom of the ocean buried.
Now are our brows bound with victorious wreaths;
Our bruised arms hung up for monuments;
Our stern alarums changed to merry meetings."

From Richard III
WILLIAM SHAKESPEARE

I had one of those 'it came upon a midnight clear' moments. I say *one of* when it was the only such moment I'd ever had.

As I stood on a windless night in Eeyore's field after visiting with Edward and Puck, my pulse quickened at the unmistakeable sound of sleighbells ricocheting off the surrounding treeline.

Feeling whimsical, I asked Eeyore a question in the guise of a Christmas carol *"Do you hear what I hear,"* I sang. And then because he ignored me, I cleared my throat and repeated my question. "Eeyore, do you hear sleighbells, or have I gone doolally?"

Eeyore shook his mane. "You are most definitely the quintessential poster child for doolally." He sniffed. "As I suspected, snow is in the air," he said.

I looked up at the same starless night. "No, it isn't," I said.

Eeyore shuffled closer to me as if to tell me a secret he didn't want Lucy to hear. "There are creatures like Puck in some enchanted forests that ring sleighbells for fun. I'll race you to the cabin before the snow flies. Do you need a head start?"

We both knew it was an empty challenge. It was Eeyore's way of pointing out our age differences and degrees of agility. Racing through a dark forest on a moonless night was asking for a stubbed toe or suddenly kissing a tree trunk. A thousand exposed roots tripped up the nimblest of travelers, neither of which described either of us.

The perfect timing of a fat snowflake landing on my nose heralded a swirl-pool of white crystals that filled the air. I was never going to hear the end of this. Eeyore loved coming off as a mystical seer.

"You're on," I shouted. "Try to keep up old man." But neither of us ran. We sauntered toward the treeline through warm helium flakes as if inside a snow globe.

"I happen to have a nose for weather," Eeyore remarked. "What's for dinner?"

I let my tongue catch several flakes before answering. "I rather think this is chicken soup snow," I said after another mouthful confirmed my findings.

Eeyore wanted to know if there would be dumplings and if so, we should have invited Edward and Puck to stay.

I inhaled deeply. "Yes, I believe there will be because in case I haven't mentioned it, I happen to have a *nose* for *dinner*. I closed my eyes and waved my arms for psychic effect. "I sense plump fluffy dumplings and fat noodles served with crusty French bread fresh from the oven."

"Leela, I like how your mind works." Eeyore brayed softly. "And may I add a little magic of my own because I see an apple cobbler served with lashings of custard for afters."

"We make a good team," I said, brandishing a flashlight. "Why don't you send Puck a message to join us for dinner. By the way, I used to hear strange music and what I imagined were fairy bells when I was a child. I was never able to see where it came from. After meeting Chesire and Absolem, nothing would surprise me in Veratopia."

The moment we entered the forest the snow stopped and by that, I mean it kept snowing, but the forest canopy blocked it from falling *on* us. "The more it snows," Eeyore said, and paused for my response.

"Yes, yes, I know, tiddley-pom, the more it goes on snowing."

"Correct. You see, we're attuned."

"It's hardly surprising considering who lives here," I said, and we tiddley-pommed the rest of the way home. As the cabin came in view, Eeyore stopped. "I was kidding when I ignored your question earlier about hearing sleighbells," he said. "But I *was* serious about liking how your mind works. We're always in sync, so, of course, I heard sleigh bells. I can read your mind. It's still full of sleigh bells, isn't it?"

"They never stopped," I admitted. "Does that make me completely doolally, then?"

"Oh, you can't help that. I'm doolally. You're doolally. We're all doolally in here."

There came a gentle swoosh of wind as Owl pushed off from an upper branch. A fine dust of dislodged snow filtered down through the pine needles like dust motes caught in a sunbeam, leaving a pattern of microscopic diamonds on Eeyore's back and the sleeves of my navy Peacoat.

"Soup's on, Vera called from the doorway. "I hope you two are hungry. Sorry to drop by unannounced, but I made far too much Chicken Noodle so, I've brought you the extra. You're just in time. I was about to take a loaf of bread out the oven. The apple cobbler is already cooling. And Edward and Puck are seated at the table."

Eeyore stretched out by the fire sleeping as I let the flames hypnotize me. And then it happened. Suddenly I was back in the Shadowlands, and it was midwinter, and I could do nothing but let the dark memories close in. There was nothing for it but to let them unwind their unmerry way, hold onto Eeyore's tail, and hope for the best.

The terrors of Christmas past shook the room, revisiting me like a Dicken's ghost... the nasty one. Any winter where snow was welcomed for its poetic beauty was a far cry from my Shadowland winters where snowy weather had brought nightmares of slipping on ice and fears of breaking a hip.

Sidewalks were slippery enough for pedestrians, but the roads were treacherous for a sliding bus where one had to cling to the sides of seats as it careened around every hazardous corner.

I'd had no choice but to ride the number 61 bus to put in a day's work and shop for groceries. In all my years I had never taken any trip that could be classified as a joy ride. There hadn't been a single scrap of joy in being old and alone, out in the shadows on bone-shattering ice.

I remained focused on getting home and hurried through the frightful weather until I reached my front door, greeted by the loveliest sound in the world – a donkey braying joyously on the other side of the door at the sound of my key turning in the lock. In seconds I was finally home wrapped in my mother's old shawl while the magic of Otherwhere turned my work clothes into a fleecy robe and slippers. When fat snowflakes fell soft and silent it was time for hunkering down until it melted, and my runners could grip the sidewalks once more without fear of injury.

I always wore a man's grey overcoat from a thrift store two sizes too big that looked especially shabby next to genteel old ladies wearing black leather boots trimmed with fur. I had sat apart, a lonely old woman, jealous of smiling faces and their conversations. Suddenly my almost brand-new 'Doctor Who-length scarf' from a charity shop looked ridiculous.

Christmas lights from the neighbors' trees left me feeling more abandoned than usual. Their cheerful decorations made the inside of my apartment, as sterile as it was, with its spartan hotplate, a wonky can opener, and chipped plates reminiscent of a London slum.

On the worst days I wore spiky pads on the bottom of my boots, but they made walking clumpy, almost as precarious as the ice. I used two canes to keep my balance like a pair of ski poles, prodding deep snowdrifts ungainly – an ant on a landscape of flypaper. Wading was difficult. I felt like a ship marooned in the jaws of an Arctic icefloe. Life flashed before my eyes before I took another step wondering if the drivers of passing cars noticed my predicament. I'm sure some had but failed to rescue me what with Christmas being a busy time.

There were many Christmases by the time the bus lectured me. I was sixty-one, but none truly belonged to me. I experienced the season of cheer as a penniless window shopper hypnotized by store front displays and the occasional Sears catalog left on the bus. I was easily unnerved by boisterous children hyped out on sugar, and completely panic-stricken by the local brass band in the Santa Claus parade that I always forgot until it was upon me.

The flashing lights of the street decorations gave me headaches. I tried to smile at the passengers *bus*tling about carrying shopping bags stuffed with treasures. But they looked away, embarrassed. I resented their pity, filled with bitterness and shame. And it was then I realized with a shock, I wasn't avoiding them; they were avoiding me.

In any case, I had to redouble focusing on staying upright to navigate the deep snowbanks left by the snowplows and over icy sidewalks too slippery for oldies without a cane or an arm to lean on.

The promise of tea with Eeyore kept me moving forward but all the general pushing and shoving, and fake jollity wore me out.

The first thing after hugging Eeyore like a lifesaver, and before taking off my threadbare coat, I adjusted the thermostat control that released the whoosh of an exploding flame captured behind a glass door in the fireplace and put the kettle on.

It only took a moment to hang up my coat, spread out my new charity shop scarf to dry, and don a robe and slippers before Otherwhere came into focus. By the time the tea was ready, a few friends had wandered into my cabin to say hello and were already nibbling the stack of buttered toast Alice had made for Pax's elephants. I pulled my chair to the fireplace and helped myself to toast, content to warm my toes and listen to everyone's news of the day. Peter raided the larder and brought back sardines, a plate of sharp cheese cut into thick wedges, strawberries, clotted Devonshire cream, and a pot of marmalade.

"Don't let your tea get cold," Piglet said holding a strawberry so big he had to hold it with both hands. "You always do that, Leela."

"Is that a new scarf?" Alice asked. "It's just your color. Oh, you *are* clever at finding nice things."

Pax's voice carried over Piglet's. "Alice quick, she's closing her eyes, grab her cup."

The last thing I heard was the happy drone of conversation. "Leela has had a long day, Piglet. Let her take her afterwork nap. You can show her the drawing you made later. Are you sure I can't help you with that strawberry, dear?" and Peter's triumphant "Woo-hoo, I found a chocolate cake" as Alice tucked a blanket around my legs.

Comfort food was something on toast or just as toasty, toast without anything on top shared with my family.

I relived the same happy Christmas over and over every year. It was Eeyore's favorite memory of the Christmas he'd been a gift for Christopher Robin and how he'd found Piglet who had gotten himself lost under a mountain of wrapping paper and ribbon and was very nearly thrown away. It was a story that never failed to excite and unnerve Piglet into a state where he required a mirror to prove he was still here.

Piglet whimpered, snuggling deeper into my armpit, excited and terrified by the story where he'd nearly been lost forever, wanting its telling to be over but thrilled to be the star attraction for once.

The old bag lady had felt like kindred the precise time I needed a human friend. I thought we could have tea and discuss the pros and cons of becoming homeless together. The voice on the bus tricked me with a hint of friendship, but in the end, if it hadn't been for Eeyore's encouragement, I would still be the same grumpy old woman with illusions of grandeur and an overimaginative mind.

It isn't a foregone conclusion that I am here celebrating Christmas. I'd grown plenty belligerent living in the Shadows forty-four years. If Eeyore hadn't run off ahead of me things would be different because Verity told me the Lady Flora had strict rules regarding my return. It had to be of my own free will.

My first Christmas in Veratopia arrived in due course after I'd lived here four months, celebrated with cake and candles and was full of the joys of writing. It was different and the same. I asked Cheshire how long he'd lived here.

"I arrived when I stopped trying to get here," he said. "The path of least resistance works wonders if you keep to the rules."

"I've always been here," Absolem echoed. "I can sometimes still see the pyramid that used to be where the ruins of Tirings used to be."

The tree sprites made miles of paper chains and hung them in the trees connecting them with garlands of tinsel. The fairies dressed in festive colors held hands adorning the forest as dancing strings of light. I came to appreciate freezing temperatures as a welcome prelude to warming by the fire intoxicated by the scent of pine boughs and gingerbread while sipping hot milk infused with cinnamon and nutmeg.

For a week, Eeyore's memory of his epic Christmas experience eclipsed my own so much I woke up on Christmas morning believing I was a gift under Lucy that couldn't wait to be unwrapped. I was still half asleep when Eeyore whispered Merry Christmas.

Vera stood beside him holding a tray bearing a pot of Earl Grey tea, a plate of mince pies, and a red rose in a bud vase.

Pooh, Tigger, and Kanga had arranged themselves at the bottom of the bed covered in tinsel and ribbons. When I applauded their efforts, Piglet bounced out of Kanga's pocket like a jack-in-the-box. "All present and accounted for," he squeaked and took a theatrical bow so sweeping he would have fallen off the bed if it hadn't been for Eeyore's nose waiting to break his fall.

I winked at Vera. "So, I see."

"He's been rehearsing that for a week," Eeyore whispered in my ear.

"I taught him how to bounce," Tigger boasted, eyeing the tray. "Tiggers love mince pies." But after his first bite he looked up at the ceiling and said, "Do you know, I don't think I can quite finish this, after all," to which Pooh shed some of his decorations and volunteered to help. "Oh, do step aside and let me show you how it's done, Tigger, and don't go scoffing all the chocolate fingers, there's a good chap."

"Tiggers definitely love chocolate fingers," he said.

Piglet nibbled on a large rose petal as big as one of his ears.

A loud popping noise came from the forest where several friends, as I discovered later, were pulling Christmas crackers.

After breakfast, Eeyore and I built a snowman that towered above the cabin with the help of Puck's magic but when I went inside for the biggest carrot I could find, it ambled off into the forest.

The others arrived with a story how they'd barely missed being trampled by a giant snow-donkey that was, in truth, Pax's lead elephant, Martha, covered in snow. They wore paper crowns from their crackers. Pax's was gold with red feathers. Alice's was fashionably blue to match her dress. Pooh's had fallen into a green collar with a pattern of silver glitter stars. "Like Edward used to wear," he said. Edward appeared wearing his purple crown as an armband. Puck twirled Piglet's pink crown on his finger as it covered the little chap from his ears to his toes and threatened to trip him up at every turn. Vera wore a circlet of holly on her head and presented Eeyore with a wreath made from a dozen daisy chains and a headband of red teahouse roses for me.

I excused myself and visited Lucy's field to hang some baubles in her low hanging branches, where sure enough the snow had settled into a white sheet deep enough to make my first snow angel. Eeyore and I raced about leaving footprints that mingled with hoofprints emitting a supernatural glow that lingered until Boxing Day.

Absolem's hookah smoke had melted any flakes that threatened to cover him, and Cheshire floated under a sprig of mistletoe with a wreath of colored lights around his neck, his fur snapping with sparks. "Last one to the cabin is a rotten egg," he shouted, and snap, he was gone.

"That will be me," Absolem moaned, sounding like the old Eeyore. "Not the rotten egg bit but a cold snap as the last to arrive part."

When we were all gathered by the fireplace sharing our favorite

Christmas stories I was reminded of the scene in 'Wind in the Willows' when the mice children were asked inside to warm themselves by Mole's fire and eat the wonderful things in his larder after singing carols at his front door.

Pooh ate a bowl of marshmallows. Piglet smuggled one out of Pooh's sight and sat beside it wondering what to do next. Edward and I sat cross legged on the floor sipping cocoa and Eeyore lay beside me with his head in my lap while Puck played his flute. "Can it stay as wonderful as this," I asked him. His answer was one word brayed loud enough to startle the dryads on the mantlepiece "Yes, Leela there is Santa Claus!" he said.

chapter 45

OMNISCIENT MARTYR

"If you can meet with Triumph and Disaster
And treat those two imposters just the same,

Or watch the things you gave life to, broken,
And lose, and start again at your beginnings
And never breathe a word of your loss,

or walk with Kings – nor lose the common touch,
Yours is the Earth and everything that's in it."

selected lines from 'IF' by
RUDYARD KIPLING

Moments after the bluebell summoned Edward, Peter, and I to class Vera stood, arms crossed, legs planted slightly apart in the stance of a genie commanding an army. She glared at each of us in turn. Clearly, she meant business. "Listen up everyone," she said. "We have a lot to get through today, so we need to make a start."

Her desk was piled high with pillows of different shapes and sizes and an assortment of chocolate biscuits on a three-tiered plate. "We'll leave our comfy armchairs empty today," she said. "Please take a pillow and make yourself comfortable. Take as many pillows as you like. We're going to play a game. I want you to sit on the ground and look up at me. Remember our exercise where we sat still with our eyes closed and listened to the forest?"

"Meditation," I said.

"Precisely, well this time it will be concentration. So, keep your eyes open, and listen carefully. Block out all other sounds. Visualize. I will assign each of you an imaginary writing room with a table and chair, writing paper and pens. Let me know when you're there."

Edward sat leaning against a tree trunk, legs outstretched with a neckroll behind his head. I sat on my pillow, hugging my knees and immediately felt like a child listening to a bedtime story. Peter warming to the game, used his pillow as a lap desk and sat cross-legged. He grinned at me. "This is fun. Better than books and memorizing things. It isn't quite what Tink had in mind but that's not unusual for a domineering fairy. You know what she's like."

"Like a mother," I said. "But a strict one."

Vera faced Edward. "Edward, your room is equipped with a long oak table with carved legs upon which there's a roll of parchment, a quill and an inkwell. It is a winter day. The snow is deep, and your room is toasty from a roaring fire."

"Leela, you're writing room is a walled garden on a sunny day with a wicker chair, an easel with a canvas, an assortment of oil paints and brushes, and a diary."

"Peter, I give you a treehouse on a rainy day, you have a lap desk, a slate and a box of colored chalk and another of wax crayons."

Vera's expression softened. "Edward. What if I had the power to have you killed? Please answer this question. Am I a sorcerer, an enemy, or a tyrant?"

Edward yawned and glared back indifferently. "You're a queen."

"Leela, I give you three doors. Behind one of them is a library. Behind another is a bedroom with a nightmare. Behind the third door is a stagecoach and horses and a winding road leading to a fairy tale castle. Am I a witch, a genie, or a trickster?"

"You're a storyteller."

Peter looked nervous. "I'd rather just…"

"Peter, stop. I know what you're thinking. But more than this I know *why* you're thinking it and what you're going to do or not do about it." She lifted her arms wide to the sky. "I can make it rain. I can make you do whatever I want. Am I a witch, a bully, or a mind reader?"

"You are definitely a fairy."

This last question is for all of you. I make each of you into a wicked liar determined to hurt an innocent protagonist.

Am I a criminal, a magician, or a monster?"

"You are a psychopath."

My punishment is wearing the letter A embroidered in red silk in plain sight on my coat for all to see.

What has happened? Am I a victim, a sinner, or am I a bystander in the wrong place at the wrong time?

"You are a doomed bystander," Edward said. The others agreed. "Doomed!"

"Well done, full marks. There are no wrong answers but there are wrong assumptions and attitudes, and I needed to prove a point." Vera nodded to Puck to hand out the chocolate biscuits.

Eeyore ambled up to audit the lesson, snag a chocolate digestive or two, and ambled off again with Puck. "I'll meet you at four o'clock for stoa tea," he whispered. "Sorry to intrude, Vera. Puck invited me."

"The game is almost over," Vera said. "A few rhetorical multiple-choice answers remain before we open the floor to discussion, and you can resume your armchairs. I needed to speak from a position physically and metaphorically above you. A metaphor is something that means something else to make a point, Peter."

Peter looked lost and waved his hand nervously in the air. "Please Miss, could you tell me what rhetorical means."

Vera smiled sweetly. "It's a question not requiring an answer."

"Does anyone know what wearing a red letter signifies?"

Edward looked uncomfortable and rose to leave.

"Sorry, Edward, you must stay. We're both aware you know the answer."

Edward … "I'd rather not say on the grounds that…"

"You might incriminate yourself?"

"Yes."

Vera persisted until I was outraged with her tormenting Edward, and Peter cowered behind his pillow. "But what if telling the truth sets you free?" she said.

Edward stood to go. "It won't. It didn't, and it never will." He looked as if he might burst into tears, but he sat down and banged the back of his skull against the tree, hard.

"Edward," Peter asked. "What happened?"

"I cheated on my wife, and made another woman pregnant who had a child I couldn't openly acknowledge. Many suffered. A woman wore a red letter 'A' – the scarlet letter for cheating on a husband."

Vera read from her notes without looking up.

"A scarlet letter is a plot twist often used by an author to create a problem for an innocent protagonist, involving the birth of a fatherless child, leaving the mother branded a scarlet woman. The man more or less enjoyed the positive reputation of being a womaniser and went about free to continue his indiscretions at will. It was somewhat a badge of honor amongst men."

"Guilty as charged," Edward said staring into Vera's eyes without shirking. "So, now what? Are you going to punish me?"

"Oh, Edward, I couldn't punish you more than you've already punished yourself. You have a good heart, Edward. And now you must set yourself free as an honest one by forgiving what was and letting it go. Slates exist to be wiped clean.

Did you think the woman in question was an innocent. She was not. She plotted for your attention. And she played the wronged party the way a fine actress delivers her lines. Furthermore, she paid the price for her performance with winning a sound marriage with a husband who wanted public permission to be a philanderer. It worked out for everyone except you, Edward. And now, my dear, it's time to let it all go.

The next chapters of your life begin here in Veratopia if you choose to accept them. Do not write them in red ink, Edward. Write them openly with your head held high. You deserve nothing less. Indeed, you deserve much more."

"You sound an awful lot like your older sister," Edward mused. "I miss her."

A falling pine needle could be heard as we wrote our memoirs as if we were other people. I was in essence Chlora the wood sprite. Peter abandoned his role as the savior of lost boys. Edward, looking older than seventeen, dabbled in iambic pentameter.

Vera, the commanding chief, resumed her tack of illusive answers to meaningless questions. "What does a protagonist know? What do they give up? What do they want in their heart of hearts?"

None of us answered.

"Sorry," Vera said. "That was a trick question. So, extra points for your silence. A protagonist knows nothing until their writer *tells* them what they want. It's a contract.

Speak with your protagonists. Listen to them. But remember you're in charge. You, the writer, have the final say. You can erase as much as you create. Assemble your cast. Demand silence and deliver your commands clearly by stating *I will write your story, and YOU will act it out accordingly*.

Here is the contract: "I shall keep some of you in the dark. I shall favor one of you beyond the others but will make things difficult for you. You will resent me and fear me. Your lives are under my control. I will give you unholy terrors. I will put you in danger and I will cause you to lie to each other. I will think for you because you cannot second guess my plot. You will read your lines as written and if you're foolish enough feel the need to improvise, bear in mind I have the power to edit you. You can guess and assume what each other is *thinking* to your heart's content, but you can never know what each other *feels*. Fight amongst yourselves off the page but when it's time to perform, fail to follow my script at your peril. You can beg me to save you and pray to me all you want. But I have already decided your fate.

Now… think again and tell me who I am."

"You are an author."

"Yes, and so are you."

"It takes courage to be an author. An author must also be an actor," she said. "You are the director and set designer. Actors have no choice but to follow you even if they balk at first. Why? Because you know the end of the story and they don't. They may have ideas, but you have the plot.

And before I forget, I want to direct you to an all-important plot point called 'all is lost' because at some point your protagonist will face a challenge, she or he will be unable to surmount. You will write them onto a high window ledge where jumping appears like a solution.

Your reader must be worried for them. *You* must be worried for them. But you must also divine a way for them to overcome a death wish with a genuinely creative solution. Letting it wait too long will kill your story stone dead with no survivors. The past cannot be eliminated, it's a done. Your rough draft is an entity in a state of flux. But it is a living entity that can evolve. The future is always in your hands.

Peter has never drawn breath, but his story circumstances were no less traumatic than Edward's or Leela's because they were written by a human genius with one foot mired in suffering. Edward and Leela, you have died and been reborn several times. As such, you retain the vocabulary, fears, and the wisdom of multiple lifetimes. Since you, like me, here in Veratopia are unfinished."

Vera's rhetoric diatribe continued.

"Edward? You are a master wordsmith. But your life flowed erratically beyond your control. You could either accept or deny situations as they arose. And although you may have been intuitive, you could never have foreseen the cutthroat madness that lay in wait for you. Name one secret in your life that destroyed your destiny?

As the author of your new life, what would you change if you could go back in time?

A writer is a dictator. A writer is both creator and underdog. Ultimately, I'm speaking about omnipotence and omniscience. Characters will love and die on your pages. They will betray each other and perform acts of compassion. They will win and lose without warning. Indeed, without warning is the best way to hold a reader's attention.

I am talking about power, martyrdom, sacrifices, creative license, and the divine right of authors. Edward, I won't ask you something that's none of my business. But I *can* ask if there is anything you'd care to volunteer about your life. And as I understand it, you've done that already amongst friends. But curiosity begs to be heard. Is there anyone in your past that you want to confront for your peace of mind? Look them in the eye right now and tell them something to set matters straight?

One perk, pardon the paradox, about *'living'* in the afterlife, is processing one's life with perspective, as a story about someone else. Philosophically, all stories are about everyone, and all biographies are about a stranger we've never met. We write characters to discover ourselves.

Edward, you deserve to know how loved you've been for the four hundred and twenty years since your death. Does that help assuage the wrongs, both self-inflicted and conspired, against you? Perhaps not but accepting the conditions of your death may have brought you peace today. Revenge is overestimated."

Vera looked around her, as if startled she was in the middle of a class. She repeated the words tomorrow and tomorrow and tomorrow like a broken record. Suddenly she snapped awake. "Ignore peace at your protagonist's fate," she mumbled to herself. Then louder, in her teacher voice. "What is martyrdom for? Are secrets better aired? Should silences be broken? Is all in love and war fair after death? Reincarnation is often a deeper sea of troubles. Do you want to reincarnate? As a writer of ciphers do you want to dot every 'i' and cross every 't'? Do you want to reveal the pointless mathematics of life?

Peter, since you were unsure. Those questions directed at Edward were rhetorical."

Peter stood calmly like a child in a witness box. "They're questions Edward answered for me when I never asked. We are friends for life. I was never real. Edward was never make-believe. But millions of people believe in us."

Edward resumed his form at the age of his death in 1604 – a tired, grey-faced man of 54, saddened by betrayal. "I never told my *invisible* son, Henry, I was his father," often enough he said. "And another time I pretended to be someone else's father. I never asked my mother if she caused my father's death. I never confronted Leister about returning the legacy I was born with. I never slapped Elizabeth's face and called her a bitch. I never openly admitted I was a murderer, and since I've never bumped into any of the liars and loves of my life in this afterlife, I assume my guilt was mine alone.

I should like nothing better than to honor my family motto. 'Nothing is truer than truth' is difficult when trying to survive the Elizabethan court. In all honesty, even I have my doubts about some of what conspired. No question, I wrote the sonnets, but I was pressed into studying the mysteries from the age of twelve by Master John Dee who I now believe, was never completely of sound mind. I fear there's been too much water, too much mud, and too much bad blood, to render truth *'accidentally'* lost. That said, nothing is completely irretrievable.

Later generations of 'muddiers' had a go, and to this day there are lost documents vying with falsified documents and portraits wiped clean of signatures and cyphers. My self-centred family paid teams of mud slingers who made great sport of confusing King James. Henry Wriothesley who should have been the 'Henry IX' had grave doubts (as in death defying thoughts) his mother was the Queen. Master Dee played so many intrigues within intrigues he had Elizabeth almost believing she was a virgin… and *that* she and I knew to be utterly untrue.

We were all court jesters, playing for laughs. I played the roles of multiple writers as part of the ongoing war debates that arose from the mud like dragons to be slayed. I also succumbed to old injuries and ill health but by then I didn't care so much.

I lived a life so complex it took dozens of actors to play the parts, many of whom I invented as pseudonyms. And each performance was altered to be more evasive, more intriguing, more deceptive. And then my works fell into the hands of a man who I can unequivocally declare was not William Shakespeare Almighty.

Power, wealth, and praise, each one in turn took the lead. But most of all staying one step ahead of the axe kept all of us busy. Elizabeth had a bloodlust that would have killed a dragon outright with one look. I make no excuses. I lived in fear for my son's life.

I left clues. Truths disguised as poetry. Legends disguised as history. Hints disguised as accusations, poisonous breadcrumbs that led to or away from the scaffold. I kept my head in ways that mattered to a poet. It was fortuitous timing that saved Henry, and ill timing that lost my heart's work to a bumpkin without the wit to steal or the wherewithal to spell his name."

Vera looked pale and had to sit down. "We may have done too much for one day," she said. "I feel quite dizzy."

chapter 46

GENIOUSITY

"That which is an impediment to action
is turned to advance action.
The obstacle on the path
Becomes the way."

MARCUS AURELIUS

For quite some time Eeyore and Puck decided they were birds of a feather. Pranks were pulled on a daily basis. And because Eeyore was such a sweet open book it was easy to catch them out.

So, when Puck dropped by to ask if Eeyore could come out to play, if I hadn't known what a tease he was, I might have answered, Eeyore is a grown donkey. He comes and goes as he pleases.

Of course, it *was* a ploy. Edward and Peter emerged giggling out of the trees with a chocolate layer cake and three bottles of ginger beer.

Edward doffed an imaginary hat with a flourish. "Mad mademoiselle, we're a scriptorium of cake-eaters who write stories," he said. "May I present a lost boy who can fly."

"Indeed," Peter chimed in. "We're a writing team. All for one and one for all."

Peter leaned in close until our noses touched. "Leela, do you ever feel you've been called to serve the world?"

I took several steps backwards until I could uncross my eyes. Peter, in focus was a formidable opponent. "Well," I answered. "Verity once hinted I could be the queen of a brave new forest. Was she being funny?"

"Everything may contain humor, but not everything is a joke," Peter said. "I'm here to evolve which is harder than growing up. It's why any of us are here. It's why Leela is writing a book about a tree sprite after sixty-one years of blank pages."

Edward cheered enthusiastically. "Bravo, Leela, take a curtain call."

I gave them a wobbly curtsy. "Whenever I reason why Veratopia isn't overrun with a million souls, I'm afraid I'll wake up in the world of shadows in an asylum. The real ones that house the wounded with neurological disabilities and the living dead suffering from depression. The condition Edward Lear called the morbids."

Peter pushed his luck. "And what pray tell is the lighter side to *that* story?"

"It's too fine a day for morbid thoughts," Edward said. "And Peter's question was meant to spark a lively conversation after yesterday's dark lessons on sacrifices and martyrdom. I for one can't help but chastise myself for being both."

It was the time for a meaningful smirk. "Great," I said. "Three ghostwriters in a *lively* conversation. Why is there a slice missing from the cake? I detect Puck's handiwork and Eeyore is especially partial to chocolate."

"Then, shall we away to Lucy's meadow where all will be revealed?" Peter said.

I was happy to nod yes. I had a few questions that hadn't been resolved and ones that required an overnight ponder. "By the way, Eeyore has renamed the meadow his *energy field*. I'll just grab some plates and my thinking cap."

Lucy welcomed us with a vigorous wave of her branches that were apple-ing, so, windfalls were added to our repast.

Edward interrogated me in the hotseat. What ensued was an

interview, an accusation, a lecture, more questions, and a surprising confession.

Edward got right to the heart of his thinking. "Tirings was no less outlandish than Timbuktu or Utopia or an invisible silk road on the high seas. Spritewood sprouted from Leela's creative mind as assuredly as Otherwhere rose from the ashes of Verity's despair, and as surely as Athena sprang from Zeus's forehead. Chlora and Wick are Leela's gifts to the shadow children beyond the grey West Coast Road between Veratopia and Shadowland.

That is how unselfish and brave Leela is. It takes a courageous writer to imagine beyond the map dragons. Writers who live on the outreaches of reality are trailblazers."

It was my turn to defend my favorite trailblazers. "Authors like Lewis Carroll, T.S. Lewis, and James Barrie were compelled to create bizarre new worlds like Wonderland, Neverland, and Narnia especially since most of them shared their personal traumatic experiences to tell a story based on truth.

Did you think it was easy for our favorite authors to write wonderous stories? In some cases, writing an intangible premise got them into trouble. Once upon a time, intuition defied the laws of reality and made their lives difficult. Living between genius and doolally is walking into ethereal quicksand. When you think on it, reading tealeaves is no less irrational than a dormouse living in a teapot or an odd puddle duck wearing a bonnet," I said.

"They were geniuses," Cheshire answered frozen in mid-apparition. "But their motives and methods were different."

Edward slammed his fist on the table. "Did they think it or believe it? *That* is the question."

Absolem coughed from within the tall grass. "Genius brings joy or unbearable suffering. Geniuses like Edward, Cheshire, and I are more real than ordinary humans which is why we have retreated here to endure. Raised voices are pointless."

"Let's not forget that Leela is a genius, too," Eeyore said. "We owe her a lot. Much more than she knows."

A stream of agitated smoke rings rose from the grass. "I didn't mean to leave her out," Absolem stuttered. "My apologies. Of course she is, or she'd still be in Otherwhere."

"It's also why parents cite books as role models and why children respond to them so easily. Even the best parents can't do that," Edward said. "In my time, there were no children's books. Parents were deliberately distant, in favor of servants and tutors who were paid and ordered to care.

Olive Rand (Nou), Christopher Robin's nanny, was his mother during his formative years. Toys are real to children, nannies are more real than parents, and the Queen of England is the top dog on the pyramid of reality. Being compared to a dog is a compliment, and by the way, don't even ask about cats."

"Well, that explains Cheshire," I said, careful to check for Lucy's newly-abandoned branches. "But how do you explain the Green Man?"

Lucy's branches shivered with feline irritation. "One doesn't explain the unexplainable," Cheshire snapped, back in business. "Leela, by now you really should know I'm invisible until I feel the absolute need to interfere. Energy is impossible to describe which is why most people don't give Gaia a second thought. Magic? That, they accept, but only in diluted storybook form. The stories that saved you were called fairy stories for a reason."

"How can anyone explain the phenomenon of Queens without hearts," Absolem said. "Or, for that matter of caterpillars transmuting into butterflies."

"Because we're all demi-dogs," Edward declared, pacing like a lawyer delivering a final statement with a theatrical air, patting Peter on the shoulder. Peter was never born. But he represents the very essence of childhood humanity so how could he not be alive?

Only something exceptionally out of the ordinary gives the dreams of wunderkinds their substance."

"Were you always this smart?" I asked.

"Yes." Edward answered. "Please don't think me arrogant, but yes, I absolutely was. Millions of children are born with both feet in the world of shadows, but once in a blue moon a child like me or Leela is born with their soul permanently grounded in the world of spirit. We're not 'all here' but we are, in essence, more here than anyone. We are also blessed with more troubles as well. Suffering awakened my soul. Genius is never a curse even when it feels like one."

"Spoken like a poet."

"Incorrect," Cheshire hissed out of sight. "Spoken like a lawyer."

I tried not to feel outraged, but Peter started to cry, and I couldn't resist a small criticism. "Surely such an overwhelming sense of being better than everyone else..."

Edward stopped me. "Wunderkinds are not better than anyone else, nor do they harbour such narrow thoughts. Wunderkinds simply listen more closely to the silences between words and never give up.

It serves no purpose to fake humility. What is, is. Why deny who you were born to be. Owning one's birthright is not being arrogant but using it as a weapon for personal gain is a terrible misuse of power. Feeling unworthy of one's destiny is a crime against nature. I may have been born into noble privilege, but hindsight tells me social entitlement is almost always a punishment for being greedy in a previous life.

I was once a dream of Zeno's student, Endless, and Zeno was born a poor wunderkind with a message for humanity. He couldn't possibly have kept such certainties to himself. He was a true 'soul of his age', an honor I proudly carry as the lifeforce we briefly shared."

Peter seemed revived by the first bite of a Lucy apple. "Please, Edward, all kidding aside, was Shakespeare's canon meant to be or not to be?" One thing I know for sure is that you are the mad demi-dog who wrote it."

Edward looked Peter in the eye. "I promise you that I, now gone, compelled for all time to honor my highest truth, directed a scriptorium of writers, do hereby proclaim the universe wrote the Shakespeare canon *through* me."

ZENO HIGH

THE LAST CURTAIN CALL

chapter 47

MELANCHOLY BABIES

"And all our yesterdays have lighted fools
The way to dusty death. Out, out, brief candle!
Life's but a walking shadow, a poor player,
That struts and frets his hour upon the stage,
And then is heard no more."

WILLIAM SHAKESPEARE

Meanwhile... back in Athens, Verity reported the curtain to first class had no substance.

"The unfiltered light that met me was so bright I felt I was inside the sun," she said – "a visceral first impression hitching a ride on Silkie's fear. I found myself evicted from her consciousness, standing behind her on a stadium bleacher so high into the clouds it rendered the term 'seated in the gods' meaningless.

I steadied myself and shaded my eyes. An unseen entity touched my shoulder and handed me a parasol. "Standard issue," it said. "I was too overawed to speak, so, I thought the words thank you and shielded my face, already burning from the noonday heat.

The sky was veiled in blinding white light until a vivid trace of blue materialized in the mist turning the world from white hot to a cloudless canopy dotted with seabirds. Their wings beat the lemon-scented air into a froth of expectation. A raw sunbeam wrapped itself around my eyes like a scorching blindfold. Unbelievably, it settled me.

As white on white shapes came into focus, I planted my feet on a stone step of white Carrara marble as others above and below it materialized in tiers. I was wearing sandals far too big for me.

Silkie's recent bout with bunions and corns were a painless memory. I knew them well."

"Painless," a voice boomed. "No need to thank me." It was Zeno's way of introducing himself.

Silkie sniffed her disgust. "Thanks, but I'd like to go home now Mr. Bus."

Zeno's reply carried a faint suggestion of humor. "This *is* your home, Silkie, until you find a better one." He scoffed, "Homes aren't that easy to come by as you will soon discover." His voice grew louder as he turned his attention towards me. "Welcome old friend. So lovely to see you. Let me show you around." A bare arm extended from his blinding aura. "Welcome to Athens."

I stood on the highest tier of steps that radiated in a circle as seating in an amphitheatre – a vast theatre in the round. The term for lofty seating 'in the gods' made me smile. Zeno always did know how to make a point, and as in times past, he'd outdone himself. I was suitably impressed.

The sky, now a blaze of electric blue showed through the thin cotton of the parasol tinting it lilac. A comforting buzzing sensation suffused my body. I was not truly present. I was elsewhere. *'What a great name for another fantasy world,'* an unfamiliar voice teased. *'Do you plan on creating it for Silkie? I believe she's in need of a new home.'* It certainly knew how to taunt my granddaughter. Silkie stamped her foot. "Well, Granny, is this the school with bullies and no desks you envisioned."

I couldn't answer because the vista of a dazzling turquoise sea stretching to the horizon and an endless white beach left me speechless.

"Did you say something," Endless asked a little way off.

"Sorry, your name slipped out," I replied. "Are you seeing this?"

"Athens is a familiar sight. I lived not far from here. Zeno's stoa is less than a mile away." He gestured towards Nike's empty clifftop and waved his arm. "In that direction. I believe Zeno wants to direct our attention to the stage."

Actors moved on the stage far below and I floated down to see.

Zeno stood to the side with his students. Four new players were ushered in stage right. Three were women: one old who seemed vaguely familiar, one young, and a version of you, Leela, who fluctuated between sixty-one and seventeen. I recognized the fourth as Seneca Aurelius Greenwood. Greenwood was joined Siamese style at the hip to a woodcutter whose body hung like a limp ragdoll over his arm. Except for the woodcutter who looked more like a suit of clothing than a person, the newcomers were sleepwalking, eyes open, staring inwardly from another dimension.

As doppelgangers they had been unconsciously drawn to our debut performance to unroll the roadmap of our lost souls. Leela, you had to be here and in the forest at the same time. I shall explain all in due course.

A great voice boomed a warning while Zeno directed several stagehands to position half a dozen identical cradles into a circle. *'Take cover. The tempest approaches,'* it roared.

There was no time to argue. The Aegean Sea whipped its calm surface into choppy waves and the sky darkened as a cosmic dimmer switch reduced the sky to inky black. Without stars, the canopy above us churned with malevolent blood-red streaks. The word cumulous formed behind my eyes. *'Not cumulous. Not yet,'* Mr. McCloud shouted from far away.

Strong winds sucked the parasol from my grip and spiralled it away into the arms of a tornado funnel that touched down precisely where I had been standing moments before. "Yes, Verity, you were correct," Zeno said. "We are in the hands of the gods now. But know the eye of a storm is the safest place to be. Remain calm. Psychic nosebleeds are common at this height. Parachutes are available by request. *The storm is a ploy to take everyone's attention away from the stage until it's set for our class reunion to begin.*"

I smiled. "One can only *remain* calm if one is calm to begin with," I said.

"Breathe," Zeno instructed. "Trust me, despite appearances a plan is unfolding as it should." I smiled again. Zeno often quoted the Desiderata during his visits to the forest. Zeno's eyes twinkled. Some poets declare we have a right to be here," he said.

"No less than the trees and the stars," I countered.

"It's time to play," he whispered directly in my ear. "Good girl. I knew you would understand."

A spark of light penetrated the darkness, emanating from the center cradle. It drew my attention illuminating the stage like a sole lantern burning in the night.

"That lantern is your group soul," Zeno said. And as I watched, the other cradles flared one by one.

Our acting troupe melted into the backdrop waiting for a cue. Zeno commanded we face centerstage until every cradle glowed with newborn infants – an eery garden of babies in a theatrical nursery setting. They sent up a collective squall of hunger cries caught in the curtains like trapped seagulls.

Zeno's voice commanded we look and wait. Without moving my legs, I drew close to the nearest cradle.

The nursery ward of cradles burned steadily but a single cradle flickered and went out as swiftly as a blown candle.

Childless screamed "Save her" and had to be restrained from rushing to her stillborn child.

"Approach, Childless," Zeno said gently.

Childless's cries ceased but she continued to reach for her child. The light from the other cradles glowed brighter picking out the agitated outline of her white robes.

All of us were similarly draped in white cloth that blew wildly from the swirling tempest above us. Peripheral vision showed two entities supporting Childless. They led her towards the nearest cradle. "Open your eyes," Zeno directed. "Look upon the child once kept from you. Your daughter still dreams, waiting to meet you once more."

The darkened cradle sent up a blue spark and Childless's attendants let go of her arms. She approached the cradle, her eyes swimming with tears.

"Your child's name is Truth," Zeno said.

A warmth surged through me as I stared down at the infant that had once been me not so very long ago. I dropped Childless's hand and swooned inside her stillborn infant blinking up at my grieving mother and the transparent shadow of the empty woman beside her.

Each cradle blossomed. One by one, we actors gravitated to them. Most found a child lost to memory or a memory lost to a child. Only two actors left the stage.

Zeno addressed us: fathers, daughters, mothers and sons, lovers and allies, and nemeses. "Dear ones," he said. "We may not constitute a traditional bloodline like a genealogical tree, but together we are reunited as a group soul. All of us have been drawn together through the gift of rebirth."

"You mean, the curse of rebirth," a disembodied voice shouted from the wings.

The cradles disappeared as the sunlight pushed away the storm with a single luminous breath.

Zeno charged us to link hands. And once the chain was complete, I floated back 'to the gods' where I joined the others, milling together. All but two glowed with inner power.

But looking down, it conspired that none of us had left the stage.

We'd been transformed into stone statues glowing with energy. I was reminded of Stonehenge under moonlight as it appeared on the summer solstice midway between light and dark. We had become a sculpture of human standing stones. The stage lights dimmed.

The first rays of the sun broke through the clouds and warmed our bones. We had become a single student body separate but no longer apart. That's when the tears threatened to come but we found ourselves dry-eyed on the white beach kneeling in the sand, building an enormous sandcastle.

I reached out to help Silkie. The moment I touched her arm, Zeno intervened in a private conversation. "Please don't coddle Silkie," he said in a stern tone. "She's here to awaken into the real world she claims to crave. She will resist until she has no choice but to follow the truth within her. Until she lets go, she will suffer from the self-inflicted memories she has bottled up inside. Please don't be alarmed, but her explosive nature will get worse before she grows up."

Zeno left us with a brief message. "We've made a second start, yet there are many roadblocks ahead. For now, each of us must battle ourselves. Not until the empty cliff summons the return of Nike will we be victorious. In some ways that resonates equally for Veratopia."

"I had just enough time to wave hello in your teacup, but I couldn't stay. I'm in a fractious state of overwhelm. My apologies. Sorry to cut and run. Much love to Eeyore."

But Verity returned instantly.

"In hindsight," she began, "I should have delayed a little longer because I heard the answering urgency in your voice as you shouted *wait*. But Zeno closed my mind. He knows best and I am in his hands now. I can only hope this extended message will float between us and reach you later.

I returned to my expanded group of new friends, abandoned and neglected children, desperate unworthy mothers, promiscuous indiscretions, absent lovers, and one reluctant father, most of them aware of their transgressions. I was left to face the guilt of my impetuous actions bordering on soul abuse.

I see the error of my ways and have accepted the guilt for my selfish adoption of Silkie. She truly hates me. I don't fault her. My actions destroyed her promise of human life. I'd thought I was saving her, but I was saving myself to assuage my own loneliness. I have paid the price for my transgressions yet again. Oh, Leela, will I ever learn.

I summoned you at such a late hour because sometimes you have tea at midnight, but when you failed to appear, I left a message blindly flapping like a bat in your empty teacup.

On return to the theatre, Zeno approached me trying not to smile. "Hello, young lady. Where did you get my sandals?" he said.

"They were a gift," I said. "Thank you, old friend."

Apparently, a deranged woman named Beatrice hates me more than Silkie does which is truly saying something. I've been notified that she's a danger to herself, but she can't physically harm anyone while Zeno guards Veratopia. He means to dispatch Beatrice and Greenwood in a fair-minded tribunal after the present emotional release has been duly processed. Although I had not been officially invited by Zeno my appearance didn't seem to surprise him.

And I must say he made the best of it to help a childless woman. So, my interfering was not entirely in vain, my presence made a sad woman, happy.

But the fact remains my meddling has left me feverish. All I want to do is sleep. There's no need to wait by your teacup, dear ones. I will be home as soon as I'm well. For the time being, your open invitation to afternoon tea has been quashed. I send my heartfelt gratitude when I say, 'there's no point in leaving a light in the window.'

I was transported to an overdue healing dream from the back of Zeno's bus, fussing like an impatient child but instead of snivelling *'are we there yet?'* I asked, *'Where do we go from here?'* in a steady voice as clear as a bluebell. I had grown up.

Zeno's answer was pure Buddhist. "The finger that points to the moon is not the moon," he said.

chapter 48

THE DARK KNIGHTS OF THE GROUP SOUL

"All the world's a stage,
and all the men and women merely players.
They have their exits and their entrances;
And one man in his time plays many parts."

WILLIAM SHAKESPEARE

Edward shocked us by arriving in class brandishing a spear. He strode defiantly, shaking it at Vera who failed to see it being lost in thought. Edward made sure she was watching when he thrust his spear violently into the ground between her feet. "The lie stops here," he bellowed. "It's time to let go of your guilt too horrific to remember. "Come out foul demon," he shouted like a faith healer.

"What are you playing at," Peter shouted. "Have you gone mad?"

Edward paraded about the trees using his spear as a walking stick. "Quite the opposite," he said over his shoulder. "My attack is meant to provoke a *return* to sanity. Vera has been barely coherent for the last month. And don't tell me none of you hasn't noticed her absentmindedness. She's been half awake and she's getting worse.

This is a long overdue intervention. Verity charged me with this assignment before she left. She told me to spring it on everyone without notice. It will be made clear why when it's over."

"You do love theatre," Cheshire remarked.

Edward couldn't help looking pleased.

Vera stirred and answered Edward timidly with a question. "Greenwood was a terrible employer?"

"That we know," Edward said. "I'm referring to Alice."

Vera blinked. "Wonderland Alice isn't a secret. She became one of us after Mr. Carroll died, everyone knows that."

Edward circled Vera three times and shook his spear in her face. There was compassion in his menacing. "I was referring to *your child*, Vera. Her name was Alice."

"But I didn't... I wasn't." And then a vision of a child materialized before us. A cherubic face stared at Vera from a bundle of swaddling clothes, and she remembered.

"My Alice. She had to leave us, didn't she."

"Who is us, Vera? "Who was Alice's father?"

Vera's legs buckled and she fell to her knees. "Greenwood," she shrieked, "What have you done with Alice?" She turned to Edward. "Did Greenwood murder my child? Edward, please, you must tell me the truth."

The words *'Verity had a child!'* rang through the clearing like a shockwave sending the rabbits into confusion. One by one they hared off in fear.

"We knew, of course," Cheshire said, smugly.

Edward's voice softened and he took hold of both Vera's hands. "Vera, listen to me. Greenwood didn't murder Alice. He murdered *you!*"

The forest buzzed with relief. "Finally, Vera is to be set free." But the words *'Greenwood murdered Verity'* tied itself in knots as it wound its way to the Nozone.

Vera flinched. She looked at Edward in a daze. "My headaches?"

"Are the result of being bludgeoned by the handle of an axe. Greenwood was too squeamish to spill blood."

"Is the woodcutter, here to finish the job?"

"My dear, woman, the job was finished a long time ago. The past is done as much as history can ever be. Verity feels responsible for your sanity. She is protecting you as an older sister would. As a surrogate mother who let you down, would.

Indeed, her purpose in Athens was to find Alice and bring her home. Greenwood's violent crime spree is almost over. There's a final matter of comeuppance befitting his crimes that must be adjudicated properly this time, in Athens.

The woodcutter is under Greenwood's control – an innocent caught in Greenwood's trap. We never see him without his axe because Greenwood is unable to let go of the violence he caused. The woodcutter is condemned to carry an axe for Greenwood the way Death carries a scythe."

Edward motioned Peter and I to join hands in a circle of protection around Vera. "Greenwood's savage cruelty towards Verity indirectly led to Alice's premature death. Her sacrifice will not go in vain." His voice softened. "Vera, you remained here so Verity could spare you from the heartbreaking memory of motherhood buried inside you until the worst of it was over. She accompanied Silkie to Athens to save you and Alice as much as Veratopia. As such, your stoa served to keep you focused on teaching Leela, the woman who may one day take Verity's place."

Vera slumped into a faint. "She can still hear me," Edward said. "Keep holding hands."

Vera revived as her memories returned, heartened by the fact that Alice would be in her own afterlife or reincarnated by now. A ghost can manipulate the ether to find a lost soul.

Edward coached her. "Remember the day Greenwood forced himself on you. It was a diabolical punishment conceived by a sociopath. You must process the full extent of Greenwood's cruelty to be free of him. We're here to support you.

Greenwood gave Alice to a pair of unsavory peddlers who sold her on to an even worse fate of being housed in a tenement within the plague quarter of London.

Scuttlebutt survives in London for generations as old wives' tales. Zeno sent word to me a long time ago, but we had to wait for the right time to bring Greenwood to justice and clear Zeno's conscience because he killed Greenwood's ancestor, one of his students nicknamed Relentless, thinking to prevent the tragedies inflicted on you.

I am still here to fulfill a promise to reincarnate with Verity, and as Zeno's representative, to divert some of his guilt. Verity needed a tutor for Silkie and called upon Zeno for help. Zeno in turn, needed help and called on me. A group-soul is a close-knit family no matter how much time separates us."

Vera revived quickly after the first shock wore off and related her returning memories.

"Greenwood threatened to fire me and destroy my career. He said he would see to it that my reputation as an unwed mother would result in poverty that would surely affect Alice's health and her chance for a full life. I stayed with him to save her from such a fate. He knew of a wealthy childless couple who wanted a child. And so, Alice was to be given away. *There would be other children he said.* I replied, over my dead body.

Greenwood sent me on an errand and when I returned, Alice was gone. I hadn't been able to say goodbye."

"Vera, the whole truth is almost out," Edward said gently. "We're in this together. Your freedom impacts our entire community."

With that observation a bitter wind whipped through the trees raining down leaves. *'It isn't over'* they cried out. *Verity says it's always darkest before the dawn'.*

Vera's ordeal suspended our class but opened new possibilities for Veratopia. Her intervention rejuvenated the air that had become stagnant with suppressed rage. Lucy, privy to all things Veratopian, offered her umbrella as a therapeutic meeting place. Even Pax's elephants attended.

Eeyore and I were still coming to terms with Verity's last truncated message but despite the absence of her teacup chronicle, 4 o'clock tea resumed as our traditional ritual, often presided over by Puck when a message was in the air. Today, he'd hinted at Verity's return.

I downed my first cup fast. Not to get to Verity's message faster, should there be one, but to experience the therapeutic ritual of pouring and stirring more than once.

Lately, the ritual began with a lighthearted glance inside a cold empty cup and my declaration *'my teacup is bare'* signaled I was open to receive an incoming communication. But today, due to the aftermath of shock, Puck promised to read our leaves. Perhaps Verity would show.

The time was 4:30 when Puck materialized. He took one look in my cup and declared "Your cup is belligerent. IMPatient". He emphasized the first syllable. "Imp is a sign. Your incoming message is delayed."

"So, Verity isn't coming?"

"Not necessarily. A delay is always more significant because it calls for patience."

By the position of his ears, Eeyore was already on high alert.

"A storm in a teacup," Puck said helping himself to biscuits. "Time fluctuates after a major disturbance. Vera has been at war with Greenwood for ages. Peace needs time to reset itself. Tea is a sensitive plant; there's no telling how long yesterday's shockwaves will disrupt the patterns of the tealeaves. Even so, I feel Verity's powers building. I sense she has something *imp*ortant to say."

"Another IMP?"

In answer to my question the shallow puddle at the bottom of my cup rippled like a rough sea.

Emotions swirled around the interior of the bowl as if being stirred with a spoon.

A few garbled words sputtered nonsense. But eventually, Verity's last truncated message came in hot for ten seconds, minus her reflection which was puzzling.

The guilty expression on Puck's face made it clear he expected trouble. "I'm sorry, Leela I'm not always permitted to tell you everything I know. Timing is tricky. All I know is the events that are coming cannot be stopped. They must be endured."

I stirred my tea in slow motion widdershins, unnerved while Eeyore and Puck spoke in whispers.

"My dear ones," Verity said at last through a buzz of static. "I know you've had a shock. Don't blame Edward. He was brave to do my bidding. He always is.

I have more disturbing news. But you must bear it well and try not to worry. Events are accelerating faster than I expected. I hardly know where to begin. Puck was here in spirit."

Puck made an impromptu bow, beetled off into the forest, and Eeyore followed without saying goodbye. I had no choice but to listen through the static.

"Eeyore and Puck have been given instructions to leave you alone while we talk. I have upsetting news of Alice. I'm so pleased I got through, but I may not have long. Our connection is crackly. So, for now, just listen, I have a lot to tell you.

I remain undetected when I stand beyond Silkie's peripheral vision. I stood watching Zeno's darkened abandoned stage when a spark of light fluttering centerstage put me in mind of Tinkerbell addressing a pantomime audience of Peter Pan. It grew larger and floated towards me, changing colors as it came. It was Puck. By his violent color shifting it was obvious he didn't want to be here.

He gave me one of his impish grins although I could see his heart wasn't in it. "I am sent by my master, to announce that the time is right for your main event," he said. "And then he shrank to the size of a newborn, circled my head like a cherub, before seating his normal self beside me.

Childless was captivated by Puck's appearance and reached out for a hug but Endless took no notice. He displayed his usual indifference around children. It was a practiced façade that fooled no-one, but it was his safety valve to compensate for a surgical crime that had haunted him for two thousand years.

But Puck is no child. He never was. He's an ancient forest spirit who has lived for many thousands of years, and as you know, well-versed in the art of magic.

The main event is a betrothal as well as a map charting soul-connections stronger than death. Reincarnation plotted on paper like a genealogical family tree except that none of the family share a bloodline. I propose we follow it together when I get home. Veratopians form a group soul, and someone must break the curse on our respective houses.

Zeno appears muddled. Unlike the man I knew to be unflappable. He's distracted. He reminds me of Vera before I left. I'm sure you've noticed her increasingly erratic behavior.

I orchestrated a simultaneous event: Zeno's voice issued from Nike's trumpet at the exact time Edward confronted Vera."

As Zeno spoke, a figure I recognized as the definitive image of William Shakespeare climbed the steps, sat next to me, and held my hand. Puck took my other hand after he bowed low in deference to his master. "Patience, Verity. The truth will out," he said. "There is nothing to do. What's done is done."

"Methinks this list is all about me," Silkie whined in my head.

"Silkie's word 'methinks' triggered my anger. I'm afraid I turned on her. 'I love you to death," I said, "but everything is not always about you." Then I begged Zeno to dispatch Greenwood to hell so we can go home. Vera needs me. Please help her.

My big news is that Vera's Alice reincarnated as a woman named Beatrice and gave birth to twin daughters. She's your mother, Leela, and she's deeply unhinged. But be forewarned. She's on her way to Veratopia where she intends to take out her anger on Vera."

Verity's voice waivered into static. *I ... I... home... if... if... but... but but*

Eeyore nipped my arm. "Leela, please wake up."

"How long have you been back?" I asked. "I must have blacked out." I was dismayed to find my favorite three monkeys cup neatly broken like the sections of an orange."

"What was the message? Puck said it was bad news."

"If you'd stayed you could tell me. All I remember is you and Puck deserting me, and one enormous windstorm. I don't understand when Verity speaks as if she and Vera are two separate people. Can you explain it to me?"

"Sorry, we were following Zeno's orders. You were unconscious when we got back. Verity's message arrived on a massive jolt of electricity. Puck and I felt it in the meadow as horizontal lightning. Did you not hear Verity?"

"Nothing but ten minutes of white noise."

"Such a condensed spilling of psychic beans must have shattered our cups, teapot, sugar bowl and all, as well as bending a few spoons for good measure. What was Verity thinking."

"She wasn't thinking," Absolem said in my head. "Well, there goes the neighborhood. Beatrice has sent the forest into an uproar, and in so doing, an *imp*-ending thunderstorm is now approaching at full speed where we happen to be standing. It should...*SLAM*... hit us momentarily."

The impact of high velocity winds churned the tree canopy into a state of panic.

Eeyore nosed me forward. "I came back for you. We must take cover under Lucy. She has opened up a tunnel for us. Pooh and Piglet are already there, safe. We have to go right away."

"Does Lucy speak directly to *you*, now?"

Eeyore set off without answering. He called to me over his shoulder. "Follow me and don't look back."

Lucy brought us up to speed. She had shed an entire bale of leaves in one great dump frightening Pax's Ellies so badly they shriveled to the size of mice. The birds stopped singing and went into a furious nest building mode. Consequently, several new nests displaced Cheshire into an enormous pink sulk ranting "mark my words. There will be *imp*-lications. Zeno's voice is muffled but I can still hear him. He's threatened and that's never good."

"If I ate birds," Cheshire shouted, "and by feline rights I should, my *best* branch would be empty. And now miniature elephants are rampaging through the grass making an awful racket, Piglet is a basket case, and Absolem is missing."

"He can't crawl far," Lucy said. "He'll turn up. I showed Piglet where to hide but it seems he's more terrified of roots than heffalumps. What a to-doing."

The forest let out an agonizing groan as the rain unleashed itself full force, lashing plants into a quivering green carpet and pulverizing the remaining Tirings bricks into pulp. Hurricane winds tore the treetops, bent low to the ground. Cheshire found refuge deeper inside Lucy's crown as Absolem wriggled under the earth snuggling beneath her roots as his last official act as a caterpillar.

SENIOR HIGH

TROUBLE IN PARADISE

chapter 49

A SCARLET HERRING

"It is a tale
Told by an idiot, full of sound and fury,
Signifying nothing."

WILLIAM SHAKESPEARE

The aftermath of Hurricane Beatrice left steaming hills of rotting vegetation in Veratopia, but the trees recovered quickly from shattered limbs and bare branches. It was decided between them that a cleansing fire would be needed once the flotsam dried out.

"Something doesn't half pong," Eeyore said, sniffing the air. "I say, writing is a bit fishy when you're writing about someone you know. Are you writing a fish out of water story, Leela? Are you writing about me?"

I sent him a look of frustration. "I am a little. But if anything, I'm writing about my own childhood, and since you were a part of that..."

"Were?"

"Sorry, I meant that you are a large part of my life as well as any others that might come along. You always said you would edit my first book, so, well spotted, editor. What you sense is true. It's probably the red herrings, I've been a bit careless with them. I may have used too many. You may think your eyes are weak, but they see everything that must be brought to my attention. I'd be lost without you."

"You're a fish finding your perfect swimming hole. No worries, and just so you know, silver herrings smell like roses."

Eeyore's ears twitched as he continued to sniff the air. He shook his head and sneezed. "Sorry, Leela, I have to go. Something smells terribly wrong. The trees are restless. Absolem will know what's up. I think you should come along."

The expression on Eeyore's face told me red herrings could wait.

Absolem, reprieved from an early chrysalis, *did* know. By the time Eeyore and I found him, the forest was in an uproar. Absolem, being overly sensitive, was babbling. "If interrupting a grove of trees discussing the identity of Shakespeare is tantamount to treason, then trees must take sides. And taking sides implies the discussion has progressed to an argument. An argument suggests one or more trees is for and when one or more trees is for it stands to reason that other trees are against."

He was clearly in a state of uncontrolled panic. Only Cheshire could reason with him.

This was all made clear in Absolem's unique ability to put two and two together and make a thousand and one excuses for treachery... another word for treason pertaining to forests. "It's elementary dear Absolem," Cheshire hissed, "since the word trees plus reason equals the big bad T-word. A message written with a poison pen is a bogus missive sent by an idiot, full of sound and fury, signifying trouble."

Eeyore plodded at his normal speed towards Lucy. 'There's no need to race," he said. "What's happened has already happened. Lucy will know what to do. Mice mean well, but as a rule they're an awfully distracted lot. As for ants, why bother trying. You're only wasting your breath."

"You look worried."

"I can't help my face, Leela. It's rather set in its ways. People expect me to exude gloom which is deeply hurtful considering happiness is welling up inside me as we speak. Whatever *has* happened, somehow, I feel quite uplifted. In fact, I am elated. Rather high spirits than high jinks, I always say."

"Well, that's the first time I've heard you say it. Pity it doesn't describe your friend, Puck. One assumes his jinks can go no higher... and then, they always do."

Lucy blushed a reassuring shade of green when she saw us. The forest was vibrating with hundreds of feet from tiny to enormous. Mice and Pax's Ellies swarmed along the same crowded pathways galumping their way through without a sense of destination. Procrastinating destiny, Eeyore called it. Lucy bade us sit without delay.

"Someone has started a rumor in the worst possible place – the Dryads' Grove, and the dryads are terrified," she said. "My roots connect with their rather stumpy ones, so I heard the scuttlebutt right away."

"I think it's called that because mice scuttle and it was the mice that ran higgledy-piggledy into the woods bearing bad news to Vera's school," Cheshire said. "If Verity were here, she might have been able to calm such unbridled panic. I'm doing what I can. Absolem is nigh catatonic. Vera has retreated into accelerated aging and is in no mood to save herself."

"I thought trees were wise."

Lucy shook her leaves. "For a start, dryads are not trees," my dears. "Tell them, Cheshire. I have to go. My roots are ringing nonstop. I won't be a second."

Cheshire circled Lucy widdershins three times to unwind the stress of her tree sprites. "Trunk calls are far too intrusive," he shouted to Lucy. "Just hang up. I suggest you rewrite Chlora with a sturdier grip on reality, Leela. The little lass will make herself ill if you don't. As for me, I never hang up. But I will continue to hang upside down whenever it suits me."

"Dryads," Eeyore bellowed. "I believe you were about to enlighten us, Lucy? You were about to tell Leela that dryads have dead leaves for brains. And if that isn't enough, they're simply unable to process gossip with an open mind. When dryads were alive, they were flirtatious nymphs, silly creatures gaga over the satyrs. The forest was in a state of lusty shenanigans all the time."

Puck thinks it's a lark to pick locks and let the woodcutter out. This time the woodcutter ran amok through the dryads in a last hurrah, waving his axe chasing a woman none of them had seen before. And before Absolem could say Jack Robinson, she'd told them Verity was gone and never coming back. Other than losing their protector, there's nothing more distressing to a dryad than a mad woodcutter waving an axe amongst a grove of nervous trees.

They sent their fears underground in all directions via their roots and alerted the mice living burrowed within them to spill from their homes and fall about like so many skittles."

"Panicked mice," Absolem piped up, materializing out of puff, suddenly focused. "What a to-doing. The greater trees have responded with good sense but some of them were too young to speak slowly and clearly. After all, an accusation is only words. And certain words beginning with T stir up trouble when it comes to a queen.

Several mice kept shouting let's ask Owl, he'll know what to do. Which goes to show how distracted they were. Owl is rather partial to eating a few mice for breakfast as a rule."

"It's perfectly logical," Cheshire said. "I've said it once, but I'll say it again: trees love to reason and if you put the word trees and reason together what have you got?"

"Treason. That's what," Eeyore said. "And where there's treason heads will roll. Any king or queen is sure to lose their composure. And since the Queen of Hearts has never had a smidgin of tolerance in her entire ditzy life, let alone composure, her guards caught wind of an uprising and promptly reacted more erratically than the mice. They're rather more 2-D than is necessary if you get my drift. Without barely a foray they blustered into trees, knocking themselves out, and vanished into thin air from over exertion."

Eeyore took one look at his energy field littered with armor and spears and card-shaped bodies and roared with laughter. "Oh, the humanity!" he said.

chapter 50

SAVOR YOUR DARKLINGS
a fighting chance

*"Oh, what a tangled web we weave,
when first we practice to deceive!"*

— SIR WALTER SCOTT

Lucy lowered her branches without making a sound. "Leela, please bring Absolem and Eeyore close under this hide I've made. My chlorophyl is strong. It will keep hostile energy out and we can speak freely without fear of interruption from the evil forces gathering in the dryads' grove. The hubbub is still very much localized there.

I believe we're still under siege from Beatrice. The good news is unable to move as freely as her lies."

I settled Absolem and his hookah on a flat boulder just as Cheshire slunk onto a low hanging branch touching the ground.

"You look like a real cat under here," I said. "It's very snug."

"I'm always real," Cheshire growled. "I'm a special feline with the extraordinary ability to camouflage, not unlike a caterpillar on a leaf or a butterfly on a flower, as you shall soon discover, Absolem."

Lucy sounded like a mother hen. "I heard Vera in my dreams again," she said. "I'm sure it has something to do with what's happened. Have you noticed anything out of the ordinary in the classroom?"

Eeyore looked asleep on his feet. "Not being overly focused on writing, I observe things," he said. "I've noticed that Vera is getting old. She's much older looking than Verity was when she left. And she's aging at an alarming rate. Her energy is flagging accordingly, and she depends on Verity's walking stick. She never used to bother with it other than to wave it at Puck when he was in the way."

"And now Vera has retreated into accelerated aging," Lucy said, "she's in no condition to save herself."

"I sometimes forget Vera is Verity with much less knowledge and not as much suffering. I'm ashamed to admit I've been too intent on getting a sentence to work than anything else."

Eeyore snorted. "You can say that again. It wouldn't hurt to get a hug once-in-a-while."

I put my arm around Eeyore's neck, rested my chin on his nose, and whispered better luck *this* time.

"Right, so be it," Lucy said. "Pandemonium it is for the time being. We must find Verity. She was cagey about when she was coming home."

"No problem, we know where she might be at four o'clock," Eeyore said. "Leela and I will intercept her tea report with an S.O.S."

"What's a tree report?" Absolem shouted. "Will everyone please calm down. I can't hear myself think. *Puff puff.* Is it something to do with trees?"

I put my hands over my ears. "I said, *tea* report. It's to do with Verity reporting from her location in Athens via tealeaves. It's about Zeno's class and how Silkie is holding up, which so far appears dismal. That girl is a fighter. Worse still, Verity is aware that Silkie hates her. She's devasted."

Eeyore brayed loudly. "So, a worse to-doing then."

Cheshire's grin turned into brazen laughter. "Sorry to be the bearer of grim tidings but methinks the cat's out of the bag," he said. "It's no surprise that Silkie has caused trouble. That's her modus operando." He sobered. "What's more to the point is what to do about a mad vixen loose in a henhouse."

"What makes you think Vera hasn't suffered as much as Verity,"

Absolem said after a long intake of purple smoke. "The hidden truths underneath Verity's memories may be so scandalous even *she* doesn't know. Lady Flora kept her under a Styx spell for her safety. Verity was a stickler for letting things go, but no match for the Green Lady's superior powers."

Cheshire grew to twice his size. "I have feline night vision which includes long distance remote viewing. I know exactly where Verity is and why, and more importantly why she can't up stakes and head home. We are on our own my friends. A tempest in a teacup has now broken its banks."

Absolem choked from inhaling too deeply. "The grapevine is buzzing with innuendos. Vera is in no state to defend herself, let alone a pack of overwrought dryads. This couldn't have come at a worse time. Someone knew what they were doing to start a ruckus while chaos was brewing in Athens."

"Even Zeno is worried," Cheshire said. "His intervention was never designed to open a bag of caterpillars. He has a mutiny on his bus and a twitchy group soul on his hands. It never rains but it pours. Zeno is basically a referee, and Verity is in a state of shock. Comatose by the sound of it. She bore the worst of Silkie's intervention. She's definitely *not* being cagey."

"Does anyone know how it started?"

"One of the mice had it on good authority that Puck was trying to be entertaining. Quite an alarming thought, actually. That little rakehell has no filters. At any rate, Puck thinks it's a lark to pick locks. The flimsy padlock on the Nozone Gate was just waiting to be picked."

"Don't tell me. That's how the woodcutter got out."

"No, that's how a woman on a rampage got *in!* Beatrice is a malevolent spirit by all accounts, again from a rodents' point of view, with, pardon the pun, an axe to grind with the woodcutter.

It takes a woman scorned to throw a fox into a henhouse of

witless dryads. And what good authority could a mouse possibly have?"

A queen on the rampage calls for spies and the executioner not in any order. One begs the other.

"Where are our spies? I wasn't aware we needed any. But we *will* need Kanga's strengthening medicine. Piglet's ears are low to the ground but being pintsized puts him at risk of galumping feet. He'll imagine the worst."

"We don't have time to speculate what might happen. We need to take action," I said, trying to keep the panic from my voice.

"Leela," Eeyore said, "one must *make* time for pondering. Stampeding woodland creatures are like chickens with their heads cut off, the bally lot of 'em."

Cheshire materialized. "Pax's Ellies are stomping at the bit, raring to tear up anything that moves."

"Perhaps, Cheshire, you could stop grinning for a moment," Eeyore announced.

"I'm gloating, Eeyore, there's a difference. Grinning comes with the territory; one has to work at gloating. Besides, I have an inkling."

"Try not to hurt yourself," Eeyore remarked

Cheshire resumed grooming his tail. "An accusation has been thrown down – a cowardly ploy while Verity is away, with Vera too inexperienced to handle a full-blown ghost tantrum. It was timed perfectly; I'll give Beatrice that."

"Out of control and into the fire," Absolem puffed. "I'm an institution around here so, …"

Eeyore would have raised his eyebrows if he'd had any. Instead, he shook his head. "Please, Absolem. Be more aware of Leela's feelings. Institution is not a term a sensitive person would bandy about in front of her."

Absolem's hookah smoke turned pink from embarrassment. "I apologize, Leela. I forgot about your lost years in the … *ahem…* asylum." He busied himself untangling a hookah tube coiled around the stem of his mushroom. "Mark my words. Greenwood is at the bottom of all this," he shouted to hide his shame.

Cheshire's tail blossomed into the shape of a mushroom cloud. He blinked out several times and when he solidified properly his expression no longer expressed mirth. "Beatrice was in Athens, but she's been expelled, expunged and erased, so she's having a final fling of mad temper. It can't last much longer. She's a dying wind.

Zeno is aware of Beatrice's unstable mental health but is playing it cool by acting unconcerned. In any case, he's not taking messages. He's too busy juggling complex connections. Leela, your doppelganger is there too. No worries, it's simply a memory of yours spontaneously responding to Zeno. You weren't to know of Verity's stowaway game."

Suddenly I remembered. The situation was much more serious. "Greenwood is also there with the woodcutter, and I doubt either of them were just going along for the ride. I tried to speak to Verity, but she was in a trance."

Cheshire spun and stretched to dislodge the negative energy in his fur. "Verity has been injured," he shouted. "I saw an aura of black around her. She's fighting off a fever. That was all I was able to get." When he righted himself, his grin was gone. He buried his face in his tail and sobbed.

Absolem's hookah clattered to the ground. "Cheshire old boy, do calm yourself. It can't be as bad as all that. I say, pull yourself together. What can be done?"

"Nothing," Cheshire hissed, "Beatrice is filled with the most abominable hatred. We must keep our wits about us, but the dryads will have to sort themselves out. We have bigger fish to fry."

"The poor dears never could see the forest for the trees,"

Absolem said, quite recovered with his hookah set to rights, now emitting a cloud of sweet strawberry-scented smoke.

Eeyore's ears swiveled to pick up a faint memory. "When Silkie was giving us a lecture on her many accomplishments, she mentioned a legal contract hidden in the forest that Verity hid before she died."

A heavy fog lifted. Eeyore was right. I'd not been paying attention. Silkie had been on a rant to undermine my confidence, so I'd tuned her out.

Eeyore read my mind. "But what is *Vera* tuning out? What is she not saying? What does Vera, the lost years, hold? I have a strong inkling that's where you'll find the answer to this attack," he said. "No matter. What's done is done. Who will know what to do if you lot don't, that's what I want to know."

Cheshire let out an anguished yowl. "Edward, that's who. We must formulate a plan otherwise all this bally-hoo is libel to end worse than badly. Libel being the operative word for something called a legal subpoena. I know what I know because I *don't* tune people out as a rule. What I'm trying to point out is that in addition to his many talents, Edward de Vere is a crackerjack lawyer!"

I pulled Eeyore to his feet. "Oh, my god. Edward is waiting for me in the classroom. We have to go."

Eeyore brayed silently to himself, reeling and disoriented. "Leela, you're late for school," he suddenly shouted. "I'm supposed to get you there on time. What was I thinking. The bluebell was rung hours ago."

I could see Eeyore was not his usual self. "You're unwell. You've had a bad dream," I said. "It's been a rough morning. We ran here without eating breakfast. Go back to the cabin and rest. I'll be along shortly to make supper, and we can have a nice sane evening. Let Beatrice do what she must, and we'll wait things out. Edward will have a plan and if he doesn't, Verity used to say evil eventually wears itself out if it doesn't get too much attention."

Eeyore shook his head. "Sorry everyone, I drifted off. Silly really. My brain is as muddled as Pooh's these days. I must ask Kanga for her strengthening medicine. I'll see that little Piglet is recovered and meet you in the classroom."

Lucy fanned him with a leafy branch. "Dear ones. Savor your dark imaginings for therein lies our survival."

Cheshire yawned and found the remnants of his old grin. "I truly hate this ghastly saying, and I rarely use it, but Beatrice won't stand a cat's chance in a fire against Edward. It's off with her head time."

Lucy lifted her branches. "Where's Absolem?" she said. "He was right here a second ago."

Absolem is already there," Cheshire said. "When he wants to, he moves at the speed of hookah power. Va-va-Voom. I strongly suggest we reconvene in two shakes of a donkey's tail to consult with Edward. I'll join you after I have a quick cat nap to fully regain my composure."

"Everyone go," Lucy ordered lifting her branches. "Not you, Eeyore. I order you to stay here and rest. I've already dispatched Puck to deliver Piglet into owl's care."

I looked back to thank Lucy and saw Eeyore already curled asleep under Lucy's branches, lowered over him like a green blanket to keep him warm.

chapter 51

GHOST RYDERS IN THE SKY

"PER ADVERSA AD ASTRA"
Through Adversity to the Stars

It was raining when the group huddled under Lucy's branches the following day. "Hello Lucy, Vera, Piglet, Pooh, Chesire and Absolem. We come bearing news," Eeyore said.

"Good or bad?" Lucy asked.

"Precisely," Pooh answered, setting down a bottle nearly as big as Piglet. "Kanga sent this for you, Eeyore," he said. "I expect that's the bad news out of the way, then."

Its label 'extract of malt' was plain to see. "Piglet makes a tremendous fuss when he has to take a spoonful of this stuff. It doesn't half pong. It's strengthening medicine." Pooh held his paws over Piglet's ears and sang a short hum so he wouldn't hear the rest. "Kanga swears by it."

Piglet shivered under a large umbrella sized leaf. The sound of rain lulled everyone into stupor. I see none of you got much sleep last night," Lucy said. "Now, Leela, let's hear your news."

"It's all right, Pooh," Vera said. "There's no need to cover Piglet's ears again."

I took a deep breath. "Well, yesterday, when we got home, Eeyore slumped into a heap. He looked dreadful and he was making gasping noises in his throat. I covered him with a blanket and…"

"Excuse me, Leela. Sorry to interrupt. But I need to correct you. I was merely a little restless," Eeyore mumbled. "Disoriented you might say. Out of sorts. Nothing that a cup of tea wouldn't put right."

I nodded. "Which was why I headed straight for the tea canister

385

and put the kettle on. Tea may not solve the events of the day, but it will take the edge off our anxiety and sooth Eeyore's throat. And his weepy eyes were soon back as bright stars in no time."

Eeyore peered closely into the gathering. "As you can see, I am recovered. I feel quite starry-eyed."

"I found a garbled message from Verity in my teacup. No wonder she'd begged off earlier and now we know why. Verity met Beatrice yesterday and as you may imagine it was not exactly a happy ever after 'hands across the sea' encounter."

Absolem sat open-mouthed. His hookah stopped billowing smoke. "Coincidence? I don't think so," he managed to cough out. After a few puffs, pipe in hand, he was able to speak like his old self. His ever-present cloud billowed protectively around him once more. "Well, I don't mind admitting I'm gobsmacked."

"You don't have to," Cheshire said. "We have eyes."

"Quite."

"And speaking of eyes," Cheshire resumed. "The forest spies report the dryads are back in their trees, but Beatrice is still at large, stomping about like a mad thing."

Piglet's eyes became saucer-like. Vera picked him up and put him in her pocket. "There, out of harms way," she said. "Go on, Cheshire. I can see you have a lot more to say. Beatrice might wear herself out although it's more likely she'll stir the woodcutter into chopping something.

And thanks to you, Vera, I learned a thing or three last night, as well. I think it *ahem*... behooves us to retrace the past. Beatrice had to start somewhere. We may find a weapon to use against her. I mean, it's no secret that ghosts are restless. But Beatrice is quite off her head."

Piglet's muffled shout 'off with her head', from inside Vera's pocket was more of a surprise to himself than anyone. He promptly fell into a confusion of hiccups with a dollop of whipped cream still on his nose.

Cheshire preened in his damp spotlight. This is what I was able to piece together. Vera, stop your ears when you need to. This concerns you and I don't want you upset."

"I'm not upset, I'm old," Vera said in a huff. "And I was there. My mind isn't *all* cobwebs. You think you know the whole truth, but you don't. If you ask nicely, I will tell you when you're ready."

Cheshire resumed speaking into a microphone that wasn't there. "Young Verity was a tad highly strung in those early days, working for Greenwood. She was a true romantic."

"A term for idealistic notions rarely hitched to reality," Absolem threw in for Pooh's benefit, and also to prove he knew what was what."

Vera took up the tale in first person. "I dreamed of becoming a novelist after catching the writing bug from trailblazer women authors who gave themselves men's names or published under their initials. Sadly, like attracted like. I was out of my depth. My writing, like Greenwood's, lacked originality, but at least I had the sense to accept my limitations with good grace and move on. I followed the breadcrumbs of publishing into a jungle of rampant testosterone. I think you know the rest. I couldn't have known I was in the clutches of a sociopath.

"Well, that explains a lot," Cheshire purred. "No wonder you wrote bodice rippers, you poor girl. I hope that's not the genre Vera is encouraging *you* to write, Leela."

"On the contrary," I replied. "Vera has given me the freedom to choose. After asking Edward's permission to write about his... *um* situation, he gracefully declined, and happily a middle-grade story surfaced in its place. I'm eager to get stuck in."

There was a rustle amongst the foliage and Puck's face emerged. "Oh, dear," Absolem moaned. "Look what the cat dragged in."

"I never did any such thing. So, there's no need to insult me," Cheshire said scratching his chin on an overhanging twig. "As I was saying, or about to say, I've been Verity's friend a long time. In the years since we met, she's suppressed a lot of bad memories. I know a few but not all."

The story Beatrice has put about is that Verity and Silkie have run off to join Zeno's little 'circus'. They're a separate family now. Apparently, there were several expelled students, an intervention, and supposedly a return ticket. Bad Karma is certainly involved. Verity often mentioned she had a plan to help Zeno escape his present dilemma."

"Which is?" Puck asked.

"For goodness' sake, Puck, the man's a bus!" Cheshire yowled, taking a swipe at him.

Puck did a double handspring and disappeared, but the echoing howls of his gleeful laughter remained.

After a pause to clear the air and calm Cheshire's ruffled fur Absolem attempted to speak again.

But Cheshire was quick to impart her news. "The witch in the dryad's den is a woman Verity was acquainted with during the time she rescued Silkie. She'd had her hands and her mind full. Was she doing the right thing? Was she saving the infant from a life in an institution? Would the child be thrown to the wolves a.k.a. parents who lacked the skill or the desire to love and care for an orphan?" She wasn't sure.

Vera stood and walked around the table leaning heavily on a cane. "I think I'm aging right now because events have come full circle. In which case I may as well speak as Verity since I was her and she was me."

"Something still doesn't smell right," Eeyore said.

Vera stood and claimed the spotlight. "It never did. It never could. Remember what I taught you, Leela, how red herrings are designed to distract and mislead. This Beatrice creature is nothing more than a puffery of her own imagination – a giant red herring on a mission she can't win. Lady Flora officially rules here until a suitable replacement for Verity can be found. We have earned our freedom and then some."

"Humans can be flighty creatures and forest nymphs were more emptyheaded than most," Absolem mused. "Mind you that was long before my time, but some things never change. Women scheme. Men plot. Nymphs hide away in fear. It was ever thus."

Cheshire was more down to earth. "Greenwood purchased forestland where an earthmother named Flora ruled. In due course, after his death and a few glitches, Lady Flora handed Verity the reigns so she could make the rounds of several neglected overseas forests."

Vera's voice took on the timbre of feverish woman. Verity's presence had entered her body. "Greenwood coerced, begged, and finally blackmailed me into service that kept me at the mercy of his beck and call. But the worst of it was I humiliated him. I shudder to remember it.

He abused me on a regular basis until I became pregnant. He couldn't abide children or women. The bottom line of all his outrageous lunatic plans designed to punish me was that he wanted me to suffer. He wanted to hurt me in the worst way imaginable, but he needed my child to do it.

Flora said she was waiting for the right time when I was strong enough to understand the truth. Yesterday was that day."

Cheshire uncurled himself from a tightly bound ball of nervous energy and shook his whiskers.

"Greenwood waited until I bonded with Alice before springing his trap," Verity began. "I lost my cachet as a reputable literary agent as soon as Greenwood put it about that I was a slag who'd had a child out of wedlock. He painted himself as the injured party, of course, in that sly way he had. It looked as if he'd done his best for an employee and her child by giving me a position for life. I was told the child would be raised by a wealthy family. The alternative was a one-way passage to London, a street-life of unbearable poverty, and suffering for Alice and me.

But now I know the truth. Greenwood found the most unworthy couple he could find and when I was on an errand, he gave them Alice. I sank into white depression. After that, nothing mattered."

"Until now," Cheshire said, springing into action. "The sky is filled with ghost writers."

Vera stood straight as a statue. "Cheshire's quite right. Flora told me to expect the unexpected and to hang on a little longer. I still have a few last duties to perform. You see, Zeno is an old friend from my philosophical days in Athens. We were colleagues. I'm obliged to help him until he's free. He's in a bit of trouble. And good friends stick together for as long as it takes. I would say the end, but I promised to unburden myself of a terrible secret revealed to me this morning."

STOICISM

c.300 BC -
Zeno of Citium founded Stoicism –
the Greek school of philosophical thought
that developed into the most influential
ideal of the world as divinely planned
to optimize moral goodness and happiness
by engaging one's assigned role
in the cosmic scheme
of things.

UNIVERSE-CITY

THE END IS NEAR

chapter 52

MUCH ADO ABOUT LYING

"Go, said the bird –
humankind cannot bear
very much reality.
Time past and time future,
what might have been and what has been
point to one end,
which is always present."

T.S. ELIOT

"Eeyore," I asked. "Will you please escort Pooh and Piglet home. Piglet is bound to see a heffalump behind every tree."

"I'm happy to. And please don't you worry your little head about me. I'll manage to find my way there and back safely in the cold and dark."

Vera made a pot of tea while we waited for Eeyore. "Eeyore is getting old, Leela. I know how he feels. He pretends he can see things that are blurry. Although I have to say, his ears are as sharp as a tack. He can hear a pine needle drop in the forest. He needs tender loving care."

"I've always given him that."

"Give him extra, then. He's too proud to ask for it."

Eeyore arrived pretending not to be winded. 'Hello," he said casually. "Ah, is that a plate of digestive biscuits I spy?"

"There's fresh tea in the pot," I said. Vera is about to tell us what happened. She says we must prepare ourselves."

"That can't be good."

"It is what it was," Absolem said.

"Cheshire left us at a bad spot in my story," Vera said. "But I must go back further to see what I refused to see until it was too late."

"How can a bad spot get worse?"

"We're about to find out," Absolem said.

"Seeing a mistake, you needn't have made is far worse than making it," Cheshire said.

And so, it began. Verity held us in rapt anticipation.

"I worked all hours before we left England. More still after we arrived here. I was rarely allowed to sleep. As a result, I was too tired to dwell on people. People were extraneous to my work. My mind was steered to editing long dreary passages of text. It's not like I read them for content but because many others who did, found them wanting.

I count that as one of my first mistakes. I knew a good story from bad, but had I known I was working for an illiterate psychopath I would have thrown in the towel. I didn't of course. And years after scanning words that made no sense, Greenwood began to slip another's words in place of his own. I noticed, but by then I was an automaton, and Greenwood was aware his feeble stories injected with other's words passed for literature of the highest standing. More the fool me."

Verity stood formally and addressed us fidgeting a loose button on her coat. "I have a terrible confession to make," she said. "When I told you about losing Alice to save my reputation, it wasn't the whole truth. I left the worst part out. Something much more sinister occurred. Something that caught me out. Something a more worldly girl would have noticed. It was a harmless lie to get ahead. A caper. But I was naïve. I used it without considering the fallout that occurred. There was no reason to suppose a white lie would create complications. But then, I was an innocent, eager to succeed."

"What on earth."

The trees shuffled closer together. Vera moved the tea things on the table like chess pieces as a nervous distraction to postpone the inevitable.

"Come on Vera, we're all friends here," Absolem said. 'We're here to support you."

Vera toppled the saltshaker she was holding with a dramatic flourish as if surrendering a chess game and took a deep breath.

"Checkmate!" she said. "Greenwood hired me under an assumed gender. I had the frame of a lithe boy in those days. So, to get the job I wanted, I dressed like a boy, studied hard, and explained on paper that I was mute. I said very little. Editing only required a pen. Sign language filled in the gaps. Being a mute played into Greenwood's hands perfectly. I couldn't tell his secrets, and I was not to know that he had the toy boy he wanted at his beck and call.

I'd decided the career I wanted as a teenager. I was an avid reader and spontaneously edited as I scanned the text. I even made margin notes in a notebook and wrote promotional blurbs and taglines that came to me without effort.

When I was seventeen, job hunting was a serious pursuit, not to be outdone by rich girls born with silver spoon advantages. Even the lowest paid menial jobs were scarce. But the competition in the publishing world was fierce. Women were passed over all the time which made me evermore determined. I was enlivened, invigorated by the game – eager to prove my literary skills before I had established a track record.

I wore no makeup and kept my hair short to save the expense of a hairdresser. I had to keep my expenses low but that was my downfall. A first lie is insignificant, but a continual lie increases exponentially into a full-on nightmare.

My need to succeed made me bolder. In fact, I was too impressed with my progress for my own good. But it changed drastically the day I recognized the gleam in Greenwood's eye was sexual desire. I'd known there were men who loved other men as a *fairy* story, pardon the pun."

Cheshire grinned his famous grin. "Good heavens woman, it's wonderful you can still make a joke. I take my hat off to you. Humor is the best medicine, which leads me to believe that despite your overwhelming torment, you're on the mend. Now, wasn't it liberating to get that Greenwood business off your chest."

Verity smiled at last. "My reach had exceeded my grasp as the old saying goes," she said.

"My lie grew like mushrooms in the dark to the bleakest point where I thought I would die of shame. Instead, time accelerated me to a state where I no longer cared if I lived or died. I was already dead inside."

Cheshire arched his back and gave out a frightening yowl. "Puck was right, mortals be fools. A man who loathed womankind meets a woman with the maternal instinct of a female cat."

I felt my skin flash hot and cold. My expression changed from curiosity to shock. I leaned forward. "Oh, God, Verity, Greenwood fancied you... thinking you were a boy."

Verity's face burned with shame. She couldn't look me in the eye and her breath came in painful spasms of anger laced with tears. I poured her a glass of spring water and handed her a cool washcloth dipped in vinegar.

"I'm making you something considerably stronger than tea," I said. "Verity kept a bottle of brandy and smelling salts for minimizing skirmishes with Silkie."

"I humiliated him," Vera continued. "There was no simple way to extricate my guilt. I couldn't very well say *by the way, you'll laugh when I tell you... I'm a woman.* As much as I despised Greenwood, my apology nearly killed me. The words *I'm so sorry I broke your heart* lay on the ground bleeding as I left the room.

I hadn't played a devious trick; I'd accepted a challenge by picking up a gauntlet at my feet and performed the role of noble underdog proud of my ingenuity and how, by studying diligently, I'd made Greenwood a better writer considering he was a frightfully abysmal one to begin with.

Greenwood wanted a literary agent; I wanted the job, and I saw an opportunity; Greenwood saw a handsome boy.

I was a fraudulent impostor working for a fraud. Later, Greenwood called it collaborating and threw me to the lions. Afterwards he kept me on as his literary agent not because I was good at my job, which I was, but to punish me for making him appear foolish.

I never noticed a young man who hung around the office. But he noticed me. His eyes followed me, and Greenwood's eyes followed his never missing a beat. His name was Robin Clarke. He'd worked as a landscaper for Mr. Brown. I worked for Greenwood, and Clarky (that's what everyone called him) decided I was the perfect woman. He said nothing but Greenwood never missed a trick. He invented excuses for Clarky to bump into me. The day I said hello to Clarky he was that tongue-tied I thought he was choking to death. He blushed like a girl which made Greenwood laugh. He called Clarky, Luvvy, behind his back, and all ran smoothly until I became with child.

Clarky clearly felt betrayed. He never spoke to me again after

Greenwood accused him of mooning over his..." Verity faltered. The word W I F E resounded like a gunshot in the room."

Cheshire vanished and reappeared several times in succession. "Oh, dearest girl. How ghastly."

Verity spoke as if to the saltshaker. "Please excuse me rushing through the next bit to get it over with. I hardly know how to go on."

"Try dearest," Cheshire purred. "We've all made mistakes. Absolem does it all the time."

Vera gagged on a hysterical giggle. "Clarky was dismissed without pay. I gave birth, and the world went downhill. I had a daughter out of wedlock while Greenwood was being hounded for plagiarism. He adopted Alice out, played the ace immigration card, and hustled himself out of the country on my coattails.

And then one day Clarky turned up at the castle, hat in hand, fresh off the boat saying he forgave me. To say I was affronted was an understatement. But when I heard his proposal to take me off, what he called, Greenwood's 'dirty hands', I burst into tears because it was true.

I have to give Clarky credit. He was shaking but he still had the courage to confront Greenwood. "I know you're not married," he said. "I also know that Verity is under investigation for your crimes. It would be no trouble for me to lead the authorities to your door."

"I shrank into the shadows and tried to disappear. Greenwood relented with a handshake far too quickly and gave Clarky a job clearing some land.

Clarky's continual advances approved, nay *calculated* by Greenwood, sickened me. I sickened myself when I obeyed Greenwood by encouraging him. Teasing him, more like. I hardly knew wrong from right anymore. I loathed myself. I blamed the perversity of fate. Bad luck and the worst timing have haunted me all my life and continued in death.

Greenwood called me into his office on payday. I thought

nothing of it because I made out the cheques. He faked his loyalty to me. He screamed at Clarky to *get out and leave my beloved wife alone*. I cringed as if stung by a wasp when he put his arm around my shoulder.

Clarky stood his ground and searched my face for a sign before he shouted back, pay me what I'm owed. I stared at the floor hoping it would swallow me whole.

Greenwood shouted *I owe you nothing, leave my dear wife alone*. Later, I heard Clarky had booked passage back to the old country, but he hadn't.

And that was the last I knew of him until I saw him from the blind in the forest. He was strolling towards me with his axe, staring at me with a face like thunder. I said nothing and he blended into the trees like the apparition he was.

Greenwood was happy to fill me in on the details of Clarky's accident. He'd been crushed by a falling tree. Jezebel, he called me. *You were always batting your eyes at the poor kid. You have his blood on your hands. How can you live with yourself. Get out of my sight.*

So, the apparition *was* a ghost. No big deal. I dismissed Clarky for years until I died. And then I discovered the truth a poet once said that death has no dominion. The lust of two deranged men meant nothing. But ignoring them only fanned their need for revenge. And here we are."

Absolem paused puffing on his hookah which alarmed all of us including Vera. "When the worst has happened, there's nothing left to fear," he said barely audible.

Vera covered her face with her hands and sobbed her heart out. "But there is. You see, I've come to realize I *do* have Clarky's blood on my hands. And one thing I know for sure about reincarnation, is that one is given a few tries to correct a mistake but after two or three, a next life isn't granted if one's copy book is smudged. My dreams of a next life are over. How can I ever tell Edward."

Cheshire expanded to twice his size. Clearly, he felt important. "The truth of it is," he said. "I have news. We must change the conversation for something extraordinary. The woodcutter hasn't been stalking Verity to harm her, he was besotted. He's still waiting for an opportune moment to pop the question."

"Are you insane? Is the first question that comes to mind," Eeyore said, newly returned, his radar length ears picking up the newsflash to end all newsflashes.

chapter 53

GRADUALIZATION DAY

"The time has come," the Walrus said,
"To talk of many things:
Of shoes and ships and sealing-wax,
of cabbages and kings.
And why the sea is boiling hot,
and whether pigs have wings."

LEWIS CARROLL

– from 'The walrus and the carpenter'

VERITY'S LAMENT

Meanwhile, across the vastness of earth time, Christmas in Athens arrived, appropriately enough, at ground Zeno in a whiteout flurry of emotional exam papers.

Zeno's word was final. The volatile ceremony unfolded in my mind as it was no doubt destined to do under the imaginary auspices of hot snow that grew in strength from the rage of Greenwood's latest explosive tantrum – as a woodcutter snowman destined for exposure under an unforgiving sun. Soon there would be nothing left to show for Greenwood's Relentless reign of terror than a dozen metaphorical black stones from his eyes and mouth and the buttons from his imaginary clinical straitjacket.

Greenwood's outburst did more damage than the seismic aftershocks of a size 8 earthquake when he confessed to the crimes of which he was most proud – the purview of a true sociopath.

He had sealed his fate but was too unstable to be shown the door to Nowhere. Beatrice watched him go, gloating smugly until she too was ushered towards the void.

Zeno wiped his brow and collapsed into a chair. "You lot needn't worry," he said, "you've all passed. Not with flying colors mind, but no matter. A passing grade is a ticket to a next life, so congratulations are in order."

Endless found a jar of wine, poured it into eight clay cups and held his cup aloft after following the custom of wetting the new fallen snow with a libation for Athena.

Zeno refilled his cup and proposed a toast to Verity. "Truth," he said, "you inspired me to declare the end of a war with myself that has battled far too long. I took myself prisoner. I am clearly responsible for Restless's untimely death. I don't own up to such a thing proudly but with defiance. The man was a menace. He had to be stopped. But instead of removing him, his doppelganger Greenwood returned to a life corrupted tenfold, so my crimes exist today as a monster grown out of control. I've learned much about demons, but it was too late to do anything other than wait for a natural break in the universal flow of karmic comeuppance."

Endless stood beside him with his own cup, filled with guilt. "I helped Zeno," he confessed. "There were two prisoners. Zeno and I have been shackled together in guilty leg irons ever since. It's time to stop hobbling around our mistake."

Zeno as the accused, judge, and executioner overturned the guilty sentence to a casualty of war, pardoning himself and Endless in one fell swoop.

"It's time we were exonerated as heroes under pressure. I release you and you release me. What was done was done for the highest good. Would that I'd seen fit to carry out my crime earlier, and with more finality so the residue of hate that has pursued the rest of our group soul might have been avoided. But once done, a path is set. As Chesire would say, the cat is out of the bag. And speaking of cats."

Zeno clicked his fingers and Fetch materialized in the room shaking sparks from her fur. Silkie was about to ask where Chase was, when he bounded into the room hot on Fetch's tail. "Finaly he's chasing something," Silkie said. "Who's a clever boy, then."

Fetch took the floor and confronted Zeno. "Sir, it's urgent I speak with Silkie and Verity alone. Sorry, Zeno, but as Silkie's *Fetch*, I've had an important job to do for sixty-one years now, and I'm excited to deliver it."

"Yes, of course," Zeno said staring at the floor. "I understand perfectly. Silkie, you're free to go. I sense your confusion, little girl. Dream along with Fetch and she will see you safely to the low door in the wall. There's nothing to fear. Resist nothing. Bow to the green energies collecting around your estranged sister – she is a goddess in waiting.

Perhaps far-fetched is a more appropriate word than urgent, Fetch. Your task is more than Silkie imagined, but your timing is perfect. She and Verity are celebrating their reincarnation diplomas. Come along everyone, it's a perfect day to build a sandcastle. Let's give Verity and Silkie the room."

"Not too farfetched I hope," Fetch said. "Although perhaps now my sacred task is apparent."

"As a student well-versed in mythology, I know what's what," Verity said. "There's nothing to fear about dying. I know what a fetch is."

"Easy for you to say, grandmama," Silkie remarked. "Since you're already dead."

Zeno beckoned the woodcutter forward. Mr. Clarke, woodcutter extraordinaire, before we take our leave, we have old business to complete. You are here as a hapless attachment, a falsified document as it were, by your own admission, to Seneca Greenwood.

You were a victim of circumstance that resulted in a shameful display of poor judgement. I grant you a last chance for a better life on the condition that you cease and desist plaguing, hounding, harassing, or otherwise upsetting Verity from this day forward, since death already parts you." He paused smiling. "My proposition sounds like the future wedding vows you once cherished, do they not? Although with less rings and a prenuptial agreement."

You were ill served, and Verity was ill-used. As such you will be issued a boarding pass to the roving nursery Chrysalis Mundi of Veratopia. Please use it wisely. Love given too soon is rarely a successful match. Do I make myself clear?"

"Yes, sir. Indeed, you do. There's no need to explain it twice. Being in Greenwood's Forest once was more than enough."

Clarky released his grip on his axe, and it clattered to the stage. As we watched, it squirmed away like a snake, turned into a small ice pick, then a Swiss Army Knife, and finally, a harmless letter opener.

"Mail call," Cheshire called out dripping with sarcasm from the ether as he slowly materialized from the tip of his tail first. "I always say it only takes one bad apple to spoil the barrel."

Zeno's tone was shrill. "Relentless Greenwood, do you have anything to confess? Beatrice, have you any last words that may comfort your daughters or William Jonson?"

Both stood tight-lipped, their arms crossed, defiant to the end.

"Does anyone feel the need to say goodbye, good riddance, or good luck? Apologies anyone?"

"Forgiveness is not an apology," Endless said. "I could almost forgive shamefulness without losing any sleep. As for burying the hatchet? Not a chance."

Relentless's rage was building. "Wait," he shouted. "I'd like to face my executioner... pardon me, executioners." His presence percolated into a column of white heat. But then his shoulders relaxed, and he looked smaller as the wind left his sails. One could see it in the veins of his neck as much as his tortured bloodshot eyes. He worked his mouth, and I thought he was about to deliver a curse but the words "Sorry, Mother," tumbled out before he shut down entirely.

There was no melodramatic farewell. Only a sad little pop like a balloon half-filled with foul air. Psshhht, it was over. School was out.

chapter 54

CATCH 61

POST HOC, ERGO PROPTER HOC
(After this, therefore because of this)

I was left as Silkie had gleefully predicted, with the responsibility of a troubled forest coupled with my own unfinished story of profound transcendence. But where to begin? Where to finish? Would it ever finish?

In hindsight, the act of Silkie leaving marked my formal induction to Veratopia.

I was so looking forward to Silkie's absence all I could think of was having the forest to myself. Consequently, I forgot to listen to the cautionary alarm bells that warn of danger when something is too good to be true. Slowing down to smell the buttercups never occurred to me.

What I hadn't count on was the inevitable catch 61 of being too greedy.

There was no excusing being self-centered but still I reasoned that after many long seasons of psychic starvation I deserved to be in a winner's circle of some kind.

I was gripped in the total eclipse of right and wrong. Not only a situation that I couldn't see, but for a while one I had no interest in seeing.

What did Eeyore know? His shy words came back to me, *you'll know everything when the time is right. Best not ask too many questions.*

In my heart of hearts, I was fully aware that being giddy with power required the balancing effects of selflessness. But I hadn't reckoned a new set of literary challenges would so completely overshadow my devotion to Eeyore or that I would repay his self-sacrifice with my selfishness. It shames me all over again each time I replay it in my mind.

I was lightheaded from newfound possibilities and sadly, the amazing benefits from Verity's fountain of youth reduced me to a temperamental princess.

The rules of Verity's riot act, were harder to tame, hidden as they were in memories, forbidden secrets, and rubbing shoulders with ghosts who demanded serious restitution. For one thing, I'd regrettably assigned Eeyore an overabundance of editing hours that were hard on his eyes.

Cheshire said I was making up for lost time, which as he pointed out, was rather ironic in a forest where time stands still. He was right as usual. I'd lost track of being kind. Unforgiveable. Cheshire pointed out creating Chlora was a call for help. Her 'birth' was necessary to release my suppressed sadness from living in the true asylum that had been my mother's house. I was blind."

Eeyore was aging at a phenomenal rate. Like humans, toys grow old from lack of attention.

Eeyore was no exception, but he was humble and resilient. As such, he'd refrained from verbalizing his needs. He never demanded anything, having grown used to being singled out in the Hundred-acre Wood to make do with discomfort and neglect at the mercy of the elements. A feeble pile of sticks was a pathetic excuse for shelter.

A.A. Milne wrote bad luck exceedingly well and dumped the lot of it on Eeyore as his designated comrade in arms to ease his guilt from surviving in a war that claimed thousands of lives. A sadly overburdened downcast donkey was the perfect scapegoat to atone for the sins of the father.

It took Vera and Puck to show me the error of my ways. And by then it wasn't so much as too late but where to begin lavishing compassionate care on my best friend.

Negative consequences known as catch 22's or as I called mine, the catch 61's – the *'damned if you do and damned if you don't' laws* – Do this and that happens. Fail to do that and this will surely result in the classic excuse of *I'll do it later*.

Writing saved Alan Milne from the worst of guilt by transferring his overwhelming despair from his pen to his son. How telling that literary success made Alan jealous of the fame he'd unwittingly heaped on his overly sensitive, boy.

Christopher Robin bore the brunt of the intrusive publicity of the insatiable press core and obsessive fan adoration. As unintentional as it may have been, Milne was blindsided by embarrassment from writing a phenomenally successful children's book at the expense of legitimate acceptance within his old fraternity of professional humorists, dramatists, and journalists.

Balancing the inevitable good with terrible sacrifices is a tough call. What to forgive... what to sacrifice, and what to protect. For Eeyore, it was fully assimilating my lost years, his sense of duty, leaving well enough alone, and indulging in a daily ritual of forest bathing. A buttercup a day kept the reproaches at bay.

I wondered if Beatrice was aware that she died so she could be recycled as a new growth sapling? But those thoughts led directly to understanding how I'd been selfish so Absolem and Cheshire could teach me a valuable lesson about compassion.

Edward could only be reborn from the ashes of truly accepting defeat as a victory. His legacy as William Shakespeare is being publicly reclaimed as I write this, from the phenomenal discovery of missing documents indirectly uncovered from Eeyore nosing about the woods searching for Roo.

The bookmobile had to be buried in a consecrated landfill in a public display of social responsibility for a new library to be born and an old school to end.

The concept of *last but not least* finally came home to me. Good had come from bad when a remnant of Beatrice's mercenary firebrands was sniffed out by Wick and extinguished.

Pooh, in a staggering display of owlish wisdom wondered if Veratopia was *'praps* one of those *furnominal* Bermuda triangles where small animals like Roo purposely go missing so they can be found.

chapter 55

A NEW YEAR DAY'S PROMISE

"Do I dare disturb the universe?
In a minute there is time
For decisions and revisions
which a minute will reverse."

T.S. ELIOT

I woke the second before our cuckoo clock struck 2025 with three magic words on my lips, threw on a robe, and grabbed a saucepan and lid to wake up the New Year. Outside, the dew sparkled on every blade and leaf, and I closed my eyes, a green goddess in waiting.

My first official words required uttering a mystical incantation that called down the universal energies of healing. Once quickened, the troublesome accumulation of negative energy of the forest's turbulent past would be purified at last.

"RABBITS RABBITS RABBITS," I shouted. And *crash* answered the cymbals of cooking pots and lids from every surrounding hollow and burrow where all homesteads above or underground honored the Lady Flora for the previously turbulent twelve months in exuberant displays of gratitude for surviving them.

I had already prepared myself the night before by reading 'Watership Down' to get in the mood. In my dream I wandered through a field of fragrant clover that extended the boundaries of Veratopia's liminal space. Every rabbit that ever lived was present in spiritual form, rabbiting in every direction while the great Pan sat cross legged in their midst, his eyes closed welcoming in the beginning of a new cycle.

I walked towards him waving, and the rabbits parted so a green avenue of new grass materialized before me. I levitated a few inches off the ground in a state of euphoria. Pan's love for his forest filled me with the feeling of belonging. I had come home.

I'd been in Veratopia since Verity, the embodiment of truth, called me. Well, it turned out she called Eeyore first and I followed her to rescue him from her clutches. Or so I'd thought. But there'd been a conspiracy of friends and I'd been gently nudged towards my lost destiny.

The crashing celebration of metal against metal, the commotion of a braying of a donkey, and raucous trumpeting Ellies, resounded through the cabin's sacred grove. When it stopped abruptly, the trees encircling the cabin briefly turned to stone in deference to our ancestors forming a sacred henge of standing stones that energized the clearing.

Every bird sang their sweetest song, every squirrel and tree sprite, every mouse and rabbit gathered to pay homage to the rising sun. Storybook characters joined them, moving in a trance like a procession of ancient druids, responding to venerate Silvany's elemental god, Pan who rose with his arms held wide to embrace the first sunrise of Terra Nuova.

The party that followed resembled a wedding breakfast of well-wishers. Edward held hands with his beloved Verity– a tall, beautiful, silver-haired woman, wearing a simple shift of dark green wool.

Pax arrived with his Ellies in tow, now grown to the size of brontosauruses, suitably subdued for the occasion. They loaded their trunks without incident, and took their spoils back to their allotted grove to chow down a truly magnificent array of foodstuffs where a food fight was not only common, it went a long way to trumpeting the forest clear of recent unwelcome spectres.

Eeyore and I rubbed noses, not to acknowledge *better luck next time* but to express how lucky we were in the moment.

The Ellies surprised everyone by cleaning up the aftereffects of a particularly lively food fight, so that their grove looked as peaceful as any other. Pax prophesied it wouldn't last, and it didn't, but it was a much-appreciated concession to refined behavior. The next day they resumed their regular size, which wasn't that much smaller, and loud unconstrained revelling issued from their section of the woods once more.

chapter 56

THE TUNNEL OF LOVE

"What you imagine, you create,
What you feel, you will attract,
What you think, you become."

BUDDHA

Earlier that morning, I'd opened the scratching at the door to find a Dalmatian wagging its tail, clearly delighted to see me.

"Who is it," Eeyore called out from the kitchen.

"A lovely big dog," I called back.

Eeyore shuffled up behind me trying rather unsuccessfully to wag his tail. "Well, bless my soul," he said. "If it isn't Wick, my understudy. You must have written him so well he was able to jump off your pages. Come in old boy. Welcome."

Wick bounded past me and rubbed his nose against Eeyore's, and they performed the customary canine ritual of *'how are you I'm delighted to make your acquaintance what did you have for lunch'* sniffing formality.

"Leela will get you your own water bowl, won't you, Leela?"

"Already doing it your highness. Dost thou require anything else, sire?"

"Food would be most appreciated. Any dog who scratches at a stranger's door is starving. Food first… affection second… third, more food."

"I'm not a stranger. I created him. I guess that kind of makes me his mother."

"You were a stranger until the door opened, Leela. Dalmatians are quite clever compared to… say, a piglet."

I filled a clean bowl with leftover macaroni and cheese, to which Eeyore commented "All I ever got was thistles."

"And a case of amnesia," I said. "If you think back, you will recall I gave you porridge and you're forgetting all the digestive biscuits," I reminded him. "I shall have to buy some special doggy ones for Wick."

"Bacon flavored, please," Eeyore said. "I'd like to try those myself. Where will he sleep?"

Wick dug his nose deep into the macaroni and scoffed the lot. I hazarded a guess. "Most dogs like to sleep in front of the fire."

"What? Both of us?"

Wick slurped his water and whined at the door to go out. "Fair's fair. You share Wick's bacon treats; he shares your hearth rug. And in hot weather, we have tile floors and a lovely field of cool grass. I wrote Wick, so, I happen to know he prefers sleeping outdoors in all weathers. Let's leave it for him to decide."

Eeyore pawed the ground. "Perchance you're right. I'll show him my field and explain Absolem's rules of etiquette. He's none too thrilled about being barked at."

Eeyore used the word barking to mean the sound dogs make. My definition was usually reserved for barking mad or shouting in someone's face. "Aren't we all," I said using the shouting designation.

"I dare say Lucy won't mind Wick's …*ahem*… extra curricular *bathroom* habits."

Wick gave a short sharp bark in search of Chlora who, upon hearing with her spritely extra-sensitive ears, fairly flew from the herb garden and flung herself at his neck where her twiggy limbs stuck like Velcro.

I grabbed the shopping basket, donned my bag lady persona,

and headed to the town center. "You three have a nice visit," I called over my shoulder. "Teatime is at …"

"Four…" Eeyore answered. "Of course it is, Leela. Everyone knows that."

"Dinner will be at 5 o'clock."

Eeyore was more contrite when he asked if I could (changing it to would), bring home something chocolaty flavored.

"So, chocolate, then. Normally I wouldn't, but I've already written that Wick was privy to chocolate when he belonged to the firefighters and that he thrived on it."

"I wish old A.A. had written that sort of thing for me. Pooh got honey. And whatever Pooh had Piglet ate…"

"Acorns, if I remember correctly," I said.

Eeyore brayed his shock in a strangulated "*Eeeew* and I thought thistles were bad. I swear I heard Piglet mention having cream teas at Owl's every Tuesday afternoon and teacakes with Christopher Robin on Saturdays."

"Oh, he said it all right," I said, "but he daydreams his wishes out loud, does our Piglet."

It wasn't long before the rabbits heard of a celebrity character in their midst. Word spread to Alice and on down the food chain to Pax and Peter who loved dogs and Cheshire who didn't as a rule, thinking them empty-headed, but tolerated them because they couldn't reach him.

Absolem was so uneasy he had to inhale several long puffs from his hookah pipe before he allowed Wick to sniff him which worked out well because as it happens, dogs and hookah smoke are not mutually compatible. So, a line was drawn. A trippy spaced-out caterpillar on one side and the Ellies, Parker, Tigger, and Wick on the other.

Piglet made himself scarce whenever Wick was around. He had

reason to be nervous as he'd once been mauled by a terrier. His little piglet face showed the aftereffects of teeth marks after being shaken like a rat; his soul carried the psychic toothmarks of terror.

Later, in front of the fire, a pensive Eeyore asked me something that had been worrying him ever since the characters in my book joined us. "Leela," he said, "I was wondering what, if any, other animals you might be writing into the forest."

"Would you like me to write you a donkey friend?"

"Perhaps a unicorn," he said. "If it's a little one."

The Ellies followed behind Pax who rode to Lucy's meadow on Eeyore's back shouting "make way for our latest peace march" whereupon I greeted them by placing a wreath of bluebells around Martha's neck.

The rabbits sniffed the wind for any lingering traces of the woodcutter. But Clarky was history, and the rest of us embraced the purging of Veratopia's forest as a new world named Terra Nuova.

I held my arms wide to the meadow filled with Terranuovians. "Welcome, to our tunnel of love, party, to celebrate Eeyore's coming of age," I shouted. "There will be one or two cursory speeches after which food will be served."

Cheshire opined from above "You know, to some of us *celebrities*, speeches are fun," he stage-whispered to Chlora, waving ecstatically from her favorite branch.

I shushed her with a finger on my lips and was about to introduce the first speech when Absolem, chuffed beyond measure with his blue wings, landed on Eeyore's bluebells and proceeded to wax particularly eloquently befitting the occasion of Eeyore's formal debut.

"I'd just like to remind everyone that our little get together, named after the ethereal tunnel of white light that represents the transition from death to life, is the perfect metaphor to honor a tumultuous year of changes."

Absolem lifted to hover on a passing updraft. "Heading towards the white light at its far end literally embodies the end of life that leads to positive changes in a new physical form. Eeyore will soon attest to this better than anyone, although as you can see, I've recently experienced reincarnation again, but that said, I'd like to add that my tunnel was a lovely spherical chrysalis."

"Enough to fill a book, wink, wink," Eeyore said nudging me in the ribs.

Cheshire giggled and stretched out a paw to bat one of the first baby apples. The apple, not technically a windfall, fell to the ground and rolled into Eeyore's front hoof where the dismounted Pax retrieved it and took a bite before feeding it to Eeyore.

I stood, wineglass of ginger beer in my hand, to give a toast. A passing Sparkly tapped it to grab everyone's attention. "It has been an eventful six months," I said. "Let us welcome Roo back into our family. Thanks to Eeyore's brilliant sleuthing and the trees giving up a dangerous secret, he's sitting here. Do you have a few words to say, Eeyore."

Eeyore lifted his neck and bowed solemnly. "First, I have Lucy to thank for my discovery. The woodcutter amused himself by drawing out his dastardly game, but because trees, connected at the roots as they are, they all knew where Roo was but were afraid if they spoke up, they'd be chopped down. Christopher Robin had left Roo behind under an apple tree on a summer picnic.

"Huzzah," Piglet shouted, and immediately took a step backward behind Pooh, so as not to be identified as being too overenthusiastic.

"Kanga won't mind me saying," Eeyore continued, "considering I say it as a compliment, that she's a little single-minded about children. And may I add, it was a blessing in disguise that she never noticed Roo gone. Piglet being the same size, wasn't about to tell her. So, we have Piglet to thank for Kanga never being sad."

Piglet, as excited as he was, from our smattering of applause, took a bow without falling over, and pulled his ears over his eyes.

Kanga, wearing her new reading glasses, pushed Roo forward. "It's all right, dear, it's your turn. I'm right behind you."

Piglet, quite revived, and reinforced by a generous teaspoon of extract of malt, stood as tall as he could and spoke up in a brave voice. "Actually, that's me *in front of you*," he corrected. "Roo is in your pouch. Kanga, you need to wear your glasses *over* your eyes. They're no good on the top of your head."

Eeyore gave Piglet an affectionate shove, "You might consider not using your ears as a blindfold."

Roo, de-pouched, reached for Piglet's hand and told us what happened. "It was a hot-ish sort of day. Christopher Robin placed me in the shade of a strange apple tree a gazillion miles from Cotchwood Farm, and as I'd grown drowsy after several doses of strengthening medicine, I wriggled into the roots above ground for a cozy place for my afternoon nap and fell asleep. The next think I knew was Eeyore's wet nose poking me awake. He carried me home and placed me inside my mother's pocket as a surprise, and here I am."

"Well done, dear," Kanga said petting Piglet's head instead of Roo's.

Piglet, mellowed after his brush with celebrity, was about to be bounced by none other than Eeyore, of all animals who whispered in Wick's ear that it may be an opportune moment to help cure Piglet of an old fear.

So, after Chlora, gave her word, doubly empowered with a 'piggy swear' that he'd be safe, Piglet stayed still as a statue while Wick sniffed him gently and backed away without a bark.

I gave Wick a bacon-flavored dog treat while Pooh serenaded Piglet. *"Sing ho for Piglet. Piglet, ho,"* he sang, and the rest of us clapped in unison which made the song more rousing. At which point, Piglet fainted and was revived with another spoonful of strengthening medicine that Kanga always carried in her pouch.

As the party wound down, Edward raised his glass in a final

toast. "I can safely report that Verity and I burned her Greenwood contract under a full moon. My documents and original plays rest in peace in London and will come to light when the time is right and not one moment before."

Cheshire cheered on Piglet, who now comfortable with giving impromptu speeches, bowed respectfully to Edward. "They will be no doubt be a wonderful Sir Prize," he said.

chapter 57

LEAVING FOR GOOD

"Take charge and stake your own claim."

ZENO

My diary entry reads as follows: The Queen of Hearts left for good yesterday. It was followed with an ecstatic row of exclamation marks and a large happy face.

We held a madly extravagant tea party to celebrate.

The tree sprites formed teams to see which family could make the longest paper chain of black paper hearts in the least time. The results festooned the trees surrounding a long trestle table loaded with cream cakes and watercress sandwiches.

In hindsight, 2024 has been a time of unprecedented purging. First Beatrice, then Greenwood, and finally the woodcutter. Our flash deforesting took a turn for the miraculous. Through patience and a great deal of happenchance, Veratopia was freed from four long-term residents who never ceased to maintain an aura of destructive unease.

Edward had chanced to be confronted by one of them on his way to our writing class.

As usual, the Queen of Hearts was on a pointless mission to round up anyone she deemed in need of beheading – ever an unlimited quantity. Everyone in her royal path was subject to execution without trial. It would have been grisly, he noted, had her bumbling knaves been capable executioners.

Edward had been minding his own business picking daisies when the words 'off with her head' flew out of the forest. Following close behind was the redheaded shrew herself.

She'd shrieked her usual warning. 'Anyone picking daisies belonging to the crown without my written permission must be punished'.

Edward told the old witch she could have the flowers back and tossed them at her feet but apparently that worsened his sentence although, as he commented later, it's impossible to imagine what could be worse than having no head.

Edward pleaded his case, articulated in plain English, something Edward rarely did in front of an audience. I believe he called her an horribillously grotesque creature or words to that effect. And sin of sins, he ordered her to step aside and neglected to bow.

No-one calls Edward de Vere a boy without serious backlash so when the queen spat 'you there, boy, hold up,' it got ugly. "He bellowed back I AM NOT A BOY," and proceeded to brag, that as an Earl, he'd always spoken thus to his Queen Elizabeth. "You're as disagreeable as the queen I once knew", he said. "Not that it matters but your hair is an even ghastlier shade of red which I didn't think possible. You are a repugnant upstart. There is nothing majestic about you. And if you think to frighten me, you, madame, are sadly mistaken."

The Queen of Hearts stood, at a loss for words, her mouth gaped open gasping for breath. Not content with silencing her, Eward continued to bait her bellowing "You are a madwoman. Your knaves are witless. You waylay me at your peril madame. Pray step aside, disgusting harlot, I'm late."

"For a very important date," a voice catcalled, followed by laughter.

Edward smiled and continued. "The queen greatly mortified, flounced about in a speechless rage, and as she did so, her wig slipped sideways, further humiliated by the stays of her dress popping like corks from a bottle. All she managed to shout was a weak 'well I never', without an exclamation mark and promptly tripped backwards over a bluebell.

At that, the queen's knaves turned tail and scattered, leaving her defenceless. "Jackanapes," she shouted after them. "You will all be executed at dawn, tomorrow."

The Queen of absolutely nothing important had to roll onto her knees to rise but fell back when no help was proffered. She scrambled, graceless, tripping over her own shadow that had detached itself and stuck its tongue out at her blocking her path, and while tying her shoe Edward had a clear shot at booting her out. It was pure farce, and he admitted he played it for a cheap laugh as if we'd been there watching. She was a sorry sight, landed on her knees, bald as an egg, groping for her wig – an orange mop trapped beneath her voluminous petticoats.

The knaves, assembled outside the gate bumped into each other like stumblebums. Edward couldn't resist turning toward the treeline and taking a bow.

Edward beamed from Cheshire's enthusiastic "Ding dong, the witch is dead!"

"Atta boy," Absolem said. "Well played, sir."

I asked Cheshire if he'd deliberately made a theatrical pun to which he replied helpless with laughter. "What else could it be? A playwright plays. Once stagestruck; always a star."

"All hail the conquering hero," Puck shouted, taking his own flamboyant bow.

For a nice touch, Puck played Edward offstage with his flute.

Pax straightened his pith helmet and shouted, "Let the revelry begin!" Immediately the Ellies joined the party by trampling a table of cream cakes into mush.

Edward had long-since abandoned his starched lace collar and balloon pantaloons for blue jeans, a black T-shirt and sneakers, but since he'd recalled his old leather doublet, he looked like a rockstar – the Earl of hip with the romantic cachet of a buccaneer. His theatrical prowess allowed him to parody the carefree teenagers of the local school to perfection. Showing off being a professional stage performer's ultimate glory.

The comfort of soft unrestricting fabrics did wonders for his angry mood swings. Clearly, clothing made the teenager. Edward strutted his best pose teasing Alice into a fluster whenever she was around. Likewise, but to a lesser degree, Peter swaggered with an air of the pirate about him.

But as the festivities wound down, Edward's confident mood surprisingly changed for the worse. He withdrew, charged with supressed anger that soon turned maudlin.

"There is nothing romantic about being uncomfortable," he declared, "I've decided to stay here for good." It was shouted like a nobleman to a lacky. His next order 'bring me a roast swan, hither, knave' was in jest. Noting that a swan was an Elizabethan name for an actor, I wondered if Edward was referring to an actor being burned at the stake, an unheard-of crime, but nothing entirely out of the question if Elizabeth had so much as a toothache.

His theatrical declaration earned a genuine smatter of applause. He bowed his thanks, but I could see he was grumpy, and for the rest of the day when he spoke, he spoke as if to himself, but something had unleashed the actor within, and once released he delivered an impromptu command performance into the breathless forest that rendered us speechless. His voice grew louder to reach the trees in the back row.

"Whatever nonsense historians like to fantasize, I was there in Elizabeth's court," Edward proclaimed. It was obvious he was alone, centerstage under a spotlight, delivering a long-suppressed soliloquy.

There was nothing to do but to honor Edward's truth spilling out.

The forest theatre grew still. The wind died down enough to tickle the leaves as a gentle reminder that life vibrated under the forest canopy. Puck put his arm around Piglet, and Pooh counted the bees that had gathered around his unopened jar of honey.

In the silence that followed, Edward spoke his truth clearly. "The court was never the jolly merrymaking romantics imagine," he began. "We lived in fear for our lives at Elizabeth's whim. The truth is, only one secret kept me from the block, but it never saved me; it outed me."

"Omigod, he's not acting. This is for real," Cheshire said. "We must hear him out and prepare for the worst."

Edward paced an invisible stage like a restless bear. "The screams of dying prisoners haunted my childhood," he said. His eyes glazed, viewing an England only he could see.

He bent low to deliver a spicy bit of supressed bitterness to the trees in the front row. "Did you know that as a ward of Elizabeth's chief executor William Cecil, or should I say, her chief executioner, Lord Burghley, I resided in Burghley House, near enough to Whitecourt palace to hear the cheers of the crowd following the thud of a decapitated head."

Eeyore and I couldn't imagine the horrors that Edward had seen every day of his life. The Queen of Hearts pathetic games, terrorizing the small woodland animals and Piglet were the tantrums of a spoiled child in need of attention that paled in comparison to Edward's encounters with jeering bloodthirsty crowds calling for torture.

Absolem's sudden fit of coughing overwhelmed him. When he was quite recovered, he managed to declare "London was ground zero for plague and torture. Defying Elizabeth was never an option."

"Did you ever make Elizabeth cry?" I asked Edward.

Edward shook his head remembering. "No. I specialized in making her furious many many times."

It was then that Cheshire did something I never thought possible. He materialized on the ground and encircled Edward protectively with his tail. "True or false, that is the question," he said. "Daring to tell the truth or choosing to lie to save your head begs an entirely different question that you never have to ask yourself again."

The rest of us gathered closer as a family and sat with Edward until he talked himself out, learning more about his heroic battle with truth until the moon faded to sunrise.

"Burghley declared it educational for me to witness gore on a regular basis. Torture and punishment were commonplace. Animals were slaughtered in every bear pit, cockfighting arena, and courtyard. The streets ran with blood, offal, and the contents of piss pots. Everyone was desensitized to stench.

Those mindless schoolboys we saw in town would never have survived a hanging let alone a drawing and quartering or the many times a blunt axe failed to separate a head cleanly from its shoulders with one swing. They amuse themselves with games of violence in a tiny box – a coward's way of being a warrior. Fingers crossed the Shadowland never has to face another world war.

Living in a luxurious manse may have awarded me fine rooms and rare books but I grew overdependent on my status.

My zenith as a royal favorite waned as the years passed partly due to Elizabeth's guilty conscious for being an insatiable harlot with a roving eye and a license to pick her lovers at will. Elizabeth modelled her image on the queen of heaven, but her lusty needs invariably won out over chastity. More like a Virgin Queen despoiled a hundred times," he sneered.

"Producing a male heir was the first duty of a queen and to my lasting regret, my shame. But our son, Henry IX, was never meant to reign. His presence destroyed Elizabeth's perfect performance as the Virgin Mary in Tudor clothing. Henry was fobbed off on a noble family too terrified to refuse her and too greedy to ignore her gifts of titles and land.

When Elizabeth was born, her father King Henry was furious for her failing to be the son he craved."

The opposite of Christopher Robin and his mother a voice shouted.

Elizabeth's mother, Anne Boleyn was as good as executed for the treason of birthing a daughter. In a mad scheme, Elizabeth was determined to please her father posthumously by becoming his son who died at fourteen.

King Henry was never easy to please in the years Elizabeth knew him considering his bloated condition with a purulent oozing leg that stank of rotting flesh. No distractions of sumptuous finery could overshadow the realities of Henry's obesity and irrational temper. Henry's pain threshold ruled his court; Elizabeth's fear overruled hers. Like father like daughter.

Given her druthers, Elizabeth might have fared better as a wench in a tavern. But she saw herself as a Tudor prince and therein lay her inhumanity. Elizabeth never cared for the title princess.

She was three when Henry beheaded her mother, hauled off to the tower on a contrived charge of treason – a grim reminder of her own shaky succession. So, when Elizabeth's day of deliverance arrived at age twenty-five, after lingering in the Tower believing she awaited imminent execution at the hands of her older sister, Bloody Mary, Queen of Scots, she embraced the attitude of an entitled spoiled teenager.

Her crown sat on uneasy shoulders; her nerves permanently ready to snap.

I organized amusements, pageants and plays to delight her, but she was single-mindedly determined to suffer. Assassins hid behind every tree. Burghley made sure to catch at least one a week to keep her majesty on high alert, and more importantly in his debt.

Assassins were easy to create. Confessions wrung from tortured bodies were commonplace.

Fabricating treasonous deeds was an art form best performed by Burghley, a callous fearmonger who used everything to lever his position as first minister. He was a greedy bejewelled toady whose hatred drove him to destroy me."

Edward cowered defensively, drained of energy.

"One big unhappy dysfunctional family," Absolem declared overcome with emotion. "You're here with us, dear boy. You're safe now. Let it all go." And as he spoke, Edward took the form of a twelve-year-old orphan. Whereupon Puck took his hand and led him into the forest.

Elizabeth was not unlike the Queen of Hearts except Heartless's threats were idle and merely caused the woodland creatures' unease and the rest of us irritating delays.

Elizabeth wielded serious power to behead whomever she chose. Her whims were insatiable. Her moods were lightning fast. One moment she was lavishing praise upon the head a favorite courtier... the next day it was impaled on a spike atop Tower Bridge.

Some queens end up as caricatures, but Elizabeth started out as one. How could she not. One day she was a hapless prisoner and the next, a dizzy reckless girl suddenly released from house arrest with a free pass to absolute power, freed from a pending death sentence.

Alice's mad Queen of Hearts was last seen leaving our backwoods with her knaves, terrifying the trees en-route and spilling forth into the unforgiving world of shadows headlong into a police cruiser. She was unceremoniously swept up, arrested for creating a public disturbance, parading without a license and carted off shrieking about treason and her absolute divine right to rule as she pleased. Queeny, unwisely gave her pseudonym, ' *Queen Ruby-locks of no fixed abode at the present moment, not that it's any of your damn business*'. Letters may be left for her in The Tower of London and no she wasn't sure of that street address either.

Pax commanded his Ellies to wait quietly in a grove of trees which they obeyed immediately without a single trumpet. Wick calmed down enough to investigate, sniffing their leathery hides without incident and trotted back to report they were a tad intimidating but really quite sweet and harmless if treated with respect.

Eeyore watched the confrontation with an air of caution, not being overly thrilled with animals ten times his size. "No offense to you, Pax, but even Puck doesn't overturn as many apple carts as your lumping great pets."

"Ask Edward. I'm as tame as a midsummer's day, I am," Puck said.

"And honest as the day is long, I *don't* think," Cheshire added. "Magic tricks are just fancy illusions, and honesty is more often deceptive by nature, two sides of the same wooden nickel, if you ask me, fool's gold is *dangerous* gold."

Puck did a somersault, materialized bareheaded, and produced a shiny coin from Alice's ear to prove his point. "And what half-a-crown would that be, Cheshire?"

"The one you just made disappear," Cheshire answered, rolling his eyes. "Why do fairies, still think they can outsmart a cat?"

When Edward's performance was over the trees gave their foliage a shake and their limbs reached higher into the blue to warm in the sunshine.

"It's all well and good," Absolem said, "to celebrate an old forest is always fresher after a reshuffle of sunshine and chlorophyl."

I stood and stretched my limbs imitating the trees. "Come on then, stir your stumps. There's work to be done."

"No need to act haughty," Eeyore muttered.

"Oh, dear me. I'm afraid you couldn't be more wrong," Absolem said brandishing his hookah pipe like a sceptre. "Stuff and nonsense. Haughty is an artform dear boy."

Eeyore, not about to be dissed by a caterpillar, countered with "Mr. Carroll's Queen of Hearts and Mr. Lewis's Snow queen were the mirror images of Edward's Queen Lizzie, the axe trigger fiend. For a while it was all off with their heads and Turkish Delight."

Absolem wriggled uncomfortably and curled into a woozy ball. "Sometimes, I despair of you, Eeyore. You take what I say far too literally. Although I can understand how you might assume that I'm a master philosopher. An educated difference of opinion is never a mistake. After all, a caterpillar can look at a queen."

In the end, writing 'Spritewood' transmuted my sad childhood into a positive message from Eeyore and the ghost of the twelve-year-old boy, Nate, who so loved books that he died of his injuries. I see him wandering the grounds of Parallel Park where the bookmobile rests peacefully under the foundations of the Nathaniel Sloane Memorial Library. A large portrait of Nate greets children and their parents at the entrance and his ghost waves them goodbye as they leave with arms full of books.

After Edward unburdened himself, I told him he was a fine example of human evolution reaching for the stars.

"That reminds me," Absolem said. "When Puck was knee-high to a grasshopper, reading tea leaves was ..."

Cheshire got the last word by vanishing before Absolem finished his sentence. But one could still hear Absolem's bemused voice muttering through Lucy's foliage for days: "What do you expect from a fairy that reads his own tealeaves."

TERRA NUOVA

WHAT DREAMS HAVE COME

chapter 58

CRUCIBLE TIME

CRUCIBLE
*An alchemic container able to withstand
the intense heat necessary
for the transmutation of lead into gold.
A metaphorical melting pot for
enduring human tests both physical and spiritual.*

Veratopia was ablaze with more than news. Absolem said not to worry. "A forest is a phoenix. It burns when the time is right, and new trees rise from the ashes. Fire brings new life."

Cheshire brought me up to speed. "Veratopia as we knew it is gone. A flash fire picked up speed and raged out of control. The Nozone is now a field of desolation – a clearing of charred tree stumps, twisted roots, and a host of widowed dryad's skeletal ghosts." He sniffed his tail and grimaced. "I smell of soot. Never mind," he said. "It's nothing a long bask in sunshine won't cure.

As we speak, black ashes are raining down on an area that temporarily reeks of despair. Crowflakes, Absolem calls them. Fortunately, he's used to choking on smoke. As immortals we've witnessed them many times. Now buck up. It's a time for celebrating.

Fire is a natural crucible for purifying our sacred forest desecrated by malevolent energies. It's about time, too. Enchanted sectors reincarnate instantly. You'll see. By the end of business today, the domain of Terra Nuova will reign as a new earth."

My first thoughts were of Lucy. Instantly, Absolem reassured me "No need to fear, Leela. Lucy is spared. She is our earth mother. Even as we speak, she's comforting the animals.

Our old growth forest understands they're protected as a single entity rooted to each other deeply underground. Even the charred tree stumps are alive. They will be absorbed by the earth and rise as saplings without waiting for spring."

He continued to read my thoughts. "Cheshire has safely escorted Pooh and Piglet to Eeyore's field. It's like a birthday party over there. The woods will smell like smoke for a while, but it will be green in the shake of a donkey's tail."

I was relieved. The snowstorms I'd experienced in the dead of shadowy winters had left the landscape bereft of green. Even lone straggles of pine trees had been whitewashed.

I never saw a Christmas card landscape as winter wonderland as others did. Even as a child I had no desire to build a snowman. I'd been dressed roughly and pushed outside. I huddled close to the house out of the wind, but sometimes Mother forgot about me until dark.

Eeyore's first instinct was to visit Lucy. Mine was to race him to the door.

The first thing Lucy did was give us hope. "Go to what you will surely see as devastation but know it for an optical illusion. Look for me, there. As true as I'm growing here, my daughter has been born in rich new topsoil. Her name is Lucinda. As my seedling, she will be the new princess of the Nozone. Please think of a joyous new name to honor her."

"I will."

By the time Eeyore and I reached the Nozone the fire was still smouldering. Lucy's voice came to me calm and steady. "Take a deep breath, Leela. All is well. You were brought to Veratopia to learn more than writing. What you see is the kindest teaching to prepare you for your destiny."

"I'm not aware of any such... what destiny?" I said.

"Verity left explicit instructions to protect you. Eeyore knows."

"It has come," Eeyore said, looking more sheepish than a real donkey should. "Verity foretold of this. I was directed to take you to Lucy where all would be made clear. Well, that's been accomplished except for the being made clear part. All I know is that I am meant to guide you as your appointed, for want of a better word, shaman. The Green Man himself thought it wise to ease you into what can often appear violent to unaccustomed eyes. All I can say with my limited knowledge of natural lore is that the view we see here will have transformed into one of serenity by nightfall.

I've not been plotting against you," he said. "I've been awaiting further instruction on how best to help you transition from any persistent old dark shadows to new lighter ones."

Lucy looked more beautiful than ever. Her energy surged up my spine in wave after wave of bliss. I lay in her shade as instructed, so that her foliage filled the sky. She lovingly fanned befouled air from my clothes with a low sweeping branch.

"This is my lesson for both of you," she said. "Look up. Choose a small patch of blue and concentrate. Become what you see. Expand into the loving spaciousness that is your truest home."

Absolem materialized on my arm in his butterfly coat, Cheshire materialized above me, and Eeyore acted like a kid on Christmas morning, rolling in leaves.

"What remains will come as it comes," Absolem said. "A trial by fire is a blessing, my dear. Tell them, Cheshire."

Cheshire spun like a furry tornado before he righted himself in his default position of lounging on invisible pillows. "It's a blessing,

Leela. As Edward would say, 'All's Well that Ends Well'. That boy certainly knows how to turn a phrase."

Lucy began to teach as soon as I entered my patch of sky. "The fire acted as a crucible for purifying our forest desecrated by malevolent energies. It is the way of all forests, that from time-to-time a select grove is razed to the ground. It is done swiftly without harm to the mother forest or its fauna. I didn't want to alarm you. You're a sensitive young girl still processing a great deal of recent dramatic events. The aftermath of a spiritual cleansing looks shocking, but I assure you there is no permanent devastation. Deforestation makes way for new trees to thrive."

I pictured the word deforestation written in the sky, amused that the letters descrambled into the words 'frost' and 'defrosting'.

"Words used powerfully are specifically uttered to clear the air," Absolem remarked. "What comes to mind is mindful, do you see?"

"What goes around comes around," Cheshire purred. "Aint *that* the cat's pyjamas."

"A veritable chrysalis," Absolem finished, nostalgic for his good old days.

A thousand rabbits gathered to encircle the NoZone in a chain of energy to protect its rich topsoil. In place of charred stumps were translucent sprouts no more than an inch tall, glowing like lime-green Christmas tree bulbs flooded with electricity.

We found Lucinder easily. She spoke to me in the sweet leafy voice of a child. "Hello, Aunt Leela. Please may I call you that. Mother says it will serve for the moment until we are better acquainted, although in truth you are my own dear fairy godmother."

"I'm honored. Perhaps I should call you Cinderella or Cinder for short?"

Lucinda giggled as only a baby tree could. "I'd like that very much."

Eeyore sniffed her gently. "You smell like chocolate, Cinder," he brayed softly "because it's one of my favourite things." He sniffed again. "Ah, now I smell apple blossoms. What a delightful creature you are. Lucy told Piglet about you. He's over the moon to meet you. Piglet adores apple blossoms even more than I delight in chocolate. He will no doubt look up to you even though he's presently twice as tall as you are." He bowed his head low. "Welcome to Terra Nuova, little lady. We renamed the nozone the 'Grove of Brides' after you," he said, "because brides carry bouquets of apple blossoms to celebrate their new lives.

"Before you go," Cinder said, blushing dark green, "Eeyore wants you to meet another sapling."

I was puzzled. "Eeyore, you never mentioned another sapling. Is it important?"

"It is, Eeyore said refusing to make eye contact with me. "I've been carrying a secret that you should know. First, the sapling in question is over there in the corner. Her name is Beatrice."

"The crazy woman who terrorized the dryads?"

"The very one. She's been forced to turn over a new leaf. Verity said it was important you know she's here. She won't remember you or what she did."

The tree sprites Sapdragon and Leif gathered the baby rabbits into a circle and told them a story about new warrens dug in soft fresh earth with walls lined with sweet herbs until they fell asleep.

Verity's old walking stick lay abandoned in the grass before it slithered snake-like, morphing into a bough of apple-blossom that heralded Lucy's finest crop of apples the size of watermelons. The apple deva gathered her energies freed of Greenwood's blight and Terra Nuova blossomed.

chapter 59

THE TRAGICOM

*"Truth is truth
at the end of reckoning."*

WILLIAM SHAKESPEARE

Edward stood proud, all of seventeen years old, everyone's favorite boy wonder. As always when he spoke, the rest of us were in raptures. "First," he said. "I'd like to air the truth about two lost pseudonyms, and then 'fall on my sword to reveal a truth I've kept secret far too long."

We sat up eager, assembled for a tale of intrigue and woe. Whenever Edward revealed a secret, it was juicy. Not only had we been rewarded with killer confessions but were also privy to the blatant misusages of royal power and toxic betrayal. Edward paced back and forth in front of us, a paradox of restless excitement in a one-man show.

Piglet, overexcited more than usual, couldn't help but blurt out huzzah! – his favorite word for 2025. The rest of us, Wonderland Alice, Peter Pan, and me, along with Milne's animals from the Hundred-acre Wood, and Mr. Carroll's sentient characters, waited like children for a bedtime 'once-upon-a-time'. But it turned out to be a confession.

"It has been my experience," Edward said, "that the mottos of the British nobility are all too often pufferies designed to lie. Mine, 'nothing is truer than truth', was the biggest lie of all. I could leave it there and have done with my ...*ahem*... confession, but I entreat you to read the introduction in the first folio of my surviving collective works. Perhaps the only truth evident in its ersatz pages is the command to disregard the hideous 'Droeshout engraving' that mocks me from its frontispiece and to read my words, which were written by someone else.

So gathered my false friends, enemies, mercenaries, jealous rivals, ex-lovers, and my trusted scriptorium fellows, once happy to live safely in my pocket to save themselves. Their collective conspiracy backfired into a myth that made many people rich but left my legacy in tatters.

The designation 'Swan of Avon' has been a spear in my side far too long. Let me just say: in my day, actors were called swans, and we performed for the queen in the palace of Hampton Court – known as The Avon. It was a clever smokescreen to shield the powerful and sacrifice the compassionate.

The first folio was written in code. Surely, nothing further need be said on the matter, and yet it does.

Liars and fools continue to hang their history on a book where every word doth tell a false tale, and every false tale hides a profound truth.

He gestured, pointing off stage. "And yon 'lies' barefaced Stratford – a place where I was never born, nor lived, nor, like its native 'son', William Shaksper, an unscrupulous moneylender who bought and sold wool in addition to moonlighting for a scant season or two as an amateur actor. Ever my *'dumb man'* on the de Vere payroll, albeit written in invisible ink with a crooked pen.'

I am said to be a learned scholar, an impossibility had I been educated in Stratford-Upon-Avon's grammar school where rare books didn't exist written in languages that hadn't yet been translated.

Shaksper worked his way up from the illiterate son of a glove maker to the status of illiterate lacky – a devious unlettered dogsbody mildly useful for 'creatively' managing box office receipts, shuffling papers, sorting props, peddling old manuscripts, and standing close enough to confuse my identity for generations to come, content to accept all manner of nonsense on the face of researching nothing.

In hindsight, he was a covert jackanape known for his cunning sleights of underhanded business transactions – a 'chancer' ever on the lookout out for a few extra shillings who, I might add, amassed a substantial fortune far in excess of what he might have earned as the honest playwright so many naively assumed he was.

He lived off my spoils 'pulling his wool over everyone's eyes using my false identity as a cover. All the while appearing historically seamless as lies go, because his name, William Shaksper, was so similar to my pseudonym, William Shakespeare, as to defy comparison."

Edward pointed to Peter. "Lady Luck sucker punched me, Peter. I believe that's the correct term we learned in our forays to 'Havenford's dimwit school', was it not?" Peter gave Edward an enthusiastic two thumbs up.

Madame Luck created a simpleton from sheep's clothing (please study the 'Droeshout-*impossible-tailoring-portrait*' to confirm.) Never more than a cheap obsequious 'ployright' of the worst stripe. And speaking of simple, which he most certainly was, Shaksper, an uneducated upstart, spelled his name with an X.

Money speaks louder than blood. And blood money there's been aplenty from the thousands of fools who'll believe anything while knowing nothing. Gullible tourists in search of cheap thrills continue to jostle each other to stand in Shakespeare's footprints from first to last. Beginning in the room where he was said to have taken his first breath, they digress to an unnamed wall plaque overlooking an empty faux grave in Holy Trinity Church.

They sidle past his second-best bed, down the narrow staircase of remarkably fresh timbers (after 400 years), pausing to marvel at the very cup, no less, in which he enjoyed a morning cuppa with cream and three spoons of sugar, perhaps scribbling a quick poem, before making their way through the chicken yard to his father's workshop to sew a quota of gloves.

These same sightseers then venture down Henley Street to the grammar school to ogle the carvings of bored schoolboys in search of initials beginning with W and ending in S. Except, the 'Shaksper' fellow was likely unable to spell W.S.

And, just to be clear, tea had yet to be introduced in my time, so best change the visual of a cuppa to a tankard of warm ale.

It is, of course, only the beginning of a tale created by stumblebums signifying the incandescent fury of a family, literally up in arms over an invisible child.

But so much for the unvarnished truth. The varnished truth is lazier, and so much easier to remember if you can't write things down.

He paused to sip a cold cup of tea. "But let us begin at the beginning, as Leela's favorite, Lewis Carroll, is wont to say, and go on to the end, revealing as we go, the many faces of betrayal along the way.

The first was the stunningly pasty white face of a woman with a penetrating glare and flaming red hair presented to me as a goddess adorned with jewels who ruled the world by divine grace. Children and courtiers alike are impressed by grandeur. In Elizabeth's case, opulence covered a multitude of heinous sins of a crass vain creature.

In hindsight, Elizabeth Tudor was a self-centered, terrified, little girl all her life, dizzy with power after years where fawning fearmongers made sure she stayed frozen in fear for her life. Eliza's depravity fuelled her insatiable appetite for gory theatricals, heartless spectacles of animal brutality, and excessive punishments that turned the merest rumor of treason into a public torture chamber.

Even so, 'Venus' the queen of everything, lived centerstage, blindly magnified by an unflattering ever-present spotlight to illuminate her somewhat exaggerated charms. Distracted by fashion, music, dancing, and lust to satisfy her fulltime occupation of being admired, Elizabeth Tudor relentlessly preened under the ministrations of her calculating ladies. Portraits of Elizabeth show her with flawless lily-white skin. Clearly, artists were as keen as anyone to keep their reputations in a land where hands were lopped off at the queen's pleasure.

As a young woman, Scarlet Fever had left the queen's face pockmarked and her scalp marred by bald patches and angry scars. The face she offered the world had to be constantly refreshed by toxic cosmetics. A paste applied with a trowel formed a facemask that dried and cracked throughout the day and fell off in scabs. Beauty swiftly degraded to a mockery of fusty garishly red wigs adorning a scarlet-lipped, toothless hag. I do not exaggerate when I describe a pair of infected bloodshot eyes squinting daggers from a complexion tortured by lavish quantities of bleach and lead.

By the end of her life, Elizabeth, a grotesque shadow of a decomposing clown with teeth blackened by sugar, had no mind of her own.

Just as disturbing, is the deformed caricature chosen by ill-wishers to falsely represent my true image as a pudgy expressionless dullard of no fixed abode, watching over an empty grave in Holy Trinity Church that was never there.

To summarize: I arrived in Elizabeth's court as the 17th Earl of Oxford, a twelve-year-old orphan. Under the laws of the land, underage children of noble families became official wards of the queen. I was placed under Elizabeth's *'care'* which essentially gave her permission to do with me whatever she *cared* to do and moreover whatever her ex-lover, Leister, *cared* to do. His first pleasure was appropriating my inheritance. His second was to watch them crumble in disrepair.

Leister's first pleasure was appropriating my inheritance. His second was to watch my properties crumble in disrepair.

Elizabeth Tudor coached me in her exclusive mutual admiration society. The second of her pleasures was to misappropriate my virginity at her earliest opportunity. I won a romantic lead in the queen's theatre of hapless rumpy-pumpy – a box-office disaster.

My core belief from the age of four was my determination to shine as a perpetual champion. Sadly, my rakehell nature backfired in my teens. Elizabeth found bad boys irresistible.

But young as I was, I was wily enough to gravitate without hesitation towards power handed to me on a silver platter. Power is addictive, and if you're born into a bejeweled goddess's court, power becomes a goal as much as a privilege. But I was too arrogant for my own good. I spat in the face of Burghley's authority at every turn, safe within an exclusive stratosphere of academic superiority that I presumed safeguarded me from the direst of consequences. It didn't.

Lord Burghley was an arrogant untouchable powermonger who operated above, beside, and behind the Tudor throne. As such, my perverse actions vaulted me to the top of his most wanted list that earmarked me for the cruelest of executions, that of losing my destiny, my son, my bloodline, and my literary canon, but keeping my head so I could remember it all.

Edward stopped pacing, straightened his doublet with a harsh jerk, cricked his neck, and proceeded, shoulders back with soul-crushing dishonor, his eyes shaking spears at us, his shell-shocked audience. "But I digress," he said, feeling bewildered.

"You look bewildered," Piglet shouted. "Does this mean our interview is canceled?"

Well spotted, Piglet. Just give me a moment to have my little whinge. No worries, our interview is absolutely on.

Some of you, *I'm looking at you Absolem*, are aware of the covert stipend the queen awarded me at the eleventh hour that paid me an annuity of a thousand pounds for the duration of my lifetime. It was a bribe. But somewhere in the foggy recesses of Elizabeth's guilt-ridden mind I thought she may have been saying she was sorry.

"A chance would be a fine thing," Puck called out.

"A sudden windfall of a thousand pounds a year was an unheard-of expense from a tightfisted Queen bankrupted by war and running a vast spy network that covered the entire known world. But Elizabeth needed my pen, and there were intimate secrets between us she couldn't deny to God, who was only slightly more powerful than her astronomer, John Dee. And in an act of unprecedented effrontery, she set me to polishing my history plays to quash her growing reputation as a failed monarch. I was secretly paid to salvage her waning popularity. I thought she was proposing, if not marriage, then hatching a plan to elevate our Henry from an embarrassing mistake to 'Henry Apparent'. I couldn't have been more wrong. What does one do with a besmirched, tarnished, dishonoured goddess of the living dead?"

She was different but ever the same, an extremely old, bald harridan – tawdry and bawdy who had baited her last bear.

Pooh startled the way he always did at the word bear and scratched his head. "Is that a *'realstorical'* thingy? he asked Eeyore.

No, my astute little bear," Cheshire said. "Edward is asking our advice. I don't know about you but I'm ..."

"Shocked," a voice rang out. It was Puck. "Master, I know all, and your story pales in the retelling."

Eeyore's ears flattened. "Should I be worried, Leela? I can regress to melancholy if gloom is called for."

"Is it *praps* time for chocolate fingers do you think?" Piglet said hopefully, his lop ears matching Eeyore's. "Because if it is, I know where they are."

"Here comes the confession I never wanted to divulge," Edward said. "The truth is, after I'd effectively destroyed my position at court I became a dead-beat dad, a failed entrepreneur, and a cuckold. They were not my finest hours.

Time spent during the process of transmutation is intense. Most scandalized souls don't reincarnate. It would seem that only the guilty who are cursed with telling the absolute truth when they're barefaced lying, live again to tell their tales.

But there's a truism to surviving guilt. I have set aside my motto 'nothing truer than truth' for a new one: IF YOU DON'T REMEMBER SOMETHING, IT NEVER HAPPENED!"

After a moments awkward silence, Piglet, as Verity's once assigned junior reporter, bravely waved a pencil in the air and shouted "Now?" as forcefully as he dared.

Edward, looking drained, took a deep breath and managed a wan smile. "Now is as good a time as any, Piglet."

Piglet wasted no time. "Do you have anything to say about something?" he asked, a sharpened pencil held suspended above his notepad.

"Well, the burnings take care of the details: letters, diaries, manuscripts, legal documents, wills, and sad memories purged of regret and hate. It's a long winding alphabet from adversity to Zeno. But they led me here.

I was a proud de Vere. I took my family's motto far too literally. As such, my truth lies buried under an era of obsessive lying, greed, and bloodshed."

Piglet's ears waggled in several directions at once. "Were they? Are they? Excuse me, Uncle Edward, are you telling porky pies right now? Vera said I need to *Vera-fly* facts for my interview."

"I swear I am not," Piglet. "I may have appeared tight-lipped on my worst days, but guilt has a way of stealing one's tongue."

Piglet stage whispered what no doubt was meant to help me.

"No worries, Uncle Edward, I was often tongue-tied as a nipper, but I grew out of it."

"That's an exclusive," Puck interrupted. "Write it down, Piglet. It's important. Wait for it."

The look Edward gave Puck, meant to chastise him, made him grin all the wider. "I regret failing to live up to the true ghost of me when it counted most, and subsequently it took me thirty-one years to die."

Piglet dropped his pencil and fell over backwards. "Oh, my *w w w* word. That is, I mean *your* word. That's heff heff hol huff hollerable," he said, upset because he had no idea how to spell subsequently.

Puck nodded me to go on. Edward picked up the pencil and placed it firmly in Piglet's hand. "I can say with certainty," he said, "once a fearmonger violates the art of living, they die twice."

chapter 60

THE DEAD AUTHORS' SOCIETY

"Do not be afraid;
our fate cannot be taken
from us; it is a gift."

DANTE ALIGHIERI

– 'The Inferno'

I dressed slowly for the last day of term. Pleased to be finished; apprehensive of saying goodbye to Vera who was preparing to travel a great distance with Silkie. The Chrysalis Mundi awaited their departure but there was no telling when the actual call to their next life would come.

Vera's form comes and goes with Verity's impending retirement. Edward says it's only to be expected after her recent 'rude' awakening. So much for the truth will out. In real time is one ever ready? Ironically, Vera reports that preparing for ethereal limbo takes physical stamina.

For weeks, I hadn't known who I would find in the classroom on any given day. On one occasion, Vera was a pre-school child too young to teach us, so we looked through a picture book together and she told me what she thought the story was about. Her innocent point of view proved to be a great lesson to never assume words were universally true.

Case in point. The word retirement is far deeper than retreating. It means letting go. It indicates sustained rest. Edward described it to me as the drowsy state of transition, known as 'leaving before actually going'. In effect, the art of becoming someone new without leaving anything behind. He knows those shifts of personal power, perhaps a little *too* well.

So, I was relieved when Vera the younger met me at the clearing. She'd decided to hold her final open-air stoa in Eeyore's 'force field' resplendent with bluebells and the majestic Lucy growing from their epicenter like a tall leafy umbrella. Two amazing forces to be reckoned with.

There were days I'd come to view Lucy as my designated babysitter. Eeyore referred to her as the ringmaster of our multi-ring circus.

Pooh, Piglet, Absolem, Cheshire, Pax, Peter, Alice, Chlora, and of course my knight in shining armor, Eeyore, were in attendance to celebrate the end of my beginning and the beginning of Verity's ending.

Lucy was exceptionally vibrant for the occasion. A temperate breeze invigorated her leaves with ozone encouraging her branches to reach higher than ever before. Her roots glowed incandescent through the black earth, radiating lightning bolts headed to the stars.

Absolem was as high as he usually was by 9 a.m. and Cheshire floated as high as a kite (of the bird persuasion) as he usually did when auditing my class. Although by audit, I mean he did most of the talking, listening for long periods not being his most eloquent default mode.

Vera tapped her ruler on the makeshift picnic table podium. "Well, our last official school day is upon us, and it couldn't have come too soon. As they say, I'm neither here nor there these days, which feels more like being there *and* here at the same time." As ever, she was being modest. Her radiant smile grew more dazzling with each passing day. "But you *are* here, Leela. And your life as a published author, draws near." She steadied herself with Verity's cane. "But before I dismiss you, I have arranged a special story circle to celebrate this auspicious day. My going away present to the class of '24."

She rang the blue bell for so long I thought she may have forgotten who or where she was. Its ring warbled in slow motion in keeping with her molecular structure's state of flux. She spaced out for longer periods of time, now. Dissolving. Experiencing erratic shape shifts. Nevertheless, I felt privileged to witness her transmutation... her literal *undoing*.

"I know how she feels," Cheshire stage whispered.

"It's for luck," Piglet said tugging my hem. "Ringing the bell is for luck. Edward told me."

I closed my eyes the better to feel its unearthly sound resonate inside me. It was easy to follow it ricocheting from tree-to-tree and looping back on itself like an echo burbling underwater. Time standing still described it precisely. Its ethereal boomerang effect brought several families of rabbits and mice scurrying to join us. They wiggled into the dozens of spaces between Lucy's exposed roots like excited children. Vera addressed them as such. "There's no need to fidget, tinies. Lucy has kindly sprouted a crop of clover between her toes for your dining pleasure."

Vera's form briefly glowed incandescent as the first unexpected buttercup sprouted behind her with a popping sound. The alerted rabbits stood upright, their noses quivering, and sniffed the air for predators until the grass was dotted with tiny explosions of yellow.

And so, we were assembled. The mice hunkered down to nibbling, and the older rabbits hopped into the meadow to *silfray*[*] on a carpet of parsley and lettuce leaves.

---

[*] *Silfray is the term Richard Adams explained in 'Watership Down,' that describes the appointed time wild rabbits leave the safety of their burrows to eat above ground. Fiver is his protagonist rabbit with a sixth sense. A yearling is a teenage rabbit. Four is the highest number a rabbit can count. Hrair covers any number above four.*

Vera wasted no time in a guided meditation. She was out of time. "Please link hands in a circle," she said.

"That means paws too, doesn't it Pooh?" Piglet said in a nervous whisper.

"Focus on the empty space in the center. It represents your first thought, the beginning of all stories which will appear as a physical white light."

Vera nodded to me with a smile. Her lithe form, now as transparent as glass made her look like an ice statue of a Greek goddess. The dark trees shimmered through her as frosty sage green. Edward stood far off on the horizon bearing a spear. Verity, the elder manifested inside me. *This is your initiation,* she said. *Just breathe, Leela. All is as it must be. You have done well my child.*

I felt lightheaded as the peal of the school bell returned to vibrate inside my chest and for a moment my body trembled pleasantly. And then I was back with the others and Vera was still speaking.

"As the light dims your connection will intensify," Vera explained. "It will take our collective focus to call down the guests I've invited. They will arrive slowly, one at a time. Take deep breaths, listen to the forest, and keep your eyes closed until Lucy tells you to open them.

She waggled a schoolmarm finger at the mice. "So, no-one is going to slope off home behind my back, are they? We're all going to sit in silence and see what happens. I think you will be pleasantly surprised. A cream tea will be served, nursery style, in due course. And no, Piglet it doesn't look like rain, and contrary to popular belief heffalumps give cream cakes a wide berth. Now empty your minds." She pursed her schoolmarm lips. "There's no call for rude remarks, Peter. It takes all kinds to make a world. Pooh, take no notice of Peter."

She needn't have worried. Pooh as usual, was entirely absorbed by the promise of tea cakes and condensed milk.

Lucy rustled her leaves and whispered to Piglet. "Piglet dear, I have a special task for you. It's a secret for now. Will you help me, please?

"Mm m me?" Piglet stuttered. "Yes, my lady, you only have to ask."

"Take one of my windfall apples to the Nozone field and eat it tomorrow."

"The N n n no zone. Is it safe?"

"You have my word, little one. After you consume the fruit, bury the apple core in the epicentre of the field. You will find a spot between the trees. I will make it glow so you can't miss it. I'm grateful, little one. Now, go and join the others. The party is about to begin.

"Come along, Piglet," Pooh shouted. "We have to join the circle."

At first a few grey-haired old men approached individually through a natural break in the trees, then in twos, and finally in small groups, exhibiting surprise at their chance meeting. An overall impression of muttonchop whiskers and leather elbow patches completed the general impression of a literary pantheon.

One by one, they discarded their top hats and frock coats as they came through the bluebells. Subsequent generations of military uniforms, velvet smoking jackets, country tweeds, and riding breeches followed suit until the field was littered with monogrammed handkerchiefs, stiff collars, bowties, dickies, neckties, and cravats, as well as their cares of the day that tenaciously clung to them, peeled and tossed like so much orange peel.

Their congested lungs filled with tobacco smoke were refreshed in the Veratopian air. They were soon gazing enraptured at the blue skies and buttercups with an eye to the silver tea service and fine porcelain china, twinkling in the sunshine.

The unexpected expedition called for holiday attire of white rolled up sleeves, schoolboy trousers, and bare necks. One old boy manifested a fishing rod over his shoulder. An oversized Sherlock Holmes magnifying glass protruded from another's waistcoat pocket. A few dangled butterfly nets and carried empty specimen jars from their boyhood forays into the countryside. I sensed their pockets filled with useless bits and bobs. Lengths of knotted string, lint covered licorice-all-sorts, leaky fountain pens, paperclips, stubs of HB pencils, conkers, and the occasional golf tee.

Some had come straight from their gentleman's club nursing snifters of brandy and puffing on cigars. The closer they came to the amphitheatre in the grass, a collective weight lifted from their shoulders and smiles lifted furrowed brows.

The approach of muffled conversations ceasing abruptly meant they were upon us. They stopped in their tracks as a single entity from the spectacle of a hundred entranced animals and children arranged in concentric circles with their eyes closed basking in an aura of white light.

I opened one eye to see Vera waving an enthusiastic hello to someone behind me. She held a finger pressed to her lips. I wasn't sure if it was meant for me or the arrived stranger I couldn't see. "Thank you," I mouthed. She closed her eyes and nodded *you are most welcome*.

The sensation of being surrounded by quickening life was exciting. Who was behind me? What would I find? One thing was certain whatever or whoever it was, it was Verity's going away gift to herself as much as my graduation present. The word present echoed inside my head – another word for this moment called now.

A gentle breeze wafted the scent of red apples over me which meant Lucy was '*apple-ing*'. She was under Verity's spell as much as I was.

When Lucy bid us open our eyes, we beheld two things simultaneously. Her green crown glittering with juicy red jewels and an assembly of spellbound gods and goddesses who stood transfixed watching us with as much awe as we acknowledged their presence. We almost remembered one another.

But it took one of us to break the silence. It was Piglet. "Is one of you, my grandfather?" he squealed.

Eeyore gave him a nudge forward. "Oh, well played little Piglet," he said. "But you may need to repeat your request a little louder. Not everyone may have heard you."

"No bother, Piglet. It's what comes of being a very small animal in a very large space," Pooh said peering high and low. "Now, where is that cream tea Vera mentioned? It must be well past elevenses."

That eased the tension. Laughter brought us closer in age. We were a mutual admiration society of writers and the written, illustrators and the illustrated on a school picnic.

I was being launched in style. It was a happy birthday for my impending book but more to the point, it was New Year's Eve for Veratopia.

A dear old lady with a twinkly smile, caught my eye. Beatrix Potter was a stout darling who I knew from her memoirs to be tenacious as a bull when she wanted to be. She'd come bundled for a stormy hike in the fens of the Lake District, wearing layers of scruffy shawls and a battered weather-beaten hat. And she'd brought Shep.

Eeyore knew Shep right away and led him off to show him Absolem's mushroom. "No sudden moves," I heard him say. "And for goodness' sake, no barking."

Mr. Lear came forward and shook my hand. After that the introductions were steady. We were 'perfect' strangers who could almost read each others' thoughts. We didn't require name tags because we either said our names with each handshake or someone introduced us. In every direction there was a C.S. Lewis, a James Barrie, or the likes of AA Milne, J R Tolkien, Rudyard Kipling, Hans Christian Anderson, Antoine de Saint-Exupéry, E.B. White, Richard Adams, Kenneth Grahame, Beatrix Potter, Lucy Atwell, and Enid Blyton. A veritable feast of adults who never grew up, waiting to say their belated *fancy meeting you here, have you fared well*, and sometimes genuine apologies for being self-centered.

Mr. Carroll found Alice immediately and she brought him to me. I was tongue-tied. All I could manage was "Such a galumping pleasure to meet you, sir."

"Burblier and Burblier," he replied cheekily. "I do hope Verity's tea party is properly insane."

"Let's find out," I said and took his arm. "What can I get you, Earl Grey or Lapsang souchong?"

"Ginger beer, if you would be so frumious," Cheshire answered inches from his shoulder. "Right this way. Absolem is waiting, and you know what an old mimsy he can be."

"He does like a good burble, does Absolem."

Lucy's sweet red windfalls had the full attention of the rabbits who couldn't decide between clover, buttercups, or apples, although I caught Richard Adams laying in the grass eating an apple as yearlings played hopscotch around and over him without fear. Lucky for him, Tigger was occupied elsewhere bouncing Pooh to the pastries out of his reach.

Now, here they were, large as life albeit younger, perpetual old boys with skinned knees and ink-stained fingers, juggling math proofs and fantasies to soften the horrors of war. Blissfully out of sight from starched nannies and even more starchy parents. Parents shaking their heads. Schoolmasters shaking their whips, rivals shaking their fists, and nannies shaking their fingers in a concerted effort to discourage whimsical writers into steady husbands and wives. And, of course, Edward de Vere, a literary star in their midst shaking his spear shaped pen.

Tables laden with shepherd's pie, fish fingers, rice pudding, boiled eggs with bread-and-butter soldiers, sausages and mash, sardines on toast, and Jam roly-poly, greeted them. Heart stopping calories and brain clogging nut butters. The mind-boggling consummation of sugars and fats continued undiminished: Bakewell and treacle tarts, pink and white checkerboard squares of Battenberg, marzipan mice, Victoria sponge, Turkish delight, walnut whips, Jaffa cakes, blancmange, meringues, and eclairs, washed down with Ovaltine, ginger beer, lemonade, and orange squash.

Not to be lost in the spoiled-for-choice deserts, towers of insubstantial paper-thin English cut Hovis sandwiches of watercress, cucumber, and egg that teetered when the earthquake of Pax's Ellies stampeded by on the way to the ice cream. I calculated wryly, it would take a hundred crustless triangles to balance the weight of a single American burger with its eleven spices and a secret sauce.

The savory table balanced the dominant sweets with sharp cheeses. Lobster paste, salmon spread, and marmite enlivened the blandness of cucumber and watercress and lettuce.

All the same, I sensed, to a man or woman, they would have been just as happy with baked beans on toast.

Warm fizzy bottled ginger beer replaced brandy snifters and sherry glasses.

Writers were strangely insensitive concerning the realities of life and death smoothed over the sad truth that rabbits had a tendency to be baked into pies and stews and that owls preferred mice to toast and marmalade for breakfast. Substituting thistles and gruel for buttercups and honey was an act of omission that could have easily been rectified with a little compassion, especially after experiencing the rationing during the war.

The landscape was suddenly populated with anthropomorphic animals wearing yellow bonnets, blue coats, and red mittens, escapees from illustrators' inkwells and fountain pens and the chewed stubs of pencils, weightless as the Cheshire cat or as grounded as a green caterpillar stoned on his own imaginative fumes, spouting philosophy steeped in whimsy.

One of my favorite characters, a particularly pleasant water rat wearing a fisherman-knit pullover led a shy bespectacled mole who peered myopically into the crowd periodically pointing and saying, *is that him?* every few minutes. All the while they searched for Mr. Grahame, they were secretly hoping to see Pan.

I read some of their thoughts. None imagined their advanced years as ancient academics on their rickety knees, playing tic-tac-toe with a teddy bear or hide-and-seek with a heffalump, let alone uncovering pirate treasure and finding the north pole before teatime or visiting Africa after breakfast.

I leaned on Lucy's trunk and listened to the comforting echoes of wind in our own willows, the splash of Ratty's oars as he rowed a blue and white boat down the river, and an owl serenading his lady love. But most of all, I strained to hear the panpipes that stilled birds and beasts and gurgling streams into a peace that surpassed all human understanding.

I searched in vain for Alan Alexander Milne.

Visions of *expotitions* undertaken in dappled sunshine, and Piglet wriggling snow from behind his ears, and a donkey left out in the rain filled my head like sugarplum fairies.

Rabbits who never once stood upright on two legs other than to sniff the air for predators chased their literary cousins Benjamin bunny, Flopsy, Mopsy, Cottontail and the Velveteen rabbit.

My childhood friends milled around the legs of the writers eating cake as if their lives depended on it. Which is odd because I've given enough childish tea parties in my time with empty plates and teapots filled with air to know full well that toys don't eat gumdrops or ham sandwiches. Yet, Pooh has a larder full of ceramic pots filled with honey and condensed milk, and albeit somewhat clumsily, he eats cake one slice at a time.

Owl, hailed as the wise oracle of the forest – a sage who couldn't spell for toffee, put in a brief appearance. Not so sharp-eyed the time he'd been oblivious to his door pull being Eeyore's lost tail, considering a bird of prey can pick off a fieldmouse from a great height.

Verity had been a professional editor who appreciated a deliberately planted wrong word in its time which brings me again to the masterfully inventive mind of Mr. Carroll.

"Who," I asked Eeyore, "would use the word lumbering to describe Pax's heffalumps when Mr. Carroll's word 'galumping' was available?" Piglet on the other hand wasn't fussy about his grandfather's name, but then, neither was 'Wol.' Trespassers Will became the title of an intrepid explorer. Which reinforced how refreshing it was to be taught in Vera's classroom where no-one received a black mark for misspelling Chattanooga when, as she put it so succinctly, hardly anyone lives there.

Vera spied me alone and waved me over for a cup of tea where we happily resumed our discussion about Alan Watts' warning against the indiscriminate use of 'spookery'. He believed children wouldn't be fooled by nonsensical magical flimflam.

"I totally agree," Lewis Carroll mused. "Children require sensible flimflam."

I wandered through the party taking mental notes for a future book. Snatches of conversations floated amidst the 'hello' --- *Tiddely Pom*, 'how are you' --- *Tiddely Pom* --- 'you look well' --- *Tiddely Pom*, and the 'we must do this more often' --- *Tiddely Poms.*

Pax sat cross-legged a way off doodling a treasure map in the dirt with a stick. He looked like a boy in khaki trousers wearing an explorer's pith helmet because that's exactly what he was. Behind him a mountain of colorful ellies formed a protective wall against his mother who, as mothers are wont to do, often slipped through the portal of his imagination with things like toothpaste and hairbrushes.

Pax's peace-loving Ellies had already consumed a ton of custard and apple pie and were snoring their trunks silly.

Pax approached his author bravely, and kneeling reverently, placed his pith helmet on his master's head. His ensuing mad powwow woke up his wall and at Pax's command, his ellies formed a row, lifted their trunks in salute and enthralled the party with a moving trumpet blast.

Many writers suffered from 'the morbids' as Mr. Lear called them. Which is why so many of them deliberately injected their personal battles with melancholia into their stories.

Neverland's lost boys were permitted to pine for their mothers but not enough to grow up. None of them dreamed of biding their time in a green leather armchair in a gentleman's club being waited on by a staff of ancient grandfathers. They were busy fighting off pirates and loneliness.

Mr. Barrie knelt beside Peter Pan and said he was frightfully sorry. He stayed there a long time resting his hand on Peter's shoulder before Peter allowed himself to be drawn into a teary hug. He hadn't lost a mother. His feather-brained mother had left him behind in a shop.

Likewise, Mr. Milne finally showed himself by bringing his dark polished memories into the circle and stood behind Eeyore. Milne's subconscious regret for denying an innocent donkey a straw shelter or a windbreak of trees hovered unsaid in embarrassed silence. A tormented woodcutter presented himself. I saw a transparent figure holding an axe, but Eeyore recognized him and ran off kicking up his legs braying fit to burst.

Mr. Milne must have noticed the wear and tear of Eeyore's

ravaged body needlessly subjected to real battles with the elements to beleaguer a point. Was he sorry for subjecting a sweet loveable donkey to misery and torture? If he could write him again, would he write him a warmer drier life rather than what passed for humor at his expense? I think not.

Milne had no excuse. Sunshine is far easier to write than a torrential downpour. Yet Eeyore had grown into a wise loving creature in spite of being the scapegoat for a troubled man jealous of his boy's fame eclipsing his own.

Sir Arthur Conan Doyle looked in to ask if anyone had seen a chap named Seneca Greenwood and hastily retreated after a resounding shout of "A chance would be a fine thing. Huzzah!

At long last, as the sun dipped low in a splendiferous curtsy of red and gold, the gathering of souls well-met in Eeyore's bluebell meadow, drifted off towards the trees, collecting their discarded bits and pieces. Mumbled farewells of *we must do this again, soon* floated back to me, suddenly overwhelmed with the realization I was alone, released from the joys of formal education with a sad lump in my throat.

Whoops of revelling Ellies having a food fight with the cupcakes they'd filched, came back to me. I can still picture them in my mind's eye trumpeting uproariously smothered in cream and jelly. Later, they marched in single file to wade in Eeyore's pond and sprayed icing off each other that turned into more of a game than a bath.

Birds swarmed the leftovers as Vera, looking painfully transparent, put the kettle on. Eeyore, Edward, and I toasted her approaching rebirth adventure with Camomile tea, suitable to the late hour. I realized with a rush of happiness that Vera was whole without her older half as was Edward, a teenager full and complete without his famous identity. And I shivered at the same instance seeing Eeyore in a sunny flashback during the festivities when he'd wandered ahead of me, that his gate was wobbly. And when he'd turned to check if I was following his happy eyelids were droopy.

I reached out and snuggled into Eeyore's neck. The thought he sent back was *Don't be such a fussbudget.*

Vera and Edward didn't leave so much as evaporate into the evening without a word.

Piglet wandered about his head in the clouds after completing Lucy's mission, happy to have survived the ordeal. He'd eaten his apple and buried the core. He was so pleased with himself he dropped in to the cabin to celebrate. "I can't *'splain*," he said, I'm not *illowed*, but I've been a helpful little piglet so, I should think a cup of tea and chocolate fingers might be in order.

"What did you think of Mr. Milne today," I asked Eeyore.

"I suppose it was like old times… and by that, please don't misunderstand me, Leela. I don't mean the good old days. Nothing like. I remember Mr. M as a troubled soul, back from the war. Well, most of him, anyway. I believe he left the better part of his happy thoughts in France.

One could hardly call his delegated hidey hole of a writing space a room let alone a study.

It was dark and smelly from pipe tobacco. Stuffy. Airless. Curtains saturated with foul smoke. But that's what he felt he deserved. The space was crammed full of gloomy mahogany desks and bookshelves. I called it 'Dark Woods Corner' a spot fit for a subservient donkey."

Not even Eeyore knew the extent of what happened overseas. Suffice to say Alan Milne was injured and slipped into a depression known as shellshock quite outside the scope that Mrs. Milne's delicate little rich girl's nerves could handle.

Christopher's father was compelled to create some sort of house for Eeyore, so, he effectively bequeathed his writing space to him as his gloomy place. Nothing for shelter but a pile of measly sticks.

Eeyore got lumbered with Milne's grim thoughts from the dank trenches of his night terrors. The farm was never more than an extension of the battlefields he left. He *tilted at windmills,* as they say. Solitude suited his anxiety. It did nothing for Eeyore who wanted a meadow with cornflowers and buttercups which would have been easy enough to write.

But Milne was damaged enough to believe he was exorcizing a few pesky ghosts by passing on his sad memories to an innocent toy donkey. Both Christopher Robin's parents were selfish and needlessly tactless, but that was their privileged upper class generation's attitude of entitlement. Christopher couldn't help being spoiled.

"Happy birthday to me, I *don't* think," Eeyore muttered to himself. "Many *unhappy* returns were more like it. Many wet, un-cheery, chilly returns. I mean, the man *did* know how to write an umbrella and pots of honey, didn't he, Leela?"

I fondled his ears. "Yes of course he did."

Dear old Eeyore's plight was even more hurtful because Christopher often left him outdoors in the rain. *Nanny had to rescue him,* he'd told me, *but never until the morning. A grey donkey in a grey field behind grey fog is not so easy to pick out as one might think.*

The Christopher Robin I met when I first arrived had taken me aside as an act of mercy. Heads up he'd warned, *don't become too complacent,* but I fear this writing game has made me selfish. It was a sticky moment where I deeply regretted the all-consuming novice writer I'd become. I had taken Eeyore's love and loyalty for granted. Many unhappy returns, indeed.

Pooh had come with an unfortunate disgruntled expression as mass produced bears often do. I wondered if that was why Milne had chosen him out of all the others. I wouldn't doubt it.

Eeyore had explained the dynamics of emotional alignment to

me long ago. "You see," he'd said. "The placement of a toy's eyes and nose are critical. Frowns and smiles are implied."

I knew this well from my unsettling pareidolia days and the fearful face in the bath taps.

Eeyore read my thoughts. *You were going through your own nightmare when we met. Partners in crime, I thought. But the crimes were theirs', Leela. You and I were victims. We saved each other.*

"We did," I said rubbing his ears. "We still do. Every day."

Eeyore lifted his head from the pillow. "In hindsight I probably should have confronted Milne and simply asked him outright to write me stronger legs and a sturdier neck. All around I'd say much drier legs and a more substantial tail."

"Oh, Eeyore, any writer worth their salt can do that."

"Are you offering?"

"I'll do better than that, you sly old fox. I shall write you new legs tonight while you're asleep."

Eeyore's sly side surfaced as it did whenever he needed a favor. "Leela, do you suppose we could have buttercups for breakfast tomorrow?"

With great relief I replied with a hug. "We'll have cornflowers and clover, and bluebell pancakes too."

"This is why I love you so," Eeyore mumbled. "You take the trouble to understand me."

Eeyore's contented snore relaxed into the gentle purring sound I loved. I would have to pay him more attention now that my manuscript was done. I kissed his nose and whispered *I wouldn't have missed you for the world either,* in his ear.

But in the morning, he was gone. I looked and called until Cheshire showed up, still half asleep. "Don't worry, Leela," he said. "I know where he is. Eeyore's safe. Lucy has him. And Owl told me Eeyore's woodcutter was Mr. Milne stalking by way of a backhanded apology. In any case, according to Owl ALL ENDED WELL! One less woodcutter is a good omen."

And then I found Eeyore's farewell note left under my pillow:

Gon out Backson
Bisy Backson
– E

I burst into tears. He was saying goodbye, and then it dawned on me, Eeyore was saying thank you.

chapter 61

A MIDWINTER NIGHT'S WISH

"If we shadows have offended,
think on this and all is mended."

WILLIAM SHAKESPEARE

– A Midsummer Night's Dream

Eeyore had been keeping to his dell more and more, out of sight. I sensed his need for privacy and took Lucy's advice to heart. He was not hiding from me. How well I understood Eeyore's need to feel his power without distraction. His changes advanced quickly while I had a story to finish. Chlora claimed my time. She was real, now. And although a tree sprite is no bigger than a newborn squirrel, she took up space on my desk, both physical and psychic. I found it difficult to separate myself from the gargantuan task of completing a novel.

Eeyore reassured me he would be well soon if he could be repaired. "My coat is wearing thin at the seams. Moth holes have weakened my ability to walk. I need to be written with stronger legs and a sturdy neck. Puck, you know who to ask for help. Will you do that for me?"

"Dear one, Puck is not here. It's me, Leela. I've been in the cabin burning the midnight oil. Time gets away from me when listening for words. I had no idea how much. But I wished for this writing business. Perhaps I should have been more careful. Perhaps I wished for it too late."

Eeyore cheered at the sound of my voice. "Leela, you've come to visit me at last. I've missed you. I too, wished the writing for

467

you. And your wish could only have been answered according to divine timing. You know that, so, no regrets. It's the same situation for Edward. Take heart from what another Edward said. Edward Lear knew a great deal about time and timelessness when he wrote *'It's time to speak of many things'*.

Cheshire floated closer. "Can you not see me, old boy?"

"I admit you're a bit blurry," Eeyore said, "but then you always were."

"I say, are you feeling quite well?" Absolem said manifesting from the top half of his body down.

Eeyore continued to look for Cheshire in the wrong direction. He tried valiantly to locate Cheshire's voice, helplessly turning his head this way and that. "Can you not hear me, dear one," Cheshire asked gently.

"I appear to be coming apart at the seams. I need to rest. But I'm not worried. This happens to all toys. Puck says the mending fairy isn't picking up her messages."

"And Cheshire, there are two reasons why I couldn't see you, earlier. First, I had my eyes closed. Second, and this is the clincher, you were *invisible!*"

Absolem's peels of laughter spiralled above him in rings of smoke. "That's what I love about you, Eeyore," he said. "There's nothing wrong with your sense of humor. Perfectly wise and as generous of spirit as ever," he said, but his thought *'Alas poor Eeyore I knew him well – a donkey of infinite jest'* hung in the air in smoky letters.

"I'm not trying to be tiresome, Absolem, but do I look shabby? Tell me the truth." A crow laughed. The trees gathered closer together. "I feel awfully thin. Maybe one day I'll simply disappear into thin air like Cheshire. My stuffing has collected into lumps. It's most uncomfortable."

Cheshire's disembodied words spilled out from behind a clump of foliage. "Not a pretty sight either."

I closed my eyes, and their voices receded, strangely clearer in the distance.

"There's magic around you Eeyore," I heard Tink say. "It must be Leela. I believe she's growing into the goddess she was destined to become. Sadly, it's you who manages her energy, and now she's making up for lost time."

"Tink, please remind Leela that her years have been reset to conform with a timeless forest. She has all the time in the world. She's happy. I sleep more; she writes more. We're still in sync."

The birds stilled and the trees ceased waving their branches. "When Leela falls asleep at her desk she calls out for you," Tink said.

Eeyore tried to raise his head. "She misses her bedtime ritual. I was rather good at stories."

"You spoiled her."

"How old is she today? Ballpark?"

"Leela's growing like a weed, blossoming like a flower, and she has the aura of a young vibrant woman, which has not escaped the notice of Pan," Absolem said slyly.

Cheshire yawned. "I dreamed last night that Pan was courting her, so it must be true. I feel her happiness giving the forest the strength to evolve now the woodcutter is gone." He swooped low to the ground and swept his tail over Eeyore's muzzle. "Capital old friend, rest up, come with me to Lucy's field."

"You mean *my* energy field?"

"The energy field you share, then. You take the low ground and metaphorically speaking, Lucy holds the high ground. And I'll keep holding up the sky," Cheshire said with a smug grin.

"Leela is a true writer now. She loses time, lost in listening. Words come from a silence deeper than the woods. Verity told me this would happen and not to take it personally. She can't help herself. You see, Edward is pushing Leela to perform. His critiques often upset her, but she gets up and begins a new page. Some mentors are relentless."

Speaking of relentless," Absolem remarked. "Thankfully, Master Edward is looking more at ease. Have you noticed he's wearing more blue. But, *blue jeans*, I mean, I ask you! Quite beyond the pale. Something big is happening in the forest. Vera is aging fast. The trees say she will soon be Verity in Sparkly form."

Eeyore chortled. "Zeno says Life in a forest is endlessly, one might even say *relentlessly*, verdant."

Cheshire floated down to inspect Eeyore's seams. He sniffed and flew into a somersault causing a passing swarm of bees to dissipate in a frantic buzz. "I was sorry to hear Verity had to terminate her chronicles. But nothing lasts forever, even the past." Cheshire sighed. "Nine lives aren't nearly enough. I'm on my sixty-first. Do you think that's some sort of meaningful coincidence?"

"It's called accelerated synchronicity," Absolem said. "Eeyore, don't worry, Mr. Milne gave you literary immortality."

"Pity he can't be summoned to write me new stuffing."

The sun was getting on for setting into red and gold.

"Verity hinted we should expect a surprise any day now. Zeno is back in power but he's immortal and his philosophy acclaimed for posterity. Edward's power is undiminished. It sleeps.

Ironically, the bard's body of work *is* also immortal, but the body of the poet walks like a ghost in buildings that no longer exist. He's biding his time, waiting for something. Only Zeno knows who and what. But then Edward is partial to winding plots where no-one gets out alive."

"Well, other than me," Absolem said. "I always get out alive. I transcend, you see. It's a caterpillar thing. I made sure Leela heard me the other day in class. But I was crawling on a leaf at the time, and without my hookah I'm not as coherent. Not less wise, you understand. Just not so happily distracted. But I managed to call out a profound truth that Mr. Edward told me: when you write, he said, you must give life to the fairies and spirits on the page. I hope she heard me."

Eeyore hung his head. Not from sorrow or regret but because his head was too heavy for his neck. His legs buckled while he was in the middle of the sentence "Don't mind me. I'll be my old self after a cat nap," he brayed. "Roll on 4 o'clock. I guess we'll be having one last communiqué and some form of chocolate before the afternoon is out."

I jolted out of my reverie, seamlessly rejoining the conversation. "I have a packet of Jaffa cakes I've been saving," I said. "This calls for our best china."

"We always use our best china, Leela."

"Then, I guess you'll be getting a bath."

Eeyore tried to stand. "Oh, I see what you're doing," he said coyly. "You're toying with me. What have I told you about that?"

"Never toy with a toy."

"Correct."

"Okay, no bath. But a nice brushing wouldn't hurt."

"I happen to love being brushed. Leela, by any chance do you have time to buy a cake? It's not your regular shopping day, and I'm not asking you to bake it, but reincarnation rather calls for a rich chocolate cake. I say, can you help me up. All I can see is sky."

I was nearly asleep… in that shimmery in-between time when important thoughts try to sneak in hoping to become true. "It's almost over, Leela," Absolem said. "Go back to sleep, dear. Tomorrow never comes."

I dreamed of a full moon in a purple sky where Puck led Eeyore and I to Silvany's liminal threshold that met the outskirts of Havonford. Eeyore's tormented woodcutter was waiting there. All I saw was a transparent blue figure holding an axe, but Eeyore recognized A.A. Milne. "It's Blue!" he shouted, in surprise. They communicated in silence until Eeyore pranced around me braying tearfully. "I understand, Blue," he said, happier than I'd ever seen him.

THE EPILOG'

THE TRUTH IS NEARER THAN YOU THINK

THE PRICE

TWO FUNERALS & A WEDDING

"Shall I compare thee to a summer's day?
Thou art more lovely and more temperate.
But thy eternal summer shall not fade,
Nor lose possession of that fair thou ow'st,
Nor shall death brag thou wand'rest in his shade,
When in eternal lines to Time thou grow'st.
So long as men can breathe, or eyes can see,
So long lives this, and this gives life to thee."

WILLIAM SHAKESPEARE

I made my way to Eeyore's meadow carrying Verity's bag-lady-basket full of carrots, a thermos of Builder's tea, and a packet of plain digestives, chocolate not being the best thing for flesh and blood donkeys.

From a distance, Lucy's crown glowed like a green sun. Sunlight dappled the tips of her leaves and painted her a new skirt of bluebells until Eeyore's energy field, abundant with clover, blue cornflowers, and Sweet William, was suffused with white light. I drank in the permanent scent of summer that wafted from the hedgerows succulent with wild raspberries.

Eeyore's body lay in a grey lump on the grass. A newborn donkey stood over it sniffing its fabric coat and nudged its right ear. Absolem made music beating his new wings. "He smells like fresh air," Cheshire said. "Not a bit musty. Not anymore."

Eeyore heard me approach and looked up. He cantered a victory lap around his body, leaping over puddles from a recent shower, and trotted towards me, braying hello.

His new ears made him taller. Eeyore snorted with pleasure

when he saw the carrots I'd brought, and I felt his breath snuffle my hand. I rubbed my face in his velvety ears and smoothed his silky hide stretched warm and soft.

After tea and biscuits, I sat watching Eeyore examine an empty toadstool. A blue butterfly alighted between his ears sunned its wings and flew up to a cat shaped cloud where Cheshire played cat and butterfly with Absolem free of gravity.

Unencumbered by his jelly body, Absolem dived and looped gracefully, evading Cheshire's paws. I'd never heard him truly laugh until now.

Piglet continued to sob until Pooh had an especially roly-poly-moth thought. "Eeyore may be a little larger than he was in his old life, Piglet, but he's still our dear old Eeyore and now our new *young* Eeyore. This is the form he wished for all those years when we wandered together over the pages in Mr. Shepard's sketchbook. Isn't it wonderful."

A tearful Piglet succumbed to a bout of nervous hiccups. "Does this mean I will be a real pig someday? I wouldn't like that."

"Then you won't be," I said. "What's *your* dream little Piglet?"

"I shall be an explorer who leads *expotitions* to the North Pole instead of lagging behind and getting lost. You see, I quite like my size. I'm happiest when my ears turn bright pink. And you won't change, will you Pooh? You're safe in a library in New York. And so is the body of dear old Cotchford Farm's, Eeyore."

"Well, Eeyore was never intended to be a toy," Absolem piped up. "Owl told me to keep the secret lest Eeyore feel even less wanted. Billy Moon asked Father Christmas for a real donkey like the ones he saw at the seaside. Indeed, he prayed a little too hard for it according to Nanny. It was lucky Christopher Robin never set his heart on things. He wanted a puppy too. But Mrs. M quashed that notion pretty quick."

"Ooh! Do tell."

I shushed Piglet.

Absolem's wings quivered. "It was a secret so Eeyore wouldn't feel worse than he was written to be."

Piglet nodded but his eyes blinked with questions.

"Mr. Milne intended to buy Christopher a real donkey for his sixth birthday," Cheshire said. "But Mrs. Milne being fussier than Kanga, put her foot down and went shopping in Harrods toy department and there was Eeyore, small and grey and already saggy."

Piglet blushed. "And... and...and... I was there, too, wasn't I, Leela?"

"You were small and given to jumping at shadows only you could see, and I heard tell, you were bouncier than Tigger."

Piglet's ears flushed red with pride. "We must have been on separate shelves for we only met on Cotchford Farm. It was Christmas. I hid under a carpet of wrapping paper, and it was Eeyore who stood amongst the ruins asking where the little 'pink chappie' was. He nosed into the wastepaper basket and there I was, trembling in tears under a mass of tangled ribbons. He picked me up by the scruff of my neck and deposited me in front of Kanga and I was *'dopted*. Kanga thought I was Roo. After that she couldn't keep the two of us straight.

Cheshire interrupted with his approval. "My mother carried me that way. It's the only way to carry one's offspring or a dead mouse without dropping it."

"Kanga was always a bit confused," Piglet continued dreamily. "She had to count her children several times a day, and considering she only had one, I was often mistaken for not being me.

Every evening after Roo's bath she gave me a spoon of Roo's strengthening medicine, extract of malt, for my nerves. Well, for *Roo's* nerves, really. I was an over x'citable piglet when I first came to the forest and being of similar size, Roo and I were, as you might say, and others often did, a pair. It was nice having a mother and a brother." Suddenly, a tear escaped and ran down his snout. "Roo was lost in 1930 in an apple orchard which is why I'm afraid of apples and picnics. In any case, when there was just me, Kanga never noticed. She never worried where I was after that."

Cheshire floated down and licked Piglet's ears. "Sadly, that didn't stop *you* from worrying where you were half the time."

"Well, that explains a lot!" Absolem puffed. "Piglet at the happiest of times had night terrors all day long. His nerves were always enfrazzled into knots. Come to think of it, Roo's were a bit off the beaten track, too. Not being of the toy persuasion himself, Owl always said toys were a lot of bother, generally being lost or left out in the rain, as in Eeyore's case, at the end of the day. He and Rabbit were real, don't you know."

Eeyore shook his mane and kicked out his back legs. "I'm real. Leela's a writer. The woodcutter who shadowed stalked me is gone. And only this morning the Green Man's face appeared in Lucy's bark. He'd been gadding about in Europe for centuries until Leela's magic called him home."

"Nothing is realer than real," Pooh said suddenly, staring at the sky.

Absolem dropped his pipe in astonishment. "Brilliantly put, Pooh."

Piglet, not to be left out of such a miraculous occasion, spoke up. "And I was once bouncier than Tigger. Leela said so."

It's pretty interesting to hear a caterpillar laugh and a pig with the hiccups. Piglet's poetic story changed the somber mood. "What joy," I declared. "The trees are appleing and the dryads are doing what dryads do, which I have to say isn't much, and the tree sprites are treeing. The dark night is over. I have grown up."

"And I can fly," Absolem fluttered, showing off by dive bombing an unsuspecting beetle.

It was bound to happen. Even a magic bus must die. Rust presently mulches the bookmobile into toxic compost as landfill under a new children's library. Zeno, poetically returned to its final resting place in Parallel Park, its engines stripped, its tires recycled, its driving force expelled to the Never Never.

I've had several visions of its revitalized spirit as the newly incarnated number 61 bus. It has new zip in its engine that delivers a smooth ride with silent brakes. Its interior is impressive with the latest Global Positioning System maps; its exterior has matured into a double decker painted vibrant pea green, the color of a boat I once knew in a poem.

By all accounts it arrives on time, reaches the exchange as scheduled, and heads back to Havonford in record time.

For weeks the rumble of heavy machinery in the park had rattled the roots of the trees causing much excitement in the burrows and warrens. An influx of displaced rabbits and their relations arrived in a welcome home ceremony. Additional tunnels were dug hastily in a frenzy of good cheer playing animal games that I dubbed the 'Bunny Olympics'.

Back hoes ploughed Zeno under a ton of fresh topsoil, levelled it smooth, and compressed it with a steamroller preparing Zeno's tomb for a tree planting ceremony.

I'd taken the form of an anonymous old bag lady, who had won the town's raffle as honorary ground breaker and invoked the spirit of old Capability Brown to work through me. So, it was he who expertly dug the first sod with a shovel painted gold.

I beamed at the impressed crowd and took a bow. The spectres of Nathaniel Sloane and Edward de Vere waved at me from a group of onlookers that Piglet called spectral-tators, as my picture was taken for the local paper which, thanks to Puck, was over-exposed. We had a good laugh over that.

Someone or some *thing* had thrown a copy of 'Paddington Bear' minus its cover into the forest entrance that marked the boundary of our liminal threshold. I had an inkling of who it was.

Its decrepit condition reinforced its age. Wet pages had warped into a fan of swollen paper. I laid it under a bouquet of bluebells beside the ceremonial sapling. I looked back over my shoulder in time to see the ghost of little Nate Sloane pick up the book and stow it in his backpack.

I noticed a tall nature spirit standing apart from the frivolity of my coronation, watching me, pretending to examine a shrivelled leaf on the forest floor whenever I caught his eye.

Puck, meanwhile, performed an acrobatic dance inviting much enthusiastic competition that set the dell alive with merrymaking. I singled out Pooh and Piglet on the sidelines.

Pooh was having a serious think, arms crossed, amongst the jollity of noisy unleashed exuberance. Piglet waved hello with a sprig of orange blossom, tapping his toes to the music. I blew him a kiss. Both of them were looking thin, inevitably beginning to fade as I knew they would. I quickly diverted my attention to the trees swaying to the music of enchanted panpipes.

I was home at last, no longer an intruder, but come to be crowned queen. I expected the assembled guests to launch into a 'Happy Birthday to you' tribute, after all, the handfasting of two gods was not considered a wedding. Nevertheless, it *was* a birth of sorts, with me the only birthday girl aged seven-going-on-seventy. Instead, Auld Lang Syne rocked the treetops.

My elusive nature spirit stayed distant under a shower of party streamers that rained down from the night sky. Fireworks exploded inside my chest in time to the sparkling constellations bursting in the sky.

Eeyore appeared like a noble stag silhouetted against the

horizon, his ears perked upright at last. The word father formed behind my eyes. Once again, I wished he was here.

"I *am* here, child," the lone spirit spoke inside my head.

My father never asked to approach but materialized suddenly beside me with Puck and took my hand. "Dearest girl," he said. "I am Moonspin. Please believe me. I've never left your side."

That was when my beloved donkey lifted his head high and brayed in a moving tribute that made Absolem cry. Not to be outdone, Cheshire disappeared to wipe his eyes.

The presence of Pan loomed over us, guarding my back. He whispered gently in my ear. "Come, my love, we are one. Here is Moonspin, come to lead you to the broom-jumping."

"Go on, girl, it's your destiny," Cheshire called out. It was all the encouragement I needed. My body evaporated as I became the immortal Virgin Queen of Terra Nuova.

Edward and Perpetua Jonson truly wed in parallel time in Jabbers Walk, a few precious yards across the West Coast Road – the cement river dividing our worlds. Their only witnesses were my old menacing trees, now tamed, bowing over them in a canopy of protection.

Absolem gave a mischievous toast. "Here's to Leela and Edward, whose twin stories, have *Panned* out, still ever the same," he quipped.

WHEN HE WAS SIX

"We shall not cease from exploration
And the end of all our exploring
Will be to arrive where we started
And know the place for the first time."

— T.S. ELIOT

Now... when Edward Jonson was very young, he started to speak with an entity only he could hear. Sometimes it was me, but more often it was Puck. And when he was six, through Puck's artful cunning, Edward saw a Shakespeare play for the first time.

'Hamlet' should have been beyond his comprehension, but Edward was transported to distant memories, recalling characters from Shakespeare cannon he knew as pseudonyms.

His parents, professors of literature, were astounded. Their boy was experiencing an extraordinary phenomenon, and wonder of wonders, they stopped to listen.

Puck's artfulness advanced Edward to a performance of 'A Midsummer Night's Dream'.

It so happened that Edward suffered from recurring nightmares and frequent migraine headaches until he woke in a panic screaming, he had to go home. As ever, following Puck's lead, the family traveled to England and visited Castle Hedingham, where for the first time, Edward's headaches and nightmares miraculously plagued him no longer.

Edward took to languages like a duck to water, some said, but they never called him an odd duck. Instead, Edward was given the space to swim at will until eventually, at seventeen, he was given a scholarship to a prestigious University where he stunned his masters and charmed a girl named Perpetua.

And that's where we must leave him for now, in the care of Puck.

Revealing more would be a breach of privacy although I will say, at this juncture, Edward is under no delusions of being William Shakespeare in a former life because at a cellular level he is aware no person of that name ever existed.

Suffice to say, Eeyore is with me still, and now, quite naturally, a steady stream of homeless donkeys make their way from the Shadowlands to his sanctuary of bluebells overseen by a grandmother tree named Lucy.

MUCH ADO AFTER EVERYTHING

"Take kindly the counsel of the years,
gracefully surrendering the things of youth."

MAX EHRMANN

While I wrote Chlora's sequel in a budding new growth of apple trees, I kept my promise of making Eeyore a heroic protagonist. And as luck would have it, the recent deforesting inspired me to write how Eeyore chased Wick into a grove of charred roots exposed by the forest fire in Spritewood, and found Roo, still asleep, dreaming of becoming a full-sized kangaroo.

Eeyore dictated his memoirs to Alice at the same time Absolem dictated his guide 'The transmutation of transcendental metamorphosis' to Cheshire who claimed front page credit for endurance beyond the exceptional.

Publishing is almost as tricky in 2025 as writing publicly ever was under the reign of Queen Lizzy's overactive fears, although with less executions.

Roo loves to sit on a shelf above my desk and bask in Shinrin Yoku to make up for ninety-four years spent underground in damp leaves. After a gentle hand wash and being gently squeezed dry with towels, he emerged in a vibrant shade of brownish grey as his fussy mother.

Kanga wears spectacles designed by Absolem and is proud of her two sons, Roo and Piglet who play make-believe as happy children will.

Christopher Robin's spirit showed up in the guise of a tree

surgeon who gave our traumatized forest something he called Styx therapy. Soon their memories of the woodcutter will be no more. Any day now the trees will be apple-ing, pine-ing, cone-ing, and seedling with the best of them and telling stories under my bedroom window like the ones I used to hear when I first arrived.

Wick, whose name means the quickening of life forces inherent in all plant forms, has become a beloved house pet. He and Eeyore act like proper twins, inseparable and full of energy.

Aging is but an imaginary curse of a bad fairy waving a magic wand over one's birth. We may delay the truth, bury our heads in sand, and postpone the inevitable until we tire of the game and the futility of staying young overwhelms us and we give up our ghosts to dream of better things.

For what else could we be on a star named Terra Nuova where 80 years is a blink of the universe's eye. Whether we live 80 years as a six-year-old or 6 years as an eighty-year-old!

I'm over the moon to declare that a pair of magnificent white birds, *swan* in from time to time and have settled in the gurgling brook that flows freely under Pooh Styx Bridge.

At long last, I sat musing with Eeyore beneath Lucy's shade while Chlora chased Cheshire's tail from branch to branch. I looked up at the bouncing branches. "Yes, I see you Cheshire, torturing my Chlora." Cheshire sent me his famous *cat caught the canary* grin. "Never torture, your highness. We're making up a new game. Chlora blew a raspberry at me, so, I had no alternative but to teach the little minx a lesson. I cannot abide disrespect."

It was true. Chlora was turning into an imp. As her writer, I'd become lax developing her character. "I'm the Queen of the castle, Chlora. Come down you cheeky rascal," I commanded, and got an extended raspberry for my efforts.

I pulled Eeyore's tail playfully as he wagged it in front of my face.

"Please go easy with my new tail, *your highness*. It can be painful if one is a tad exuberant. Tails don't grow on trees you know."

A yowl from above declared Cheshire managed to corner Chlora, who tweaked one of his whiskers and got away.

Eeyore, deep in one of his ponderings, let out a solitary sigh. "You know, it would have been out of character if the woodcutter had apologized but he did thank me for being his scapegoat. I finally understand why Mr. Milne used me to ease his pain. In the end I forgave him. Grey may not be the cheeriest of colors, but it serves as a stubborn place where difficult decisions must be made."

I laid my forehead to his. "My pseudonym, if I recall…"

"And she does," Absolem interrupted, appearing as an out-of-the-blue butterfly to take Chlora's place.

"… was Cheerless," I finished. "Cheerless was our path to happiness as I recall, and my darling silver donkey, have you forgotten that you recently shapeshifted quite magnificently in honor of your selfless service recognized by the Lady Flora… no small feat, Absolem assures me."

Absolem flew down, alighted between Eeyore's ears, and folded his blue wings. "Spoken like a true writer, Miss Capability Swann. A catchy pseudonym if I don't mind saying so."

"He doesn't," Cheshire said," always chuffed to have the last word. "Absolem is becoming a pest… always in my face. Now that his caterpillar days are behind him for a while, he's higher than ever, my Lady, but then life is still predictable because as Eeyore has come to admit 'pooh happens' all the time." With that, he promptly abandoned his lopsided grin hanging like a crazed rainbow in the bluest of blue skies.

In Cheshire's absence, the sky clouded over in patches of smog – the aftermath of a spectacular fireworks display. Absolem shouted, "show off" at the Cheshire-shaped cloud of electrical sparks falling to the ground in a shower of hot raindrops.

True to form, Cheshire's last word filled the sky. "Well, aren't *you* the perfect *monarch*... butterfly."

Absolem giggled cattily, fluttering to where Cheshire's smile had been, performed a perfect loop de loop, and whispered into an ear that wasn't there. "No Pooh, Sherlock!"

NEVER ENDING CONSCIOUS RIPPLES
(of a universal family tree)

"Whose soul do I have now?
Do I have that of a child, youth, a tyrant, a pet,
or a wild animal?"

MARCUS AURELIUS

As the Age of Aquarius's newly appointed agent royale, I duly accept the provenances of Silvany's eternal green bloodline as both architect and archetype. I represent the symbolic Tree of Life, as grounded as the sparks of falling stars absorbed by Lucy and her attending bluebells in Eeyore's energy field.

Beatrice & Co.'s calamitous meeting of the addicted leading the plagued has been neutralized in Silvany's 'Grove of Brides'. Similarly, as a grown up, it's time to put away my beloved toys allowing them a chance to rest awhile in their own dreams with my heartfelt gratitude for their selfless companionship, as well as on behalf of children everywhere, who if they're wise, never truly grow up.

My reach stretches root-to-root to neutralize the human storms that seep in through the low door in my forest's wall from the Shadowland.

Eeyore naps under Lucy's leafy umbrella with his toy-hood friends and the baby rabbits grown into yearlings that *silfray* on buttercups in peace. Chlora feeds the latest newborn Absolem with succulent leaves bursting with wick. Huzzah! Life is good.

Energy rises up my spine like sap; Lucy's branches hold up the sky – upraised arms filled with nests of baby birds and newborn apples. My skin in symbiotic union with Lucy's bark creaks in the wind, expanding and contracting, breathing in the evergreen life of chlorophyll. And when night falls, I dance in the moonlight as a green lady is wont to do with her green man.

I learned the best way: I grew old, then young, then wise.

Que sera sera
whatever will be will be

The official summary: After the great bargain when Edward agreed to disappear, he came to the realization that, after death, every human gravitates to their perfect afterlife. Consequently, he emerged in Veratopia, 'the land of truth'.

When he died in 1604 from the lack of willpower to live, he blacked out from anger, bitterness and shame, and woke in a dense forest with Puck at his side.

Many years later, in the warm glow of a different forest, Edward was well met by a fair maid named truth. Together, they explored their parallel forests, as if for the first time.

Verity and Edward gave each other the permission to lie until, in the afterglow of the universe dreaming a new dream, a second wind of creative immortality blew across the prow of Edward's ship. Once relieved of its cargo of guilty regrets, Terra Nuova's cocoon of Anima Mundi released Edward and Verity in 2104 as the founding parents of a new bloodline.

Puck continued to live under Edward's skin after he sprang sentient, fully formed as elemental entities are wont to be when born from a creative mind. As Athena sprang from Zeus's forehead, Puck shook an enchanted spear into Edward's literary life. But as hard as Puck could shake, Edward could never have been the soul of an age so much as a soul arising from a perfect moment in time when the stars aligned to form a cosmic stairway to universal greatness that he could only have ascended after centuries of forced humility.

In 'A Midsummer Night's Dream', Bottom, a man in a donkey's hide conquered a spoiled queen, truly proving, there are more things dreamed of in everyman's philosophy that decree art must ever imitate life.

Elizabeth Tudor's reign of terror ended. All was as well as could be expected from the hysterical chaos. At any road, Edward was thankful there was no going back.

Veratopia's parallel chaos ended with the gentle locking of a forest door that sealed a love match made in Havonford.

I wake early and, in the silence, I recall with some wonder, the uneasy day in Otherwhere when I'd dared a scoop of mint chocolate chip ice-cream to take its best shot.

Verity maintained that authentic human truths worth waiting for were purposely fraught with suffering. She'd made it clear from the off that if writing was not a passionate undertaking, it was not my highest truth. I'm delighted to report that during a period of due diligence, time passed gently like summer clouds scudding overhead and I knew writing was for the me of me.

Technically, Shaksper was not a usurper. He lived by chance and burbled into Edward's destiny when Athena was looking the other way; Lila's universal play resumed seamlessly under the spell of maya whereby happenchance shook a false spear; and a Stratford man was used, some might say ill-used, by his betters to keep a noble family safe from persecution (royalty being too fickle to be borne). Twas a dangerous game played by egos fuelled by jealousy and greed, signifying everything, so Verity said.

Edward's cache of lost manuscripts, personal and politically damning letters, hypersensitive admissions, and deep confessions survived the great fire of London in 1666. Amongst them is a contract on yellowing parchment with a broker named Shaksper who signed his name with an X.

The world of shadows is born in freedom and playful creativity rather than necessity. Leela, aligned to spontaneous divine play, caused the last will and testament of the dark scapegoat, mistaken for the literary genius of the Elizabethan Age, to come to light.

And when Edward lost the *will* to live, Puck hid *his* last will and testament, deep in the forest of Silvany where misty apparitions ever wander out of time and space.

The 17th Earl of Oxford's truth was challenged; Shaksper of Stratford's lie was promoted.

To be grievously challenged or not to be, that was the paradox!

But one thing remains truer than true: The moment Edward de Vere gave up the ghost, his cause was taken up by a symposium of 21st century champions who continue to work tirelessly to restore his legacy.

THE TEACHINGS… *an afterword*

"Nothing is real… everything is a reality!"

LADY FLORA

It was my destiny to change. Not to change history but as Eeyore, ever the one to pin the tale on poetic justice, often reminded me, to adjust my attitude.

"Destiny will wait in the wings as one's understudy," he said. "It will rehearse its lines, listen for the stage director to declare 'you're on', and give you a push. The cues will come. The performances given. Accolades, cat calls, and curtain calls will pass. The only laurel worth winning is the honor of being a 'swan of the universe' whether one's afraid of ice cream or not."

The most important thing Eeyore taught me was that I was never alone. From the moment we met on Cotchford Farm we were inseparable. But teacher is too small a word for a dedicated mentor. And a genius mentor with a sense of the theatrical is the best teacher anyone could have hoped for. He was a star performer.

Behavior is the key to survival instincts. Body language and silence are learned skills and in a war of wills they're weapons. Eeyore was a survivor. Underneath his scripted curse of depression lived a compassionate soul who believed luck to be an inherent part of fate especially if you made your own.

Eeyore took his species seriously and teemed up with Puck to turn his 'energy field' into a sanctuary for shadow-free donkeys. Thanks to Peter's mathematical genius, his 'Twenty-four Carrot Trust Fund' plan for abandoned homeless donkeys will surpass all expectations.

Eeyore was the master of using sarcasm as a defense

mechanism. 'Don't be an ass,' he once advised the Queen of Hearts, and like his hero Marcus Aurelius, Eeyore turned adversities into advantages he dubbed 'ass-ets'.

Dignity is overestimated. Falling down is fine as long as you don't stay down. Be of good cheer and eat bluebells, feeling sorry for oneself denies destiny's ability to find you.

Be wary of supernatural magicals, powerful tricksters not to be confused with mysticals or mythicals, who mislead humans as fairies of old were wont to do, waylaying many a mortal into a trap of sleeping past Lachesis's allotted life spans by hundreds of years.

Puck taught me that there was more to meet the eye than honesty. He manifested his own destiny and as such, his positive trickster dreams came true.

Tink, in many ways Puck's fairy opposite, had an axe to grind. She was a feisty self-centered fairy who manipulated humans to get her way. Case in point, she commanded children to believe in fairies so she could believe in herself. She desperately wanted Peter Pan to remain a boy. Her grown-up feelings confused compassion with possession and her jealousy almost derailed his happy ending.

Peter taught me that even sad memories were important to mine for clues and made sure to fly me safely over the River Styx high enough to escape notice. We suffered mothers whose less than exemplary attention created a confusing distrust of women in charge yet a soulful longing for maternal care. Peter found it in Wendy Darling, a visiting 'older sister' trained to sew and cook and mend scratches.

I learned the importance of sewing, as in binding things together, from shadows to ideas and donkeys' tails, and when to unpick the threads and fly free.

Peter's shadow soul broke free of its moorings and had to be sewn onto it's boy matrix by Wendy the same way I mended Eeyore's tail. Even so, by refusing to age, we grew up the hard way. We withdrew, hiding our light away from everyone but most of all from ourselves to escape the inescapable shame of abandonment. We dared time to leave us alone until acting our age was the cruelest thing of all. Peter grew up despite being tripped up by a rebellious shadow sewn to his heels; I grew up from the drudgery of dragging a gloomy shadow sewn to mine.

Shamans come in all sizes and temperaments. My two, Absolem and Cheshire, formed the cornerstones of forest lore. Absolem, my woozy guru explored the smoke and mirrors of altered states of consciousness. His wisdom, offered in plain sight behind philosophical smokescreens, enabled me to think beyond words for transcendental solutions when dreams go up in smoke.

Absolem lived high on a hallucinatory mushroom cloud in a state of euphoria all the while knowing transmutation, the ultimate reward, would reunite him with the ecstatic psychedelic experiences of his past.

Cheshire's playfulness was the bridge that connected them. Cheshire taught me the Art of Cattiness. He described it as intelligent sarcasm underscored by truth imbued with wit, and fully understood that feline arrogance in general, was a right earned from endless evolutionary adaptations within the food chain. Overall, his biggest lesson was to disappear when it was appropriate and appear when insight was necessary.

Edward de Vere whose family motto was 'nothing truer than truth' discovered the undeniable truth that 'poo' happens, randomly and often. His Shakespearean words will live until the sun burns out and Leela dreams a new dream.

Verity, Edward's counterpart in truth, confused motherhood with ownership. I learned to let go of Eeyore from watching her torture herself. Fate decreed Verity lost her infant daughter, and so, besotted with guilt she neglected me in my cruelest hour. But, as

Eeyore pointed out, her rejection was the last straw I needed to push me into growing up. Go figure!

I learned through many silent observations that Pax's magnificent Ellies were meant to roam at will, flattening the Jungle undergrowth in perfect peace. Pax found peace in exuberance, and I learned that of all the animals, Pax loved elephants most of all because they never forgot where they left their children.

Wonderland Alice's boundless curiosity and adventurous spirit taught me to explore fully, trust whatever turned up, adapt by asking questions, and to never give up.

By reading me the story of Snow-White so many times, Eeyore taught me mirrors were scrying bowls that delivered answers to important questions before I asked them.

Tigger taught me to test boundaries with joyful exuberance.

Every village, castle, and forest needs a wise 'fool' like Pooh to set life on a roar.

Christopher Robin who survived his 'picture-perfect' childhood taught me to see beyond someone's biographical story to encounter their true feelings.

Piglet, the eternal innocent, taught me that by scampering at will on endless *'expotitions'*, love overcomes fear because true courage is independent of size.

Lucy's philosophical windfall was wise. Chlorophyl is the heart's blood of the earth, she said.

Marcus Aurelius advocated the therapeutic value of fully accepting circumstances without protest by never shirking from the truth and remaining even-tempered working through challenges peacefully, one step at a time. He taught me to be grateful for the grace of adversity – the vital elements for illumination: that true humility only comes *after* a fall, patience is a virtue, and to consider moderation in all things through the arts of perception, right action, and willpower. 'Ignore common gossip,' he wrote, 'and accept abandonment as an invitation to connect to one's personal power rather than a call to arms.'

Zeno, a polymath of the human psyche, founded stoicism on the rules of conduct best befitting a universe of divine power that inspired humans to transcend the limitations of natural selection. He advocated leading a better life through self-mastery, perseverance, and acceptance, and that taking a noble cause upon oneself for the greater good quickens the synergy of an entire group soul.

MOONSPIN'S VISIONARY QUEST

Gentles – we nature spirits of Silvany are here, as we have ever been, to dismiss the shadows that hamper your spiritual progress. My all-seeing plants have waited for eons to serve you. They await you still. So, I bid thee 'well come' to the forests of earth where trees keep humanity's conscience safe, and your doors of perception are eternally open to evolve in peace.

Yoda, a story-wise nature spirit, inspired by Shakespeare, once advised a troubled human 'to do or do not; there is no try'. And therein, as day precedes night, lies Shakespeare's original thought 'to be or not to be', truer than true in Hamlet's tortured universal outcry paraphrased by Absolem: *There are more things in heaven and earth, Zeno, than are dreamt of in your philosophy.*

And so, I leave you to reflect on the profound sentiments of Lewis Carroll – a celebrated shaman and extrasensory visionary of the highest order, paraphrased below, by the Green Lady, Queen Leela of Terra Nuova, to evoke the soul of the arising Aquarian age.

The time has come the Universe said
To put away our childhood toys and dream of better things,
of love and peace and blissful days,
and caterpillar's wings.

THE ZENO GROUP SOUL

ATHENS c. 300 BC – the physical dimension
Zeno's class dropouts

CHILDLESS	RUTHLESS	ENDLESS
A mother grieving for a stillborn child	a greedy powermonger sociopath	a savant healer in crisis as a surgeon re: a HOMELESS plague child

SHADOWLANDS the physical dimension
the Group Soul backlash

EDWARD DE VERE 1550-1604
a.k.a. SHAKESPEARE

VERITY RYDER 1858 – 1924 …. mates with …. FRANK BARREN / 1848 – 1925
a.k.a. **S.A. GREENWOOD**

ALICE RYDER 1880 – 1882

BEATRICE 1945 – 2011 ………………………… 1962 - mates with ………………………… WILLIAM JONSON 1943-2024
(past life - the homeless plague child) and **MOONSPIN** – *a nature spirit in charge of hallucinogenic plants in Silvany*

SILKIE RYDER 1963 – 2024

*ENDLESS's ghost
*meets Silkie in 2024 at
ZENO of Citium's class reunion*

LILA SWANN 1963 – 2024
The CHANGELING princess

SILVANY the spiritual dimension
the Immortals

LADY FLORA
VERITY RYDER *in transition
THE GREEN MAN
PUCK
MOONSPIN
ZENO
LEELA of TERRA NUOVA ascends the throne - 2025

THE BACK MATTERS

MUCH ADO ABOUT FICTION IS
THE ART OF TELLING LIES

THE GLOSSORIUM

'Meditations'	Marcus Aurelius
'The Essential Alan Watts' / 'The Watercourse Way' and the YouTube recordings of Alan Watt's lectures	Alan Watts
The books and YouTube recordings of lectures	Rupert Sheldrake
'The Power of Now' / 'A New Earth'	Eckhart Tolle
'The Daily Stoic' / 'The Obstacle is The Way'	Ryan Holiday
'The Tao of Pooh and the Te of Piglet'	Benjamin Hoff
'The House at Pooh Corner' / 'While We Were Young'	A.A. Milne
'The Lion the Witch and the Wardrobe'	C.S. Lewis
'Alice in Wonderland'	Lewis Carroll
The nonsense poems of	Edward Lear
The entire 'Tales of' series	Beatrix Potter
'Peter Pan'	James Barrie
'The Wind in the Willows'	Kenneth Grahame
'Watership Down'	Richard Adams
'The Desiderata'	Max Ehrmann
'The Monument'	Hank Whittemore
The Works of William Shakespeare	Edward de Vere – the 17th Earl of Oxford

WORD POWER

Lila: (Leela): the nature of divine play

Lachesis: the goddess who allots one's lifetime by a length of string

Myasthenia: a medical condition of droopy eyelids and the lack of strength holding the head upright suffered by Christopher Robin and Eeyore

Nihil: nothing

Veritas, Verity, Vere: truth

Xenophobia = xenos (stranger or guest) plus phobia (flight or fear)

Zenophobia = Silkie's term for her fear of Master Zeno

Silva = forest / silva novus = new forest, new trees, saplings, seedlings

The Tao Te Ching (the I-Ching) book of changes to aid decision making and increasing intuition written by Lau Tzu – c. 3,000 BC

Stoa: a covered portico used for public lectures and debates and formal open-air classrooms

The Stoic Trinity: doing, being, and thinking – in addition to humility, discipline, reason, perception, intention, fortitude, patience, non-judgemental, and the power of silence

Empty mind: Zen mind

'Capability Brown' (**Lancelot Brown** 1716 –1783), was an English landscape architect, known as 'England's greatest gardener', best known for converting the homes of the wealthy into classic 'stately homes' set in natural parkland enhanced with water features and follies. Nicknamed 'Capability' because he told his clients their property had 'capability' for improvement.

LEWIS CARROLL'S 'NONCE' words:

Slithy: a blend of lithe and slimy

Snark: a mysterious imaginary animal

Mimsy: prim, underwhelming, and ineffectual. A blend of *miserable* and *flimsy*

Chortle: a blend of *chuckle* and *snort*

Frumious: a blend of *fuming* and *furious* that means wonderful, elegant, superb, or delicious

Burble: a combination of *bleat, murmur,* and *warble*

Bandersnatch: an imaginary wild animal of fierce disposition

Boojum: particularly dangerous snarks

Galumph: to move along heavily or clumsily

THE SPIRITUAL QUALITIES of ANIMALS

Fetch – the feline principle = the bringer, catcher, deliverer, spirit guide, shaman,

Chase – the canine principle = the importance of holding one's ground, remaining calm, non-reactive, loyal, selfless, forgiving

Together Fetch and Chase represent the 'throw and the catch' – the movement of life, travelling through space and time in perfect order.

Dryads: a nymph (or tree spirit taking the form of a human woman) that inhabits an oak tree.

Devas: ethereal beings of light that rule plant life

Donkey: horse…courage. Determined. Persistent, unmoveable, steadfast, a beast of burden, a scapegoat, true service, hard work, over-confidence, affection, empathy

Monkey: spontaneous, nervous energy, busy mind

Butterfly: rebirth

Caterpillar: transformation, rebirth, transmutation via a chrysalis into a butterfly

Owl: wisdom

ANIMA MUNDI: the SOUL lifeforce of the world

THE LOGOS: The divine intelligence implicit in the cosmos

Athena: the Greek 'spear-shaking' goddess of literature, poetry, wisdom, courage, inspiration, justice, strategic warfare, science, mathematics, and crafts

Aurelius: bringer of light

Gaia: Mother Nature, earth mother, the feminine counterpart, consort of Pan – the Green Man.

The Green Man: the immortal elemental god of forests and animals

Wick: the life energy in plants

The I-Ching Subconscious guidance through 64 hexagrams of yielding broken lines and resisting solid lines

The Eight Ball: a toy that offers random answers to simple questions

Crucible: an alchemic container able to withstand the intense heat necessary for the transmutation of lead into gold. A metaphorical melting pot for enduring human tests both physical and spiritual. For example: The fire in Veratopia acts as a crucible for purifying a sacred forest desecrated by malevolent energies into the sacrosanct domain of Terra Nuova – a new earth.

Runcible Spoon: an eating utensil combining the tines of a fork with a spoon.

OTHER BOOKS by V KNOX

The Fine Art of Haunting, Ghosts in the Gallery, Historical Fantasy, Paranormal Romance, Time-Travel & Middle-Grade Adventures

'LISABETTA'– *a fanciful biographical trilogy of Leonardo da Vinci's historical half-sister, Lisabetta.* To reclaim her true identity, the embittered spirit of the 'Mona Lisa' trapped in her portrait for 500 years must join forces with an autistic boy and his  troubled mother. A picture isn't 'worth a thousand words'… it hides a thousand secrets. **THE 'MONA LISA' MAY BE PRICELESS… NOW SHE MUST BECOME A WOMAN WORTH SAVING**

'DISAPP'EARRING TWICE' – Aurelia Marcus, an aging eccentric shadowed by the spirit of a girl from a famous painting, rents a castle by the sea to write a novel before she forgets the story she feels compelled to write based on her recurring dreams of a past life. **AURELIA MARCUS DISAPPEARED LONG BEFORE SHE RAN AWAY FROM HOME**

'WOO WOO – the posthumous love story of Miss Emily Carr' – the artist Emily Carr, an eccentric spinster, comes to her senses sixty-seven years after her death and calls down the energy of her animal totem, Woo the monkey, to rekindle the love of a rejected suitor – *a fanciful homage to Emily Carr inspired by her memoirs.* **SUPERNATURAL MONKEY BUSINESS**

'THE UNTHINKABLE SHOES' – *a story of reincarnation and extraordinary sacrifice inspired by a museum exhibit of child's shoes from the Titanic.* When death separates two children on the

Titanic who were destined to marry, the barefoot ghost of the boy chooses to remain earthbound as the surviving girl's invisible childhood companion. Finding a pair of lost shoes is their one chance to stay together. **A 'LOST BOY' FROM THE TITANIC LOSES HIS SHOES BETWEEN HEAVEN AND THE DEEP BLUE SEA**

'DOGGED STAR' – A star-crossed woman haunted by a lucid dream is aided by the ghost of a dog whose unwavering loyalty to her master, Leonardo da Vinci, transcends death and hounds her to life. **AN INVISIBLE 'SEEING-EYE-DOG' GUIDES A WOMAN GOING BLIND TO SEE THE TRUTH IN HER STARS**

'THE INDIGO PEARL' – *a story of YOUNG LOVE & OLD SOULS - *book one of two:* When the consciousness of Delphi Sharpe, an autistic woman with the extrasensory ability to converse with paintings and birds, is transplanted into the circuits of an android programmed to retrieve famous works of art lost in the distant past, intelligence is no longer artificial. Delphi must fight her way back to love, one pearl at a time. **AI = AUTISTIC INTELLIGENCE – 'STATE OF THE ART' TIME TRAVEL JUST BECAME TRANSCENDENTAL**

'PEARL BY PEARL' – *a story of YOUNG LOVE & OLD SOULS - *book two of two:* Two rivalling 'art whisperers' become single-mindedly obsessed to consummate the love of Delphi's life – a teenage boy in a 500-year-old portrait. But while the spirit of Delphi wants to rest in peace with her beloved, her counterpart intends to exact revenge on the art syndicate that exploited them. **SOMETIMES IT TAKES TWO LIVES TO MAKE ONE WOMAN**

'ADORATION – Loving Botticelli' – The romance between a retired art history professor and a five-hundred-year-old portrait leads from obsession to seduction. **LIFE CAN BE AN IMMORTAL COMEDY**

THE BEDE SERIES: – *ghosts who invite readers to come alive*

'TWINTER – the first portal' – a magical realism time-slip adventure *book one of four:* Bede Hall, an abandoned and disgruntled stately home, is desperate. It must rally its dispersed family before it's sold to developers. Its new residents, a pair of thirteen-year-old twins, seek out a girl lost in time whose apparition has haunted the estate for generations, but meeting her opens a time portal that reveals a terrible secret. In order to rescue her and protect the planet, the teens form a team of otherworldly allies called the 'Twinters'. Bede Hall is Alive, but All is Not Well! **GHOSTS ARE NOTHING COMPARED TO THE CHALLENGES HAUNTING A CURMUDGEONLY BUILDING WITH A DESIRE FOR ETERNAL LIFE**

'TIME FALLS LIKE SNOW' – a magical realism time-slip adventure *book two of four:* The secrets of Bede Hall's timely past continue with the sixteen-year-old twins working in league with a team of ghosts and 'twice-borns' who have been monitoring Bede's secrets for hundreds of years. It falls to the rules of twindom, the Great Sphinx of Egypt, and a colony of mystical cats to save the future. **THE 'TWINTERS' ARE RUNNING OUT OF TIME IN A LANDSCAPE WHERE HISTORY IS POSITIVELY ANCESTRAL**

'TOMORROW AGAIN' – a magical realism time-slip adventure *book three of four:* To save Bede Hall, a disgruntled stately home nestled against Hadrian's Wall in England, a pair of telepathic twins, at odds over logic and metaphysics, must fulfill an ancient prophecy, and rescue its resident ghost. But sending one of them to ancient Egypt, Pangea, and Mars turns out to be the shortest route to saving the planet from a nuclear winter. **MAN SAYS TIME PASSES; THE PYRAMIDS SAY MAN PASSES**

'SNOW BEHIND THE DOOR' – *book four of four* documents the *time-slipped* memories of the abandoned ghost-child of Bede Hall, named Snow, in search of the family she glimpses in dreams and the dusty mirrors of a stately home that has sheltered earth's time portals, guarded by an ancient line of royal Egyptian cats for thousands of years. **THE MEMOIR OF A CHILD GHOST WITH AMNESIA**

'VIOLET SEABORN'S UNFINISHED SOUL' An S.O.S. arriving a thousand years too late is right on time for an extraordinary infant to wash ashore from a shipwreck to save herself, her ancestors, and enable a mythical nature spirit to survive immortality. **AN OLD SOUL AND AN OLD WOMAN RESTORE THE IMMORTAL SOUL OF SCOTLAND**

'SHAKESPEARE AT POOH CORNER' a tale of whimsy and history where Edward de Vere known to posterity by his pseudonym William Shakes-peare, and Lila Swann, an abandoned child hiding inside a beloved children's book, meet 400 years apart in an enchanted forest populated by the characters from 'House at Pooh Corner'.
MUCH ADO ABOUT FICTION IS THE ART OF TELLING LIES

AUTHOR'S BIO

 Veronica Knox writes multi-layered stories under the name V KNOX that reconcile historical facts with imaginative fiction: eclectic historical fantasies, art history delivered in ghost stories, paranormal romances, and 'THE BEDE SERIES' a 4 book magical realism time-slip for ages 14 and up in which a disgruntled stately home nestled beside Hadrian's wall (in the north of England) has a mind of its own in a mystical landscape that shelters a pair of teenagers, resident ghosts, mythical elementals, and sentient animals.

Her novel 'VIOLET SEABORN's UNFINISHED SOUL' is an historical, supernatural, time-slip romance for readers 18 and older, set in the Highlands of Scotland about a mythical Water Horse.

Veronica, a member of the Shakespeare Oxford Fellowship explores her fanciful take on the ongoing Shakespeare identity question in her latest novel 'SHAKESPEARE AT POOH CORNER' – a tale of paranormal fiction about a changeling six-year-old child who creates a fantasy world populated by characters from her favorite children's books and the ghost of William Shakespeare. But after refusing to grow up as her friend Peter Pan advises her, she continues to age – a social outcast coping on the edge of madness until at age sixty-one a disembodied voice on a bus offers to restore the life she was meant to live in an enchanted scriptorium that teaches the three Rs: Reading, Righting, and Reincarnation.

Ms. Knox dips into the creative inner worlds of autistic savants and master artists, and in one case, the unknown child in the Titanic cemetery. By tapping metaphysical resources such as the discrepancies between reality and lucid dreams, Veronica fishes the depths of the subconscious, the afterlife, reincarnation, the anomalies of parallel lives and dimensions, and the classic psyche of 'the ghostly lover'.

Studying for a university Fine Arts degree inspired an imaginative take on art history that led to other untapped avenues for stories. She discovered inanimate objects are rarely bereft of life and portraits have juicy secrets to tell – snapshots of what was and more importantly, who left their ethereal 'I was here' imprint on the world.

What if two children aboard the Titanic were meant to marry, and a pair of baby shoes from an exhibit in a museum could reunite them? What if the 'Mona Lisa' was Leonardo da Vinci's kid sister?

Veronica resides on Vancouver Island channeling ethereal echoes from objects in museums and the stifled voices of the Italian Renaissance – the artists as well as their anonymous subjects and companions. She grants them second chances to air their grievances, tell their stories, and together they set the dreariest history books on fire.

WEBSITE & CURIOUS ART HISTORY BLOG
https://veronicaknox.com

Thank you for reading
'SHAKESPEARE AT POOH CORNER'
If Edward de Vere's betrayal
moves you please support
The Shakespeare Oxford Fellowship
and
The de Vere Society

and please consider donating
to an animal shelter for donkeys

Veronica Knox

May 3 – 2025

SILENT K PUBLISHING — Vancouver Island, Canada
https://veronicaknox.com

www.ingramcontent.com/pod-product-compliance
Lightning Source LLC
Chambersburg PA
CBHW071957110726

47910CB00005B/1566